a
girl's
gotta
eat

a girl's gotta eat

michelle valentine

St. Martin's Griffin
New York

A GIRL'S GOTTA EAT. Copyright © 2007 by Michelle Valentine. All rights reserved. Printed in the United States of America. No part of this book may be used or reproduced in any manner whatsoever without written permission except in the case of brief quotations embodied in critical articles or reviews. For information, address St. Martin's Press, 175 Fifth Avenue, New York, N.Y. 10010.

www.stmartins.com

Library of Congress Cataloging-in-Publication Data

Valentine, Michelle.
  A girl's gotta eat / Michelle Valentine. — 1st ed.
    p. cm.
  ISBN-13: 978-0-312-36059-7
  ISBN-10: 0-312-36059-2
  1. Young women—Fiction. 2. Hollywood (Los Angeles, Calif.)—Fiction. 3. Motion picture industry—Fiction. I. Title.

PS3622.A442G57 2007
813'.6—dc22

2007023911

First Edition: November 2007

10 9 8 7 6 5 4 3 2 1

in loving memory of

my gramma russ

acknowledgments

As with all my blessings, I thank my Heavenly Father for giving me the talents, the will, the drive, and the determination to accomplish yet another goal. Thank You for bringing these words through my hands onto the paper, for giving me the patience, courage, and diligence to pursue my dreams and for giving others the ability to see and believe in my vision. Without You, I can do nothing, but with You I can do all. And so I am.

To my one and only baby girl, Morgan Dorothea—it is for you that I continue on this quest. We rarely get exactly what we want, but with you, I got just that and so much more. You have shown and taught me so much. I love being your mom because the joy you bring me is indescribable. Thank you for giving my life continuity and purpose, for the day you were born, so was I. Just as I am, you too will *always* be a "Momma's Girl," I love you, Cooki.

To the most wonderful mother on Earth, Dorothea McKenney. Thank you for your unconditional love, loyalty, and support.

You are my biggest supporter and my very best friend. Thank you for your never-ending encouragement and for always having my back. Without you, surely none of this would be possible. You're the best mom on the planet and ain't nothin' change—I'm still and *always* will be a "Momma's Girl."

To my baby brother, Larry, Jr.—know that I stay on that ass because I believe in you and want you to be happy and successful. Trust in me 'cuz I would never steer you wrong. To my dad, Larry, Sr., who as I grow older I'm becoming more and more like. Scary, hunh?

To the Epitome Group, LLC; Doug Walrond; Aunt Barbara; Uncle Michael; Anthony "A-Blitz" Botter; the Stephens family; Daddy Milt; Michelle Hudson; Trouble; Capone the Gangsta of Comedy; Grand Puba: David L. "Money Train" Watts; Messiah Lozado; J and W Seligman; Tori Titus and family; Zane, Charmaine, and everyone at Strebor Books for helping me get my feet wet in the literary world; Judith Curr and everyone at Atria Books/Simon & Schuster; Mark Anthony and Q-Boro Books for your interest in my talent; Teri Woods for your words of wisdom and advice; Laurinda Brown; DV Bernard; Timmons; Sal Abiettello; Luz Perez and family; Emmanuel Baptist Church; Mt. Zion Baptist Church; my true sister-friends, who understand me and the true meaning of friendship and who have shown me a tremendous amount of support and love for so many years; Jeanine, Daliah, Diane, Shonda (and family), and Kenyatta Toler (and family); my radio inspirations—Wendy Williams, Miss Jones, and Michael Baisden—for thoroughly entertaining, enlightening, and cracking me up while I write; Eric Dickey; Sarah Camilli; Heather Hunter; and all of the other amazing people I have met during my literary journey!

Tracey Moore—Marable of The Spirited Actor—my wonderful acting coach whose class has validated many of my already existing emotions by teaching me so much about acting and life.

Monique Patterson, Kia DuPree, and everyone at St. Martin's Press for believing in me and helping to make a good book great.

Yvette Hayward and Nancy Flowers of Flowers and Hayward Management—my agents, publicists, and friends. Yvette, thank you so much for supporting my work from the very beginning. Words cannot express how much I appreciate you both.

Special thanks to all the book clubs nationwide—especially the *fabulous* Yellow Roses; Rawsistaz; Readincolor; Karibu Bookstore; Sisters Uptown Bookstore; Hue-Man Bookstore; Nubian Heritage; Black Expressions; all national and local retail bookstores that support authors of color as well as all published and unpublished authors who have a story to tell; and most of all, YOU—my readers, who support my work and keep asking for more. If you keep reading, I'll keep writing!

To all the intelligent, beautiful women out there who know they have to get up, get out, and get some. Just be careful how you get it 'cause one day it might come back and bite you on the butt.

I thank you all for completing my universe.

Now sit back, relax, and enjoy the ride.

a
girl's
gotta
eat

1

*S*he's *a* brick . . . howwwse . . . ," blared the nasal voice of Lionel Richie from the speakers of her Bose sound system. It really didn't matter that the words were over two decades old. "Brick House" was her theme song and the only tune that could accurately describe her.

As Rementa Renee Broughton performed her weekly ritual of getting ready to hang out at some trendy New York City night spot, she danced around her sparsely furnished one-bedroom apartment, located in Spanish Harlem—or El Barrio—wearing only a crimson-colored thong. With her feet tucked neatly inside a pair of strappy black stilettos from the East Village boutique, Petite Baton, she waited for Shannelle to call her to say she was on her way before throwing on the rest of her outfit. She didn't want to risk getting a drop of unnecessary perspiration on her getup, especially since tonight it would be the off-black Gucci mini wrap dress that she'd boosted from Jeezy's video shoot.

She felt a little bad for lifting it, being that they had been so nice to her on the set and all. They'd even sent her home in a Lincoln Town Car after they'd wrapped at nearly 4 A.M., which is something they rarely do for extras. Usually Shannelle came to get her. But this time she was treated like a star. Maybe it had something to do with that red metallic bikini thong set she'd worn for fourteen hours straight that had almost split her ass in half. She had nursed three hemorrhoids for two weeks afterward, but it was well worth it. Jeezy's manager had taken her number and assured Rementa that she'd be in his next video.

"Next time we might even pay you." He smiled.

And she'd gotten her hands on this three-thousand-dollar dress—the one she'd be wearing that night. Life couldn't be better.

"Be downstairs in ten," Shannelle ordered through the phone. Remmi, as she was called by everyone who knew her, quickly hung up the phone, pressed replay on the CD player, doused herself in all the right places with some more J'adore, and threw on the dress, which barely covered her 34Ds.

It would definitely be on tonight.

O h my gooooodness . . . ain't that that nigga, Nitro? He's the muthafucka that had my ass all up in the clinic last May. I ain't seen his triflin' ass since I told him I was pregnant. I *knew* that nigga ain't have no money—frontin' like him and Kanye West was all tight. He's a muthafuckin' lie! I need to go over there and make him give me my damn money!" Shannelle spat then downed her fourth Cosmo.

It was quite obvious that her friend had had far too much to drink, and Remmi was in no mood for beef that night. She didn't have a bra on, and knew that her ample breasts would be flapping in the wind if she and Shannelle started a fight. Besides, she'd told Shannelle a million times to use condoms. It didn't matter if a nigga *looked* like he had money.

She better be glad all she got was knocked up, Remmi thought.

"Girl, I ain't in the mood for no beef tonight. Y'all are both drunk, and my titties'll be every-fuckin'-where if we have to scrap with that nigga. Plus, Diddy is in here with no bodyguards, and I been tryin' to get at that nigga forever. Let it go," Remmi instructed her friend.

rementa Broughton and Shannelle Anderson had been inseparable since the first day of the second grade. When they both walked into Ms. Washington's class with the exact same Theo Huxtable lunch box, they knew they had a bond that would be the glue of their friendship over the next fifteen years. "Theo's mama *and* daddy got money!" they exclaimed. Even at seven years old, they knew they wanted to be around money. Blame it on their broke absent daddies, blame it on being the only children of two gold-digging mamas, blame it on whatever. The fact of the matter was that from an early age, these girls knew what they wanted from the opposite sex, and they pretty much knew how to get it.

So, while Theo Huxtable was what brought them together, over the next decade the Dynamic Duo, as they dubbed themselves, did things together that only strengthened their bond. From experimenting with cigarettes and weed to losing their virginity to the Dobson twins from apartment 4D—you name it, they did it together. And aside from their career aspirations, they both wanted the same things out of life: a nigga with money and—a nigga with money. And neither of them would stop at anything to be in the company of those who fit that bill. Although exceptionally beautiful on the outside, their high school diplomas from Julia Richmond offered them very limited career options. With no desire to go off to college, Remmi decided the day after graduation that she wanted to be an actress, while Shannelle began working four nights a week at a strip club in the Bronx. With her diploma in her right hand and a dean's list certificate in her left, Remmi registered at a temp agency whose forte was Fortune 500 companies.

"Who wouldn't want to see your pretty face when they walk up to the front desk at a multimillion-dollar firm?" Teddy, the middle-aged, horny white employment agency rep lustfully smiled. And so her journey began.

Each week when she'd come to the agency to pick up her check, Remmi could feel Teddy's eyes unbuttoning her blouse and sucking her nipples raw. Getting a kick out of his behavior, Remmi pushed the meter to see what additional benefits she could get from the situation. She began wearing tightly fitted blouses just to entice him. It wasn't long before no matter how many days she worked—one or five—the paycheck she received remained the same. If she went to auditions three days out of the week, Teddy made sure her check still represented forty hours. It was their little unspoken deal—she'd inconspicuously allow one of her top buttons to pop open, revealing just enough of her satin-covered bosom to give him a serious hard-on beneath his desk while he eyeballed her nipples, which always stood erect from the office air-conditioning. And once he'd received his gift, he'd make her check look like she worked a full week. Hell. After a while, she'd work only one day a week whether she had an audition or not. And since she was his favorite, she got the best assignments—fashion houses like Ralph Lauren and DKNY, companies with summer Fridays, and *record labels*. And it was at one of these labels that Remmi got thrust into the world of hip-hop videos and became a "video ho," a title that she took to a whole 'nuther level . . .

i t was a late summer morning and Remmi's first day as the twenty-sixth-floor receptionist at Def Jam Recordings. She sat quietly at the switchboard, looking stunning. As usual, her shoulder-length jet-black mane was impeccably done, without a hair out of place. Her flawless complexion sparkled as it glistened with a richer caramel tone than usual (those Saturday mornings at Jones Beach with Shannelle having done her justice). In a tight-fitting white spaghetti-strapped tank, she looked like she could have graced any magazine cover. But she was feeling down. She had gone on four open calls and hadn't gotten a single call-back. She just knew she had been perfect for that McDonald's commercial—but nothing. Not even a smile from the director or producer. As she sat reading yet another story about the trials and tribulations Mary J. Blige had made it through, all she could do was shake her head and say to herself, *Well, at least ain't nobody kickin' my ass.*

Her concentration on the article made her oblivious of the handsome young black man in his late twenties who stood above her.

"Excuse me, ma. Sam Court to see Marcus Vissat," he said. Remmi looked up and became immediately intrigued by the sight of this tall brown-skinned brotha with a rock-hard body and pearly white teeth that glistened so brightly, she thought the ceiling had opened up and let the sun shine in. She could tell that he'd taken his Crest Whitestrips with him everywhere he went, and after she buzzed Mr. Vissat's extension, the two locked eyes for nearly three whole minutes.

"His assistant'll be with you in a moment." She smiled as she filled out his visitor's pass.

"You a model?" he questioned.

"An actress." Remmi smiled again coyly, sensing his interest.

"Is that so? Well, I'm a video director."

"Oh, are you?" she flirted. "What videos have you directed?"

"Too many to name, baby girl. Too many to name," he arrogantly replied.

"Well, why don't you put me in one of your videos?"

He smirked. "One of my *home* videos?"

"That, too. Maybe we can star in it together." Remmi laughed. Just as she scribbled her name and phone number on a Post-it note, the executive's assistant entered the reception area. Remmi quickly passed her admirer the yellow sticky and said, "I expect to hear from you tonight."

Three days later she was flown to Trinidad and featured in a Jay-Z music video. Five days after that, she and Sam starred in their own production. The rest was history.

Shannelle, on the other hand, liked the quick and easy money of stripping, and with the measurements of 36-26-36, she was one of the top earners at Shirley's Temple.

"Videos are okay," she'd say to her best friend. "But I need to get paid every time I put in some work. Rubbin' elbows with rappers don't pay no bills. I can make over five hundred dollars in four hours at the Temple. You be on those video sets all night long!"

But in her own defense, Remmi would always retort, "Yeah, I may not get paid every time I do a video, but I have so much fun. Plus I get free trips and get to be around those fine-ass rappers and I'ma get one of 'em to fall in love with me yet. Then I won't havta work nowhere. Who you gon' find at the Temple, girl?"

"Whateva, bitch. I need dough *now*. I can't wait for some rapper to fall in love with me. Besides rappers don't fall in love, and I got rent and a car note. Look, you ain't even got no car. You can't make no livin' doing rap videos. That's why you still tempin'. And I don't know what you talkin' about. There ain't nothin' but ballas at the Temple. And not those penny-ante rappin' muthafuckas either. I mean doctors, lawyers, and politicians. Shit, that blind congressman was in there last week—ain't that some shit? You know we some baaaad bitches when *blind* muthafuckas are comin' in! We the baddest bitches in the whole tri-state area!" Shannelle would cackle.

"Whateva, bitch! What the fuck eva!" Remmi chuckled.

"Don't worry, girl. When you get tired of shakin' those titties for free, there'll always be a spot for you at the Temple, if you want it. Just let me know, and I'll talk to Shirley for you!"

"No thanks!"

It was a never-ending debate between the friends. Two very attractive young black women, they were loving life and living it to the fullest. They made it out of the club without incident that night. But much to Remmi's dismay, she didn't get to hook up with Diddy.

"He ain't neva leaving that bitch Kim Porter anyway, girl." Shannelle shrugged.

2

hello?" *Remmi* moaned into the receiver of her cordless phone. She squinted at the digital clock sitting on her nightstand. Her blurred vision revealed that it was three thirty in the morning—just a few hours before she had to get up for work.

"Whatchu doin'?" a low, masculine voice mumbled.

"Huh?" Remmi moaned again, the sleep in her voice evident.

"Whatchu doin'?" the voice repeated.

"I'm sleeping. Who the fuck is this?"

"It's D."

"D? Well, why you calling me at three thirty in the morning? I haven't heard from you in weeks."

"Been outta town. But you know I been thinkin' about you."

Remmi adjusted the down pillow behind her head as she cradled the receiver between her neck and shoulder. "If you been thinkin' about me, why ain't I heard from your ass?" she sleepily questioned.

"You know how it is on the road. Shit is hectic. But never mind about that. I'm about to leave this club. Why don't I slide through and check you for a few?"

"Naah. I gotta get up in a coupla hours."

"Oh. I wanted to see you 'cause I'ma be outta the country for like two months and I have something real serious I wanted to talk to you about."

Oh, shit. Is he gonna propose? Remmi asked herself. Maybe he *had* been feeling her, even though he always hit it and never called for weeks, sometimes months, later. Maybe Remmi was finally gonna get that six-carat diamond she'd been wishing for. God knew, as the president and CEO of one of the most successful hip-hop labels of all times, D could afford it—and since his fiancée had been killed in a recent skiing accident, maybe now was her chance.

"All right," she replied.

It was on the set of R. Kelly's "I'm a Flirt" video that Remmi had met D'Aundre Collens. His eyes remained fixated on her for the entire shoot, and from the blinding light on his left wrist, she knew that he was someone she should get to know better. After being wined and dined for two months straight, Remmi definitely thought she had caught her man. Little did she know, he was very much engaged. When confronted with the issue, he told Remmi he was planning on calling the wedding off—that he just needed the right moment—that although he wasn't ready for marriage, his fiancée was "good people," and he didn't want to hurt her. But he never called it off, and then the fiancée died—skied smack into a naked oak tree on the intermediate slope of an exclusive resort in Vail, Colorado. You would have thought D'Aundre would go into hiding as he mourned the death of the woman he was supposed to spend the rest of his life with—*not*. Two weeks later, he was doing the freaky mambo with Remmi on her kitchen sink. So much for true love.

Knowing how he drove his CLK, Remmi had less than fifteen minutes before he'd get to her place from downtown Manhattan. So she set her cordless phone onto its base and immediately jumped up from her queen-sized bed. Then she sprayed the bed and herself down with Issey Miyake, changed out of her sweats and into a red silk Vicki Secret's teddy, brushed her teeth, washed her face, and waited for the doorbell to ring. And it did. Almost to the minute. She knew her niggas.

"So, what up?" D asked as he stepped across her threshold.

"Ain't nuthin'. What's up with you? Where you been?" Remmi asked.

"Told you. I been on the road. And I'm about to go back out in the morning." D'Aundre looked Remmi up and down, licked his lips, and chuckled out loud. "Rementa, Rementa, Rementa— always a sexy muthafucka. What's up, ma?" He grinned as he took off his mink jacket, tossed it onto Remmi's black leather sofa, and sat down beside it.

"You tell me. You the one who said you had something to talk to me about. Well, what the hell is so important that I needed to get outta my bed at damn near four in the morning?" she sassed, standing before him half-naked with her hand on her hip. Like the cat that swallowed the canary, D'Aundre kept smiling but said nothing.

"You drunk?" Remmi questioned.

"I'm nice . . . ," he replied.

"So, what the fuck is up? If you ain't got nuthin' to say, you might as well go 'cause I told your ass I gotta get up in a coupla hours. I'm starting a new assignment at Epic Records in the morning."

"You still doin' that temping shit? I thought you was a star. I just seen your ass all up in Ne-Yo's last video."

"Yeah, I know. I only temp at labels or fashion houses now—to get connects, yaknowhatImean? A girl gotta eat, ya know."

"I hear dat. An independent woman. I like dat." He grinned some more, licking his lips again as if he would devour her at any moment. "So come on over here and give me a little suga." Remmi sat down beside D'Aundre, who immediately began rubbing her butt and kissing her neck. No stranger to his skills, Remmi couldn't help but give in when he ran his hand up the inside of her teddy, touching and gently prodding all the right places. The chill from the ice on his fingers and wrist added to her excitement as she quickly began to feel hot moisture between her legs. She climbed aboard his muscular body, aggressively gyrating herself upon his jeans until she could plainly see his bulge ready to burst through his zipper. He softly bit her nipples, and she did her best to push his dark blue 575s and boxers to his knees before she slid down between his legs and slipped his pulsating ten-inches into her mouth—balls and all. As he moaned in ecstasy, a voice inside her head screamed, *That's right, I got this nigga now. Gimme my mutha-fuckin' six carats!*

It wasn't long before their bodies became as intertwined as a Boy Scout's knot. They rolled from the leather sofa to the hard-wood floors, from her computer chair to the windowsill, fogging up the glass. After a good twenty minutes of hot, sweaty, funky sex, D'Aundre pulled himself out of Remmi, ripped off the con-dom, and squirted a million of his unborn babies all over her face and chest. He was the best she'd had in a while. He always was.

Yeah, I think I can do this shit for a lifetime. I could get with being the Mrs., she thought. As he caught his breath, Remmi threw on a satin robe while D'Aundre lay on her floor in his birthday suit. Then she silently positioned herself beside him and began playing with the tip of his penis.

"So, baby, now that we're both feeling good, I wanna know— what did you need to come here at damn near four A.M. to talk to me about? It must be pretty important if you couldn't say it over the phone," Remmi began.

"Yeah, it's important," he mumbled as he started putting on his clothes.

He's going for the ring! He's going for the ring! It must be in his jacket pocket!

"Yeah, well—um, ma—I know you and I been fuckin' with each other for a while now, and I think you real special."

"Uh-huh."

"And you know Tonya's death really fucked me up, right."

"Tonya?" Remmi thought a minute. "Oh, yeah—your ex."

"Yeah, Tonya was wifey." He paused for a moment before continuing. "Anyway, that shit got me thinking 'bout how precious life is and shit and how tomorrow ain't promised to nobody, na mean?"

"Uh-huh."

"So I started counting my blessings and shit."

"Uh-huh."

"And I decided that I'ma marry Peaches."

"Peaches? Who the fuck is Peaches?" Remmi demanded, dropping his dick on his leg.

"You ain't gotta stop, ma," D replied, focusing his attention on his now limp penis.

"Who the fuck is Peaches, D'Aundre?" Remmi snapped, annoyed.

"My daughter's moms," he said, as if she should have known.

There was near silence in the room with only the hum of her refrigerator in the background. Remmi just knew he could not be for real. Not after she had given the performance of a lifetime.

"Excuse me?" she asked, and stood her full five feet five inches.

"Yeah—um, she was my high school sweetheart, and I realize that I always loved her. Even more than Tonya."

"Get the fuck outta here! Then what the fuck did you just fuck *my* brains out for?"

"Oh—that was 'see ya' sex—I'm not gon' be doing no more shit like that—I'ma settle down, maybe even have a couple more kids if she's wit' it. But I definitely had to have one for the road. Chicks don't fuck like you anymore, Rem. Bitches don't be wanting mess up they perm and shit. But not Rementa. You got skills, B. And it was good as shit, wasn't it?" He smiled.

"Are you serious?"

"What? Why the fuck you trippin'? I *know* you ain't think we was gonna *be* together or somethin' like that." D'Aundre chuckled. "Come on, now. You know you my jump-off chick. Thought that was understood."

Remmi grabbed D's jacket from the sofa, pushed it into his chest, and softly whispered, "Good-bye, D."

"Why is you trippin'?"

"Good-bye, D!"

D'Aundre slipped his arms into the sleeves of his coat, shook his head, and walked toward the front door.

"You buggin'. Gettin' all emotional and shit. What you think? I was gonna wife you?" He shrugged with a last chuckle as he exited the apartment.

"Fuck you," Remmi muttered.

She placed her forehead on the wall, and her eyes welled up

with tears that she refused to let fall. It was all part of the game, she told herself. Remmi waved her hand in the air and locked the front door before climbing back into her bed for one last hour of sleep.

3

too fat . . . too skinny . . . too dark . . . you need a touch up . . . your legs are ashy . . . you need a pedicure . . . ," the stout middle-aged director pronounced with a strong European accent as he walked up the line of hopefuls. His crossed arms rested above his protruding belly while he looked each girl up and down with a raised and scrutinizing brow. There had to be over two hundred girls anxiously awaiting approval, all wishing and hoping to be one of the fifty who would appear in the pool party scene of Ludacris's new video.

As the director approached Remmi, she could feel her heart pounding a mile a minute. And when he stood before her, it stopped completely.

"You. Step over here," he instructed almost as emotionlessly as he had spewed his insults to the others. But Remmi didn't care. She had made the cut and was damn proud of it.

The director continued his process of elimination, and Remmi's line began to fill up with her soon-to-be coworkers, all smiling as if they had hit the jackpot, each one more scantily clad than the next. Once he'd made his final selection, the director dismissed those not chosen and announced to those remaining that they should report to 125th Street and Park Avenue at 5 A.M. where a bus would be transporting them to the shoot location.

"And, ladies," he continued through his silver megaphone, "you need not bring wardrobe."

"So, what you saying is that you gotta be on 125th before the sun comes up to get on some bus that's gonna take your ass to West Bubble Fuck?" Shannelle asked Remmi as they sat in a public atrium on Madison Avenue, sharing a sandwich. Shannelle had just come from a doctor's appointment not too far from where Remmi was temping and decided to join her for lunch. As much as she liked having lunch with her best friend, Shannelle hated going up to the record labels where she worked. All the interns and fake-ass wannabe execs were always staring at her as she waited for Remmi, especially in the summer when she liked to put her long legs on display. But this particular day she happened to be in the city and decided to suck it up, and meeting up with Remmi was a good way to pass the time before she headed to the Bronx.

"Yeah, they said we shooting at some mansion in Connecticut," Remmi replied, taking a sip of her Dr. Brown's Cream Soda.

"You crazy, girl. I wish I *would* get up at the crack of dawn to shake my ass for free."

"Oh, here you go again—and for your information, this time I'm getting paid."

"Oh, really? How much?"

"Don't worry about how much. Do I ask you how much you bring home from that god-awful dungeon?"

"Bitch, please. Call it what you want. That dungeon pays every single last one of my bills and I'm sorry but two hundred fifty dollars for twelve hours of work does not qualify as getting paid, Remmi. I make that shit in two hours."

"Who said I'm getting two fifty? I *said* it's none of your business how much I'm getting paid," Remmi snapped.

"Must be two hundred." Shannelle chuckled.

Remmi sucked her teeth and rolled her eyes at her best friend, who'd actually hit the nail on the head—she was getting two hundred dollars.

"I'm meeting Dale after work tonight. That's why I'm going in early. He's picking me up at nine," Shannelle continued.

"Dale? I thought you kicked his trifling ass to the curb a long time ago."

"I did. But you know I got a weakness for him. I figured we'd just go get something to eat and chill. We can't do nothing anyway. I'm on my period. Not to mention I'm still dealing with this cold that I can't seem to get rid of."

"Girl, your period won't stop a nucca from asking you to suck his dick. You need to leave that cat alone. Don't you remember all the drama that nigga brought to your life? The crabs, the chlamydia, the psycho baby mama? Damn, you have a short-ass memory."

"He ain't wit' her no more. They split up. And I told you, I ain't even sure I got those crabs from him. Plus, he got his own place now and everything. In Queens. And he just started doing publicity for Baby Phat. I was thinking I might be able to parlay us into getting some free gear."

"Hmm. I really don't give a shit what he's doing now. Ain't no orgasm worth a sick dick, and that nigga is dirty."

"You right."

"You just like his ass 'cause he got so-called good hair."

Shannelle chuckled—her friend was right.

"Bitch, a lotta niggas got good hair. . . . Shit, yo' ass got good hair. What the fuck you need his for?"

"Girl, it ain't just them jet black silky curls he got goin' on. The nigga got da magic stick, and he knows how to use it!" Shannelle replied, licking her lips as if she were tasting him at that very moment.

"Whateva. That shit ain't hard to find. And magic sticks ain't worth it if there's an STD at the other end. I just don't like that muthafucka—and he ain't neva liked me."

"I don't think he ain't like you. He felt you was too much in our business."

"He's damn skippy! He ain't gon' be doggin' my best friend out and think I ain't got nuthin' to say about it. Fuck that."

"Well, I think he changed. Sounds like he's trying to get his act together. I don't know. He sounded different."

Remmi shrugged. "His ass is trouble."

"You probably right. But what's the harm in me letting him buy me dinner? I gotta eat tonight anyway. Might as well let him pay for it. And like I said, we can't do shit, 'cause I'm on my period. And I ain't suckin' shit."

"Yeah, let's see what story you tell me tomorrow. 'Remmi, I couldn't help myself! Remmi he seduced me! Girl, he ain't care that I was on my period! We did it in the shower!'" Remmi mocked her friend.

Shannelle couldn't help but laugh as Remmi mimicked her, almost choking on a potato chip. As Remmi patted her on the back, the two young women were interrupted by a short heavyset guy who stood before them and knocked three times on the table.

"Hello, Rementa. Who's your friend?" he asked, adjusting his expensive rimless Versace glasses.

Remmi looked up to see one of Epic's senior VPs standing above her with his belly jiggling two inches away from her elbow. Remmi quickly replied, "Oh, hey, Marc."

Not taking his eyes off Shannelle as he mentally peeled off every stitch of her clothing, he asked, "You gonna make an introduction?"

"Oh, sure—um, Shannelle, this is Marc Roosy, senior vice president of A&R at Epic. Marc, this is my best friend, Shannelle Anderson."

The two firmly shook hands as a mesmerized Marc sat his fat ass in the empty chair beside Shannelle.

"I don't think I've seen anything as fine as you all month." Marc smiled as he looked into Shannelle's eyes. Remmi turned her head a bit to keep from laughing. Marc looked ridiculous as he tried to mack Shannelle, whose three-inch heels made her stand almost a whole foot above his four-foot-eleven-inch frame. He wasn't a bad-looking guy. Just short and fat. He had charm and dressed exceptionally well, but those attributes could not hide the fact that he clearly possessed a Napoleon complex and found his ability to mack tall females an incredible ego booster.

"And you're not gonna see anything better for the rest of the month, either." Shannelle smiled, humoring Marc's midgetron ass.

"So how can I get in contact with you?" he asked, licking his lips as if he'd just eaten the juiciest pork chop on the planet. Shannelle scribbled her cell phone number on a half-crumpled napkin and placed it into Marc's tiny piglet fingers.

"I'ma call you." He smiled.

"Okay."

The corniness of the scene tormented Remmi as she repeatedly cleared her throat, hoping to interrupt the dialogue between them. She knew damn well Marc's ass was married, and it was burning a hole in her tongue not to mention it. After all, his wife had been up to the office two times since she'd been working there, looking like she could be the captain of the WNFL. Needless to say, Mrs. Roosy certainly did not appear to be one to fuck with. After Marc walked his portly body away from the table where they sat, Remmi blurted out, "What the fuck are you gonna do with his stunted ass when you're damn near twelve inches taller than him?"

"I happen to like little dudes—especially ones with *big* wallets. He'll spend a lot 'cause he's got shit to prove, and plus he's closer to my kitty cat," Shannelle laughed.

"Well, he's married."

Shannelle shrugged. "That's his wife's problem, not mine."

"I gotta get back upstairs. . . ." Remmi shook her head, rose from the table, and dumped her trash in a garbage can nearby. As she walked back over to where Shannelle sat, her eyes bulged and her impeccably manicured fingers covered her mouth—a soiled sanitary napkin was sitting on the ground beside her best friend's right foot. Remmi leaned in close to her friend and irately whispered, "How many times have I fuckin' told you *not* to wear a Kotex with a thong?"

"Wha—," Shannelle exclaimed as she looked down to see what Remmi had spotted from afar.

"Girl—let's go," Shannelle cried out, and jumped up from her seat.

"That's what you get for not listening to me. You know my ass is smarter than you," Remmi said.

"Do you think little man saw that shit?" she continued as they made a hasty exit.

"I hope not, girl," Remmi howled.

he clock struck 9 P.M., and Shannelle hustled out of Shirley's Temple with a spring overcoat thrown over her revealing costume. She didn't want to keep Dale waiting and was anxious to see him after so many months. It had been a very good night. The early evening crowd had been extremely generous, and she'd come away with close to seven hundred dollars after her four-hour shift. Happy as she was about her earnings, she could not help but think about Dale, who was supposed to be outside waiting for her. She looked at her watch, which read 9:10. They hadn't seen each other in a while, but Dale had never been one to be late. As she made her way over to where her car was parked on the street, she dialed his cell phone number, but it went straight to voice mail.

He's probably driving through a dead zone, she thought to herself as she climbed into the driver's seat of her Volkswagen Passat.

Patiently waiting, Shannelle turned on the car radio to keep her mind occupied. She hadn't spoken to him since the night before, but considered their plans to be solid. So when her watch read 10:15, she gently stuck her key in the ignition and turned it, overwhelmed with disappointment and slightly concerned. He was a schmuck, but Dale had never actually stood her up before. She wondered if some chick had cock-blocked her. She wondered if he had gotten tied up with work. Or maybe his psycho baby mama wasn't really out of the picture. However, she wasn't about to wait another moment in that parking lot. She pulled off and headed home.

---

adies, your trailer is to the left. Do not come out until you are told!" the production assistant instructed. As the girls walked to the cabin, Remmi felt like the star of the show. She knew she looked better than the other girls on the set and was determined to be all up in the camera with Ludacris.

Remmi and her forty-nine coworkers piled into a thirty-foot trailer like cattle waiting to be slaughtered, and she could feel a lot of eyes on her. Remmi acted as though she didn't notice the jealous looks as one of the makeup guys took her by the hand and sat her in his chair.

"You need to be in the front." The muscle-bound Latino stylist—with far too much sugar in his tank—smiled. "I am going to make you look *extra*, girlfriend." He quickly wiped Remmi's face with an astringent-soaked cotton ball, and she noticed that both his nipples were pierced—it was obvious even through his red spandex T-shirt. A little on the freaky side herself, Remmi became immediately aroused. He was fine, too, but she was clearly not his type—having female parts and all.

Still, Remmi could not help feeling flattered by his attention. He obviously thought she was something special. She always knew she had an edge on a lot of girls but was ecstatic when others confirmed it. After twenty minutes of feeling like the queen of the Nile, while stylists and makeup artists relentlessly fussed over her, she saw the director of the video make his way to the back of the trailer. It was the same stout middle-aged director with the European accent who had picked her out of the lineup at the audition, but for some reason, today he looked even more portly. Perhaps it was the ridiculous-looking black wool tam that sat upon his balding head.

What could this fool possibly know about hip-hop videos? Remmi asked herself, letting out a small laugh.

While Remmi stood before him, scantily clad in a black lace teddy and four-inch spiked heels, the director circled her with one hand on top of his protruding belly and the other beneath his double chin, looking her up and down like a slave owner about to purchase his most fertile investment. Remmi stood perfectly still as she was observed, eagerly awaiting the next compliment. Needless to say, she was taken aback when the director opened his mouth and began his spiel.

"She's the lead?" the director asked the head stylist, as if Remmi wasn't even standing there.

"Yes," the petite caramel-skinned girl replied.

"She's overdressed," he continued.

"Overdressed? She's wearing a G-string negligee, Evret," the stylist pointed out. "What do you want her to be—naked?"

"Yes," he snapped.

Silence came over the trailer, as if everyone had stopped to tune in to the conversation that was brewing before Remmi. Remmi herself could not believe that this director actually wanted her to walk out onto a set filled with people, wearing nothing— lead or no lead. She was already practically nude. The teddy she had on barely covered her breasts, and the cheeks of her ass were completely exposed. Did they really have to go to the next level?

"This is a bedroom scene. She doesn't need to wear anything. Her face is beautiful. Her body is beautiful. That's enough. The other girls in the lounge scene can wear what she's wearing. She needs to stand out from the others. She is the lead," Evret firmly stated.

Shaking her head, the stylist looked Remmi in the eye and asked, "Are you willing to be naked in this video?"

"Of course she's *willing to be naked*. Look at the skin she's in," Evret ranted. "She's probably *used* to being naked. *Right?*"

Remmi was so taken aback by his frankness that she was actually at a loss for words.

"What are you? A stripper or something?"

"Uh, um, no," Remmi finally mustered up enough courage to reply.

"Well, you should be. You could make a lot of money. Look, sweetheart, you're the finest babe in here. That's why you're the lead. You're gonna be in Ludacris's bed. Don't you wanna be in Ludacris's bed?"

Remmi still couldn't manage to speak. She knew the words she wanted to say, but she could not get them out.

"You'll be under the sheets. Nobody out there in TV land is gonna see anything but cleavage. I know you've shown cleavage before, haven't you?" he continued.

Still silent, Remmi stared right at the director with a look of disbelief on her face. The stylist's only response was to shake her head in disgust.

"What's the matter with you, babe? Are you mute? Well, it really doesn't matter if you are. In fact, the less you say, the better. Look, if you don't wanna do it, I'm sure there's plenty of other babes in here that will—where's that babe with the platinum tongue ring?" he called out, looking around the trailer.

"No, no, no—I'll do it," Remmi weakly responded.

"What was that, babe?" the director questioned.

"I'll do it," Remmi replied more firmly.

"Oh, you'll do it . . . oh, okay—I thought so. Don't be shy, babe. The skin you're in can make you a lot of money. Use it while you have it because one day it'll be old and wrinkled." The director snapped his fingers as if he was losing his patience.

"Somebody get this babe a disclaimer and release form!" he called out as his stubby little legs carried his corpulent body out the trailer door.

ll eyes were on Remmi as she lay beneath the purple satin sheets with the video's star. The stylist was kind enough to convince the director to let Remmi at least wear a thong as she lay under the covers. Initially extremely uncomfortable, Remmi tried with all her might to keep her breasts covered with the top sheet. She did look beautiful, but her obvious uneasiness annoyed the director, who yelled and threatened to replace her several times before she finally got into the swing of it.

However, by the time the shoot wrapped, Remmi was a seasoned vet, comfortable with exposing her perky voluptuous breasts and on her way to being video ho royalty. Before leaving the shoot, Remmi exchanged numbers with everyone she thought was anyone, including the abrasive director, who promised to feature her in all his future projects. It was a turning point for Remmi's career, and had she known that showing her titties would make her a star, she would certainly have done it a whole lot sooner.

Shannelle will be so proud of me, she thought to herself.

ow long have you been holed up in this apartment, and why you ain't call me?" Remmi asked Shannelle. It had been nearly two weeks since the Ludacris videotaping, and Remmi had been so busy, she hadn't had an opportunity to have a real conversation with her best friend in all that time.

The Ludacris video had been Remmi's big break, fully thrusting her into the world of music videos and placing her name and her breasts in extremely high demand. With the connects she had made on that set, Remmi's next two weeks were filled with three rap videos, all with leading roles and major pay. But when Shannelle had left a message on her voice mail telling her that she was suffering from a bad case of the flu, Remmi rearranged her schedule and made it her business to get over to Shannelle's apartment to take care of the only sister she had ever known.

"'Bout time you got over here," Shannelle softly began as she took a sip of tea. "I left you that message last Thursday."

"I know. I just couldn't get out of that Eminem video. But I'm here now," Remmi replied, adjusting the pillow behind Shannelle's head. "Ya know, he really is a fine-ass white boy. I'd never fuck him, though."

"I would." Shannelle laughed and coughed at the same time.

"I'm sorry, but I love the brothas, even though they get on my last nerve. I read in *Vibe* magazine that D'Aundre got married down in the Bahamas. I *hate* that nigga. Still, black dick is the best, though."

"Girl, forget that nigga. I never knew why you was fuckin' wit' him in the first place. He's somebody else's problem now. Don't be surprised if his ass be calling you in a couple of weeks. That's how niggas like him are. But on the real, dick is dick. It's the size that counts, not the color."

"I don't know. I ain't neva fuck no white boy. Don't think I could." Remmi scrunched up her nose.

"Girl, like I said, it's the size that matters. And all brothas do not live up to the myth, ya know. One of the best fucks I ever had came from this white boy named Ross Kaufman when I used to strip up at the Hidden Treasure. He was the owner's nephew. A Jew boy. He started catchin' feelins, too—but he was engaged to some little white bitch names Suzie and could have *never* brought *my* black ass home. We used to still hit it every once in a while on the DL even after his ass got married. I didn't give a shit—it wasn't like I was dissin' no sista or anything like that and like I said, that dick was good. Not to mention he used to hit me off lovely—paid any bill I gave his ass. That muthafucka was loaded. He used to bring lobster dinners to my house and shit—since we could never be seen in public. But I ain't care. I haven't heard from him in a while. As a matter of fact, I need to call his ass." Shannelle laughed again.

"You are such a ho." Remmi shook her head.

"Well, it sounds like you about to become the head video ho in charge."

"A little sumthin'." Remmi smiled.

"I told you if you showed a little more ass, you could go further. See, they all checkin' for you now 'cause they know you got heart and ain't afraid to get gully. It takes a certain kind of confidence to parade around naked, ya know. And most bitches ain't built that way. Maybe I should be your agent. You sure you don't wanna come down to the Temple? Shirley's always looking for new chicks. Together we could run that place. Maybe even start our own shit."

"Girl, I ain't tryin' to dance butt-ass naked for no nasty-ass, hard-up, can't-get-no-pussy-for-free, pantin' muthafuckas! What I do is *acting*. It's an *art*."

"Bitch, give me a break!" They shared a hearty laugh until Shannelle began to cough violently.

Struggling to hand her friend the cup of tea that sat on the nightstand without spilling it, Remmi was taken aback by Shannelle's fit of coughing. "Damn, girl—you sound like you dying!" she snapped.

"I'ma do a lotta things real soon, girl—but dying ain't one of them," Shannelle replied as she regained her composure.

"Well, I hope not, 'cause we haven't made our first cool million yet."

"Say word."

4

You were definitely the finest chick on the set," the medium-built dark-skinned brotha bellowed at Remmi over his drink as she sat perched on a bar stool in Club NV. It was clear that he wanted some ass, but Remmi had to see what he was working with before she gave him that type of consideration. Sure, his wrist was laced with diamonds that glittered in the darkness of the nightclub as the sounds of Mobb Deep blasted in the background. But that wasn't enough for her. He hadn't bought a bottle of Cristal to prove that he was serious, nor had he refilled her apple martini that he'd sprung for twenty minutes ago. He claimed to own some recording studio in the Village where everyone who was anyone was supposed to have recorded at some time or another, and had seen her on the set of Sean Paul's video—but Remmi sort of got the feeling that he had seen her in the video on BET like all the other regular brothas out there. After all, it wasn't like she'd been hidden in the background. She'd been the lead.

It was the first time the Dynamic Duo had been out on the town in a while. Shannelle had finally squashed her flu bug, and the girls wanted to catch up on some much-needed partying. And since Shannelle's new flava of the month was the head bouncer at the club, the girls had decided to spend their Sunday evening getting their swerve on.

At the stroke of midnight, Shannelle dipped off with Omar for a little freak session in his office while Remmi sat perched high like the mother of all peacocks, looking like the beauty queen she was at the crowded bar. It didn't take long for her to have company, but she was selective about whom she let buy her drinks, and the first four brothas who came along didn't fit the criteria. By the time the fifth knucklehead had sauntered into her sphere, the thickness of the air had gotten the best of her, and she was thirsty. It could have been a snaggle-toothed cyclops with a prosthetic leg, and she would have given him the privilege of spending his money on her. But it wasn't. It was Byron Barnes. Now, he wasn't an ugly brotha—but a little shorter than Remmi liked. Still the bling on his wrists was enough for Remmi to listen to what he had to say. And even though she got the feeling that he was actually somebody's sidekick, her throat was drier than the Sahara.

"What were you doing on the set?" Remmi asked, clearing her throat and eyeballing her martini glass, insinuating that it was time for a refill.

"I was chillin' with my mans and them. SP uses my studio whenever he's in New York," he replied, not taking her hint about the drink.

"Well, I didn't see you there." She shrugged.

"How could you? There was a swarm of people around you like killer bees," he laughed.

"Well, if you was checkin' for me so hard, why you ain't come up to me *after* the killer bees flew away?"

"Not my style. I figured if it was meant to be, I'd see you again. Guess it was meant to be." His smile displayed a mouthful of platinum teeth. Remmi was a little put off by his Cash Money–ish grin. She was a stickler for good hygiene and couldn't imagine that platinum-covered teeth could actually contribute to that—no matter what kind of hood status they demanded. But it was a double-edged sword for her. It had been her experience that platinum teeth usually translated into platinum pockets. And while she knew that Byron's teeth were probably rotten underneath all that metal, she was also smart enough to know that his wallet was probably very healthy. So what she had to give up hygiene for bling bling. She just wouldn't kiss him.

Everybody has to sacrifice something at some point in life, she reasoned.

"So, you having a good time?" he questioned, looking her up and down like she was a ham sandwich.

"I'd be having a better time if you refill this fuckin' apple martini you bought me over thirty minutes ago. Can't you see it's watered down? Dang."

He summoned the bartender to refill both their glasses. "And a bottle of Cris," he added.

Now that's *what the hell I'm talking about*, Remmi thought.

Twenty minutes later, another apple martini and an empty bottle of Cristal truly had Remmi hot under the collar. To top it off, she had no idea where the hell Shannelle was. Thus she had no choice but to stick with Byron for the night, which only put him in his glory. And she really didn't mind that much, since the drunker she got, the finer he got. With a clouded view of the scene before her eyes, Byron led Remmi to the dance floor with her hand in his. As they grinded to the sounds of Beenie Man, the reggae beat sent Remmi on an out-of-body experience. It was almost as if she were watching herself on the dance floor from the bar, as she never even remembered climbing down from the stool. But there she stood, nevertheless, with Byron's right hand on her naked inner thigh inching its way up to her apple bottom and then around to her shaven crotch. She'd decided not to wear panties that night, since her Ferragamo minidress fit her like a second skin, showing the panty line of even her tiniest thong. The bareness under her dress made Byron's voyage inside her easy, and the crowded dance floor was none the wiser as he fingered her moistness and licked his finger, then used his left hand to do the same. She wanted to tell him to stop, but she couldn't seem to get her lips to form the words. His thick manicured fingers felt good as they moved in and out of her, but exhibitionism was not her style.

"You need to stop," she finally panted, grabbing his hand and pulling it from under her dress.

"You know you like it, baby." He breathed heavily into her ear. "I can feel how wet you are."

"I'm not into public sex acts, muthafucka," she snapped.

"Then let's leave this dump. I got a four-point-six outside that we can finish this up in," he replied, still holding her close.

"Nah . . . I'm not interested," Remmi groggily answered.

"I already tasted your pussy, and I like it. Ain't no way I ain't fuckin' you tonight," he grunted. Offended that he would actually have the audacity to think that it was up to *him* whether or not he was getting some pussy—like *he* was calling the shots—Remmi turned around and, in her most disgruntled, drunken ghetto-girl voice, screamed over the music, "I *said* back the fuck up, muthafucka—you ain't gettin' none of this! I don't know who the fuck you thi—"

Before she could put the *ink* on *think*, Byron's massive paw came crashing down on her face with the intensity of an Amtrak locomotive. It happened so quickly that Remmi almost didn't even realize that she had been slapped with the same thick-ass fingers that Byron just had in her coochie, sending her flying at least five feet, knocking everyone in the path out of the line of fire. As a huge commotion broke out and Remmi tried to regain her bearings from the sting of the blow, before she knew it, Byron was on her ass again, causing her to see stars like she was straight out of some Bugs Bunny cartoon epic, all the while yelling, "I don't know who the fuck you think *you* is, bitch—you betta recognize, *bitch*!"

Trying desperately to block her face from his attack, Remmi felt like it was forever before security came to the rescue, pulling Byron off her and restraining him.

The two minutes that it took to guide Remmi from the dance floor felt like an eternity. Drunk, fucked up, and embarrassed, she saw the faces of Omar and Shannelle through her swollen eyes, as she sat in the old, dingy security office. In a daze, Remmi was seated behind a rickety wooden desk in a chair that could barely support her weight while the distant sounds of Lil' Kim's "Queen B" could be heard from the other side of the steel door. Usually the anthem of the Dynamic Duo, tonight the song's lyrics pierced through Remmi's eardrums like daggers as a female bouncer held an ice pack to the left side of her face. Remmi could feel the throbbing of her cheek as it continued to swell. Shannelle could not apologize enough for leaving her best friend unattended, and assured her that vengeance would be theirs.

"Have a fight with your boyfriend?" the female bouncer asked.

"That ain't her muthafuckin' boyfriend!" Shannelle screamed. The female bouncer looked Shannelle up and down before Omar instructed Shannelle to relax because the cops would be there any minute.

"Do you want to press charges?" Omar asked Remmi. Unable to speak, Remmi merely nodded her head.

"Hell, yeah, she wanna press charges! And somebody need to call an ambulance! Look at her face!" Shannelle continued to shout.

"Do you want us to call an ambulance?" the female bouncer asked Remmi. Remmi shook her head but could not ignore the fact that her head was throbbing and the bass from the music in the club wasn't making it any better.

The police came through the steel doors with a forceful entry—two uniformed members of NYPD with smirks on their faces and their heads shaking from left to right in disgust.

"Was the perpetrator your boyfriend?" a fat red-haired officer asked Remmi.

"That *wasn't* her boyfriend. What the fuck is up with you people?" Shannelle snapped.

"Who are you?" the other officer, a medium-built Latino, dryly asked.

"Her sister," Shannelle replied with much attitude.

"Well, if you want to help your sister, you'll be quiet and let her answer the questions," Officer Morales continued.

"C'mon, ma. Why don't you wait outside," Omar suggested to Shannelle.

"I ain't going nowhere! The reason why all this shit happened is 'cause I left her in the first place. Fuckin' wit' your two-minute ass!" she ranted.

Obviously embarrassed, Omar tried to calm Shannelle down—to no avail. Needless to say, the yelling was far too much for Remmi's already aching head. In pain, she lifted the ice pack from her face and said, "I don't know him. I met him here tonight. His name is Byron Barnes, and he owns some studio downtown. That's all I know."

"Are you intoxicated, ma'am?" the red-haired officer questioned, scribbling in his pad.

"Yes, well, no—well, a little bit. But I know exactly what happened," Remmi replied.

"My sister ain't drunk! That muthafucka couldn't take no for an answer, that's all, and instead of being in here questioning the victim, you *need* to be out there arresting his ass!" Shannelle spat.

"Look, ma'am, if you're not going to be quiet, we're going to have to ask you to leave," Officer Morales informed her.

Shannelle shook her head and sucked her teeth. Then she pulled up a chair next to Remmi.

"Where is he now?" Remmi asked.

"He managed to slip away from security, so we need as much information as you know about him," Officer McFee stated.

"What the fuck you mean he managed to slip away from security?" Shannelle yelled, jumping up from her seat. "Omar, he managed to slip away from security? What type of shit is that!"

Omar shrugged his shoulders and couldn't explain why his staff had failed to hold Byron until the cops got there. As Remmi tried to recap exactly what had happened out on the dance floor, the red-haired cop effortlessly scribbled all her words into a little black spiral notepad.

"We'll do our best to try to catch this person, ma'am. Hopefully somebody in here knows him and will be willing to talk to us," Officer Morales told Remmi after taking down her contact information. Meanwhile, all Remmi could do was sit there in pain, looking more and more like the Elephant Man with every passing second, her formerly flawless face swollen beyond recognition.

5

a*lthough Shannelle* had gotten over her bout with the flu, she still couldn't kick the tired feeling that overwhelmed her. She also still hadn't recovered from the night Remmi had been assaulted at the club. She felt guilty about leaving Remmi by herself. She loved making a lot of money at Shirley's Temple and usually put her all into it, but over the course of the following week, it was as if she were a robot mechanically going through the motions during her shifts at Shirley's Temple. She was skeptical of every dude who placed a five-dollar bill in her G-string, because he could be a potential psycho. To add to her paranoia, the police still had not picked up Byron Barnes—whom they claimed did not even exist. According to their investigation, there was no Byron Barnes who fit the description of Remmi's assailant who owned or who was even connected with any recording studio in the tri-state area. He had obviously given Remmi a fake name. Determined to have him arrested,

Remmi had even gone down to the police station to look through mug shots, but to no avail. After two hours of thumbing through photos, every medium-built dark-skinned brotha looked the same to her. It seemed that this psycho had gotten away with first-degree assault, and the cops couldn't have cared less. They took one good look at Remmi and Shannelle, assumed they were strippers, and developed a "these things happen to girls like you" type of attitude. Needless to say, Remmi felt like her ass had been kicked twice.

At work, Shannelle now gave an old balding white man dressed in a dark blue suit her most lackluster lap dance. Unable to concentrate, all she could do was hope that her shift would breeze by swiftly so that she could crawl into her bed and drift off into dreamland.

"Silky," Shirley whispered the stage name in Shannelle's ear as she quickly went past her on the floor. Though it was only four in the afternoon, Shirley's hot breath was already tainted with Hennessy and nicotine. From the way Shirley's 350-pound torso brushed by Shannelle's naked bottom, she knew Shirley had beef. She didn't feel like being reprimanded by her boss, but she also knew she hadn't been on her feet lately. For the past week, she had been late every day. Earlier that week, she had even forgotten part of her outfit, having to borrow a pair of shoes from one of other girls. Not to mention the fact that her pole and lap dances had been real sloppy. Shirley was bound to have something to say about her recent performance.

As Shannelle made her way off the club floor, down the corridor, and into the lavishly decorated office of her superior, her chest vibrated to the sounds of "Thong Song"; her heart was beating a mile a minute. Not feeling very confrontational and knowing she was in the wrong seemed to take away all her usual feistiness.

When Shannelle entered the office—which looked as if it didn't even belong in the dingy club where it was housed—Shirley sat quietly behind a huge expensive mahogany desk, slowly rocking back and forth on her deep brown leather throne; her impeccably manicured claws neatly formed a hollow triangle.

"Have a seat, Silky," Shirley softly stated with a raised brow. Her voice was deep and husky from years of inhaling Black & Mild cigars. It was rumored that she was a dyke, although no one had ever seen her with a lover and she was far too smart to hit on any of her workers. But her mammoth size—she stood an even six feet two inches in flats—perfectly lined fade, and masculine demeanor made no one question what her preference was. The only daughter of a Harlem powerhouse numbers runner, Shirley had pistol-whipped her share of dudes and could tussle with any man. Many a night, the girls at the Temple saw Shirley rock some out-of-control patron's world for getting out of line with one of her girls. Gay or straight, Shirley was not one to be fucked with.

"What's up, Silky? You're one of my best girls, but lately you really haven't been on your job," Shirley began. Shannelle was taken aback by her mild demeanor, thinking that Shirley was going to bawl her out.

"I know. I've been going through a lot lately," Shannelle responded.

"Well, I don't wanna get in *your* business, but whatever it is you're going through is affecting *my* business," Shirley continued, reminding Shannelle of the Shirley she knew. A moment of silence passed before her boss pressed the butt of a Black & Mild cigar into her crystal Mikasa ashtray, took a deep breath, and shrugged. "And you need to snap out of it. So consider this your warning."

Shannelle slowly lifted herself up from her seat with her lip slightly twisted to the side, pouting like a five-year-old who had just gotten caught with her hand in the cookie jar. She wanted to walk through the front door of the Temple and never come back. She wanted to disappear. Whatever ailment had come over her body had really gotten out of control. She didn't even feel like herself. All she knew was that it was really starting to get to her.

i t took nearly two weeks for Remmi's face to get back to looking somewhat normal after her assault in the nightclub. Checking herself in the mirror ten times a day, hoping to see improvement was driving her crazy. Being in the house, missing out on her money was driving her crazy. After all, there's only so many talk shows you can watch during the daylight hours before you go half out of your mind. Needless to say, she was ecstatic when she could finally put on some makeup to hide the last few blemishes left over from her violent encounter. Although out of commission, Remmi made it her business to keep her ear to the street, staying abreast of everything that was going on out there in the industry that she so proudly called herself a part of. Her homegirl, Gayle, had called her to let her know about an open audition for John Singleton's new film. Although Gayle could by no means take the place of Shannelle in Remmi's life, they had become fast friends over the months that Remmi had become fully integrated into the video scene.

Gayle, a tall, slender, exotic-looking Hollywood-starlet wannabe, seemed to be the only other girl unthreatened by Remmi's overnight success. Standing an even five feet ten inches, Gayle had a beauty that was undeniable. Her face reflected diverse ancestry. High cheekbones, thick jet-black hair, which she kept in a midlength bob, and perfectly proportioned body made her a force to be reckoned with. Her flawless complexion resembled the color of a newly pressed penny, an obvious contrast to her sparkling green eyes. Physically, she definitely gave Remmi some competition—but Remmi had the sex appeal and charisma Gayle lacked. However, Gayle definitely made up for her few shortcomings with the abundance of gulliness her personality possessed. The girl would do *anything* to get what she wanted. And since they were probably the two in the greatest demand, they ran into each other very often on video sets and at auditions—they could either hate each other or bond. With cattiness and jealousy being so prevalent throughout the business they had chosen, they opted for the latter. In fact, it was Gayle who Remmi had called to fill in for all her shoots while she recuperated from the incident at Club NV. Thus, the least Gayle could do was tip off her audition friend when she heard about this open call.

"I'll see you there, girl," Remmi said into the phone before quickly placing it into its base.

the line for the casting call wrapped around the block of Times Square Studios. The sticky humidity that filled the New York City streets had chicks with hair weaves looking like Frankenstein's brides—everyone except for Remmi and Gayle, that is. The two beauties arrived with their thick ebony manes softly slicked back into ponytails, à la Sade—showing off their sultry but angelic good looks. They had gone to enough casting calls in hot July weather to know that free-flowing dos were simply not an option. As usual, there were glares from the other hopefuls, but they were used to that. It was for this reason they sought refuge in each other.

Although the ad in *Backstage* said the auditions would begin by 8 A.M., at nine fifteen, the doors had still not been opened. Security guards clad in Sean John nylon warm-up suits did their best to keep the crowd in order, but the heat was starting to become too much for some, as many of the girls began voicing their disgust for the lack of consideration shown to them by the staff. Remmi and Gayle were numbers seventy-two and seventy-three in line, although they had arrived well before eight o'clock.

"Ain't you the chick from that Ludacris video?" the burly toy cop questioned Remmi, interrupting a conversation she was having with Gayle.

Rolling her eyes at his rudeness, out of the corner of her mouth she snapped, "Probably."

"Probably? What that mean? Either you is or you ain't," Rent-a-cop snapped back.

"She is. She looks better in person, though, don't she?" Gayle said.

Wiping his forehead with a white handkerchief, the brawny beast with an obvious asthmatic condition skeptically looked Remmi up and down with his beady little eyes before words karate-chopped their way through his steaming hot breath. "Yeah, she a'ight. Her attitude is stank, though," he mumbled.

"Man, it's ninety-five degrees out here and we been standing in the same spot for almost two hours. Every bitch out here got a stank attitude! What's going on? Are y'all having auditions or not?" Remmi interjected.

"Yeah, we'd be in much better moods if we were inside underneath some nice cool air. Who do you work for? The director or the studio?" Gayle asked, batting her long eyelashes above her emerald-colored eyes.

Magilla Gorilla chuckled as he leaned in close to the two girls and whispered, "The director. And we actually about to open the doors in ten minutes—"

"It's about time," Remmi and Gayle chimed together.

"—to the first fifty chicks," he finished.

"What!" Remmi gasped.

"Shh," the guard instructed.

"What the hell you mean, the first fifty chicks? Do you see our numbers? We're seventy-two and seventy-three!" Remmi loudly whispered.

"And we been out here in this heat since seven forty-five this morning!" Gayle continued.

"A'ight, a'ight—I'ma do y'all chicks a favor, 'cause I liketed that Luda video," he whispered as he looked around to see who was watching. "Come wit' me," he said.

"What?" Remmi asked with major attitude.

"I *said*, follow me," he said again.

Gayle grabbed Remmi tightly by the wrist and pulled her as they followed the guard to a door around the corner from where everyone else was standing on line. Remmi didn't feel too comfortable about the situation but figured since she was with Gayle, there was strength in numbers. Still, after what had happened to her at NV, she couldn't be too careful, and she definitely didn't want to be the victim of another assault. If the guard tried anything, she had a rusty box cutter in her Kate Spade bag that she knew how to use very well.

The two girls followed the guard through a dimly lit doorway, the back entrance to the Times Square Studios. She could hear talking over a microphone coming from someplace down the hall, but the guard led them to a small office upstairs.

"Why the fuck are we coming up here? Sounds to me like the auditions are downstairs," Remmi questioned as the guard closed the door behind them.

"Did y'all hear what I told you? I said we're cutting off the auditions at fifty. Mr. Singleton don't wanna see no more than fifty chicks. He's only looking for someone to play the star's sister," the guard told them.

"So, like I said, why the fuck are we coming up here?" Remmi asked again, her arms tightly folded across her chest.

"'Cause I know y'all ain't think I'ma just take you bitches to Mr. Singleton without getting a little something for myself." He snorted, the phlegm from his porky chest swirling around in his throat.

"What?" Remmi said, appalled that he would even think she would degrade herself by touching him just so she could play the main character's sister—the starring role, maybe, but some side character? That was completely out of the question.

"Look, I took y'all bitches off the line. Y'all are numbers seventy-two and seventy-three. Y'all wasn't even gettin' in this piece if I ain't bring y'all asses up here. So go 'head. Turn and leave and watch the casting crew turn you bitches away after he brings in the first fifty. 'Cause that's what he gon' do."

There was a moment of silence in the room, as the foul stench from his foul breath made its way to their noses.

"Or y'all can give me a little sumthin' sumthin' for my trouble," he continued.

"Well, what do you want us to do?" Gayle asked.

"Girl, is you crazy?" Remmi retorted, hitting her friend in the side with her folded elbow.

"Let's hear the muthafucka out, girl. Let's hear the muthafucka out," Gayle replied.

Magilla scratched his crotch, chuckled, and smiled, displaying a mouthful of gold fronts that covered a set of rotten teeth, revealing the culprit of the horrid stench that seeped from beneath his cracked and crusty lips. "I really just wanna finger you. I ain't trying to catch nuthin'. Plus, I gotta girl and five kids already. I ain't even trying to risk payin' no more chile supote." He belched.

Remmi and Gayle looked and each other and tried to hold in the laughter that so desperately wanted to come out. Shaking her head, Gayle looked at the guard and softly asked, "You mean to tell me, all you wanna do is touch my pussy and then you'll take me and my girl downstairs to meet John Singleton?"

"Uh-huh. That all," he replied.

"Will you wash your hands first?" Gayle asked.

"I could do dat." He grinned.

"All right." Gayle shrugged. "I'm wit' it."

"How 'bout you?" he turned to ask Remmi.

"I don't know." Remmi chuckled as she looked him up and down, eyeballing his dirty fingernails. Even if he did wash his hands, he needed to soak in a bucket of bleach and ammonia before his grimy fingers would be clean enough to touch her. As quick as Remmi was to fall into bed with someone for a purpose, she was still an unmitigated funk-phobic who was totally paranoid of catching any kind of social disease. Visible nastiness was a complete no-no, and she just didn't know if she could go through with what he was suggesting. Plus, it was only a side role in a John Singleton movie—not a starring role with Spielberg.

"Come on, Rem. A John Singleton film could jump-start our careers. Look at what it did for Morris Chestnut—with his fine chocolate self," Gayle coaxed.

Remmi didn't like the idea of spreading her legs for someone whose hygiene was so poor and who she wasn't sure could help at all anyway. After all, she could meet the director and still not get the part. Magilla Gorilla would get his pleasure and she might still walk away empty-handed.

"Well, I'm down." Gayle smiled as she slid her thong down

past her thighs, her knees, and onto the floor. The guard exited for a few moments to wash his hands. When he returned, Gayle spread her legs after hoisting herself onto the bare metal table, the white Christian Dior minidress allowing easy access. He then licked his lips and rubbed his still grimy paws together as he slowly inched his way toward Gayle. When he reached her, he gently slid his right index finger in and out of her vagina while moaning in ecstasy, as his left hand aggressively stroked his own crotch. Gayle's face, on the other hand, looked like she couldn't wait for the whole thing to be over. In silence, Remmi observed the entire scene from the other side of the room. After about five minutes of the exchange, the guard let out a noise that sounded like some sort of animalistic mating call. Remmi thought surely all his friends from the jungle would start banging the door down at any moment.

As the guard gathered himself and regained his composure, Gayle put her thong back on and stood before him. He eyeballed her like he wanted more.

"No way, muthafucka. I upheld my end of the bargain. Now it's your turn," Gayle said, straightening out her dress. Seeing that it hadn't turned out so bad, Remmi decided to let him do her next. After all, Gayle was right about Morris Chestnut.

"All right, I guess you can do me now. But go wash your hands again," Remmi said.

"Naah, I'm good. A big nigga like me can only come once every coupla days anyhow. Your friend was enough for me." Magilla waved Remmi off.

"What?" she replied in amazement.

"Beat it. I already got my shit off." He shrugged.

"Well, come on, nigga. Take me to Hollywood," Gayle huffed.

"Yeah, yeah. Right this way. Lemme just stop by the john and clean off a little," he panted. As they walked toward the door, the guard turned to Remmi and said, "You get out the same way we got in."

"Excuse me? I don't know what way we came in. It was dark." Remmi sucked her teeth.

"Do like Toucan Sam," he stated as he and Gayle walked down the hall.

"What?" asked Remmi.

"Follow your nose," he continued.

"Catch you lata, girl!" Gayle called in the distance.

So much for strength in numbers.

6

Shannelle had missed so much work thanks to her episode with the flu that Shirley put her on probation. Her boss was being so insensitive that Shannelle asked herself if Shirley really was a female after all. She had given that woman three good years of flawless work, and now that she was having health issues, Shirley was unsympathetically all over her ass. Shannelle was definitely one of the Temple's top-earning girls with regulars who came there only to see her. The very least Shirley could do was be more understanding.

It wasn't like Shannelle liked missing work. Damn, she sure as hell needed the money. If she didn't work, she didn't get paid. And whether she brought home two thousand dollars a week or not, her rent and car note still had to be taken care of. None of her suga daddies had been stepping up to the plate lately, so all her expenses were on her own shoulders. Her being out of commission was definitely not a good thing for anyone.

When Shannelle strolled into the Temple after being out for two days, she was summoned back to Shirley's office—the Lion's Den, as all the girls called it. She knew she was gonna hear it, but there was no way she could have made it to work—puking her brains out every half hour and all.

Shannelle hadn't put on her costume yet, but when she saw Shirley's note on her locker door, she hurried to see what her fate was going to be. Dehydrated and woozy once again, she slowly made her way down the dimly lit hallway that led to Shirley's office. She knew she was either going to get docked or fired, neither of which she could afford. She was also exhausted and in no mood to be chastised, especially when she was legitimately ill.

When she opened the door, Shirley was already seated upon the throne and as usual, vigorously puffing on a Black & Mild. Shannelle silently sat before her boss, ready to defend herself and her job if need be. But she wasn't gonna kiss Shirley's fat ass. She had done enough of that over the past three years and was in no mood to do it that day. After all, the Temple wasn't the only strip joint in New York.

"We meet again under less than favorable circumstances," her boss began.

Shannelle gently tilted her head from side to side, knowing what was coming next. "I'm sorry if me being sick hurt the club. But I have really been sick," Shannelle explained.

"You know you have regular customers, Silky. Ones that come in and ask for you."

"Yeah, I know, but there's nothing I can do if I'm puking my brains out all over the place. I don't know about you, but I don't think puking in a nigga's lap is all that sexy." Shannelle huffed but regretted her statement as soon as it hit the air.

"Are you trying to be funny?" Shirley questioned as she placed the butt of her cigar into the ashtray on her desk.

"Not at all. I'm just saying that I been really sick. You act like you think I'm lying, and I'm not. I can even get a doctor's note to prove it."

"Do you think that I would trust you giving me a doctor's note? Do you know how many doctors come in this joint? You're probably screwing one of them and could get him to give you anything from a note to prescription drugs," Shirley waved her off.

"Whateva," Shannelle replied as she rose from her chair. Having had enough of this interaction, she was more than ready to leave the Lion's Den. Shirley could fire her if she wanted to, but she wasn't about to be disrespected. Just as Shannelle was about to make her parting statement, the office door slowly squeaked open. It was Lopez, the head of security.

"Got a drop-off, ma," Lopez said before he realized that Shannelle was in the room. Lopez, a muscular dark-skinned Puerto Rican from Brooklyn with pearly white teeth and a smooth bald head, was one of the Temple's most important employees. He had been there since the doors of the club first opened, and it was rumored that he was in some way related to Shirley, although no one quite knew what the relation was. He hired and fired every bouncer that came through the club and took pleasure in beating up rowdy, drunk patrons who caused trouble or violated the no-groping rule. It was also rumored that since he ran the door, he moved a certain amount of illegal substances in and out of the establishment—for a pretty hefty cut, of course. He was handsome and always clean as the board of health, looking more like a professional football star than a bouncer. He definitely had a thing for Shannelle, but never acted on it, thanks to an ironclad policy Shirley enforced, forbidding employees to date each other.

And although they flirted relentlessly, nothing had ever happened between them in the three years that Shannelle had been working at the Temple.

"Oh, what's up, Silky?" Lopez smiled.

"Hey, Lopez." Shannelle blushed, almost forgetting why she was standing in Shirley's office to begin with.

"Gimme whatcha got and get back to work. You know niggas don't know how to act on the weekends," Shirley grunted. Lopez made his way over to Shirley's desk and handed his boss three sizable stacks of one-hundred-dollar bills bound by thick navy blue rubber bands. Shannelle was amazed at the amount of money the club had already pulled in for the day. It was only two o'clock in the afternoon, and she knew there would be at least five more "drops-offs" before the night was over.

"Lata, Silky." Lopez beamed and exited the room.

Shannelle waved her fuchsia-colored fingernails at him before turning back to Shirley and sarcastically stating, "Look. I been sick, but I'm here now. So either you firing me or I need to get to work. There's *obviously* a lot of money to be made out there tonight." She smirked, eyeballing the bills stacked before her.

"You're one of my top-earning chicks, Silky. But personally I think you running game," Shirley replied, lighting up another slender cigar.

"You can think whateva you wanna think. Just remember the beginning of your sentence: I'm one of your top-earning chicks. Now I'm sure some of my customers are out there looking for me. Is this conversation over?"

Shirley nodded.

As Shannelle's hand touched the doorknob and began to turn it, Shirley's voice hit her in the back of her head like a laser.

"I got my eye on you, bitch."

Without turning around, as she placed one foot in front of the other, Shannelle retorted, "Likewise," before she heard the silver metal door slam closed behind her.

Shannelle walked down the hallway toward the crowded dressing room, and suddenly a plan was born. Three years was enough, and she was sick of Shirley's Temple. And even more than that, she was sick of Shirley. But she couldn't quit just yet. Not until she had some security.

The night was long, and Shannelle's customers had missed their favorite girl. In order to keep them happy and make up the money she had missed, she had to do a double. Tired or not, she knew what her pockets needed, and that was to make up for some of those days. It was damn near 4 A.M. by the time Shannelle was back in the dressing room changing out of her costume. She had booty-shaked and lap-danced all night long, and her feet were killing her. While the other girls made their way out of the club for the night, Shannelle decided to take a ten-minute breather before driving twenty minutes to her apartment. She needed to catch her breath and rub her feet before walking on the concrete outside, even if she did have a brand-new pair of Nike Shox in her locker.

"You in tomorrow, Silk?" Pinky questioned as she shoved her G-string in her bag.

"I plan to be," Shannelle said, gently massaging her left foot.

"We been missing your ass around here. Everything all right with you?"

"Yeah, I just been a little under the weather lately."

"I think something is going around. CoCo was out a couple of days last week, too. Shirley was trippin'." Pinky chuckled.

"Fuck Shirley. Let her get her fat ass out there and do a lap dance."

"Ya know."

The two girls laughed out loud and slapped high-five before Pinky said on her way out, "I'll let Lopez know you're still back here. So he don't lock your ass up in here."

Shannelle smiled. "Thanks."

Shannelle had just slipped on her sneakers and threw on her velour sweatsuit jacket when she heard the dressing-room door open and close. Someone was in there with her. Scared shitless, she picked up a metal curling iron from the vanity before yelling, "Who's there?"

"It's me, Silky," she heard a voice say before she saw Lopez standing in front of her. "Hey, be easy, ma. What you gonna do? *Curl* me to death?" he laughed.

"No, I was gonna beat the shit outta you with it then burn your ass afterwards. I just pulled the plug out."

"I was just checking to see if you're ready to take that ass home. I'm about to lock this place up."

"Yeah, I'm done," she said, and threw her Coach travel bag over her shoulder.

"Damn, you fine." Lopez snickered. Shannelle was walking down the hallway in front of him.

"So why you ain't never try to holla?" she asked with a flirtatious gleam in her eye.

"I got respect. Plus, you know Shirley's rules."

"Fuck Shirley. She don't control who I give my pussy to. I'm in charge of myself. How 'bout you?" Shannelle asked and stopped dead in her tracks, causing Lopez to bump right into her back. As she turned around, their noses nearly touched, and she seductively whispered in his face, "I know a big, strong, fine nigga like you ain't gonna let some fat bull-dagger bitch tell you who you can and cannot fuck. Especially if the chick you wanna fuck is wit' it."

Stuttering and completely taken aback by her words, Lopez said, "Uh, um . . . I just don't like trouble. I have it good here, and, um, jobs is hard to come by these days."

"Oh, I see. So what you saying is that even though you have all those muscles, you still a pussy? What a waste." Shannelle reverted back to her regular voice, shrugged her shoulders, and backed up from his space.

"I ain't no pussy. I just got mouths to feed. My mama and like two or three kids," he stuttered, sounding exactly like the punk she accused him of being.

"Well, if you ain't no pussy, then fuck me right now. Unless you scareda your boss." Shannelle stared him in the eye. "Come on," she continued, breaking the momentary silence. "Ain't nobody here but us. Shirley left. I saw her. And you know you been wanting some ass from me for three years now. And I can't front. You look good as shit, too."

As she inched toward him, his demeanor made her realize that this task was going to be easier than she thought. She had originally believed that he was the man, the way she saw him busting up the customers and whatnot. But it didn't take long for her to understand what she was really dealing with was a little biatch. Still, she needed him to play an intricate role in a plan she'd just come up with, and putting it on him was a definite way to get him under her spell.

In the dark, shadowy hallway leading downstairs to the exit of

Shirley's Temple, Shannelle shoved her exceptionally skilled tongue down Lopez's Bacardi flavored throat. Unable to resist her advances and completely stunned by her seduction, he returned the favor, using his nail-bitten fingers to push her pink JLO shorts down to the floor. Shannelle wrapped her perfectly smooth legs around his waist while simultaneously removing his Versace belt. Without a moment to waste, she swiftly unzipped Lopez's expensive slacks as if her life depended on it and slid his erect eleven-inch penis through the opening of his Fruit of the Loom boxers. He passionately bit her neck and shoulders, and hoisted her slender body up on the dingy, grease-stained wall, where she hung suspended tightly between it and his torso. All in one motion, he rammed his penis in her raw with so much force that Shannelle's moans were from both pleasure and pain. She wanted to tell him to put on a condom, but hell if she could stop him now.

Sweat began to pour down his head as he drove his dick deeply into her vagina harder and harder with each stroke. Shannelle could feel a burning sensation between her legs like she had never felt before, and the pain was now completely edging out her pleasure. She desperately wanted to tell him to stop, but she was silenced by the pain she suffered. She felt a warm thick liquid ooze down her left leg, a fluid that she knew wasn't orgasmic juices, but blood. If she hadn't known any better, she would have thought he was attacking her. But then she remembered that she had been the one to seduce him and not the other way around.

It took him ten whole minutes to come, which was at least eight minutes too long. But she knew her mission. She also knew that a ripped coochie was nothing that a water and vinegar douche couldn't fix. She had to stay focused on her ultimate goal, and she needed Lopez to help her see it through.

"Baby, you da bomb," Lopez moaned as his now limp penis slid out of her body and dangled in the air.

No pain, no gain was all Shannelle could say to herself after she finally took a breath.

7

i **cannot believe** that bitch got that role," Remmi ranted as she chomped on a slice of pizza and searched through her closet for something to wear. "She's a ho," she continued.

"You a ho, too. She's just a better one than you," Shannelle chuckled.

"Well, I was gon' let the muthafucka finger me, but she let him do her too long. How was I supposed to know that his fat ass could only come once a week? A *real* friend would have only let him do it for a couple of seconds so that I could get mine. A *real* friend would have said, 'If we don't both go down to meet him, neither one of us is going down to meet him!'" She pulled out a sexy Donna Karan multicolored halter dress.

"Girl, gimme a break! That bitch upheld her end of the deal and she made that nigga uphold his, that all. You or I woulda did the same thing. You can't be mad at her."

"So now you taking up for that bitch?"

"I ain't taking up for nobody. But right is right. And besides, you the one who got it twisted. That bitch ain't your friend. You really think that bitch is your friend? I'm your only friend, bitch. Face it." Shannelle laughed as she thumbed through the pages of *Vibe* magazine.

Shannelle had come over to talk to Remmi about an important matter she said she didn't want to discuss over the phone. The two had been so busy, they hadn't had an opportunity to really hang out or chat the way they used to. Shannelle's health was up and down, and the only thing she had enough strength to do some days was work at the Temple and fuck Lopez, who was now her full-fledged man—on the DL, of course. After her vagina had finally gotten used to the roughness of his sexual appetite, fucking him really wasn't all that bad. He still perspired like a pig in heat, but she could deal with that, too. He served an ultimate purpose.

"Listen, I need to talk to you about something," Shannelle began, placing the magazine down on Remmi's bed.

"What's up, girl? Just make it quick. You know I have to meet that producer at the Supper Club tonight, and I still have to wash my hair. I still can't believe you don't wanna go with me," Remmi said as she swiftly ran a wide-toothed comb through her thick black mane.

"I'm not in the mood to go clubbing these days. Especially after what happened to your ass in NV. I can't believe you ain't learn shit from that."

"Yeah, I know. But a girl gotta eat, and this producer says he can make me the next Aaliyah. He has a label deal with Universal, so I believe him. And a little ass-kicking sometimes comes with the territory. I knew that when I signed up for this job. Shit, you can't even tell anything ever happened to me." She looked at herself up close in her dresser mirror.

"Aaliyah's dead, bitch. And your ass can't even sing."

"Neither can most of these chicks out here. They still making money, though. Why can't I get a piece of that no-singing-ass pie?"

"You are so gullible." Shannelle sighed, and shook her head.

"Yeah, remember you said that when I get my first Grammy. I'll still thank your ass, though."

"Whateva. Listen. I got a real moneymaking scheme that I wanna bring you in on."

"Really? What's up?"

"Well, you know I been fuckin' wit' Lopez from the club, right?"

"Yeah, dat nigga is fiiiiiyone. I don't know why your ass just started fuckin' him. I'da fucked him a long time ago if I was you."

" 'Cause a long time ago his ass ain't serve no purpose. Now he does."

"And what purpose is that—other than a good stiff dick? Niggas that fine are never good for anything other than that. They usually broke and crazy."

"Well he ain't broke, definitely. I found out that he's been moving huge amounts of ecstasy through the Temple for Shirley and making mad dough—over a hundred grand a night."

"Get the fuck outta here!" Remmi remarked.

"Yeah, and I want a piece of it."

"Well, ain't you his bitch? I *know* he's been hitting you off with a little sumthin' sumthin' "

"A little sumthin' sumthin' is a lotta nuthin' nuthin' compared to what them muthafuckas is pullin' in."

"Well, how much is he getting? I'm sure fat-ass Shirley ain't giving him but so much. She seems like a ruthless, cheap bitch."

"He's getting ten percent of whateva he pulls in for her each night. If she's clockin' a hundred grand, then he's still bringing home ten grand a night. Tax-free cash money. That's a lotta fuckin' money to just be buying me some Louis Vuitton luggage."

"How do you know all this?"

"'Cause the nigga is pussy and he talks more than a bitch. I know the muthafucka's whole life story, and I've only been fuckin' him for two weeks."

After a brief pause, a change of mind about her outfit, and turning on the shower in the bathroom, Remmi shrugged. "Well, what do you want me to do? I ain't selling no X. I'm not no drug dealer. I ain't built like that, ya know."

"You are so dilly sometimes. Did I say anything about selling X? No. Since when do I look like a salesclerk? I'm talking about robbing the club."

"Robbing the club? Who do you think I am, muthafuckin' Rocky from *Set It Off*? I ain't robbin' shit. You crazy." Remmi waved her hand in the air at her best friend. "You done really lost your mind now," she continued.

"Will you shut the fuck up and listen?" Shannelle snapped, frustrated now and regretting the fact that she ever decided to talk to Remmi about it in the first place.

Remmi tilted her head to the side and tightly crossed her arms as she listened with a skeptical look in her eye. There was no way in the world she was going to run up into Shirley's Temple with a mask on and a gun in her hand and risk getting caught by the police and going to jail. No way in hell.

"I'm sorry. I'm way too fine for jail. Them dykes'll be trying to eat me out every two minutes," Remmi told Shannelle.

"Listen. Tonight after I put it on Lopez real good and we start pillow talkin'—like we always do 'cause the nigga thinks I'm Dr. Phil or some shit—but anyway, after I make his ass real comfortable, I'm gonna find out where that fat bitch puts the money after he gives it to her. It's gotta be somewhere in her office 'cause she's definitely not making any bank deposits at two in the morning."

"And after you find that out, then what?" Remmi sarcastically questioned.

"Then I'm gonna wait until everybody leaves the club Saturday night. That's when Lopez locks up. And after everybody's gone, I'll dip into her office."

"Girl, Shirley is not dumb enough to leave a hundred grand in the club. When she leaves, I'm sure the money leaves, too," Remmi said matter-of-factly.

Shannelle paused for a moment. She hadn't thought of that, and Remmi definitely had a point. That's why she'd enlisted the help of her best friend—to think of things she had missed.

"Yeah, you're right. Maybe if I can find out where she holds it until she leaves—like in a safe or something—I can lift it from there," Shannelle considered.

"Well, find out the particulars from pretty boy, and then we'll devise a plan," Remmi suggested.

"So, you down?"

"Ain't I always?"

"All day, every day."

Shannelle quickly wiped off her body as she stepped onto the plush royal blue carpet in her own bathroom. It was a must that she shower as soon as she and Lopez were finished having sex. His sweat on her body made her feel nasty and uncomfortable, and she had to be very relaxed in order to con the information that she needed out of him. As she stood beneath the showerhead, her thoughts focused on how she would approach the subject, careful not to seem like she was prying or being nosy. Lopez was a talker, so she figured it wouldn't be too difficult to get the scoop off the tip of his tongue. Still she knew that she had only one chance to get it, because while he was dumb, he wasn't totally stupid.

Since she rarely asked him questions, if she started talking about it too much, he'd know something was up. Street cats never trust anybody and have a sixth sense about too much interrogation.

Shannelle walked back to the bedroom, where Lopez lay naked on her waterbed, staring at *SportsCenter* like it was some sort of science project. It was his favorite show, and she knew better than to approach him in the middle of a broadcast. He would wave her off, and she definitely wouldn't get the answers that she and Remmi needed in order to plot their next move.

As she tiptoed back over to the bed, she dropped the towel that covered her damp body upon the floor and crawled naked beside him beneath the sheets. His body still reeked of sex and his chest still glistened with the sweat he had worked up while inside her. Usually she would request that he head for the shower, too, but tonight she had a mission.

"I think Shirley might be on to the fact that we're screwin'," Shannelle began as soon as the first commercial break interrupted his program.

"Why you say that?" he mumbled.

"She's been giving me the eye a lot lately."

"Naw. That don't have nuthin' to do with me. She been giving you the eye for three years now. She just don't like you," Lopez replied.

"I know that. But it's like more than usual lately. And then the other night, she insisted that I leave before you."

"That was just because I had like six stacks of cash to give her to put in the safe. She ain't want nobody to see me handing that much dough off to her."

This was going to be easier than Shannelle thought. "Six stacks of dough? Damn, that place brings in a lot of money! I don't know why she be riding me so hard. If it wasn't for me, she damn sure wouldn't be raking in all that dough."

"Slow ya row, baby girl. I mean, you fine and all, but do you really think pussy brings in money like that? Nah. If it wasn't for *me*, she wouldn't be raking in all that dough." Lopez laughed as he rubbed his hand up and down his crotch.

"How's that?" Shannelle asked, grossed out but trying to ignore his subtle masturbation.

"Like I told you before, there's a whole lot more going on in Shirley's Temple than a bunch of booty shakin'," he continued.

Jackpot . . . "Get outta here. She's moving *that* much X through there? What the fuck you know that I don't?" Shannelle asked as she gently pinched his nipple. She knew that drove him crazy and would make him want to tell her everything just so that they could pick up where they left off before she'd gone into the shower.

"Yo, ya girl Shirley is running one of *the* most lucrative ecstasy gigs in the whole tri-state area outta that club. With my help, of course." He smiled proudly.

"You lyin'! I know what you said before, but I had no idea that it was like that!" Shannelle exclaimed, as if she had no clue.

"Yeah, baby girl. I told you ol' girl be bringing in over a hunnit gran a night."

"Yeah, but I thought that was mostly from us dancin' and the bar," Shannelle lied.

"Naah. Y'all bitches might bring in like twenty, thirty Gs a night—if we do good. But it's that X that's paying *my* bills. How you think you got them designer bags I bought you? From bouncin'? Girl, you crazy."

"Damn, and all along I thought it was us girls that were raking in the dough," she lied again, shaking her head in disbelief from side to side and putting on an Academy Award–winning performance.

"Now don't get it twisted, ma," Lopez snickered as he gently kissed her lips. "Y'all help. Y'all some baad muthafuckas, and niggas do come there to see y'all shake your asses. But it's that X that keeps 'em coming back for more."

"So if Shirley's getting like a hundred grand a night, where's she keeping all that money? 'Cause that bitch watches over us like a hawk—like we wanna steal somethin' from her and shit." Shannelle continued, secretly hoping that question would be the one she needed to ask to bring it on home.

"Man, that fat heffa is too lazy to make regular trips to her safe deposit box, so she only goes once a week. I told her ass a million times how it ain't cool for her to leave all that dough in that safe in her office. But she don't listen. To be a smart bitch, she sure is a dumb bitch."

B-I-N-G-O, B-I-N-G-O, B-I-N-G-O, and Bingo was his name-O! "Shirley has a safe in her office? I ain't never seen no safe, and I spend more time in there than a little bit," Shannelle replied with a raised brow.

"Yeah, you see that Andy Warhol picture she has on the wall behind her desk?"

"Andy who?"

"Andy Warhol—the picture with the dollar signs on it directly behind her desk on the wall?"

"That ugly piece of crap?"

"Yeah, that ugly piece of crap is worth a lot of money, baby girl. You ain't know that I'm an art connoisseur on the low, did you? Anyway, there's a wall safe behind it." Lopez huffed and adjusted his position next to Shannelle.

"Get the fuck outta here! Stop playin'!"

"True story, ma. That's where she keeps the dough."

"Wow," Shannelle sighed as she slumped her back into her pillow. She had basically gotten all the information she needed from Lopez. Except the combination, of course. She rolled over, began caressing her man's chest hairs, and in a little baby voice she cooed, "Do you know the combination to the safe, Daddy?"

"Nah. She ain't gon' tell me no shit like that. She too paranoid," he moaned, reveling in her gentle touches.

Realizing he didn't know the information she needed to bring her plan to fruition, she lightly kissed him on the cheek, pulled the covers over her body, turned her back to him, and snapped, "Good night."

"Good night?" he growled. "I thought we were 'bout to go for round two."

"I'm tired, baby. Long day. Get some sleep."

As she closed her eyes, she could feel Lopez glaring at her back. She was in no mood for him to pant and sweat all over her for the second time that night. She had to focus, think, and devise a plan. Without the combination to the safe, it would be pretty hard to get the money. What good was he if he didn't know the combination?

I'll figure something out. There's gotta be a way to get into that safe without the combination, Shannelle thought, and drifted off into dreamland.

remmi made her way through the club, trying to find Mr. Producer Extraordinaire who was going to transform her into the next Beyoncé. Her heart thumped to the beat of the music, and she slowly walked toward the upstairs lounge, ignoring the comments and attention she was getting from almost every man in the place. When she got to the VIP section, she quickly told the security guard that she was on the guest list for Snatch's private party.

"Name?" the skinny bouncer questioned in a monotone Barry White voice.

"Remmi. Rementa Broughton." She smiled. It was her hope that the bouncer would just let her in on the strength of her dress and her pretty brown eyes, which often got her over. But not today. The bouncer glanced at the list he held in his right hand and after a moment replied, "Your name ain't on the list."

"Then the list is wrong. I have a meeting with him tonight. I was on the list downstairs."

"That was downstairs."

"Okay. Well, could you go inside and tell him that I'm out here?"

"Can't leave my post."

"Excuse me, but did you hear me say that he's expecting me?" Remmi asked, now getting angry.

"Comin' out your face ain't gonna get you nowhere tonight other than outside on the curb. So I suggest you be easy, ma," the guard said without a blink or an ounce of emotion.

"Ya know, I hate when you muthafuckas take your goddamn jobs so fuckin' seriously. Who do you think you are? Otis from *Martin*? Why the fuck don't you just take your skinny ass behind that velvet rope and tell Snatch that Remmi's here? Who the fuck are you gonna secure with your skinny ass anyway? Am I supposed to feel *safe* knowing that *you're* a bouncer here? Fuck no!" Remmi bellowed, now totally out of control.

As she tried to push her way past security, she heard someone say her name. "Remmi?"

It was Gayle. Remmi looked her fair-weather friend up and down before letting out a lame, "What's up."

"Having trouble getting in?" Gayle asked with a drink in her hand.

"She ain't on the list," the bouncer replied, shaking his head lightly.

"She's with me, Vic," Gayle huffed. The guard then opened the rope and allowed both ladies to walk through into the VIP section.

"Nigga must be a homo," Remmi snapped, rolling her eyes at him as she stepped on the other side of the rope.

The lounge area was a completely different atmosphere from what she had experienced when she first entered the club. There were plush couches and pillows tossed everywhere. People were strategically placed in all corners of the room, in the center, and along the floor. The smooth sounds of Bobby Valentino resonated in the background, and Remmi pretty much forgot about the fact that Gayle was the one who had gotten her in there in the first place.

"So what you been up to, girl?" Gayle asked, ignoring Remmi's attitude.

"Same ol'. I'm meeting Snatch here tonight," Remmi replied, not even thanking her for helping her get past security. "I hope he ain't tryin' to run no bullshit on me, 'cause if me not being on the guest list is any indication of how he does business, I can't fuck with him," Remmi continued.

"Snatch is legit. He has me in the studio right now." Gayle smiled.

"Excuse me?"

"Yeah. I'm working on my demo."

"Since when do *you* sing?" Remmi questioned, her voice riddled with sarcasm and cattiness.

"Since they invented Pro Tools, bitch," Gayle snapped.

"I see. Look, I gotta find Snatch. Catch you lata," Remmi said, waving her hand at Gayle. Looking into the green eyes of her nemesis, all Remmi could hear in the back of her mind was Shannelle saying, "That bitch ain't your friend. You really think that bitch is your friend? I'm your only friend, bitch. Face it."

Remmi walked away from Gayle and spotted Snatch at the bar chatting with a Latina clad in a cheap zebra-printed catsuit. Not about to let her position be compromised, Remmi walked up to where they were standing, positioned herself right in front of the woman, and gave Snatch a hug like she hadn't seen him in twenty years.

"Snatch, baby—did you forget about our meeting tonight?" Remmi seductively asked as she placed bright red kisses all over his face.

"Remmi! What's up?" Snatch asked, startled. The woman he was talking to was obviously offended by Remmi's behavior and responded with a very loud sucking of her teeth.

"Excuse me, sweetheart but—," the woman began.

"Ooh, girl, did I interrupt something? I'm so sorry, but Snatch and I have a meeting right now—which he must have forgotten about 'cause he didn't put my name on the VIP guest list. What happened, Snatch?" Remmi inquired, tilting her head to the side and placing her right hand on her hip.

"Well, if he forgot, it must not have been that important," the pretty but tacky woman interjected.

"Excuse you?" Remmi asked, ready to jump all over the girl. She was already not in a good mood after her encounter with the bouncer. And knowing that Gayle had gotten her into the VIP section didn't make her feel any better. Now this bitch was trying to test her. Was there no end to the amount of aggravation the night was bringing to her? Seeing what was about to erupt, Snatch swiftly grabbed Remmi by the hand, excused himself from his female companion, and led Remmi to one of the plush sofas on the other side of the lounge.

"It's a good thing you cut that shit short, 'cause honey was about to catch a bad decision," Remmi announced as she plopped down on the couch. "Now why the fuck wasn't I on the guest list to get up in this piece?" she continued.

"Oversight, Remmi. My bad. I apologize," Snatch quickly replied to calm the situation.

"Yeah, and I hear you got Gayle Ford in the studio doing her demo? What the fuck is that about?"

"I work with a lot of chicks, Remmi. That's what I do. I'm a producer," Snatch explained.

"Well that bitch can't sing, and I think it's a conflict of interest for you to be working with two females who have the same image. Not that she's half as fly as me, but still. *Some* people might think we got the same kinda thing going on," Remmi informed him.

Just then a very scantily clad waitress came around requesting drink orders. Snatch ordered a rum and Coke, while Remmi asked for an apple martini.

Turning his attention back to their conversation, Snatch said, "Remmi. You need to cool out. You don't hear Beyoncé buggin' out on Scott Storch 'cause he's working with Christina Aguilera, do you?"

"Since when are you Scott Storch? You ain't had a hit since Big Daddy Kane! Tell me one top-ten hit you had on Billboard since the year 2000." A silence came over the two of them.

"My point exactly," Remmi continued, referring to his inability to dispute her claim. "Look, I ain't trying to dis you or nothin', but you need a hot artist as much as I need some hot tracks. So cut the bullshit."

"All right, all right. So what do you want me to do, Remmi? I want you to be happy."

"Drop Gayle. She ain't shit, and there ain't no way you can make both of us a priority."

"Drop Gayle," he repeated under his breath. "Look, she already paid for studio time and two tracks, so I at least gotta fulfill that."

"I don't give a shit what she already paid for. Tell her something came up. And take the tracks back. Ain't that your name, *Snatch*? Well, *snatch* that bitch out the studio, *snatch* back your tracks, and give me and my career your undivided attention. *A-S-A*-right-the-fuck-now!" Remmi took her drink from the waitress's tray.

"And why should I do that? She's not half bad, and she *is* fine as hell." He smirked, licking his weed-stained lips.

"So you fuckin' her? Oh, that's it. I see . . . ," Remmi spat, slapping her own leg and having a lightbulb moment, as if now it all made sense. "She's giving you some ass so you feel obligated," she continued.

"Nah. I don't get down like that. I just think she's cool people," he denied.

"You think I'm stupid, nigga? *All* you industry cats get down like that. But that's irrelevant. I'm talking about you doing what you have to do to make shit happen for *me*. And besides, that bitch is a ho. The only reason she got that part in John Singleton's movie is 'cause she let his head bodyguard finger-fuck her."

"What!"

"For real. I was there. He wanted to do me, too, but I wouldn't let him. I don't get down like that," Remmi lied.

"That's some nasty-ass shit."

"See, you don't even know the kind of bitches you messin' with. She's a ho, and she'll bring you more trouble than she's worth. Trust me. That bitch won't sell no records. But with me you have a triple threat—I can sing, I can dance, and I can act. Nigga, we do this shit right, and I could even have my own clothing line and perfume."

Looking as if he could clearly see Remmi's vision, Snatch was definitely feeling what she had to say. She had him open, and it was obvious. They continued to plot the details of their plan, and Snatch couldn't resist touching Remmi's soft bare legs. He'd wanted to take her home from the first moment he'd laid eyes on her at Bar 89. She'd been on a date with one of her many suitors when Snatch caught her going to the ladies' room on the DL. He slyly explained to her that he had recognized her from one of her music videos, informed her that not only did he work for Universal Records but that he was also a record producer. Seeing that he had her undivided interest, he then firmly placed his business card in the palm of her hand. When she returned to the table with her date, she and Snatch made googly eyes from across the restaurant until he finally left with his friends. Good thing her date wasn't the brightest, or else it could have gotten ugly.

Remmi's chance meeting with Snatch rekindled a desire to sing that she'd buried in the back of her head since high school. His interest in her, coupled with what she had been hearing on the radio lately, made her realize that almost anyone could make it in the music business with the right people behind them. That being the case, she knew that Snatch was exactly what she needed in her life. Although she wasn't particularly attracted to him, he did dress fly, a trait that Remmi found very appealing. She could tell that he was one of those brothas that didn't get a lot of attention growing up, but now that he was "somebody," women flocked like crazy. He was average everything—average height, weight, and complexion—but was clean-cut with a sexiness about him that reminded Remmi of the boy next door. The TAG Heuer watch that sat upon his left wrist was on the lower end of the timepiece spectrum, but it did look nice against his skin. Remmi wondered if that was his most expensive watch or if he owned anything with more bling to it. She hoped that wasn't all he was working with. After all, that watch was worth only about two thousand dollars. But his Gucci shoes somewhat made up for the oompf that the watch lacked, and that turned her on because Remmi loved a man in nice shoes. Still overall in Remmi's opinion, he was just *a'ight.*

As Remmi and Snatch sat closely together on the burgundy plush sofa, Snatch continued to rub her thighs, getting more and more aroused with each touch. It was quite obvious that she had his nose wide open, and she was prepared to use that fact to her full advantage.

"So, when are you gonna let me hear some of your tracks?" Remmi asked with a twinkle in her eye. Just as she downed another sip of her martini, Gayle came over and interrupted their conversation by sitting on the edge of the love seat where they were whispering to each other over the loud music.

"What's up, people? I didn't know you two knew each other. Small world, huh," Gayle began. Remmi could tell that she was mad, because her emerald green eyes were suddenly very dark beneath her raised brows. While Snatch tactfully raised himself up off Remmi, Remmi inched herself closer to him, making sure that Gayle got the picture that they were indeed together.

"Yeah, Snatch and I are about to start working together," Remmi playfully stated as she placed her perfectly manicured fingers on Snatch's cheek.

"Really? In what capacity?" Gayle asked.

"I just signed a deal with his label, and he's doing my album," Remmi lied.

"Really?" Gayle asked with a hint of jealousy and disbelief in her voice. Snatch sat silently, eagerly observing how the rest of the conversation would go.

"Well, if she's your artist, Snatch, why didn't you have her name on the VIP guest list? 'Cause I'm the one who let her through the ropes, ya know," Gayle continued.

"Oversight. Ya man at the door can't read. I was actually on the list. He just ain't see my name. People are very incompetent these days," Remmi said.

"Anyway, we'd love to chat, girl, but Snatch and I were just leaving. We're going to his studio so I can start selecting some tracks. My project is top priority. I only came here tonight to meet up with him. And this ain't really my crowd anyhow. So why don't you hold this lame-ass party down for us while we're gone?" Remmi smirked, grabbing Snatch's wrist and dragging him across the floor to the exit, leaving Gayle on the couch pissed off and alone.

"You got mad game," Snatch laughed as he opened the door of his silver Jaguar.

"Like Jay-Z, I'm a hustler, baby," Remmi sang, snapping her fingers and slipping her size-seven feet out of her Isaac Mizrahi slides. Tipsy off the martini and tired from a long day, Remmi tossed her bare legs upon the dashboard of Snatch's designer car, hiking her already short dress up even farther. Snatch was so turned on by the sight of her bare skin beside him in the passenger seat, he could hardly keep his eyes on the road.

"You are definitely a baaaad bitch," Snatch said as he shook his head and licked his lips.

"Badder than Gayle?" she asked.

"No doubt," he chuckled.

"Tell the truth, Snatch. Did you fuck her?"

"I don't kiss and tell, ma."

Remmi sucked her teeth. "That means yes."

"Well even if I did, what that mean?"

"It don't mean shit, 'cause you still gonna get my career jumped off, ain't you?" Remmi probed as she slid her hand up and down his crotch, instantly creating a hard-on. Feeling the bulge, Remmi started to get excited herself. She had no idea he was packing like that.

"I'ma do my best," he replied in ecstasy, enjoying his impromptu massage.

"Do your best? No baby, you have to do better than your best. You have to make that shit happen," Remmi moaned as she unzipped his Jhane Barnes slacks, gently pulling out his very ample penis. She began licking it as if it were the most scrumptious Godiva chocolate lollipop she had ever tasted in her life. Unable to control himself, Snatch had to pull over to the shoulder on the West Side Highway. The drive to his condo in Englewood, New Jersey, would just have to wait.

another night at the Temple and another warning from Shirley. But this time, getting into Shirley's office was part of Shannelle's plan—and what better way than to piss her off? As a part of her plan, Shannelle deliberately forgot the pink satin platform boots that matched her fuchsia costume, forcing her to borrow Melody's silver stilettos. Knowing how anal her boss was when it came to their costumes, Shannelle knew Shirley would immediately notice. And of course she did. Already losing patience and at her wit's end with Shannelle, as the night neared its end, Shirley called her once again into the Lion's Den—for the third time that month.

As she entered the dim room, Shannelle quickly scoped out the parameters of the four walls. She immediately noticed the unsightly print covered with the dollar signs behind Shirley's head and remembered Lopez telling her that the safe was secured within the wall beneath it. Her instincts and a mental approximation told her that the picture sat smack in the middle of the room—about thirty steps to the right and thirty steps to the left. Shannelle knew that on the other side of the wall was the dressing room, but she couldn't visualize what was there. She believed the lockers sat on that wall, but depending on what was on the other side, her plan would either be easier or more difficult to implement.

Waawaawaa waawaawaawaa—Shirley's words sounded like a grown-up from a Charlie Brown cartoon to Shannelle's ears. Shannelle didn't even bother listening to her beef, as she was far too busy formulating her master plan. She wasn't the least bit concerned. She knew from experience that Shirley's bark was a hell of a lot bigger than her bite, and all she had to do was kiss up to her after she was done with her monologue. Shannelle knew how Shirley liked to be sucked up to by her girls—the only sucking she'd probably ever get from anyone who stripped there.

"Do you understand me?" Shirley growled, snapping Shannelle back into reality.

"Yes, Shirley. I can't apologize enough. I've just been going through so much lately. But you know I've been a faithful employee of yours for a long time now. I would never do anything to jeopardize my position here. I need this job. I promise it won't happen again," Shannelle pledged with an Oscar-winning performance that would rival Jennifer Hudson's.

Surprised by her sudden humility, Shirley seemed slightly taken aback by Shannelle's change in disposition. She had undoubtedly expected Shannelle to be her normal flippant self. But little did Shirley know, Shannelle had an ulterior motive, and it was in her own best interest that her boss honestly believe she was sincere.

"This is your final warning, Silky," Shirley mumbled, waving her hand for Shannelle to leave the office. Without uttering another word, Shannelle quickly rose from the great chair.

You ain't lyin', Shannelle thought as the metal door slammed behind her.

i t was a Wednesday night, and Remmi had been in the studio all day with Snatch. It had taken them eight hours to do a chorus on one song, and Remmi was exhausted. Her session at D&D Studios was the first time she had ever actually sang anywhere other than in her shower. She wasn't used to the microphone, the recording booth, or the engineer who after forty-five minutes had grown impatient with her whining and obvious lack of talent. Remmi also wasn't used to anyone talking about her and criticizing her right in front of her face, as if she weren't even there. She was used to getting star treatment on video sets, with men dropping at her feet and treating her like a goddess from the beginning of a shoot until the end.

But this was different. She couldn't fake not being able to carry a note. She couldn't fake being tone deaf, nor could she get away with singing every word flat and out of pitch. And since many aspiring singers were pretty, she was no novelty in that department either. Needless to say, the session was a nightmare, and Snatch was clearly embarrassed. By the time 10 P.M. rolled around, Remmi was worn out both mentally and physically, unable to squeal another note—much to the delight of Snatch and the engineer.

As Snatch drove Remmi to Shannelle's apartment, her undeniable lack of talent forced him to forget all about their episode on the shoulder of the West Side Highway. It was quite clear that his attitude toward her was different. At that point, he didn't care how good the sex had been. She simply wasn't worth the humiliation or the money he'd spent on her. The session had cost him a pretty penny, and the final product was useless. She was no closer to a completed demo than she'd been the day they met at Bar 89. He hadn't known it was possible for anyone to sound as awful as she did, and began to regret letting Gayle go. At least that girl could carry a note, and she was just as beautiful as Remmi. He'd just have to figure out a way to smooth things over with her, which he didn't think would be a problem. As far as he was concerned, she could be bought—girls like her always could.

The ride uptown was as silent as a cemetery at midnight, and when they arrived in front of Shannelle's apartment building, the only words he uttered were, "I'll call you."

"When?" Remmi questioned.

"Soon," he snapped.

"Well, it better be soon 'cause my schedule is hectic, and if you gonna have me tied up in the studio all day, I need to plan for it. I do have another career, ya know," she huffed with an attitude. Snatch chuckled, smoothed out his goatee, took a very deep breath, and, while rubbing the sweaty palms of his hands together, smiled. "Remmi, I'll call you."

Still not getting the picture, Remmi shrugged and made a swift exit, slamming the car door so hard, she thought she'd shattered the window.

He just mad 'cause I said no more sex till after *the checks,* she thought as she entered the building. Giving a quick wave to the doorman, who knew her well, Remmi glided past the greenery and

mirrors that lined the lobby as she made her way to the narrow elevator bank. She had no clue that she had done so poorly or that
she had just experienced her first and last recording session. As far
as she was concerned, she was still in the running to become America's next top pop star.

8

the two best friends sat in the middle of Shannelle's living room floor chowing down on Chinese takeout as they brainstormed about the best way to get into Shirley's safe. Neither of them wanted to risk snooping around in the Lion's Den, for they weren't willing to get caught up in Shirley's domain. They had to come up with a plan that was foolproof, without involving Lopez, whom they decided they weren't going to share any of the profits with.

"I'm not splitting shit three ways," Shannelle said. "That's why I came up with the idea to set his ass up the same night we make a move. I'm sick of his rough-sex-having ass anyway."

"Girl, you gangsta." Remmi shook her head.

"Whateva—it's bad enough I gotta split the shit with you."

"Bitch, you need me."

"Yeah, I do," Shannelle laughed. "And with that nigga outta the way, we can go fifty–fifty."

"Plus your coochie should be worn all the way out by now anyway," Remmi chuckled.

"Not yet, but a couple more weeks of that shit and it will be. I already picked up some tightening cream from the Pink PussyCat Boutique."

"Dang, girl. Why you ain't tell me you was going to the Pink PussyCat? I *love* that place!"

"I went on a whim," Shannelle replied. "Look, enough of the idle chitchat. Let's get this plan in place and go over the details one more time," she continued.

"Okay," Remmi began after washing down a forkful of pork fried rice with a swig of Diet Pepsi. "It's supposed to jump off this Saturday night—really Sunday before day, right?"

"Yep. Around four A.M. The bitch leaves around two. Lopez told me that she leaves everything in the safe and comes back on Sunday morning to get it. Evidently she doesn't like carrying that kind of cash out at that time of the night."

Remmi smiled. "Perfect."

"Well, I'm gonna stop by Home Depot tomorrow and get the electric saw. I was in her office the other day and don't think that wall is too thick. Her ass is so cheap, I actually think it's a makeshift wall—like it used to be all one room. My only thing is making sure that the dressing room is empty. Shifts change at midnight, and all the girls are usually out on the floor around two A.M. After Shirley leaves, that's where you come in. You'll wait outside in my car until you see her leave the parking lot. I'll go into the dressing room around two fifteen—or as soon as you call me and tell me she's definitely gone. After you call me, wait like ten minutes and then call the cops. Tell them you wanna place an anonymous tip that you think they're running X out the club and that the head bouncer at the door—a Puerto Rican muscle-bound dude—has a stash in the lining of his bulletproof vest."

"Lopez wears a bulletproof vest?"

"Uh-huh. Every night. Sometimes them perverts get outta line and shots ring out. It's only happened a few times, but better safe than sorry. Plus that's the perfect place for him to stash the shit."

"Damn, I had no idea your job was so *dangerous*," Remmi joked. "I can't believe you're gonna set your own man up. You sure are a coldhearted bitch," Remmi continued.

"Girl, that nigga is *not* my man. I don't *love* him. If I hadn't come up with this plan, I woulda left his ass already. I just kept him around so we could do this. I'm done with him now," Shannelle reasoned.

"Well, what you gonna do when he calls you to bail him out?"

"Tell him I ain't got no money. And that's *if* they give his ass bail 'cause he already got a rap sheet longer than a double roll of Charmin."

"Bitch, karma is a mutha," Remmi warned, shaking her head from side to side.

"Yeah. That's why they're all about to get theirs."

Lopez splashed himself with a very healthy dose of Burberry London cologne as he got himself ready to leave Shannelle's apartment. It was only 5 P.M., but he had a few things he needed to take care of before heading over to the Temple. Shannelle knew Saturday was the club's biggest night and that Lopez would have usually made a major pickup in Harlem before hitting his post at seven. At his level, you'd think he would have had someone else do the transporting, but Lopez was paranoid and trusted no one. Even though they had been dealing with each other for only two months, Shannelle had his routine down pat. After all, his simple ass wasn't that difficult to figure out.

Shannelle watched Lopez prepare to exit the apartment. He wasn't half as attractive to her as he had been before she started having sex with him on a regular basis. Maybe that was because she was so turned off by his nasty habits. Since he had started staying at her apartment a month ago, he'd never cleaned anything, had her house constantly smelling like weed, and left his dirty clothes all over her otherwise very organized environment. He monopolized her remote control, always having her television locked on either *SportsCenter* or some ridiculous reality show, and she'd also noticed that he wasn't very diligent about brushing his teeth or washing his ass. Of course, all this was a serious turn-off, and she really couldn't wait until she pulled off the heist so that he could be in a cage like wild animals should be.

"Love you, *mamacita*. You da love of my life." Lopez smiled and placed a wet, smelly kiss on her cheek. Shannelle responded with a fake grin as she lounged across her plush sofa, deeply engrossed in a novel written by the infamous porn star, Heather Hunter. She had grown to hate Lopez's kisses, which always stank of the blunt he had just finished smoking.

"*Mami*, I been thinking," he continued, and sat his muscular frame beside her on the cream-colored couch. The Adonis physique she originally thought he had now reminded her of the Hunchback of Notre Dame. Figuring he was about to go into one of his usual performances, Shannelle gently closed the hard-cover edition of *Insatiable* she'd been reading, placing her right index finger in between the pages to keep her place. She was slightly annoyed that he was interrupting her just as she was about to get to another steamy paragraph, but reminded herself that his long-winded conversations would soon be a thing of the past.

"I been really feelin' you, and you know you gonna be my wife. So I think it's time that I take you to meet *mi mamá*," he continued, suddenly switching to Spanish.

"You want me to meet your mama?" Shannelle asked dryly.

"No—*mi mamá*—you gotta get the accent. Tomorrow. *Ven para una cena en la casa de mi mamá este domingo.* Translation— Sunday dinner at my mother's house—but don't sweat it, you'll be speaking Spanish in no time. I know she'll be feelin' you like I do. You'll be her *hija*—that's 'daughter' in Spanish. And she'll teach you how to cook food from my country. *Arroz con pollo, pasteles*— all that good shit."

"Food from your country? Ain't you Puerto Rican? Puerto Rico is in America, fool," Shannelle snapped, losing her patience with his dramatic spiel.

"You know what I mean. You need to learn how to cook anyway. 'Cause after we get married, don't think we gon' be eating out every night," Lopez announced as he rose from the sofa. He grabbed his keys and cell phone from the coffee table.

Married! Shannelle thought. *He's dumber than I thought.*

"Sunday—you, me, and *mi familia.* Five o'clock. I'm out. You know the Saturday-night routine. I'll see you at the club in a couple of hours." He smiled as he left the apartment, leaving only his scent behind. "And pick up a Spanish whatchama call it? One of those things with words in it?"

"A dictionary?" Shannelle dryly muttered.

"Yeah. That. Go buy one. You need to start learning how to speak my language. *Mi mamá* don't speak English, and she needs to be able to talk to da love of my life," he called from the hallway. Shannelle shook her head in disgust, relieved by the fact that that would probably be the last time she would see Lopez's face, if all went according to plan.

Giving him enough time to walk down the corridor and board the elevator, Shannelle stayed put until she heard the elevator door close. When she was certain that he had gone, Shannelle ran to the phone like a bat out of hell, to call Remmi, confirming all the details of their heist. Her best friend assured her that everything was in place and was confident that it would all go off without a hitch. At this point they had nothing to worry about.

Remmi dropped Shannelle off around six thirty, before any of the other girls arrived, assuring her partner in crime that she would be back at 1:30 A.M. Shannelle's early arrival gave her enough time to sneak the extra-large four-wheeled Samsonite suitcase containing the tools she needed to implement their plan into the club. Once in the locker room, Shannelle quickly concealed the suitcase in a vacant closet behind several old and abandoned costumes. She then opened her locker, changed into her work clothes, and tightly locked the small gray metal box that had held her belongings for the past three years.

Much to her delight, a large metal-framed mirror sat upon the wall directly where the safe was positioned on the other side. The mirror would make it easier to conceal the hole that would be left in the wall, allowing her to get away with the money long before anyone could miss it. Not to mention the fact that by calling the police and having the place raided, days might pass before Shirley would even be able to go back to the club to get the money. Their plan was foolproof, and Shannelle wondered why she hadn't thought of it a long time ago.

A little on edge and jittery about what she was about to pull off, Shannelle almost felt guilty about the fact that she had planned to set Shirley's Temple up, especially after all the money she'd made in tips that night. A bachelor party had taken over the club, and its participants were particularly in awe of Shannelle— aka Silky. She always got a lot of attention when she wore her platinum blond wig. She could feel Lopez watching her from the door as she gave her tenth lap dance of the night and wondered what was going through his mind. No one at the Temple knew about their relationship, and that was definitely a good thing. Being discreet meant that he could never hassle her in public, even though sex with him always seemed a little rougher after she'd had a good night with the customers—almost as if he were punishing her for being so good at what she did.

At 1:22 A.M., Shannelle left the dance floor and glided toward the dressing room at a snail's pace. Remmi would be ringing her cell phone in eight minutes, and she did not want to miss the call. Shannelle hadn't seen any sign of Shirley since midnight and wondered if the owner had left the Temple early.

At 1:30 on the dot, Shannelle felt her cell phone gently vibrate on the small of her back. She had taped it to her micro miniskirt with hopes that no one would notice it. All in one motion, Shannelle stepped into the dressing room, propped a chair beneath the doorknob, ripped the tiny device from the fabric that obscured it, and whispered, "Ready?"

"She left twenty minutes ago. I just wanted to wait and see if she was gonna come back," Remmi replied.

"Did she?"

"No. You have exactly eight minutes to cut the wall open and get that safe. Lopez is at the door. Once you have the safe in the suitcase, ring me once. Then I'll call five-oh."

"Gotcha."

With the speed of lightning, Shannelle ran to the closet, tossed the tattered costumes from on top of the suitcase, opened the cover, and removed the shiny metal tool. As if her life depended on it, Shannelle shoved her hands into a pair of plastic gloves to avoid leaving prints and gently removed the mirror from the hook that kept it in place upon the wall, sitting it on the dingy and gum-stained floor. She briefly tuned in to the subtle vibration that came from the music, which played loudly out on the dance floor, and prayed that the bass would cover up the sound of the electric saw as it severed the wall in two. She had tried to buy the quietest one she could find, but some noise was inevitable. Taking a deep breath, she pushed the saw into the soiled wall.

To her surprise, the job was much easier than she thought it would be. She'd been right—it was a makeshift wall, and the power of the tool went through the plasterboard like a steak knife through butter. In moments she could see the metal from the small silver safe that rested in the hollow space between two quarter-inch pieces of Sheetrock. The safe was slightly bigger than she had envisioned, but that brought a smile to her face— more could fit inside it. The rectangular box fit tightly into the suitcase, barely allowing her to lock it closed.

Shannelle quickly threw her jacket over her shoulder, tossed the cut-out planks into the hollow space between the rooms, scattered the fallen debris with her foot to blend it in with the rest of the dirt on the floor, and gently hung the mirror back where it had been. When she turned around to look at her handiwork, it appeared perfect—just as it had looked before she'd cut the wall open. No one would notice anything until it was far too late. She shoved her gloves into her pocket, and as she struggled to roll the suitcase, Shannelle softly pressed Remmi's number on speed dial and disconnected it as soon as it rang one time. Hearing her friend's signal, Remmi quickly called the Fortieth Precinct with her anonymous tip. Shannelle lingered in the dressing room for a few moments, her heart pounding a mile a minute. It was her plan to exit as the police arrived, just missing the raid and leaving unnoticed in the commotion.

Shannelle made it a point to engage in her normal routine. It was quitting time for her and, as usual, she changed into her sweats as she prepared to vacate the crime scene. Lacing her sneaker, she felt the vibration from her Motorola once again. That was her cue—her partner was on point. According to the plan, the final phone call from Remmi would let her know that the police had pulled up outside the club. The time was here for her to make her exit. Doing her best not to struggle with the suitcase, Shannelle attempted to pull the bag with ease. She didn't know how much money she'd gotten away with, but it had been a very busy night. She had discreetly watched Lopez leave his right-hand man at the door several times during her shift. His absence from his post could mean only one thing—that he was taking stacks of cash to Shirley in her office. The club was unusually packed that night, thanks to the bachelor party, and she salivated at the thought of how much money the safe must contain. She and Remmi had definitely hit the jackpot.

The entryway to the Temple was packed with patrons still trying to get inside. Shannelle could see Lopez attempting to control the crowd, throwing his weight and authority around, as always. As she headed for the employee exit, she kept her eyes peeled for anyone who might notice her departure. It wasn't unusual for her to be leaving at that time, but she knew that the sight of her pulling a large black suitcase was something that would be remembered by anyone who might see her leaving.

Nervously, she strolled down the dimly lit corridor. She rounded the corner, and her eyes remained focused on the large metal door she needed to walk through. She couldn't wait to be on the other side.

Almost home free, she whispered to herself. As her hand pushed the shiny silver bar, a familiar voice rang out from behind—a voice that made her blood curdle as soon as it touched her ears.

"Going on a trip, Silky?"

Shannelle stopped dead in her tracks and stood as still as a statue. She was afraid to turn around, afraid to keep going, and damn near afraid to take a breath.

"I hope you know that you have to ask for time off at least two weeks in advance, girlfriend," Shirley bellowed from down the hall.

"I'm not going anywhere," Shannelle stuttered. "Gotta new man. I'ma be staying at his house for a while. I'm really feelin' him," she continued without turning around. Shannelle was amazed at herself for thinking so quickly on her feet. She usually got nervous when she thought she was about to get busted, but this time she was able to rise to the occasion and come up with an excuse for looking suspicious.

"Well, as long as you do your job here, I couldn't care less where you sleep," Shirley laughed gruffly. Shannelle never looked back. She didn't want to make eye contact with her boss. She feared that if Shirley got a good look at her, she would know that something was up.

What the fuck is she doing back here and why didn't Remmi warn me? Shannelle asked herself as she rushed through the door. In the darkness, she could see Remmi's shadow behind the steering wheel of her dark blue Honda Accord. As Shannelle walked toward the car, Remmi slowly began to drive toward her while simultaneously popping open the trunk. She approached the vehicle and, without blinking an eye or focusing on her surroundings, tossed the suitcase into the trunk, slammed it shut, and jumped into the passenger side of the car before they drove off into the night.

9

Seven o'clock in the morning, and the place was already packed. On every baseboard of the wall sat some wannabe actress, hoping and praying for a four-week spot on New York's hottest daytime drama, *The Bold and the Restless*. The role of Senitra, the long-lost unacknowledged biracial daughter of one of the soap's main characters, was the most coveted role in the tri-state area for African-American actresses. Remmi just knew that she was perfect for the role, and she was determined to do whatever she had to do to get it. *Whatever!*

Remmi recognized most of her competition from local video shoots. Working frequently on the circuit, Remmi had gotten familiar with people's faces—especially those of her rivals. She even glared at her old "friend" Gayle from across the room, giving her a phony little four-finger wave. The green-eyed monster had reared its ugly head, and Remmi no longer wanted to be associated with Gayle after hearing through the grapevine that she was now working closely with Snatch—who had not returned *her* calls in weeks.

Competition filled the air, and none of the girls even attempted to make conversation with each other. You would have needed a machete to cut through the tension. Remmi hated casting calls. She felt they were useless, especially since she already knew she was better than everyone else in the room. Still, until she got her big break, she had to blend in with the masses—even if she didn't really blend in. Dressed in a pair of light blue stone-washed low-rise Levi's, a tightly fitted white Banana Republic T-shirt, and a pair of black open-toe Marc Jacobs mules, Remmi sat quietly reading the latest edition of *Black Enterprise* magazine. Her hair was pulled back in a simple ponytail, and aside from the clear MAC lip gloss that delicately sparkled on her lips, her face was completely makeup free. Her new agent insisted that Remmi's edge over the competition was her classic but sexy girl next-door look—a look that made people comfortable and not threatened. Her made-up diva look was what made people insecure. Looking like she was raised on Park Avenue set her aside from all the other hood rats no matter how ghetto she really was. This role called for a devil in disguise, not a sex kitten. Truth be told, the role called for Remmi to be herself.

Remmi was number thirty-seven. She would have been number thirty-two, but seven was her lucky number, so she asked the administrator if it was okay that she switch. He readily agreed and handed over the next number containing the number seven. The auditions were scheduled to begin at 9 A.M. sharp, giving Remmi a full three hours to practice the mock script they had given her. Unconcerned, Remmi continued to read her magazine as she finished her whole-wheat bagel and coffee, figuring that she'd start looking at the script around eight.

"So I hear you and Snatch got it on pretty heavy on the side of the West Side Highway the night I got you into . . ." a voice softly whispered to the left of Remmi's face. She was so engrossed in her article, she barely realized that Gayle had slithered down alongside the wall beside her.

"Excuse you?" Remmi replied with a blank stare.

"Yeah, that night I was nice enough to get you into VIP—I heard you gave him a pretty good professional right there on the shoulder of the road," Gayle chuckled.

"I don't know where you heard *that* from," Remmi snapped.

"From the horse's mouth. I never would have thought you'd be that desperate for a record deal—not after you were acting all chi chi fi fi at the open call. I thought chicks had stopped doing things like that anyway." Gayle shrugged with a smirk, shaking her head.

"That's funny," Remmi began, turning the page of her magazine and acting as though she were focusing on an article. "Coming from a bitch that let some fat, smelly muthafucka finger her pussy for an *audition* for a role as an *extra*."

"Bitch?" Gayle snarled, slightly raising her voice.

"Cause a scene if you want, *bitch*. This role is mine anyway," Remmi spat with a hint of evil in her voice.

"Yeah, just like the record deal." Gayle smiled, and rose to her feet. "I'll tell Snatch you said hello when I see him at the studio tonight." She smirked, strolling to the other side of the room. Remmi could feel her boiling blood pumping forcefully through her veins. It took everything she had not to jump up and punch Gayle in the back of the neck. But she knew that by doing that, she'd miss her one and only chance to read for the role. No— kicking Gayle's ass wasn't the answer. Not at that moment, anyway. But she knew their paths would cross again one day. And if the time and place were right, it'd be on.

on't you recognize me, *Daddy*?" Remmi—as Senitra—questioned with a raised brow. The fill-in actor dryly read from his script as Remmi continued to throw herself into the role with all the zest and vigor it demanded.

It was nearly noon by the time she was called into the audition room. Forgetting that she was tired from the night before as well as from the lengthy wait, Remmi became the character of Senitra and impressed not only the casting crew, but also herself. It was obvious that the Thursday-evening acting classes with Tracey Moore-Marable had begun to manifest in her ability. She was now indeed ready for Hollywood—but was Hollywood ready for Rementa Renee Broughton?

"Thank you, Ms. Broughton." The middle-aged white man casually smiled as he jotted down a few notes on his yellow pad. "We'll contact your agent," he continued. Remmi had expected more of a positive response than she was given. There was no applause, no smiles—just a room full of silence and blank stares. The casting director who had thanked her for her performance looked like a stone-faced cartoon character with thinning hair and yellow teeth. Although he couldn't seem to take his eyes off her, she couldn't find an ounce of approval anywhere on his face after she had finished. Unable to tell whether or not they'd really liked her, Remmi simply gathered her belongings from the burgundy love seat in the corner of the room. She graciously thanked the staff for the opportunity to read for the part and quietly left. On her way out, she passed Gayle, who was still waiting for her turn. Her number was fifty-nine. The two women glared at each other. She knew she was a much better actress than her rival, and when she got the part, she'd be able to gloat all over town. She couldn't wait.

———

Shannelle and Remmi couldn't believe they had gotten away with it. The news was all over the papers: BRONX STRIP CLUB A COVER-UP FOR TRI-STATE AREA'S LARGEST ECSTASY RING. The Temple was shut down after the raid; Shirley, Lopez, and all the other people left in the place had gotten busted; and "Thelma and Louise" had quietly gotten away with the safe. Ironically, the most difficult part about the heist was getting the safe open. They'd had to let it sit at Remmi's apartment for three days before they were able to get it cracked. During that time, Lopez had called Shannelle at least fifty times, but each time the caller ID displayed the Fortieth Precinct, she let the voice mail pick up. They hadn't quite come up with a plan of action for what they were going to do if Lopez actually did get released. They just hoped that with his rap sheet, a bulletproof vest, and thousands of dollars' worth of X on him, he'd be sent away for a very long time.

Unable to break the safe themselves, it took them two days to locate Shannelle's cousin—a certified locksmith—and another twenty-four hours for him to come to Remmi's apartment to open it.

"Now where'd you chicks get this safe?" Wyatt questioned as he adjusted his black horn-rimmed glasses. Wyatt was Shannelle's first cousin on her mother's side—her mother's brother's only son. Not someone the girls necessarily wanted to be seen in public with, Wyatt made Steve Urkel look like Denzel Washington. With his wrinkled high-water pants, suspenders, and Coke-bottle glasses held together by dirty masking tape, Wyatt was not someone Shannelle liked to admit was a relative of hers. Still, drastic times called for drastic measures, and Wyatt was the only person the girls felt they could trust to help them out and keep their secret.

"We found it," Shannelle lied.

"You *found* a safe?" Wyatt inquired, his head cocked to the side. "Now Cousin Shannie, if you want me to help you, you need to be honest. I have an IQ of 146. Do you really expect me to believe that you *found* a safe—filled with money? That it just dropped from the sky?"

"Cousin Wyatt—my uncle Lloyd's only son—" Shannelle copied his tone "—I *am* being honest. I found this safe, and for your information, I do not know if it's filled with money. In fact, I don't know what's in it."

Remmi wanted to bust out laughing, but she remained straight-faced as she watched the interaction between the two cousins in her kitchen. The safe sat upon the kitchen table, and Shannelle and Wyatt before it as if they were about to deliver a baby.

"Yeah, okay. I'll open it for you. And you don't have to tell me where you got it. Just don't continue to insult my above-average intelligence by lying," Wyatt snapped as he began to examine the metal box like a doctor preparing to perform a heart transplant. Shannelle did not respond. As long as he opened the safe, there was nothing for her to say. Wyatt opened his large toolbox, pulled out a magnifying glass, and looked more closely at the combination lock. After a moment of close study, Wyatt leaned on the kitchen table, folded his arms, and sternly looked the two girls directly in their eyes.

"Combination locks are the most difficult locks to open. I'll have to pop it. It's too much trouble to try and figure out the combination," he said.

"So pop it. We don't care." Shannelle shrugged, and Remmi shook her head in agreement.

"Well, not so fast, ladies. First things first. Now let's just cut to the chase," Wyatt said, crossing his legs to match his arms. "You chicks obviously have done something illegal to get this safe. And cousin or no cousin, I don't think I should open it unless there's something in it for me," he continued. Remmi chuckled in disgust at the sight of this moron making demands of them. His tone of voice and mannerisms angered her. He kept glaring at her and her best friend. Man, he should have been glad that she even let him into her apartment.

"Well, what is it that you want from us?" Shannelle asked.

"What's in the safe?" he questioned.

"We don't know," Shannelle lied.

"I don't believe that."

"You don't have to. It's the truth," Shannelle replied.

"Look, muthafucka—are you gonna open the goddamn safe or not? Ain't you supposed to be family? That's why we called your monkey ass. We coulda called my man Peto—he can break any safe on the planet. In fact, he's a mastermind safe cracka—steals all kind of shit—from cars to ATM machines. But we figured we'd give the business to you. We were gonna give your stupid ass five hundred dollars for the favor, but since you wanna act like you tryin' to blackmail us and shit, fuck you!" Remmi ranted.

"Wait—hold on a minute," Wyatt said, drastically changing his tone. "I didn't say I *wasn't* gonna open it. I just said I didn't think I *should* unless there was something in it for me."

"I just told your ass we'll give you five hundred bucks. But not a penny more. Take it or leave it, nigga. In fact, Peto would probably do it for free. He and I used to mess around," Remmi snapped.

"Five hundred dollars is fine," Wyatt replied.

In less than ten minutes, Wyatt's workmanship and know-how had the lock severed from the metal box.

"Don't open shit," Remmi spat, stepping between him and the

safe while abruptly placing her hand on the metal lid to keep it closed. "The money's on the dresser in the bedroom," Remmi motioned to Shannelle, who made a quick exit from the kitchen.

"Thanks for your services," Remmi snapped.

"I never said I *wasn't* gonna do it," he replied.

"Whateva, nigga," Remmi huffed.

Shannelle returned in a flash with five crisp hundred-dollar bills.

As she handed the money to her cousin, Wyatt began, "Ya know, Rementa—you really are looking good—"

"Yeah, I know," Remmi replied, rolling her eyes.

"Now I know you only mess around with those high rollers—," he continued.

"You mean ballas?" she interjected.

"Yes—ballers. But, uh, I got my own successful locksmith business now—so maybe you and I could go out sometime," Wyatt suggested.

Remmi laughed, still holding the lid of the safe closed.

"Me go out with *you*? Fuck outta here," she howled. She and Shannelle cackled as if they had just heard the most hilarious statement of their lives.

"Nigga, you should try hooking up with Chris Rock, 'cause your ass got jokes," Remmi managed to utter through her laughter.

"Wyatt, we'll check you later, cuz. Thanks for the favor," Shannelle stuttered amidst her amusement. Still cracking up, she placed her hand on her cousin's shoulder and showed him to the door. Once she bolted it tightly behind him, she strutted back to the kitchen, where Remmi had already started removing the money from the safe and placing it on top of the table. They had *definitely* hit the jackpot.

"It's hard to believe that y'all are from the same family," Remmi chuckled.

"I know. But girl, you crazy," Shannelle laughed, high-fiving her best friend. "And who the hell is Peto?"

"Ain't no Peto. But I had to think of something! The nerve of that muthafucka, trying to blackmail us!" Remmi snapped, placing more money on the table.

"Bitch, yo' ass is da truth." Shannelle grinned, shaking her head in disbelief at her friend who still amazed her sometimes.

"Ain't I, though?"

10

remmi ran for cover in the coffee shop just across the street from where she'd be auditioning for a JCPenney commercial. Out of nowhere, the sky had opened up and the rain came crashing down forcefully. The weatherman had not said anything about rain in the forecast, so she was assed out in an autumn storm without an umbrella. The first place she saw to take refuge was a Starbucks, which was actually a good thing. She was early for her appointment, and an Arabian Mocha Java was exactly what she needed. The tax-free unmarked $92,000 from her heist with Shannelle had given Remmi the cushion she needed to spend her days auditioning. With that kind of stash in her cookie jar, she could afford to stop temping now and forge full-speed-ahead with her acting career. Although she didn't burn her bridge with Teddy, she let him know that he wouldn't be seeing her for a while. And while a JCPenney commercial wasn't exactly big time, it was certainly a good place to start.

As she sauntered over to an empty table with a large coffee in hand, her eyes swiftly ran across the massive black-and-white clock on the wall behind the cash register. She had plenty of time to get to her audition—almost forty-five minutes, to be exact. Arriving twenty minutes early for a commercial audition was more than enough time, and she was only across the street.

Remmi tried to clear her mind as she slowly sipped on the hot syrupy liquid, savoring its silky, sweet flavor. There had been so much nervousness in her life since she and Shannelle had pulled their heist, and paranoia had set in deeply. Shannelle was afraid to go back to her own apartment and had been living on Remmi's couch for the past two weeks. Lopez somehow posted bail and had completely trashed Shannelle's apartment one afternoon while she was out grocery shopping. When she returned to her building, before Shannelle could go upstairs, the doorman informed her that Lopez had been there, left, but was looking for her. When she made her way up to the tenth floor, she arrived only to see the door ajar and her belongings in total disarray. Afraid to go inside, she quickly headed for Remmi's place and had been there ever since. They couldn't call the police because they, too, were guilty of a crime. So all they could do was find refuge in each other. Still the panic increased with every breath they took, simply because they truly had no idea what Lopez actually knew. The only thing they knew for sure was that he was definitely pissed. But what they didn't know was why. Was Lopez furious because he knew they had set him up? Or was it because "the love of his life" hadn't posted his bail? Either way, from the looks of Shannelle's apartment, Lopez was mad as hell.

As Remmi focused on her thoughts, hoping that her best friend would go back to her own apartment soon, she noticed a young man sitting directly across from her at a small wooden table identical to the one at which she sat. He looked familiar, like someone she once knew who had changed drastically since she'd seen him last. And at first, she couldn't pinpoint it. The guy's sunken cheekbones and dull copper complexion made him appear years beyond what was probably his actual age. His jet-black silky locks looked as though they had not been groomed in quite some time, and Remmi could tell that he was in seriously poor health. His eyes possessed the same hollow look that her next-door neighbor and friend, Max, had before he died—a look that indicated that there was not much time left for him, a look that had prepared Remmi for his death two months later.

As the guy positioned his bony fingers tightly around his steaming cup, it seemed to take all the strength he had to lift his coffee to his unnaturally dark and ashy lips. He frowned as he swallowed the scalding black liquid—it was obviously too hot for his taste buds. His scowl jarred her memory. She finally recalled who he was underneath all that grime.

"Long time no see," Remmi said with a raised brow as she approached his table. He lifted his head up from the cup, startled to see her standing above him.

"You look like shit, too. What—you smokin' crack now?" Remmi asked, her hand firmly placed upon her hip.

"Oh, what up, Remmi? How you been?" Dale answered dryly, trying hard not to make eye contact.

"I been good. Better than you obviously." She smirked, almost happy to see that her best friend's ex wasn't doing too well at all.

"I hear that. How's my girl?" he questioned, focusing on his cup of coffee.

"Shannelle is great. Also better than you."

"Tell her I said what's up."

"She told me you stood her up recently. Still fuckin' with my girl's head, huh?"

Dale shook his head. "Still minding other folks' business, huh, Remmi? Some things never change," Dale spewed, waving Remmi off with his long dirty fingers.

"I told my girl the same thing. Some things neva change. That includes you, Dale. That's why I told her she needs to leave your triflin' ass alone. I told her from jump that yo' ass ain't shit. But sometimes, people gotta learn the hard way." Remmi shrugged.

Silent, he remained fixated on the space in front of him as he continued to clutch the paper cup that held his coffee.

"I'm sure Shannelle will be glad to know that you're strung out now." She smiled. Remmi strolled back over to her small table, tossed her black DKNY trench coat over her arm, and headed for the front door of the coffeehouse. If she walked swiftly, she would still be early for her audition.

running out of clothes and getting tired of Remmi's couch sent Shannelle into a state of depression that she couldn't seem to shake. It had been almost three weeks since she'd been back to her apartment—being terrified of running into Lopez was keeping her glued to her best friend's couch. Shannelle knew what he was capable of, and she did not want to be on the receiving end of his fury. On too many occasions, she had seen him explode on men and women alike, and she knew he would not hesitate to unleash his temper on her, especially if he believed that she had betrayed him. Shannelle thought she would be living the good life after the heist, but fear had paralyzed her, making it impossible for her to go back home or to the Temple. She'd actually thought

about going back to the club and acting like she didn't know anything about the bust, but it had been all over the papers, and she
wasn't that good a liar. Still, the day she had decided to go see
what was going on at the Temple, she came down with a bad
stomach virus that took her almost a week to shake. Remmi did
her best to nurse her friend back to health, but Shannelle still
could not rid herself of the violent cough that accompanied the
stomach cramps that had laid her out for several days in a row.
And although Remmi loved her best girlfriend—her partner in
crime—her homie pastromie, and wanted to see her well, it was
obvious that familiarity was beginning to breed contempt. Remmi
was getting tired of seeing Shannelle lounging around the house,
doing nothing but watching talk shows and reading piles of magazines that she would buy from the newsstand on the corner.

Each evening when Remmi would return from an audition,
she'd huff and puff as she kicked Shannelle's belongings across the
living room floor. The same best friend she used to beg to stay
over after a night of club-hopping was now getting on her nerves
and annoying the hell out of her. Already aggravated because she
was wasting so much time and energy going on all these auditions
and not getting any jobs, some nights she just wanted to bask in
the silence of her own mind, in her own apartment and sulk. But
with Shannelle living on her couch, that was impossible. And the
ferocious racket of her sister-friend coughing up a lung in the
middle of the night was like nails on a chalkboard to Remmi's ears
at two in the morning. The noise was so violent that not only
did it disturb Remmi's sleep to the point where sometimes she
couldn't close her eyes again, but it also made her wonder what the
hell was really wrong with Shannelle. That chronic hacking
sounded like a jackhammer. If Remmi didn't know any better, she
would have thought Shannelle was an eighty-year-old woman

about to kick the bucket any day. *Normal people just don't cough like that*, Remmi thought.

The constant hustle of her auditions, the noisy sleepless nights, and Shannelle's mess in her living room were all starting to get the best of Remmi. Was $92,000 worth all of this? Remmi was beginning to think not. Of course the money was great, providing her with a cushion to pursue the things she really wanted to chase. But she liked her life the way it had been before she and Shannelle had set up the Temple. Although it had been only a couple of weeks, she clearly missed her quiet apartment that was big enough for only her and the silence of living alone. She'd been doing pretty well with the money she'd been making from doing music videos and even wondered if she should postpone jump-starting an acting career a little while longer. The auditions were getting tiresome, and seeing Shannelle on her couch every day was beginning to wear on her patience. Not securing roles that she thought she had nailed was also starting to make her insecure about her abilities overall. She never heard back from *The Bold and the Restless* and was simply getting tired of putting herself out there to be rejected. Most of all she missed the days when she could call Shannelle and complain about what was going on in her life, rather than feeling like Shannelle was one of the things she had to complain about.

"Shannelle," Remmi began as she tossed her keys upon the coffee table. She had thought about what she was going to say to her best friend the entire way home from her audition. Remmi didn't want to offend Shannelle, and she definitely didn't want to make her think that she was ungrateful for her cut of the loot—after all, $92,000 was more money than she had ever seen in her life—but she wanted her apartment back. She *needed* her apartment back and her own space. Didn't Shannelle have her own cash now to get a new apartment?

"Before you say anything—I know—you want your place back." Shannelle chuckled.

Remmi was a little shocked and eagerly awaited her best friend's full response. She couldn't tell if Shannelle was mad or not, but one thing was for sure—years of friendship meant they could practically read each other's minds.

"I know. I'm tired of your ass, too," Shannelle continued, letting out a hearty laugh and letting Remmi know that it was all right that she felt that way.

"Girl, you know it ain't that I don't love the hell outta you, but this here cardboard box is only big enough for one PMSer at a time," Remmi replied.

"Who you tellin'? Have you heard the way you snore? You really need to get that shit checked out," Shannelle snapped. The girls hugged, glad that they had cleared the air and were both ready to get back to their lives.

"I have to be honest, though," Shannelle began. "After I saw what Lopez did to my apartment, I could only imagine what he was planning to do to me. That's why I didn't wanna go back there. I was scared. Still am."

"I know. But what are you gonna do?" Remmi asked. "You can't stay here forever."

"Well, I've actually been looking at places around here. And it just so happens that I found something."

"You did?"

"Yeah. Real close around here," Shannelle replied with a smirk.

"How close?" Remmi asked.

Shannelle smiled. "Is the eighteenth floor close enough?"

"Get outta here! That's great—oh my God, girl! That's what's up! Now you can be close without being *close*!"

They jumped for joy and began discussing the details of how

they would get what was salvageable from Shannelle's old place into her new apartment. They also decided that it still wasn't safe for Shannelle to go back there. They'd hire a moving crew to go over to the building to pack up Shannelle's things and move them to her new place. Lopez had no idea where Remmi lived, and they figured it was far enough away from Shannelle's place for her to be safe. It was unlikely that Lopez would ever be able to find her. And with a fortune in her pocket, Shannelle was ready to start a brand-new life—away from Lopez, away from stripping, and definitely away from Shirley and that damn Temple.

The truck was ready to go. They'd contracted a professional moving company and decided not to leave any forwarding address, just in case Lopez was still looking for Shannelle. On the day of the move, both Remmi and Shannelle were on edge. They anxiously waited back at Remmi's apartment for the moving truck to arrive, with hopes that Lopez had let the entire issue go. But knowing Lopez as she did, Shannelle knew that was unlikely. As stupid as he was, by now he had probably figured out that she was in on setting up the club. The bust had been in all the papers and on every news channel, mentioning the names of all the major players in the ring—him and Shirley being up there in the ranks. On one program, they had even shown the faces of some of the dancers as they were being released from the precinct, cleared of all charges. In retrospect, Remmi and Shannelle realized that they should have let Shannelle get arrested, too. That way no one would have suspected her of any involvement. But it was too late. There was nothing they could do now. Her best bet was to simply lie low, stay away from the places she knew Lopez and his people frequented, and start a new life and career.

As the clock struck 3 P.M., the movers finally arrived and unpacked Shannelle's belongings into apartment 1801. A charming one-and-a-half-bedroom apartment overlooking Manhattan's East River, it was in a pretty nice part of Spanish Harlem. Shannelle was able to get the next available unit, and skip the lengthy waiting list, thanks to a little hand job she gave the big boss's geeky freckle-faced son one afternoon after dropping Remmi's rent check off at the office. Needless to say, she knew how to use her skills to get what she wanted, and no man was exempt from her prowess once she set her mind on whatever it was that she desired.

Shannelle made a sigh of relief once she and Remmi unpacked box after box, setting everything in its proper place. She'd lost a lot from the vandalism, but had more than enough money to replace anything she truly needed. The most important thing to her was that she was finally away from Shirley, Lopez, and that godforsaken Temple, and that she never had to lay eyes on any of them again. Once the Temple's biggest advocate, Shannelle never realized how much she had really hated the place, deep down inside.

"So what's next on the agenda?" Remmi asked when the last plate was gently placed into the kitchen cabinet.

"As far as?" Shannelle replied.

"Well, you been chillin' for almost a month, moved into a new place—what's up? Are you gonna go back to work anytime soon?"

"Eventually. But not stripping. I'm done with that."

"You gonna quit strippin'? What the hell else are you gonna do?"

"There's a lot of other shit I can do, ya know. . . . Like . . . Like . . ."

"Like what, bitch? The only job you ever had was strippin'. Do you even have any other skills?"

"Of course I do."

"What?"

"Don't worry about it. Mind ya bizness," Shannelle mumbled.

Remmi looked at her friend and shook her head. She knew when the money from the heist ran out, Shannelle would be hitting another club doing what she did best. The plan was to get into something lucrative before that happened. The only question was what?

"Well, the first thing you better do is take your ass to a doctor and find out why the fuck you been coughing for like five months straight," Remmi continued, taking a seat at the dining table.

"I told you they said I have bronchitis. Don't you listen?"

"For five months straight? Get a second opinion."

"I don't need a second opinion. Dr. Lipschitz has been checking me out since before I got my period. He knows me and my history."

"What the fuck kinda name is Lipschitz? You actually trust a muthafucka named Lipschitz? I wouldn't trust no nigga named Lipschidt. Sounds like somebody who kisses a lotta ass. Lip shit—what kinda name is that?" Remmi snapped.

"He's Jewish, stupid. He wears one of those beanies and everything, so you know he gotta be smart. You so ignorant."

"It's called a Yamaha, like the piano, do do, and *I'm* the one who's ignorant?" Remmi huffed. "Well, whatevathefuck his name is—I think you need to get a second opinion. Some days you're so weak, you can't even get outta bed. I ain't no doctor, but that sounds like more than bronchitis to me."

"I'm not weak. I'm lazy."

"Yeah right, and my name is Orville Redenbacher."

"Then pop me a bag of popcorn, will ya, bitch?"

———

much to Remmi's delight, she got a callback for the JCPenney commercial she had auditioned for. Now that she was financially stable and able to focus solely on her career of becoming more than just a popular video chick, she had a newfound burst of energy when it came to her career. She decided to go only after roles that were mainstream, auditioning for television commercials and print ads more than music videos, with hopes of one day hitting the big screen.

When she walked into the talent holding room, she instantly noticed that she was the only woman of color who had gotten called back. The other girls were all blondes and classic "California" types. Remmi wondered exactly what it was that the producer was looking for. As she gulped down a healthy portion of her Poland Spring, she sized up the others. What would give her an edge and an advantage over the competition? They were all pretty in that traditional all-American white girl kind of way—if that's what you like. In fact, they all looked very similar. But Remmi was exotic—cultural and ethnic. Her olive complexion, complemented by her hazel-colored eyes, made her stand out in a room where surfing, sunshine, and Venice Beach dominated. She knew she had a look that could appeal to the masses—people of color could identify with her, and Caucasians would not feel threatened. There was no doubt that she was black—but not *too* black—all ethnicities built into one. It simply depended on what angle and direction the producers wanted to go. She did know one thing for certain, though—the fewer girls there, the greater her chances were at getting the role.

As she looked at her watch, she made note of the fact that she had exactly thirty-two minutes before the first girl was scheduled to be called in. That's why she always arrived early. She never knew to what extra lengths she might have to go. Assessing who was probably her greatest competition for the day, Remmi zeroed in on the prettiest of the girls, a youthful natural-looking blond-haired girl with stunning crystal blue eyes and a porcelain complexion. She always had a way of accurately assessing which woman was her biggest competition and figuring out a way to eliminate her.

With a mission on her mind, Remmi made her way over to the girl, using just enough grace to emote a sense of comfort and camaraderie. She wanted to make the girl feel at ease, not threatened. She wanted to be trusted, even though she was a wolf in sheep's clothing ready to pounce at any moment.

"Hey, I'm Rementa." She smiled at the girl who sat quietly reading the latest issue of *People* magazine.

"Carrie. Carrie Fields," the pretty young woman answered as she extended a frail right hand to shake Remmi's.

"Looks like Lindsay and Nicole have a lot in common, huh," Remmi sadly began, referring to the cover story of the tabloid.

"Yeah. It's so sad what drugs can do to people."

"Sometimes you really can be too rich," Remmi remarked, although she really could not have cared less. This was just an ice-breaker for her true agenda.

"And too thin."

They chuckled.

"I've seen you at a lot of these auditions," Remmi lied. "So I just figured I would come over, say hi, and wish you good luck."

"Thanks. So many of these girls are so busy competing, it becomes like a silent catfight. It's nice to finally meet someone who actually treats you like a person instead of a threat," Carrie whispered so that the others couldn't hear their conversation. This would be easier to pull off than Remmi had thought.

"I know. It's such a shame. I know we all wanna make it, but do we have to be so cold and distant toward each other? We should really try to offer support to each other. At the end of the day, we're all women." Remmi smiled. "That's why when I saw you here and recognized you, I decided to say something."

"Well, that was really sweet of you. New York is such a cold, mean place. I'm not used to it, coming from Nashville."

"Oh, a Southern belle! I should have known! Wow, you're so brave to just up and leave your family like that!"

"Well, I'm not all alone. My aunt Sara lives here. But she's seventy-three years old. I moved in with her so I could live rent-free. She never had any children, so I also watch over her."

"Wow, that's really noble of you." Remmi looked down at her watch—as part of her act—and continued, "Oh, Carrie—I've gotta run downstairs and feed the meter. I drove into the city today and definitely don't wanna get a ticket. But listen, why don't you give me your number so we can keep in touch. I'm sure we'll be running into each other a lot. Maybe we can start our own little support group."

"Sure! That sounds like a really neat idea! Here's my cell." Carrie smiled as she jotted down ten digits on a napkin she found in her pink satin knapsack.

"If you go in before I get back, break a leg, girl!" Remmi grinned, tossed her Miu Miu calfskin leather satchel diagonally across her chest, and hightailed it out of the room. Not wanting to waste time waiting for the elevator, Remmi sprinted down five flights of stairs to the office building lobby, bolted through the revolving glass doors, and galloped over to the corner newsstand. "I'll give you twenty bucks to make a phone call for me!" she informed the guy behind the counter.

"Huh?" the disoriented, clean-shaven Arab replied.

"Twenty dollars. All you have to do is call this number, ask for Carrie Fields, tell her that her aunt Sara is in Lenox Hill Hospital and that she should come immediately!"

"Twenty bucks?" he asked with a raised brow.

"Twenty bucks." Remmi smiled as she slapped a twenty-dollar bill into the calloused palm of his left hand. She then dialed the number from her cell phone and handed him the handset.

"Carrie Fields? Yes, your aunt—aunt . . ."

"Sara," Remmi whispered.

"There's been an accident," he continued, getting all into it with his accent. Although it felt like a bad *Saturday Night Live* skit, it was working. "Your aunt Sara is in Lenox Hill Hospital. Come right away. It's an emergency!" The man smirked, handing Remmi back her phone.

"Damn, you good!" Remmi beamed, giving him the thumbs-up and wiping the oils his face had left on her cell.

"How about a date, cutie!" the newsstand guy called from behind her as she hustled back toward the building. Remmi did not even bother to respond. She needed to get back upstairs and wait for her name to be called. Now that her only real competition was gone, she just knew the job would be hers.

11

the plan worked. Remmi landed the part in the JCPenney commercial. Much to her delight, it swiftly became a nationwide hit, playing on every channel in regular rotation. Remmi was raking in residuals like never before, and agents were ringing her phone off the hook. She became known all over the industry as "the JCPenney Girl," and the success of the commercial gave Remmi the opportunity to star in three more ads. In her mind, she had now graduated from a music video girl to a full-fledged actress and model, commanding at least four thousand dollars up front for any shoot.

At the urging of her agent, Remmi decided to participate in a Sean John fashion show during the height of Fashion Week in New York City. Since she was not really interested in the world of modeling, Remmi planned not only to get up in the face of the HNIC, Diddy, but also get in good with Arthur Haddox, the president of his newly established film company. What Remmi wanted more than anything was to make the official jump from commercials and small-time parts to starring film roles. She knew Diddy and Arthur Haddox could make that happen for her, and with her agent working his magic to get her into the show, nothing was going to stop her from doing what she had to do in order to go to the next phase of her career.

As the crystal-clear New York City sky changed from azure to amethyst, Remmi could feel her heart beating slightly faster than normal. Scantily clad in a black butter-soft leather bodice with a provocatively plunging neckline and an onyx-colored mink hooded bolero jacket, Remmi was struck by a case of stage fright. Not one to normally be nervous, tonight Remmi felt her stomach churn and flutter. She made no eye contact or conversation with the other models but listened as they spoke amongst themselves about the many big names who sat on the other side of the crimson drapes.

"Did you see Will and Jada?" one girl breathlessly asked another.

"No, but I've been trying to have a conversation with them for the longest time. I would *love* a part in the new film they're doing," the unusually tall blonde replied.

Remmi kept her mouth tightly shut as she waited for her cue. She didn't want to get to know any of these women—they were her competition, and she had learned her lesson with Gayle. After all, she was not there to make friends. Her bout with the green-eyed backstabber had reminded her that Shannelle was the only friend she needed. Plus, she was in new territory. She'd done some print ads, but this was her first fashion show, and these females did this crap for a living. Remmi couldn't imagine this being her only source of income and all these weird giraffe-women being her colleagues. Adding to her annoyance, all the men were gay, making it quite difficult for her to schmooze and get over, since 99 percent of the guys were more feminine and prettier than she was. She was there only to corner whatever film connects she could. There was also something about the other models that Remmi simply could not relate to. Aside from the fact that they all seemed like space cadets, none of them seemed like real women. Their elongated torsos and necks made them look freakish to her.

Real women don't look like this. Who are they trying to sell clothes to? she asked herself.

"You're up next," the stage manager barked at Remmi, knocking her out of her trance and back into reality.

At first concerned that she might not be able to move in the very high heels, Remmi marched toward her audience as if she were wearing a pair of Nike Shox. To the rhythm of the runway song's bass, she sexily whipped her extremely long synthetic silky black ponytail from side to side as if she had been born with it and swayed her hips as if they were the devil's temptation. She had the audience eating out of the palm of her hand. They loved her, almost as much as she loved herself.

When she returned behind the curtain, she was met with adulation from all the drag queens and gay men but silence and sneers from the other models. The hate was a clear indication that she had done her thing. She didn't care about the other girls. This was about business, and she was about to handle hers.

"Girlfriend, how *do* you move in that footwear?" one very effeminate Cuban asked as he stereotypically snapped his fingers twice in the air.

"I'm a natural." Remmi smirked.

"Yes. A real diva. Let me get your number, girl. You could go places in this biz," he continued. Remmi quickly jotted her cell phone number onto a small white napkin and placed it into the palm of his hand.

Relieved and proud of her performance, Remmi felt her stomach growl and remembered that with all the backstage jitters, she'd forgotten to eat. She headed over to the food area, a magnificent spread virtually untouched by models who refused to digest anything but nicotine.

Fuck that, Remmi thought. *Those chicken wings look* good.

She ate carefully, and didn't mess up her MAC Venetian lip gloss. After a few moments, Remmi noticed a very handsome, clean-cut gentleman staring at her from a distant corner. Dressed in a trendy but professional gray suit, he held a brandy sifter in his left hand, displaying an expensive diamond-clustered wedding band. This was a man she needed to know better.

Remmi walked up to him and extended her hand. "Rementa Broughton." She smiled as they shook. "You look very familiar to me," she lied.

"You're the JCPenney girl," he replied in a smooth voice.

"As a matter a fact, I am." Remmi blushed. "Pardon my chicken. I'm starving," she giggled. There was an instant attraction between the two as their palms and eyes remained locked. Remmi felt her body temperature rise slightly, the crotch of her leather bodice get moist. She had no idea who this fine-ass black man was, but she was determined to find out.

"Art Haddox, president of Bad Boy Films, and I like a woman who eats more than rabbit food," he sexily replied.

Oh, Remmi thought to herself. She had no idea he was going to be so fine or that seducing him would be such an easy pleasure. He could not take his eyes off her, wedding ring or no wedding ring.

"What a pleasure to meet you, Mr. Haddox. I recently read about your new position in *Variety*, but I had no idea you would be so handsome," Remmi stated.

"You read the industry rags?" he questioned.

"Yes. I like to keep up on who's who in the industry."

"Do you act?" he asked.

"Of course I do. In fact, I've desperately wanted to make a transition into film."

"Never be desperate."

"Not desperate." She uncomfortably laughed. "You know what I mean. I mean, acting is a dream of mine."

"I've watched you since you were the 'it' video girl," he continued.

"Have you?"

"Yeah. Most of those video chicks never go anywhere. But somehow you've managed to do quite well for yourself."

"Well, my talent, drive, and perseverance has certainly paid off."

"I see." After reaching into his inside lapel pocket, Art extended his business card to Remmi. "Call my office tomorrow morning. I might have a role for you." He winked.

Remmi took the card from his fingers and assured him that she would be calling bright and early. As he sauntered away from her, his suit jacket gently flowing behind him, she wondered how long before they'd be in bed together. As badly as she wanted him, she knew it wouldn't be soon enough.

I ran into Chinkey from the club today, girl," Shannelle told Remmi. It was a crisp autumn afternoon, and they were spending the day at the Garden State Plaza mall in Jersey doing what they did best—shopping. Remmi was in search of shoes at Neiman Marcus, while Shannelle was stocking up on sexy lingerie from Victoria's Secret.

"Really? What's she been doing since the Temple got shut down?" Remmi asked, shoving her size 7s into the third pair of Gucci sandals.

"She said Lopez started an escort service and she's one of his top girls."

"Really? You didn't tell her anything about what you're doing or where you are, did you? Where did you see her?"

"I saw her downtown when I was coming out of my doctor's office."

"Oh."

"Lied and told her I was working at a club in Newark. She wanted to get some numbers on me, but I told her I was in the process of moving out there and didn't have any numbers yet. So I took hers and told her I would give her a call when I got settled."

"Good thinking. But I don't know. Something tells me that Lopez is still mad and isn't gonna let it go anytime soon."

"Yeah, I got that feeling, too. Like she knew something and would definitely be running back to tell him she saw me."

"I can't believe that nigga ain't do no time."

"Me either. But money talks. I'm sure he paid somebody off."

"Well, with him still being out on the street, I really don't think New York is a very safe place for you. So think about this. Art is putting me up in his condo in L.A. when we start filming next month. Why don't you come with me?" Remmi suggested.

"L.A.? I can't just pack up and move to L.A., girl! I have a life. I can't just move with you across the country!"

"Well, what the hell are you gonna do while I'm gone for all those months? Truth be told, if I like it out there, I might not come back. And it's obvious that Lopez is getting closer. You need to leave town for a minute. If Lopez finds your ass, it'll be a wrap.

You know better than anybody what he's capable of. So why don't you just come with me? We could be chillin' in Cali, hanging with the stars in our own condo in the Hollywood Hills. Come with me, girl! You could be my personal assistant!"

"What am I gonna do—move in with you and Bad Boy?"

"His name is Art, and he's hardly gonna be there. You know his wife tries to have his ass on lock—even though she ain't stoppin' shit," Remmi laughed.

"I can't believe you're allowing yourself to be somebody's mistress," Shannelle replied, shaking her head.

"Not just somebody's. Art Haddox, president of Bad Boy Films. But I won't be for long. I know it sounds cliché—but he really does love me. He's only with her 'cause he feels like he owes her, being that she was with his ass before he got money and they don't have no prenup. But mark my words: Me and Art—we gonna be together."

"Whateva, bitch. You crazy. There you go with that *Fantasy Island* shit again. Niggas do not leave their wives—especially when you talking about not having no prenup. He's using you, girl."

"*He's* using me? For your information, I have a very visible role in Bad Boy's first multimillion-dollar film. They're about to blow me up to be the next freakin' Halle Berry, I'm moving into *his* condo overlooking the Hollywood Hills, where I won't be paying a dime for anything—and *he's* using *me*? Well, use me the fuck up, baby!" Remmi cackled like she'd lost her mind.

"You're a sick bitch!" Shannelle laughed, too.

"You coming or what?"

"I'll think about it."

"Better not wait too long. Lopez is on your tail, heffa," Remmi warned.

"damn, that's some good pussy," Art sighed when he rolled his sweaty limp naked body off Remmi and sank into the mattress beside her. The air of the one-bedroom park-view penthouse suite at Trump International Hotel & Tower was filled with the stench of weed and all-night fucking. They had gone there after a night of drinking and partying at some of Manhattan's hottest nightclubs—unable to keep their hands off each other a minute longer. This normally self-controlled, in-charge businessman was a pile of mush around Remmi, and each time she spread her legs for him, he sank deeper into her realm, relinquishing all his power and forgetting about his eleven-year marriage.

Evidently his wife, a first grade schoolteacher, wasn't very adventurous in the sex department, and Remmi eagerly satisfied his healthy sexual appetite. Since the time they had met at the fashion show just three weeks prior, they'd had sex in every place imaginable, acting like two high school kids with nothing to lose.

As the sun beamed brightly through the mammoth windows, Remmi turned her back to the glare and shaded her eyes so that she could see the digital clock on the nightstand beside the California king-sized bed. It was only seven thirty in the morning, but she was famished, thanks to putting it on Art for almost two hours straight.

"I'm starving. I want breakfast," Remmi said as she pulled her bare body from the bed and walked over to the window. The view was breathtaking.

"Order whatever you want from room service. But don't get dressed yet. I need some more of you to start my day." Art groggily smiled.

Remmi climbed back into the bed and rapidly disappeared beneath the goose-down duvet. As she took his entire penis into her mouth, Art let out a moan that sounded more like agony than bliss. After fifteen minutes of performing some damn good oral, Remmi began to taste the saltiness of his preejaculation, so she spread her legs wide enough to receive him inside her. As his hardened manhood disappeared inside her vagina and their crotches met, swift as a bullet, Art ejected Remmi from him, sending her crashing into the brass coffee table three feet to the left of the bed. She felt the sting of the metal against her exposed back, and let out an uncontrollable howl. When she regained focus, Remmi saw the fiery look in Art's dark eyes.

He shrieked at the top of his lungs, "Are you fuckin' crazy!"

"Wha—What, baby? I thought you wanted more!" Remmi cried, the pain in her back resonating throughout her body.

"I didn't hear you say shit about being on the pill, and I didn't see you put on a condom! What are you trying to do? Trap a nigga? Bitch, I'm a married man, and you know that! I have a family! If you think I can be trapped by some two-bit groupie wannabe-actress trick-ass ho, you got the wrong muthafucka, bitch! Whatever we do, we do with protection! Is that fuckin' clear?" he shouted.

"Yes!" she squealed, her back throbbing even more. "I'm sorry. I am on the pill! I am!"

"Let me see the muthafuckin' pills! If you really on the pill, they'd be in your purse!" Art bellowed, lunging toward the other side of the suite, where Remmi's Coach bag rested upon the table. Like a junkie looking for his next hit, Art rummaged through her purse until he found a peach-colored pack of oral contraceptives. Remmi stared at him in horror as rage danced in his eyes. She was afraid to utter another word.

With the pills in his hand, he calmed down. "I'm sorry," he softly began, showing no remnants of the monster he'd revealed a moment ago. "It's just that, well, you know I'm married. You also know what my position is in this game. I can't afford to be having no bastard kids. It would jeopardize everything I've worked so hard for," he snapped. He jumped up from the bed, retrieved his Brooks Brothers slacks, and disappeared into the bathroom, slamming the door behind him.

Remmi sat dumbfounded on the plush carpet, trying to digest what had just happened. Art had momentarily turned into another person, like a real-life Dr. Jeckyll and Mr. Hyde. The kind, sensuous man she had been romping around the city with for the past few weeks had transformed into a raving lunatic right before her very eyes when he thought she was trying to conceive a love child with him. Of course, getting pregnant was not on the agenda for Remmi, whose sole mission was to become one of the biggest actresses in Hollywood, but she had no idea that Art would react so violently at the thought. He'd said he loved her many times during their affair, and she was beginning to have feelings for him, too. Judging by his reaction, he loved only the sex she provided.

Remmi began to pull herself together, searching for her clothes that had been scattered across the penthouse floor a mere five hours ago, in the heat of passion. In an attempt to regain her bearings, she took a deep breath, inhaling the leftover aroma of the massive blunt they had shared in the wee hours of the morning. She clumsily dressed herself, ignored the pain across the small of her back, and listened to the sounds coming from the marble-tiled bathroom. Beneath the thumping of water forcefully hitting the glass walls of the shower, Remmi could faintly hear the whisper of Art's husky voice. He spoke soothingly on the telephone from beyond the thickness of the door. "Yes, I just touched down, baby. Yeah, everything went very well. I'll be home as soon as I can. Miss you, too. Love you, too," she heard him say before he disconnected his cell phone and turned off the water. Remmi rushed back over to the other side of the room, careful not to alert him that she had been listening to his conversation. As he emerged from the bathroom, his demeanor had changed dramatically, and he approached Remmi with the loving disposition she was more familiar with.

Remmi could smell his Carolina Herrera cologne before he touched her face, clad from his waist down only in a thick terry cloth towel. His sculpted torso glistened in the sunlight, illuminating tiny droplets of water. His perfectly toned waist revealed hours of hard work and dedication at the Reebok Sports Club. He was gorgeous, temper and all . . . but damn, was he schizo.

"I hope I didn't startle you, baby. I just got a little crazy there for a minute," he began.

You got that right, nigga, Remmi thought, but remained silent.

"You have no idea what you do to me," Art continued. "But you know I have a situation, and maybe one day I won't have it. But for right now, we both have to do what we have to do to work within the restrictions of that."

"I understand," Remmi softly replied, but without eye contact, her spine still feeling the cold, thick brass of the coffee table.

"We got a good thing going here between you and me. But we wouldn't wanna hurt your career or mine, right?"

"Right," she murmured.

"And don't worry. Once we're on location in L.A., things'll be a lot easier for us."

Remmi remained silent as Art continued to dress himself.

"I have a meeting to go to. But order the works from room service. Checkout isn't for another few hours, so relax. Get a massage if you want, and charge it to the room. You deserve it." He straightened his tie in the mahogany-framed mirror. As he tossed on his black Hugo Boss single-breasted jacket and headed for the door of the bedroom, he smiled that million-dollar smile that had originally caught her eye backstage at the Sean John fashion show.

"Be sure to answer when I call you later." He winked.

Remmi silently gave him a little finger wave as she blew a tiny kiss through the air. She tried to tell herself that he'd just lost it— that the last forty-five minutes actually hadn't happened the way she'd originally thought they had. But if she had been honest with herself, she'd admit that the incident was etched in her mind, right beside what had happened to her that night at Club NV.

12

he late-afternoon California air brushed against Remmi's face as she rode shotgun in Art's Mercedes-Benz SL-Class convertible. They had just wrapped the first day of preproduction on the film, and she was flying high. She had done a great job, and the crew was already predicting a hit for the relatively low-budget independent film. The entire cast had welcomed her with open arms and were extra accommodating since this was her first major role. She felt at ease and in control, which enhanced her performance tremendously. Her acting classes had truly paid off. She was making Art very proud—he treated his protégée like the platinum doll she knew she was. Each morning they woke up next to each other, he would arrange for breakfast and fresh flowers to be delivered to her door. Thus, the violent incident back in New York soon became a distant memory.

A lifelong New York City girl, Remmi was amazed at how easily she seemed to fit into the Hollywood scene. She had been in

L.A. for only four days, but felt that she belonged there. The sunshine, the clear skies, and the warm breezes made her wonder why she had never relocated there before now. The good weather seemed to deepen her glow and improve her outlook on her life and her career as a whole—and with the movie in the works, she wondered if she would ever return to the Big Apple. If she could only convince Shannelle to come out West, she might never live in the concrete jungle again.

Art dropped her off at the condo and headed to yet another meeting, assuring her that he would return later that evening. Remmi headed up to the twentieth floor in the gold-trimmed circular elevator, feeling a little tired but like the star she'd always believed herself to be. As she watched her lover drive away, she half began to wonder if Art was really going to a meeting as he had said. However, the other half was actually grateful to have a little time for herself.

After Art's housekeeper prepared a delicious meal of grilled lamb chops and roasted vegetables, Remmi soaked her body in a cinnamon-scented bubble-filled Jacuzzi. Once she had gotten her fill, she tossed on a plush Sean John bathrobe, compliments of Diddy. She poured herself a glass of chardonnay and headed for the condo's balcony, which overlooked a sparkling unobscured view of the Hollywood Hills. Dusk was upon the city, and the sun was on its way to the other side of the planet, leaving in its place a purplish pink sky, as beautiful as one of those twenty-five-cent souvenir postcards. A gentle gust of air rustled her damp tresses, and she gently removed an out-of-place strand before it could crawl into her eye. For the first time since her career had taken off, Remmi actually took a moment to thank God for all the things that had happened in her life—the good, the bad, and the ugly.

It had been a long haul for Rementa Renee Broughton since her mother had committed suicide, but Remmi had made it. There were days when she didn't think she could or would get through it, but she did. She was a survivor and knew that if she could endure her mother's death, she could handle anything. Nothing that had happened in her life could hold a candle to the devastation of watching her mother blow her brains out over her own birthday cake. There was nothing that D'Aundre Collens, Byron Barnes, Arthur Haddox, or any of the adversaries she had met along her journey could do that would be worse than seeing her mother's head explode right in front of her.

With her hourglass figure, emerald eyes, and picture-perfect bronzed complexion, Rita Broughton was a beautiful woman who could have any man she wanted. Once an aspiring model herself, Rita stopped pursuing her career and education to care for her only daughter, whom she gave birth to at the tender age of fifteen. As she reared her daughter to the best of her ability, Rita did all she could to drill into Remmi's mind the importance of never being broke. With no education to obtain decent employment, and refusing to subject herself to the scrutiny that often accompanied those on public assistance, Rita used her extraordinary beauty to con men into supporting her and her daughter. Countless men came and went—one after another or simultaneously. They paid her rent, bought her cars, gave her credit cards in their names, and handled whatever else Rita needed taken care of. They gave her cash to put Remmi through private school, clothes on their backs, and plenty of food on their table. But eventually that way of life took its toll on Rita.

By the time Remmi was twelve, Rita had grown tired of the revolving door of men who flowed in and out of her house, her life, and her body. Some even began eyeing the younger version she had to offer: Remmi. And while Rita certainly had her flaws, she dutifully protected her daughter from any predators, always keeping a .22-caliber pistol under the right side of her mattress for anyone who decided to get out of line with her or Remmi. After all, Rita was a hustler not a pimp.

As Rementa matured and began to understand the kind of work her mother did to support the two of them, she couldn't help feeling resentful and embarrassed. Still, she loved her mother unconditionally, for she was all the family she had. There were no aunts or uncles, cousins or grandparents for her to spend time with. It was just Rita and Remmi, which sometimes made Remmi ask her mother where the rest of their family was.

But each and every time Rita would simply respond with a shake of her head. "Some folks are better off being strangers."

For years they lived in their own little world. That was until Remmi met Shannelle in the second grade and they became so much to each other—friends, confidantes, and caretakers. Remmi confided in Shannelle about her mother, and Shannelle confided in Remmi about her own mom, who was an alcoholic. The girls helped each other understand that their moms did what they did because that's all they knew how to do. And from the outside, they all lived quite well and were grateful for that. They both always had all the latest and the greatest and never wanted for anything. But as the years went by, Rita had given both girls a very clear message, and that was that it didn't matter how you got what you got—as long as you got it.

And her messages about men? Well, that was another story. Rita preached to her daughter and Shannelle every day of their lives since they could understand anything worth understanding that if they couldn't see dollar signs in the center of a man's pupils, then he wasn't worthy of a conversation—never mind some ass.

Men and money—the words start with the same letter of the alphabet for a reason. Remmi could recall her mother's sermon.

"And it don't matter how he treats you," Rita would continue. "Rich ones, poor ones, they all shitheads. So you might as well get your bills paid and make 'em feed you. After all, a girl gotta eat. . . ."

While her early years were pretty good, as Remmi approached her teens, she began to see changes in her mother. She started noticing that her doting mother, who would rise each morning to cook breakfast was now too exhausted even to get out of bed and say, "Have a good day!" But that did not concern Remmi as much as the fact that Rita would still be buried beneath the covers when Remmi returned home at four o'clock.

Finally the fourteen-year-old dragged her mother to the doctor to find out what was wrong. Diagnosed with bipolar disorder, Rita was placed on medication and ordered to attend weekly appointments with a psychiatrist—appointments that she hardly made. But she would pop a pill, which often sent her into a stupor more profound than the depression-induced sleep that Remmi had originally been concerned about. At her wit's end, confused and certainly not emotionally or mentally equipped to deal with her emotionally ill mother, Remmi began staying out, ultimately moving in with a thirty-five-year-old stockbroker at the age of fifteen.

Weeks sometimes went by without Remmi going home, and though she worried constantly about Rita, she could not face the vision of her mother quickly fading before her very eyes. The random slaps and disciplining she sometimes endured at the hands of her boyfriend were a small price to pay for not having to watch her beautiful mother deteriorate.

Then one cloudy afternoon Remmi returned home to find her

perverted statutory rapist boyfriend in bed performing anal sex on one of her classmates, a girl he must have met one day while picking Remmi up from school. In a daze, Remmi quickly grabbed the oversized Tommy Hilfiger duffle bag filled with all her belongings and headed out the door of his TriBeCa loft, vowing never to return again. And she didn't.

Hoping to smooth things over with her mother, fifteen-year-old Rementa went back to Rita's house with a new attitude. She wanted to have a better relationship with her mother. She wanted to make her mother happy and proud. She wanted them to be friends again. But not much had changed at all, and only for the worse. Not only was Rita still staying in bed from sunup to sundown, but it now seemed as though she hated the sight of her daughter.

Thinking that her normally loving mother was merely feeling betrayed by her recent absence, Remmi decided to try to make up for being gone for the past few months by preparing a special birthday celebration for Rita's thirtieth. After cleaning the house from top to bottom, placing fresh flowers abundantly around the house, cooking a wonderful meal all by herself, and even baking a birthday cake, Remmi attempted to drag Rita out of bed to enjoy all that she had done for her. But Rita was not impressed. In fact, she was annoyed that her daughter was bothering her when all she wanted to do was sleep the day away. She yelled and cussed at Remmi for disturbing her rest, even telling her that she should leave her alone and go back to her boyfriend's house.

"So what he screwed one of your little friends? That's what they do! He's a professional man. Black professional men don't come along every day! Let him take care of you! I'm not always gonna be around to blow your nose and wipe your ass, Rementa! You better find somebody, 'cause my days here are numbered!"

Rita spewed at her daughter, knocking over the meticulously set dining room table and sending the dishes crashing to the floor.

Horrified at the words coming from her mother's lips, Remmi yelled back her own venom. "What kind of mother have you become? Who are you? I don't even know you anymore! You're so mad that I ain't been here that you can't enjoy your birthday with me? I ain't been here because I don't wanna watch my mother lay in a coma twenty-four fuckin' hours a day! You want me to live with some nigga who smacks me in the face when I'm home ten minutes late from school? Who the hell are you! What the hell have you done with my mother? Where is my mother?"

"Where's you mother!" Rita snarled, her emerald eyes flickering with disgust. "Where is your mother?" she repeated as she slowly inched forward, clutching her fingers into a tightly clasped fist. "I killed your mother."

Remmi watched as Rita continued to walk forward until she was directly in her face, breathing a rancid flow of air. She dared not move away from her mother for fear of what she might do, so she remained as still as a statue, waiting for Rita to dismiss her or walk away herself. But she did not. Rita continued with a look in her eye that Remmi had never seen before—a look that let her know that this was indeed *not* her mother.

"I killed your mother," she growled. "Fifteen years ago after my brother raped me and knocked me up! I killed your mother right after my mother threw me out of the house for getting pregnant by some boy! She wouldn't believe that that boy was her son—my own brother—my *twin*! No, *I* was the slut! *I* was the whore! I killed your mother when I gave birth to *you*—my brother's child! I killed your mother every time my foster parents made me have sex with them. I killed your mother every time I had to let some strange man fuck my brains out so that I could pay the rent and keep food on the table and keep you in private school! I killed your mother last year when the doctor told me I was HIV-positive! And I'm going to kill your mother again right now!" Rita bellowed, her thick and putrid saliva spraying across Remmi's face.

Rita staggered on into the kitchen, reemerging with the cake Remmi had baked from scratch. She then disappeared into her bedroom and slammed the door so tightly, chips of cracked paint fell from the ceiling upon the carpeted floor. Remmi's heart hurt. She shook her head in disbelief. An inner voice told her to run to her mother and tell her that everything would be okay—that she would take care of her—that she would make sure that she got the very best care available—that these days people can live with HIV for decades without it turning into full-blown AIDS. Just as she rose from the couch to run to her mother's bedside, Remmi heard the sound of a single shot. With tears in her eyes and bewilderment upon her face, fifteen-year-old Remmi burst into the room where she used to cuddle up beneath her only parent's arm, to find her beautiful mother's corpse slumped over a crushed devil's food cake—the chocolate, the blood, and the flesh a vulgar mess.

The phone startled Remmi, quickly knocking the image of her mother's lifeless body from her mind. She had no idea how many times she let the phone ring before she finally picked it up, but the line was dead was she finally did. She didn't often allow herself to think about that godforsaken day when her life had changed forever. And she had no idea why she had allowed herself to go there that evening. After she popped a sleeping pill to ensure a good night's rest, she dozed off to the low sound of voices coming from the television, vowing to put the past out of her mind forever.

C ut!" the director called, signaling Remmi to release the embrace of her costar, Lamard Fisher. It was their first love scene, and Remmi lay half-naked upon the satin-sheeted king-sized canopied bed. It seemed as though everyone connected with the film was on the set that day. Maybe they were actually all genuinely interested in this particular scene, but Remmi couldn't help feeling like most of the cast and crew were more interested in catching a glimpse of her torso as she emerged topless from her dressing room, tossed her robe onto the floor, and slid herself beneath the slippery sheets.

Lamard was fine, and Remmi definitely felt chemistry as their tongues passionately intertwined, but she had Art on her brain. He hadn't come back to the condo last night, wasn't answering his cell phone, and instead of picking her up, he'd sent a car for her that morning. When she arrived on the set at 5 A.M., he was nowhere to be found. Remmi hadn't believed him when he'd dropped her off saying that he had another meeting to go to. And her senses told her that there was definitely some other chick intruding on her time.

Remmi could tell that Lamard was attracted to her, and the scenes with him went well. As they lay beneath the sheets, Remmi could feel his manhood protruding, an indication that she was definitely causing his adrenaline to rise. When they broke for lunch, Remmi headed back to the privacy of her dressing room, not in the mood to eat with the rest of the cast and crew. Remmi knew that the others on the set would think she was acting like a prima donna. But she didn't care. She needed to get to her cell phone so that she could call Art and have a conversation that no one else needed to hear.

From the moment Remmi entered the modestly furnished room, she began hitting the redial button on her Razr to no avail. Art's phone went directly to voice mail, sending Remmi's blood into a more rapid boil with each of her attempts. She paced the carpeted floor with folded arms, and her breathing quickened as her fury increased with every passing moment. She definitely felt as though she was being played—and wife or no wife, major role or no major role—Remmi made the mistake of allowing her emotions to take over, and she wasn't about to stand for it quietly. As she hit the tiny redial button for the hundredth time, she heard a soft knock on her dressing room door. Remmi immediately swung around and faced the entryway, calling to who ever was on the other side to come in. To her surprise, it was her onscreen boyfriend holding a white porcelain plate piled high with food.

Lamard was definitely a hottie. He was more experienced than Remmi, but not a well-seasoned actor either. He had done a couple of low-budget films in the past, but had yet to get the attention that his talent deserved. A light-skinned, gray-eyed brotha from the Baltimore area, Lamard had that classic 1980s pretty-boy look, and he knew it. His jet-black curly hair only added to his typical fine-black-man appearance, and his arrogance sealed the deal. He stood about six feet even, with a slightly bowlegged stroll and a moderately muscular build. He was indeed a well-put-together piece of eye candy, with a charming demeanor and a smile that could make even the most prudish woman quickly drop her panties.

Lamard stepped into Remmi's dressing room and gently closed the door behind him, ensuring some privacy. As he offered her the plate of food, he began in a low B-more drawl, "I made you a plate, yo. 'Cause ol' boy you calling ain't coming on the set today."

Stunned and taken aback, Remmi looked at Lamard, amazed

that he knew about her relentless attempts to try to reach Art. "Excuse you?" she asked, wondering how he knew her secret. Hadn't she been careful and discreet? And if he knew, who else did?

"Yeah," he continued, placing the food upon the small round coffee table. "Art's not coming on the set today. His wife's in town. You ain't know?"

Remmi looked intently at her costar as she dissected his words one by one.

"So," he continued, "you may as well stop calling and fuel up." He nodded toward the plate of catered cuisine.

Remmi looked at Lamard again, jostled her cell phone into the left pocket of her robe, folded her arms, and shook her head in denial. "How you know who I'm calling?" she probed with an inquisitively raised brow.

"Do you think you're hiding something?" He laughed. "Everyone knows the only reason you here is because you fucking him."

Remmi was shocked that Lamard would have the nerve to come into her private dressing room and toss such an accusation at her—such an accurate accusation, at that. "I beg your pardon?" Remmi spat.

"Come on, Remmi. Don't play games with me. You and I both know that what I'm saying is true. I'm just here to give you a healthy word of advice," he replied.

"And what would that be?"

"You already have the part. It doesn't matter how you got it. You a good actress, and you proving that you deserve to be here even if you did get it by laying on your back. We all have to do things sometimes to get ourselves in the door. But don't let your emotions get all involved with this cat. Be glad you here, and keep doing a good job. This film could be a huge stepping stone for you. Don't fuck it up by falling in love with a married man. Especially one like dis nigga, who's fucked every hottie on this side of the globe. You just another notch in his belt, Remmi. Believe dat," Lamard warned.

"Thanks for the brotherly concern—but mind ya bizness," Remmi replied.

"I ain'tcha brotha." He chuckled, looking her up and down and doing an LL Cool J, licking his already sexy lips. "All right, ma. I'm just trying to be a friend to a fellow actor. I'd hate to see your career go down the tubes 'cause a nigga done got you all sprung. I think you got talent. Too bad you ain't all that smart." Lamard sagaciously grinned and shook his head.

"Thanks for the backhanded compliment, but everything ain't always what it seems. As R. Kelly once said—just because you see me with him doesn't mean I'm sleeping with him," Remmi lied.

"And it doesn't mean you ain't," he laughed. "Eat," Lamard continued. "I don't need my leading lady passing out on me." He smiled at her, his hand on the doorknob. As he left Remmi's dressing room, she eyeballed the goodies he had brought her—and the goodies he had beneath his Evisu jeans. The plate was piled high with lasagna, baked chicken, and grilled vegetables—all of Remmi's favorites. She figured it would be stupid to let good food go to waste, and she was actually hungry.

Damn, does everybody know me and Art are screwing? she asked herself. Man, her down-low skills must need some work.

h ey, I just wanted to thank you for the words of advice. I had no idea I was being so obvious," Remmi said graciously into the telephone receiver.

It had been a long day on the set, and as she cuddled beneath the duvet in the master bedroom of Art's Hollywood condo, she could not help thinking of the words Lamard had said to her earlier that day in her dressing room. He was right—it did not matter how she got there. All that mattered was that she was effortlessly proving to everyone that she deserved the part. He'd been wrong about one thing: she *was* smart.

"No prob. Like I said, I think you got talent," he seductively whispered in response.

"Well, working with you is easy. I think we have a lot of chemistry." Remmi smiled, envisioning his soft full lips kissing her neck as they had in Scene Eight.

"Yeah, me, too." He chuckled.

"Well, I just wanted to say thanks. I'll see you on the set in the morning."

"A'ight. Peace."

"Yeah." She placed the telephone back upon the nightstand and clutched the comforter between her fingers. She still hadn't heard from Art, but decided to let it go. If he was with his wife, it obviously didn't matter that she was sleeping comfortably in the king-sized feather bed of his luxurious Hollywood condo instead of laying her head in some sterile generic hotel. Although the rest of the crew was staying at the Four Points Sheraton, her accommodations were far superior. She had all the opulence of a spacious magnificent condo, including a spectacular view of the Hollywood Hills and a concierge who treated her like royalty. So what she was being temporarily kicked to the curb for Art's wife? It wasn't like she was being treated like a stepchild. Once his boring spouse returned to New York, she was sure that Art would be showering her with attention again. In the meantime, maybe she could have a little fun of her own.

As a cool breeze blew the sheer window curtain against the

sliding balcony door, an idea popped into Remmi's head, and she quickly pressed the redial button on her phone. When Lamard answered the call, Remmi quickly began, "I know we just hung up, and I know it's kinda late, and I know we have to be on the set by five A.M., but—"

"I'm wit' it," Lamard interrupted.

Remmi was almost speechless at the fact that he had completed her sentence. Her heart rate slightly increased, although she honestly couldn't understand why. "With what?" Remmi bluffed. Did he know what she was talking about?

"You wanna see me, right?" he asked.

"Um yeah . . . um, so why don't you come over?" she invited, clearing the lump in her throat.

"Over where? To Art Haddox's crib?" Lamard said.

"Yeah . . . He ain't here. He's with his wife, remember?" Remmi giggled.

"Yeah, but don't you think that might be a little risky?"

"Oh, he's too busy with the ol' ball and chain. You said so yourself. And besides, I like to live dangerously." She snickered.

"Oh, do you?"

"Yeah, I do. I'll text you the address."

Before Remmi could set the cordless phone back in its cradle, the line was dead. She immediately text-messaged the location of Art's condo to Lamard's cell and began to prepare for her little jump-off. She freshened up quickly, splashing all the right places with a dash of Jean Patou's Joy parfum. She smoothed out the linens on the bed just in case she and her costar dared end up there, and lit a mango-scented candle. She initially considered changing out of the powder blue pajama shorts set that she was wearing, figuring it might be a tad bit too revealing for his first visit with her. But then she remembered that her unclad breasts had already been pressed against his bare naked chest when they filmed their passionate love scene earlier that day.

In less time than she could have imagined, the concierge phoned up to announce Lamard's arrival. He entered the front door of the swanky art deco condominium wearing a pair of baggy Red Monkey jeans and a black Calvin Klein crew-neck T-shirt, the firmness of his well-defined muscles hugged by the cotton. He appeared cool and at ease in his darkly tinted designer glasses, looking every much the part of the movie star he aspired to be. Remmi's hazel eyes were drawn to his tight round ass as he slowly strutted across the hardwood floor toward the balcony as if he were Mufasa from *The Lion King*. His black Prada loafers clattered on the oak floors. Neither of them said anything, although their bodies seemed to be having a conversation at a distance.

Remmi silently followed Lamard out onto the balcony, and they both stood motionless, looking at each other in the moonlight.

"You're beautiful." He smiled, breaking the silence.

She blushed. "Thank you."

"I was hoping you would call back and tell me to meet you somewhere. But I'm definitely surprised that you wanted me to come over here."

"Well, like I said on the phone—I like to live dangerously."

"Really? You don't seem like a bad girl. In fact, you look like an angel."

Remmi let out a cackle. "That's part of the game. Sweetie, I've done things that you would never *dream* of in your wildest imagination. One day I'll write a book," she laughed.

"What's the worst thing you've done?"

"Don't worry about it," Remmi coyly replied. She could tell that her mysterious dark side was turning him on, and like a silly schoolgirl, she suddenly wanted to impress him.

"C'mon. You tell me one of your secrets, I'll tell you one of mine."

"You first."

"Okay." He paused to think. "When I was sixteen, I had sex with one of my pop's girlfriends."

They both laughed, until Remmi shrugged. "So what? I stole the safe out of a strip joint and got away with over six figures."

The only sound that resonated through the atmosphere was the gentle draft that swayed through the air.

"Psych!" Remmi blasted, breaking the silence and laughing with her secret guest once again. "No, but seriously," Remmi began after the laughs had subsided. "On the real, I do like danger. My innocent good looks help me to be a bad girl sometimes."

"No doubt," Lamard said, looking around and taking in the spectacular view. "What do see in that nigga anyway?" he continued.

"Opportunity, that's all. It ain't like I *love* the muthafucka or anything like that," Remmi explained.

"Would have never known it by the way you was hitting that redial button on your phone today," Lamard joked.

"I don't like to be played."

"Played?" Lamard huffed. "I say both you fools are making out pretty good. You got a feature role, and he got you in his bed. I have a bachelor's degree in theater from Morgan State University. I had to go through audtion after audition. Callback after callback. You fuck the head nigga in charge, and they just hand you the role. There's something wrong with that shit." He laughed bitterly.

Remmi knew he had a point, but chose not to respond. She truly didn't want to concentrate on Art anyway. Even with Art's hip and trendy demeanor, Lamard made him look like a stuffy old businessman, and she really wanted to see if this young buck could put his money where his mouth was or put his mouth where her money was.

"You sound a little salty," Remmi finally replied.

"Not at all. That's Hollywood."

Their eyes stayed connected. It was a beautiful evening, and the Hollywood Hills backdrop was perfect for their little secret meeting. The stars twinkled in the sky.

"Money," Lamard said with sarcasm. "I always say anybody can be bought."

"It's not just money. Like Lil' Kim said—money, power, and respect. And Art Haddox has all three."

"Respect? Do you really respect him, Remmi?" Lamard asked, moving to within an inch of where she stood. She felt his warmth and a sensation went through her body as her nipples began to stiffen, screaming to be caressed. The closer he got to her, the wetter she got.

"I respect his position. But how much can you truly respect a dude who cheats on his wife and uses the aspirations of young girls against them for his own sexual gain? I'm not stupid enough to think that this is the first time he's done this. And it probably won't be the last," Remmi carelessly added.

Lamard could not take his eyes off her in the twilight. Remmi's hair softly framed her flawless face and fell to just beneath her shoulders. He became very aroused at the site of her succulent nipples and did all he could to keep himself from tossing back her tank top and shoving her voluptuous breasts into his mouth.

"So why am I here?" he asked, dragging his eyes away from her chest.

Remmi winked. "Because I think we both wanted to see each other tonight."

"So today on the set, was all that tongue action just acting, or was you really feeling it?" Lamard inquired, now standing so close to Remmi that their noses were touching.

"I don't know. It's hard to say. There was an audience, so we had to act," Remmi whispered.

"What about now?" he asked, grabbing the back of her head and shoving her lips onto his. With one swift motion, Remmi wrapped her bare legs around Lamard's narrow waist as he backed his body up against the metal railing of balcony. His strong hands groped every inch of her, sending sensations throughout her body.

Lamard gradually lifted the top of Remmi's tank above her head, dropping it to the cool pavement of the balcony floor. She in turn began to tug his T-shirt from his torso and then piled it on her garment. Perspiring slightly and yearning feverishly for each other, they gripped each other forcefully as their tongues continued to intertwine. As Lamard softly placed finger after finger inside Remmi's slippery vagina, each time licking the one he had just removed, Remmi unzipped his jeans and maneuvered his jeans and boxers down below his knees. His penis stood stiffly at attention, and Remmi could no longer control herself as she managed to slide his generous length deeply into her vagina. He vigorously pushed in and out of her body, and Remmi moaned in delight, feeling the bare friction of his raw flesh against hers.

When sweat cascaded from Lamard's clean-shaven face, Remmi used her tongue to catch each droplet of it, tasting his subtle aftershave. Initially he made very little noise, causing Remmi to wonder if he was indeed enjoying the moment. But as his thrusts quickened and his perspiration increased, he finally came to the height of his ecstasy, letting out a ferocious howl.

Afterwards, they both gasped for air. Lamard's penis slipped from inside the pulsating walls of Remmi's vagina, and they both retreated to opposite ends of the balcony. Within moments, Remmi found her clothing on the floor and clumsily tried to dress herself in the night air. Silently, Lamard grabbed his jeans and T-shirt and made his way inside the condo. Remmi followed, slightly fatigued, and awkwardly attempted to break the silence.

"That was good." She tried to smile.

"Good?" he responded, without making eye contact. "What the fuck ever happened to using a condom!" he barked.

He seemed to be blaming her, when neither of them had reached for protection, so Remmi huffed in response, "Oh, was that solely *my* responsibility?"

"All I know is that your ass better be on the pill, 'cause I ain't trying to hear no bullshit about 'I'm pregnant' in a couple months. I don't give a shit how fine you are!" he snapped, pushing his shirt into his jeans and pulling up the zipper.

"Excuse you? For your fucking information, I *am* on the pill. And who the fuck says I wanna have a fucking baby by yo' stupid ass? I ain't tryin' to trap you, muthafucka! You ain't no muthafuckin' Denzel Washington! You ain't stackin' no paper like that! You starting out just like me, and I have a career to think about, ya know! So don't flatter your fuckin' self!" Remmi went off on him as she went to the closet and pulled out a pair of thick terry cloth sweatpants.

"Well, good. I just know how bitches be trying to pull fast ones on a nigga sometimes," he replied, now more calm.

"And *I* know how niggas be tryin' to make 'keep a bitch' babies. And I ain't a bitch that's about to be kept. I gotta career, too. And according to the tabloids, mine is moving a hell of a lot faster than yours!" Remmi spat.

"Touché," Lamard replied, and glided toward the front door of the condo.

"Besides, if you was so fucking concerned, you shoulda made sure you bagged that shit up!" Remmi shot back.

He shrugged. "The heat of the moment, you know."

Remmi marched over to the front door and turned the brass knob to open it. "We have an early call, and I need to get some rest," she stated, rolling her eyes.

Without saying a word or even looking her in the eye, Lamard left the condo, leaving Remmi feeling empty, used, and embarrassed to face him on the set in just a few hours.

13

the next six weeks of shooting went over without a hitch. After the incident at the condo with Lamard, Remmi decided to tirelessly throw herself into her work; scheduling more sessions with Tracey, her acting coach, and hitting the gym two times a day. As much as everyone tried to persuade her otherwise, Remmi made a decision not to participate in the Hollywood nightlife, as she felt it would compromise her ability to rise at 5 A.M. to work out with her trainer. Tracey had also suggested that she forgo partying at this point in her career, saving all her energy for perfecting her acting methods. And her hard work, perseverance, and dedication were definitely paying off. She was in top physical condition, her skin was more beautiful than ever, and her acting was improving with every lesson. Everyone was impressed with her, and she was being pegged as the next big thing to hit the Hollywood scene, à la Jennifer Hudson—an underdog who emerged from nowhere and rose to the top of

Hollywood's elite. It was obvious that she was surpassing her costars, including Lamard, who had considerably more acting experience than she did. But Remmi's bubbly and sexually magnetic personality and angelic face made her a media favorite. She was being compared to the legendary Dorothy Dandridge, one of her idols. And the paparazzi were in love with her, splashing her face across the covers of several weekly publications. She was even named one of the top fifty people to watch for in 2008 by *People* magazine. Rementa Broughton was definitely on the rise.

Despite their tryst, on the set, Remmi and Lamard acted as though nothing had ever happened between them. They still had plenty of onscreen chemistry, but they never said a word to each other when the cameras weren't rolling. It was almost as if they had both put the incident completely out of their minds.

On the flip side, Art and Remmi's relationship seemed to be picking up a bit. After his wife went back to New York, Art became a presence in Remmi's life once again. He never offered an explanation for his disappearance, and Remmi never questioned it. After asking herself if it really mattered and coming to the realization that the answer was no, she figured there was no reason to put him on the spot. He would only lie or get angry. Either way, Remmi knew that nothing good could come from interrogating him. So again, they both acted as if he had not disappeared for nearly two weeks, and when he reemerged on the twelfth day, it was almost as if they had just been together the day before.

Over the course of her life, Remmi had grown very skilled at denying and even forgetting things that had happened to her—a talent she had managed to perfect after her mother's suicide. In fact, with the help of Tracey, Remmi was creating an entirely new reality for herself. By constructing a new past and present, Remmi believed that she would be able to establish a future she could ultimately be honest about and satisfied with.

"You and Lamard have some pretty good chemistry," Art said nonchalantly to Remmi as they lay in bed early one Sunday morning. After a very vigorous week of filming, the cast and crew had been given the day off to rest up and rejuvenate. But instead of refueling, Remmi still decided to rise early for a two-mile run, opting to chill out for the rest of the day. As Art turned the page of the *L.A. Times*, Remmi, clad only in a white cotton thong, nibbled on slices of fresh fruit.

"Yeah, pretty good," Remmi replied, placing a juicy slice of honeydew melon upon her tongue.

"You guys must be rehearsing on your days off. I know how committed to the project and your career you are, Rementa."

"No. I think it's the classes I've been taking with Tracey. She's really been teaching me the skills I need to become a wonderful actress, and that means being able to have great chemistry with my leading man," Remmi said proudly.

"But I'm sure it makes it easy that your leading man is Lamard Fisher."

"Well, I guess. I mean Lamard's okay—he ain't no Morris Chestnut, though." She giggled.

"Well, he must be better than just okay. 'Cause I haven't seen that type of chemistry since Diana Ross and Billy Dee in *Mahogany*," Art stated, never looking up from his paper.

"Or Jay-Z and Beyonce on *Crazy in Love*?—that was my jam!" Remmi laughed, snapping her fingers and bopping her head to an imaginary hip-hop beat.

"Maybe a little more like Jake Steed and Cinnabuns in *Deep Throat 2005*." Art smiled and hit the PLAY button on the remote control. The fifty-two-inch flat-screen plasma TV changed from the Special K cereal commercial it was showing to a crystal-clear display of Remmi and Lamard's hot and steamy balcony escapade. Remmi choked on a strawberry as she witnessed Lamard plunging in and out of her flesh, her face onscreen displaying the intensity of the pleasure she was experiencing with every one of his forceful strokes. She watched her sweaty body become one with Lamard's, and her heart began to pound with panic.

Art, on the other hand, sat calmly, turning the page of the newspaper and never looking up to make eye contact with her.

Remmi quickly gathered herself and rose from the bed, her plate of fruit in hand. She had no idea what was coming, but she knew it was not going to be nice. "Baby, I, I—let me explain," Remmi began. She reached to the love seat and grabbed her silk Christian Dior robe to cover herself.

"You a bold bitch, huh, Remmi?" Art's voice was calm and collected as his eyes flicked over the newspaper. The volume from the television was low, but Remmi could still hear her own passionate moans as her homemade X-rated flick continued to play in the background.

"Baby, it only happened once. . . . I swear," she pleaded.

"One time is too many in my house, Rementa," Art coolly replied, finally rising from the bed and heading over to his closet. He appeared neither angry nor hurt. He was calmer than she had ever seen him, and rage seemed like the furthest thing from his mind. Maybe he really didn't give a damn about her.

"To be honest, it doesn't really bother me that he fucked you. I know you're a whore, Rementa. All women are." Art shrugged, opening his closet door and rummaging through its contents.

Remmi's fear escalated, and she headed for the bedroom door only to have Art call behind her with a hearty laugh, "The front door is locked from the inside and the key is tucked away. Oh, and I gave Rosalie the rest of the day off!"

Remmi ran into the kitchen to search for some sort of weapon to defend herself. After quickly glancing around the spacious room, she dashed toward the utensil drawers beneath the sink—which, to her surprise, were locked. The sound of Art calling out to her as she raced through the condo scared her even more.

"Did you really think I would be stupid enough to leave you in my house without cameras watching your every fuckin' move? A whore like you?" he called. "Do you really think I'm *that* stupid?"

He was getting nearer—she could hear him. There was only one way in and one way out of the room. She was trapped.

He swung open the kitchen door, holding a thick lengthy exercise jump rope with two black wooden handles at each end. "You don't fuck other niggas in *my* house. I think you need to learn the definition of respect," Art calmly said, nearing her. Remmi ran around the other end of the marble island in the center of the room. Maybe she could run out the door and into another part of the condo. If he had locked her inside, she truly had nowhere to go—the apartment was not that big. Her best bet was to make it into one of the bathrooms and lock the door with hopes that he would go away. For the first time in longer than she could remember, Remmi swore to God that if He would let her get out of this one, she would leave Art's condo and never return—and that she would be on the straight and narrow from that day forward.

With a large portion of the rope twisted around his fist, Art jumped across the breakfast nook like a flash of lightning, and pounced on Remmi before she could get out of the kitchen. Art crashed the rope down upon Remmi's spine, causing her to let out a bloodcurdling scream. She fell to the tiles of the kitchen floor in anguish and pain. Not giving her a chance to recuperate from his blow, he positioned himself over her body and continued to strike her chest and legs while she tearfully begged him to stop.

"Don't . . . worry ba . . . by," he said between blows. "I won't . . . touch that pretty . . . face of yours. I know . . . you . . . gotta be . . . on the set to . . . mor . . . row. But I need to teach . . . you . . . a lesson . . ."

"Art, please stop!" Remmi wailed, using her hands to shield herself.

Catching his breath, Art stood motionless for a moment, as if he needed to think about his next move. Remmi weakly attempted to hold her robe closed while her body burned with every move she made. Then Art stripped himself naked, tore off Remmi's robe, kicked open her legs, and forced himself inside her. He violently thrust in and out of her body before finally pulling out and squirting semen all over her face. Before walking out of the kitchen, he spat on her battered body. She was left sprawled across the floor covered in blood, sweat, and tears.

Remmi lay limply on the ceramic tiles in a tight fetal position. Barely breathing, she moaned softly at the excruciating pain of her torn vagina. Her skin felt like it had been dragged down a highway by a speeding bus. She weakly covered herself with her bloodstained robe before she heard the sound of the front door slamming shut. He had left the condo but she feared he would return to finish the job. She dared not call the police. That would only bring bad publicity to the film and possibly get her blacklisted. She prayed that he had only wanted to teach her a lesson that she obviously had to learn the hard way—never eat and shit in the same box.

14

Luci covered up as many of the cuts and bruises as she could, while Remmi's terry cloth jumpsuit concealed the rest. Remmi's face remained unblemished, making the makeup artist's job easier, but when Remmi sat in her chair at 5 A.M. Monday morning, the woman had to be wondering what on earth had happened to the film's leading lady.

Sensing her puzzlement, Remmi explained to Luci that she had been in a slight car accident over the weekend but assured her that she actually felt better than she looked. "I always bruise easy," Remmi lied.

She didn't think Luci believed one word of her story, but was glad she opted to mind her own business.

Getting ready for her first scene of the day, Remmi could hear Art's voice on the set mingling happily with the crew. This was Art's first time on the set since the shooting had begun, so Remmi assumed he wanted to be there to make sure she'd indeed arrived as expected. And she had. Nothing short of death was going to stop Remmi from being in this movie. She had a plan and a goal, and this movie was her springboard.

Art stayed on the set for only a little while, not making eye contact or saying anything to Remmi the entire time he was there. She hadn't heard from him since he'd left the condo after brutalizing her the day before; he had not returned for the night. With no place else to go—and not wanting to jeopardize her role—Remmi made a decision not to tell anyone what had happened. She merely locked herself in the master bedroom of the condominium until the car arrived to take her to the set the next morning.

Remmi had become an expert at ignoring her pain. In fact, she was so good at being numb that she couldn't even feel the stinging lacerations on her back anymore. And that day, in all her scenes she would be wearing a Japanese kimono covering her from her neck to her ankles. It was quite easy to conceal her wounds and get through the entire day of filming without anyone, except Luci, being aware of her injuries.

two days before the film was about to wrap, Remmi sat quietly in her trailer meditating—which Luci had encouraged. After Art assaulted her, Remmi had to find something to help keep her sanity. Drugs were not an option—she would never gamble with her beauty or poise. While her cuts and bruises eventually faded, the emotional scars remained fresh. Meditation helped enable her to continue on her quest for stardom. And it had worked wonders. Still, because she remained in Art's condo, Remmi continued to be haunted by what had taken place on the floor of that gourmet kitchen.

The last few days Remmi had become increasingly withdrawn from the staff, crew, and the world at large—not even partaking in her daily sistagirl chats with Shannelle. She didn't want to risk telling anyone about what Art had done, and Shannelle had a way of getting things out of her.

Sitting alone barefoot and crossed-legged in the center of her trailer floor, with her eyes closed and her fingers intertwined, Remmi was thrust out of her deep thoughts by a loud knock on the door. Before she could invite her unknown guest in, the door burst open and Shannelle jumped across the threshold, Louis Vuitton luggage in tow.

"Surprise, bitch!" she yelled with her infamous two-mile, hundred-watt smile plastered across her face.

Shocked and amazed, Remmi leaped up from the floor and embraced her best friend tightly, a tear of joy and relief rolling slowly down her cheek. Remmi hadn't realized how much she had truly missed Shannelle until she saw her standing there in the trailer doorway. Seeing a familiar face that she knew she could trust gave Remmi a feeling of comfort that she hadn't had since she left New York.

After hugging for almost two minutes, Shannelle tossed her bags into the corner of the trailer, and the two partners in crime made themselves comfortable on the love seat.

"What the hell are you doing here?" Remmi asked with a smile.

"You think you can get away with not taking or returning my calls? Bitch, I took my ass to Kennedy, got on the plane, and came to get in your face! I know your ass ain't gettin' all *Hollyfied* on me."

"No, no . . . ," Remmi chuckled, shaking her head.

"Then what's going on with you, heffa?"

"Girl, we can't talk here. Tonight, I promise. I'll spill it all. I gotta be back on the set in ten minutes."

"A'ight—but don't front on me, bitch. This is me, girl."

"I know, I know. And how the hell you get past security?!"

"Girl, what's my name? Ain't no fuckin' toy cops gonna keep me from *my* sista!"

They slapped an energetic high five and for a moment, Remmi felt like she was in the living room of her apartment in East Harlem and that everything she had experienced for the past four and a half months had all been some kind of crazy dream.

"i cannot believe that muthafucka did that to you," Shannelle said, her fist clenched as Remmi described the brutal attack she'd endured at the hands of Arthur Haddox.

"Shannelle, you cannot tell a soul," Remmi warned her.

"Okay. You swore me to secrecy, but I still say that as soon as the movie comes out, you should go to the cops."

"If I do that, I'll never work in Hollywood again."

"How many other chicks you think he's done this shit to? I know you ain't the first—and if you don't tell someone, you won't be the last."

"Well, let some other bitch turn him in. I'm trying to build a career here, and that muthafucka would have me blacklisted before I get home from the precinct. Not to mention the fact that he'll only deny it and it'll be my word against his. That nigga's got a lotta money he can use to make a liar outta me," Remmi snapped.

"Yeah, I guess you right. But we just can't let that nigga get away with raping you."

"He'll get his. I swear he will. Just not now. Not while I'm still building this career," Remmi assured Shannelle.

"All right. I just can't believe all that went down and he's still letting you stay in this bad-ass crib." Shannelle shook her head as she looked around the condo, admiring the décor.

"I know. But everybody knows I'm staying here, and if he makes me leave now, it'll look suspicious. How would it look if all of a sudden I end up in a hotel? Like we had a lovers' spat? We ain't supposed to be lovers, remember? He's married."

"Well, at least he ain't come back acting like nothing happened, talking about 'Honey, I'm home,'" Shannelle huffed.

"I know. But I can't front. I do have that fear every night I lay my head down on this pillow," Remmi said as she smoothed out the case of the pillow that rested in her lap.

"He ain't gonna come back. He figured he got away with it. He better not push it. He ain't stupid. Crazy? Yes. Stupid? No."

"Yeah, I guess you right."

"And you been keeping this shit to yourself all this time? Girl, you shoulda talked to *somebody*—a shrink or anybody—if you felt you couldn't talk to me, which I don't know why."

"I guess I just didn't wanna put it out there. It was more about me not wanting to say it than me not wanting you to hear it."

"Well, maybe you should still talk to a shrink."

"Girl, at this point I just wanna finish this film and get the fuck back to NYC."

"I hear ya."

"So what's been going on with you? Any word on Lopez or anybody else from the Temple?" Remmi questioned.

"Nope. It's been real quiet—like they all fell off the face of the earth or somethin'. It's almost scary. I guess we really got away with that shit," she laughed, shaking her head.

"Man, we should have did that shit ages ago—if only we knew it was gonna be that easy."

"For real. But I can't lie. When he fucked up my apartment, I thought he was gonna be on my ass real soon."

"I know. Your ass was shittin' bricks!" Remmi cracked up.

Shannelle shook her head. "Man, that nigga is a beast!"

"Girl, where do we find these fools?"

"If I only knew, I'd start looking someplace else."

The movie ended on an incredibly high note, and Remmi was relieved that it was finally over. She'd gotten through her first role in a Hollywood film, and despite the drama that surrounded it, she was really proud of herself. The days that led up to the film's completion were easier for Remmi to get through than the weeks prior, thanks to Shannelle—who had decided to stay in L.A. until the filming was over.

Weeks passed with Remmi and Shannelle finally being able to enjoy all that Los Angeles life had to offer. The magnificent weather and the chic nightlife were new to the Dynamic Duo and different from the New York scene they were used to, but they were enjoying themselves to the fullest. As the days turned into weeks, the weeks eventually turned into nearly two months before Remmi looked up at a calendar and realized that she needed to make a decision about whether she would be staying in L.A. or heading back up the East Coast. She missed New York, but L.A. was certainly tempting, and if another movie offer came through, Remmi might just have to make California her new home. Then, in less time than she would have imagined, Remmi was informed that she needed to start making appearances in conjunction with the release of *Butta*. With all the media hoopla surrounding the film, the editing turnaround was swift, with the director hoping to make the deadlines for all the film festivals. And although an actual release wasn't scheduled until the end of the year, there was going to be a private screening for the cast, crew, and press, with hopes of creating hype before the film's premiere.

Anxious and excited, Remmi and Shannelle took the entire day getting ready for the first screening of *Butta*. They were armed with Art's platinum American Express Card—his assistant had dropped it off at the condo that morning. The girls spent the hours leading up to the event in Beverly Hills with hopes that a paparazzo would catch a couple of shots of Remmi and thrust her into the eye of pop culture—and bringing her to the attention of another movie director or producer who would want to feature her in an upcoming project.

Adorned in a scarlet-hued satin strapless slip dress from Rodeo Drive's Bijan, Remmi resembled a caramel-colored Princess Grace, flawless in her elegance and poise. Her hair was in a chic, sophisticated upsweep, à la Jennifer Lopez in *Maid in Manhattan*, accented with loaned Harry Winston diamond-tipped bobby pins, which complemented a teardrop diamond choker and tennis bracelet. On her feet was a pair of three-inch ruby satin Gucci stiletto slides.

Riding shotgun next to Remmi was an equally stunning Shannelle, dressed in a Chanel chiffon layered spaghetti-strap evening gown. The ginger-tinted dress shimmered against Shannelle's perfect auburn complexion, while her coordinating accessories and makeup gave her a radiant glow that truly could not be ignored. In fact, Shannelle could have passed for one of

Remmi's costars instead of her best friend. But she *was* Remmi's best friend and would not have missed her sista's debut for anything in the world. They had never missed anything important in each other's lives, and this was certainly not going to be an exception.

As they rode silently in a black stretch Mercedes-Benz limousine arranged by the studio, Remmi almost couldn't believe that this day had finally come. Her mind replayed her climb to this moment. How answering phones had led to starring in videos, to meeting men who would love her and hurt her, to meeting Arthur Haddox during Fashion Week in New York City. No matter how she felt about him, Art had given Remmi her start, and for that she was eternally grateful. After the cuts and bruises had healed, Remmi attempted to rationalize that the beatdown had been a small price to pay for the stardom she was about to embark on. After all, Halle Berry had endured a busted eardrum at the hands of someone she thought loved her, and look where she was today. Remmi figured that if she could achieve one half of Halle's success, it had all been worth it. Her only regret was that her mother could not be there to witness her achievement. Ever since she was a little girl, Rita had told Remmi that she was gonna be somebody one day. Wherever her mother was, Remmi knew Rita was watching and smiling with pride.

Pulling up in front of the Grauman's Chinese Theatre, Remmi felt her heart beat rapidly. She couldn't believe the size of the mob of people waiting eagerly behind the velvet rope. They crowded alongside the red carpet to get a glimpse of the cast. She knew the film had been getting plenty of publicity, but with so few top-name stars, Remmi didn't think fans would come out to the premiere in such droves.

She was also shocked to see so many celebrities in attendance.

She had not taken into account that anything with the Bad Boy name attached to it could easily attract wannabes and allreadyares. After all, Diddy himself was quite a star. And sure enough, as Remmi and Shannelle peered out of the tinted limousine window, they watched starstruck as Eddie Murphy and Tracey Edmonds strolled down the red carpet several steps behind Mary J. Blige and her hubby. The girls were so excited, they momentarily forgot that on this day, they, too, were celebrities and not fans. They had never been around such industry royalty before, and it dawned on Remmi that she had better get used to it. This was her destiny.

When the car door was finally opened and she was ushered out, the crowd went absolutely wild, in awe of her beauty, and she felt taller than the Empire State Building. Bad Boy's publicity department had really hyped the movie as a major industry event, and the company was determined to make stars out of everyone involved with the film. As they floated across the red carpet, Remmi smiled widely and waved like she was Miss America taking her first walk. Flashes flickered in her face a mile a minute, and as she eased toward the entrance of the theater, Remmi was pulled aside to address a statuesque Ru Paul look-alike who forcefully shoved a microphone in her face. Remmi instantly recognized the reporter as New York shock jock radio personality, Wendy Williams, and it suddenly hit her at that very moment: *I am somebody!*

"Rementa Broughten—you look stunning! And this is a pretty special role you nailed there for such a newcomer to Hollywood!" Wendy began.

"Yes, I am so blessed to have been given such a wonderful opportunity like this. I have to truly thank Mr. Combs and everyone over at Bad Boy Films for believing in me!" Remmi graciously replied.

"The movie hasn't even come out yet, and your role as Dorene has already gotten rave reviews from all the critics. You've come a long way from dropping it like it's hot in rap videos, wouldn't ya say?"

"Well, I'm proud of all the videos I've done. I wouldn't be here today if it hadn't been for those videos." Remmi continued to smile.

"But isn't it true that you have quite a—shall I say—*personal* relationship with Bad Boy's very married CEO, Arthur Haddox? I'm sure that helped get you where you are today, didn't it?" Wendy asked.

Although Wendy Williams was quite infamous for her brutal in-your-face interrogation of all who crossed her path—celebrities or not—Remmi was still somewhat taken aback by Wendy's insinuation. She thought she and Art had concealed their relationship pretty well, especially from the public. Obviously not well enough.

With all the composure under her command, Remmi took a very deep breath and with the polished charm she had acquired from her endless lessons with Tracey, returned, "Mr. Haddox has been very good to me and encouraging of my talents—as have all of the wonderful people over at Bad Boy Films. Again, I am so blessed to have been given this magnificent opportunity."

"Oh—your publicist has prepped you well, girl. . . . So who's your friend?" Wendy was referring to Shannelle. "She's as stunning as you!"

Before walking away from the first humiliating interview of her career, she really wanted to elbow Wendy in the throat, but like the lady she was now being trained to be, Remmi politely answered, "My best friend in the whole world. My partner in crime. . . ."

With that, she continued down the carpet, holding her head up high and proud of the way she had handled the situation.

Remmi could hear the interviewer from hell's voice resonating behind her as she brayed, "Best friend? Partner in crime? *Howyoudoin'?*"

15

the days following the premiere were a whirlwind. The film hadn't even been released yet, and all of a sudden Remmi was named the newest member of Hollywood's Black Brat Pack. Her plans to return to her modest apartment in Spanish Harlem were placed on the back burner, as she became the most sought-after young black actress in L.A. She couldn't imagine what was going to be in store for her once the film was officially released. After the premiere, it took a mere forty-eight hours for three scripts from top-notch Hollywood directors to arrive at her agent's office, forcing Remmi to make a decision about where she'd be living. It would be only a matter of time before she'd be booted out of Art's condo; their arrangement was only for the duration of filming *Butta.* So Remmi and Shannelle began to search for someplace they could call home, ultimately settling on a comfortable, reasonably priced furnished rental in Studio City.

Remmi moved her things out of Art's condo the same day she signed the lease at the Archstone apartment complex. She didn't have much—only a few suitcases filled with clothes, which she tossed into a cab, eager to get to her own place.

She had to rush off to an early evening dinner meeting with Allen Young, her agent, and the director of one of her prospective upcoming projects so she couldn't unpack right away. Upon her arrival at the flat, she merely dropped her bags in the foyer, freshened up a bit, and headed back out the door. With Shannelle, now officially her personal assistant, in tow, Remmi strutted through the elegant main corridor of the Four Seasons Hotel toward the double glass doors of the Gardens Restaurant.

The maître d' led the women through the lush and elegant eatery, past the bold red-and-gold-tinted furnishings to the outdoor patio, where her agent sat puffing rigidly on a Cuban cigar and engaging in conversation with a pudgy middle-aged Caucasian man. Remmi assumed he was the director.

"Good afternoon, gentlemen." Remmi smiled with her natural charm. As the two men stood to shake hands, Remmi continued, "I apologize for my tardiness, but I'm in the process of moving into a new residence as we speak."

When'd this bitch go to charm school? Shannelle asked herself, amazed at her best friend's ability to work that Hollywood schmooze.

Once Shannelle was introduced, they took their seats amongst the men, and after looking into the eyes of the director, Remmi found them to be familiar. Although uncertain about where she had seen him before, she was certain they had crossed paths before. She never forgot a face.

"I knew you'd be a star one day. I could tell you had a lot of heart," the director stated, his raspy voice heavily salted with a

European accent. He grinned at Remmi as he placed his stunted body back upon the thick and sturdy maple wood chair. He reminded her of overgrown baby attempting to climb into a high chair, his feet dangling in the air, unable to reach the cobblestone floor.

"You do look familiar to me. Where have we met?" Remmi asked.

"I directed the Ludacris video you were in. I think it was the first time you were ever nude on set. And after seeing you play Dorene, I take it that you've completely outgrown your shyness," he chuckled.

"Yes, Evret's been watching your career, Remmi. And he really likes what he's been seeing," her agent informed her.

"Oh, *now* I remember your name. Evret VonShayne. Yes, I do remember you," Remmi replied.

"So I gather you'll be staying here on the West Coast for a while," the director questioned.

"If I have reason to." Remmi winked, turning to Allen. "And Allen tells me that your movie might be that reason."

"Well, I would like to think it is. I think my film could really take your career over the top. If you do what I think you can do with this role, the industry will start saying your name in the same breath as they say Halle's and Angela's," Evret cockily predicted.

"Or Angelina's or Jennifer's?" Remmi asked.

Evret shrugged. "Perhaps."

"Well, tell me about your project and the role I would be taking on, Evret. But I must admit, I'm a little concerned about being typecast. After all, Dorene was a good character, but I definitely don't wanna play Dorene part two. And I know video directors sometimes produce movies that look more like ninety-minute music videos than feature films. After all, Halle would be nowhere near the superstar she is if she hadn't been smart enough not to do another movie like *Strictly Business*," Remmi suggested.

"You didn't tell me she had beauty *and* brains, Allen," Evret laughed, taking a sip of Pellegrino.

Nervously laughing himself, as he didn't know if Evret was serious or just making light of Remmi's suggestion, Allen summoned the waitress and whispered in her ear the array of dishes he wanted brought to the table.

"Well, Rementa—I may call you Rementa?" Evret asked.

Remmi gently nodded. Although for *Butta* she had been billed as Remmi B., she had actually been thinking of using her full name. She wanted to take this acting thing seriously.

"I understand your concern," Evret continued. "I could tell from our very first meeting that you had the desire to be more than just some video dancer. I could tell that you were by no means just some backdrop to some rapper's misogynistic lyrics. And on the contrary—I am by no means just some music video director that got a budget to do some measly ninety-minute music video. No. I take my projects very seriously, and so does Columbia Pictures."

"Wonderful, Mr. VonShayne. Then I look forward to reading your script." Remmi smiled, not the least bit intimidated by his demeanor.

"Remmi, Mr. VonShayne's film has every black actress in Hollywood vying for the lead role of Samantha. But he believes you could bring an edgier, unseasoned, and more natural aspect to the role. Vivica, Megan, and Sanaa have all read for the part, but Evret thinks your performance as Dorene showed that you could breathe a fresh new life into Samantha that the other more experienced actresses couldn't," Allen explained.

"So what y'all saying is that the only reason you wanna hire my girl is 'cause she's a new jack?" Shannelle broke her silence and questioned in her uncouth way, representing all negative New York stereotypes with one sentence.

"Well, well, uh—I doubt that, Shannelle." Allen smiled timidly, trying to make up for Shannelle's statement.

Ignoring Allen's attempt to smooth over what Shannelle had said, Evret interjected, "Inexperience is not necessarily a bad thing. It means she can be molded and coached. It means that I am more likely to get exactly what I want out of her."

"I'm interested," Remmi declared with conviction.

"Samantha is a troubled girl that overcomes many obstacles to get what she wants," Evret continued.

"Why she gotta be troubled, though? Why every black bitch from the hood gotta be *troubled*?" Shannelle questioned.

Motioning for her best friend to zip her lips, Remmi calmly inquired, "What is this role worth to me in dollars and cents, Mr. VonShayne?"

"Somewhere in the ball park of two hundred thousand dollars, Rementa," Evret replied, tapping his stubby little pink fingers upon the tabletop. Remmi's almond-shaped eyes now rounded from shock, while Shannelle nearly choked on the buttered roll she had placed into her mouth.

"Well, I guess 'troubled' ain't a *bad* thing. Damn, we *all* got troubles, don't we, Mr. VonShayne?" Shannelle said phonily.

"I'm gonna read your script today, Mr. VonShayne. And I will give you a definite answer by noon tomorrow. And I truly thank you for this opportunity," Remmi informed him. Evret agreed to see Remmi in his office the next day at noon, certain that she would claim the role of Samantha as her own with little hesitation.

uch to Remmi's delight, the character of Samantha Hill was a complex role, filled with plenty of complicated scenes and challenges—perfect for displaying Remmi's God-given abilities as an actress. Clearly contradicting the "troubled inner-city vixen" stereotype, Samantha was in fact a privileged rich girl raised as an only child in the home with her concert pianist mother and congressman father. The script chronicled the character's life and her determination to break free of the tightly held leash her successful parents placed around her neck in a painstaking effort to protect her from the real world—an effort so maniacal that it was borderline psychotic. Always out to prove that she wasn't some black Paris Hilton wannabe, Samantha eventually hooks up with Taz, an inner-city drug dealer who ultimately becomes her boyfriend and finds out what it truly means to live on the other side of the tracks. Samantha is very determined to prove to herself and everyone around her that she can make it without her parents' influence. However, when Taz ends up dead, Samantha is arrested for being an accomplice but will be granted immunity if she helps the authorities catch Taz's killers and the key players in the overall operation. Thus, Samantha gets swept up into a crazy world of drug dealers, murderers, and crooked cops, ultimately yearning to return to her privileged beginnings, only to find out that it very well might be too late.

By the time Remmi completed the final sentence of the screenplay, she'd experienced a whole host of emotions. In many ways, she could relate to Samantha's feelings of isolation and misplacement. But on the other hand, she knew that she would have to reach entirely outside of herself to become this priviledged little rich girl who wanted for nothing. Still, Remmi felt excited and eager to get started, convinced that the role of Samantha was exactly what she needed to jump-start her true Hollywood stardom. The script was good, the role was good, but at the same time, Remmi was concerned. She confided in Shannelle that she was definitely intimidated by many aspects of the character and uncertain whether or not she could really do the part justice. Tackling Dorene had been an easy task, as Remmi herself was so much like the role that she believed it was nothing more than a take-off on who she really was. But this character was another story, and Remmi secretly believed that perhaps her lack of acting experience could hurt the way she approached the role, making her transformation into Samantha a bona fide challenge.

"Girl, I don't know shit about being a rich girl who has everything she wants," Remmi revealed to Shannelle as she tossed the bulky script upon the glass-topped coffee table.

"Coulda fooled me, bitch. Niggas been buying you shit since the ninth grade." Shannelle shrugged, not even looking up from the *Jet* magazine she was thumbing through.

"That's different," Remmi snapped as she snatched the issue from her friend's fingers and threw it on top of the script.

"Girl, what you doing? I was just reading a very interesting story on my baby daddy, Tyrese!" Shannelle huffed.

"Heffa—*I'm* paying your ass to be in L.A.—not Tyrese!" Remmi laughed.

"Okay, okay—what is it? You have my undivided attention."

"I'm scared, Shanni," Remmi whispered.

"Bitch, scared a whut?"

"I'm serious. I'm scared . . . scared that I won't be able to play that role."

Realizing that Remmi was serious, Shannelle turned to her best friend, firmly grabbed her shoulders, focused in on her eyes, and began, "You have no reason to be scared. If they didn't think you could do it, they wouldnt'a called your ass. Remember, that little short funny-looking cat called *you*."

"Yeah, you know I always come across like I can do anything. But you and I both know that's a front. I just do that to throw niggas off. But this time, I might not be able to fake it, girl. That role ain't no joke." Remmi shook her head.

"And neither are you, bitch! Look, stop trippin'. You gonna do fine. In fact, you gonna do better than fine. You gonna have them other Hollywood chicks wishin' they was you! Bitch, you betta go to that white man's office tomorrow, tell him that role is yours, and like Jay-Z and R. Kelly said—when they was talking—'get dis money!'" Shannelle sang as she swiveled her tiny waist and dropped her behind to the floor like it was hotter than hot.

Unable to control her laughter, Remmi managed to utter, "I think you miss the Temple after all."

I 'm glad to hear that you feel confident you can bring Samantha to life, Rementa." Evret VonShayne displayed his crooked half smile as he sat erect behind his colossal mahogany desk, his pudgy fingertips touching to form a chubby triangle while an Opus X burned at a snail's pace in a Mikasa crystal ashtray to his left.

"I certainly do, Mr. VonShayne. I'm prepared to bring things out of Samantha that you could never have imagined." Remmi coyly grinned with a wink of her hazel eye.

"You are a very beautiful young woman, Rementa Broughton," Evret began, taking a deep drag of his robust cigar, almost as if he were puffing on a Philly Blunt. "A natural beauty, with God-given grace and talent, babe. It isn't going to take much to make you a star. You just need the right team. That's all that separates you from J.Lo. J.Lo had the right team. With me, you could be J.Lo, babe."

As Remmi looked into the beady green eyes of Evret Von-Shayne, she saw power. While he was not attractive on a physical level, his persona and aura were extremely appealing. She knew working with him could quickly put her amongst the Hollywood elite, and Remmi so desperately wanted to be there. What Evret VonShayne could do for her gave him such a sex appeal that even Remmi was taken aback by it.

"You know so much about me, Mr. VonShayne. I know nothing about you. What should I know about Evret VonShayne?" Remmi flirtatiously inquired.

"Oh, I'm a simple man, babe," he chuckled. "Not nearly as interesting as you."

"A simple man directing a multimillion-dollar film? I don't think so," Remmi replied, leaning across the desk so that they could be closer.

"It's true. I came from Germany twenty-three years ago and paid a lot of American dues before I got to this point, babe."

"Your bio must be interesting."

"Depends on what you find interesting, babe. I've worked with the best and the worst—superstars and nobodies and nobodies who thought they were superstars—the rich and the poor—the angels and the bitches. You name it, I've done it and not afraid to admit it, babe. One thing for sure, though." He paused before taking another carcinogenic puff. "I know a star when I see one. Every once in a while a director will take an actress under his wing and make her into the superstar he knows she already is inside. I'd like you to be my protégée, babe."

"I'd be so honored, Mr. VonShayne." Remmi blushed, her golden complexion turning a soft scarlet color. "But what about Evret VonShayne, the man? Are you married? Is there a family man beneath this Hollywood persona?" Remmi asked.

"Married twenty-two years to the same woman. Isabella. Beautiful girl, she is. Supportive. Uprooted herself from Dublin to follow my dreams."

"That's lovely. You must have children," Remmi pried further.

"No children. A childhood illness rendered my Isabella barren. We've considered adopting, but I could never find the time to go through the legalities. She's happy, though, with her women's clubs and charity work."

As Evret continued to talk, Remmi found him intriguing. His accent aroused her sexually, and from that moment, she became curious about what he had to offer other than his Hollywood expertise. As his protégée, Remmi knew her career could get the attention it deserved. But as his woman, she'd be unstoppable. It was then Remmi decided that Evret VonShayne was going to be hers in every way possible, and no wife with a rotten womb was going to stop that.

16

he pitter-patter of rain hitting the concrete floor of Remmi's balcony woke her up earlier than usual. The muggy air had caused her to leave the door open before she'd gone to bed, but the dampness should have been a warning that rain was on the way. Remmi hated running the air-conditioner, as it always gave her a stuffy nose and dried out her skin. She preferred the coolness of California's night breezes, but the noisy splat of the raindrops caused her to stir.

Shannelle had gone out early to a doctor's appointment. Her hacking cough had returned—not that it ever really vanished—and Remmi was insistent that she get it checked out. Figuring it was just her bronchitis flaring up again Shannelle agreed to see a doctor Remmi's friend Luci had recommended.

Remmi hadn't made many friends since she'd arrived in L.A., but she found Luci to be really cool. A master cosmetologist, Luci was a pretty Chinese-Jamaican girl who hailed from Cleveland

and was out to make it big in Hollywood. Luckily for her, she never had a problem finding work, as every studio in Hollywood needed a staff makeup artist on payroll. Her full-time gig was at the Playboy channel, where she beautified all the Playmates for on-air action—while she moonlighted on whatever film project she could. On the set of *Butta*, Remmi had met and become quite cool with Luci, promising her that she would recommend her for every project she was involved in from that point forward. She liked Luci. Her skills were impeccable, her professionalism, remarkable—and she never commented or made Remmi feel self-conscious when she'd had to conceal the bruises strategically placed upon her otherwise flawless skin during Art's maniacal rampage. Luci acted as though she were merely covering a small pimple—never mentioning the obviously painful contusions to anyone else on the set. Through their unspoken communication, the two women had somehow bonded, and Remmi began talking to Luci in confidence by phone on a regular basis. It didn't take long for Luci to inform Remmi that she had not been the first young aspiring actress to feel Art's wrath, and she probably would not be the last. Unbeknownst to her, amongst the Hollywood crowd, Arthur Haddox had quite a reputation for his temper, as well as with the ladies. It seemed as though it was commonplace for him to toy with a young unseasoned actress's emotions and then toss her away like yesterday's newspaper. What was unusual, though, as Luci explained it, was for Art to put any of these women in a film he was connected with. That being the case, Arthur Haddox must have really seen something in Remmi for him to give her a shot of such magnitude. Still, his vision for her could not save Remmi from his jealous and violent disposition, as the beatdown in his condo clearly displayed. But Luci never made Remmi feel bad about it. She never judged her or made her feel ashamed. So on the last day of filming, Luci was the only person Remmi had actually given her number to. After all, she needed an L.A. contact and someone to keep her looking beautiful in her camp. Luci filled both roles.

Remmi hopped across the chilled ivory marble tiles, her tiny Cinderella feet barely touching the surface. She gently shut the balcony doors and hightailed it back underneath her fluffy down comforter. It felt more like an October morning in New York than an early September day in Studio City. But Remmi felt good. Things were going well. Her role in Evret VonShayne's movie had been secured, and the sunshine glared brightly through the closed balcony doors even after she had shut them. Although she had less than two weeks to prepare for her role as Samantha, Remmi was ecstatic about attacking the part—a character she deemed complex, sensitive, tough, and raw. Samantha was a role she knew could catapult her into the company of the thespians she so admired. Making it even sweeter, *Moon Circles the Sun* wasn't a so-called black or urban film. It was a multimillion-dollar mainstream movie with a multicultural cast and a white costar. Remmi knew that it could have—or rather it should have—taken her years to secure a role like this in her career. And here she was, thrust into it with just one movie under her belt. Remmi could not believe her luck, but figured she had it coming after the things she'd experienced in her young life. After all the hardships she had seen, she figured it was time for life to give her a pass, and *Moon Circles the Sun* was just that. Maybe, Remmi figured, Rita was asking God for special favors up there in heaven and maybe He was finally seeing fit to give them to her. Whatever it was, Remmi was sure ready to reap the benefits.

As she clutched herself tightly, warming her body, Remmi heard the front door of the apartment open and shut. Moments later, Shannelle appeared before her, dampened from the rain and apparently tired from rising early. The hands on the Things Remembered brass clock sitting on the nightstand—an engraved gift from her old boss at the temp agency—read 9:40, but it felt more like 5 A.M. to Remmi, who had been out most of the night on Evret's arm, firmly positioning herself in her role as Samantha and in his life as his girl.

"What time was your appointment?" Remmi groggily asked, focusing her eyes on Shannelle, whose newly dyed blond hair was frizzy from the precipitation outside.

"Eight A.M. But I got there a little early, and he took me right away."

"Oh."

"Did you know Dr. Foster is black?" Shannelle grinned.

"No, Luci ain't tell me that."

"Fine, too. Overpriced as shit, though. It cost me two hundred fifty dollars for a twenty-minute visit, and I ain't even all that sick. He did take blood, though," she continued, removing her soggy sneakers.

"Did he give you anything for that gruesome cough you got? 'Cause I'm tired of you spreading your germs." Remmi stretched her arms above her head.

"Presciption-strength cough medicine. I do have bronchitis. But he still took blood just to see what else is going on with me. He thinks I might be anemic. That's why I'm always tired no matter how much I sleep. He suggested I might need to take some iron pills."

"When is he gonna have the results from the blood test?"

"A week or two."

"Cool. Look I gotta get some more rest. I'm having lunch with Evret at twelve. He's sending a car for me."

"Lunch? Weren't you fools just out till three in the morning?"

"Yeah, I know."

"Bitch, don't get caught out there like you did with that mutha-fucka from Bad Boy. Two ass-whuppins in a month—I don't know if your little body can take it. You only weigh a hunnit pounds soaking wet." Shannelle chuckled.

"Oh, shut up and get outta my room," Remmi laughed, taking the decorative pillow from beside her and throwing it at Shannelle's head.

"I'm serious. You know that white man is married."

"And white women are different from sistas when it comes to cheating. Look at that governor's wife. Shiiiiit . . . that mug came out on TV talking about he's fuckin' another man and she standin' there all tight, hair lookin' like a helmet, smilin' and shit. She ain't care. She's the *governor's wife*, and I'm sure she gets all the benefits from being the governor's wife. A sista woulda blacked the fuck out—and wouldn't a been standing there cheezin' with her doobie looking all sculptured and shit. And anyhoo, I ain't trying to take Evret from his wife. I just want the benefits that come along with being his girlfriend."

"Bitch, you right—black women and white women *are* differ-ent. And all white women ain't as calm as that governor's wife. Look at Lorena Bobbitt—Amy Fisher—and that crazy lady that ran her man over with the family car. I could go on and on. The difference is when white women do shit like that, they make movies about it. They always got a movie on the Lifetime channel about some white soccer mom taking her husband out for cheat-ing with some young silicone-tittied blonde. I'm telling you, a black bitch'll try to kick your ass, pull your weave out, cut your tires, and all that kinda dumb shit. But a white bitch'll just shoot the mistress with a piece from her husband's gun collection."

"Uh, hell-o-oh—did I say get the fuck outta my room?"

"I'm leaving, bitch . . . but you better watch your back. There's some crazy people out there."

"And now there's one in here," Remmi laughed, pointing at Shannelle.

"Okay! Laugh me off if ya wanna. But remember what I said." Shannelle shrugged, exiting the room.

"Whatevaman. A girl gotta eat," Remmi called. "And I'ma eat real nice offa Evret VonShayne—wife or no wife," Remmi retorted as she rolled over and covered herself back up from head to toe with the comforter, hoping to get another twenty minutes of rest before she started her day.

It did not take long for Remmi's plan to take effect with Evret VonShayne. The middle-aged Evret was already very attracted to Remmi's youthfulness and amazing figure, making her seduction of him extremely effortless. He quickly began spending every spare moment with her, renting rooms in L.A.'s most exclusive and expensive hotels, taking her to eat daily in Beverly Hills, and spending wads of cash on her in all the most fashionable boutiques on Rodeo Drive. But Remmi had had no idea exactly how financially well-off Evret actually was, coming to the conclusion that she had truly hit the jackpot one afternoon while they were chatting in bed after having a midday tryst in the elegant Presidential suite at the Four Seasons Hotel. As Evret lay his balding head on Remmi's voluptuous breasts, while gently stroking her pubic hair with his stubby fingers, he told her all about his childhood in Germany and how he was actually the sole heir to the most successful and lucrative vineyard in all of Europe.

His parents had not been happy when he decided to follow his dream and move to the United States to pursue filmmaking, as they had expected their only child to go into the family business—having groomed him in its development from the moment he could pick a grape. But they were supportive, nonetheless, and funded his endeavors—hoping one day to see a return on their investment. Although Evret's initial projects had not been as lucrative as his parents had wanted, he somehow eventually developed quite a name for himself amongst the urban genre of music and became the hottest video director on the scene. After many years of trying to earn his place as a director and living off his trust inheritances, he finally won an MTV Video Music Award for director of the year. His parents, although still somewhat unconvinced, decided to help their only son out with his career. Thus, his very influential and well-connected father pulled some strings, ultimately obtaining funding for two independent films that did incredibly well on the festival circuit and eventually gained him the recognition of Columbia Pictures. So in essence, Remmi figured that movies or no movies, this cat was rolling in dough. And she wanted in.

After putting it on him like he had never experienced before, she gave him thirty minutes of the most unbelievable head any man could ever imagine possible—bringing him enough ecstasy to secure herself in his life—and his bank account—forever—or at least until she didn't need him anymore.

"Are you ready for preproduction? You know we start Monday," Evret asked Remmi, his European accent making Remmi's middle wet all over again. She loved the accent and would often close her eyes and imagine that the beautiful dark-haired Pierce Brosnan was plunging deeply into her loins, instead of the portly Evret VonShayne. Good thing for her, her imagination was a powerful device, and sometimes she actually envisioned herself running her fingers through soft thick black locks instead of palming the smooth pink skin that glared at her from upon Evret's dome. While he certainly wasn't what anyone would call attractive, there was definitely something about him that Remmi found sexy. And for a stumpy man, with a midsection that closely resembled that of a Shetland pony, his bedroom skills weren't too bad.

He tried hard, and Remmi appreciated his efforts, often screaming loudly and scratching the skin from his back in an attempt to make him believe that he was doing some serious damage to her unaffected vaginal walls. She had learned early that men of Evret's stature, status, and physical appearance needed to constantly feel sexually superior, as their egos required a tremendous amount of stroking on an ongoing basis. So while she had not experienced an orgasm one time during a sexual escapade with her sugar daddy, he was none the wiser, believing in his heart that he was the best piece of dick Remmi had ever had the pleasure of receiving. Not that Evret VonShayne was the worst lover she had ever had. Eighteen-year-old Tyrik Mack had won that title from her years ago on their prom night after puking in her face an ungodly concoction of Hennessy and pigs-in-a-blanket while simultaneously ejaculating on her left thigh at a seventeen-dollar-an-hour motel on Fordham Road. Needless to say—and thank goodness—nothing and no one had been able to top that. Still, whenever Evret entered her body, she kept her eyes firmly focused on his expensive trousers tossed across the chaise, the pockets rising from the swell of his ostrich-skin wallet. Somehow, that vision made it all feel so good.

"I'm ready and so excited," Remmi replied, trying to emulate his accent. Whenever Remmi spoke to Evret, she did her best to eliminate the Ebonics from her vocabulary. Although he did request for her to speak like a "two-dollar street ho from the projects" when they had sex, when he wasn't pounding away inside her, he wanted her to speak "the Queen's English," as he put it—and had even had her meet with a linguist to ensure that it would become natural for her.

"The London premiere of *Butta* is Friday, ya know . . . and I was hoping that you would escort me, Evvy," Remmi continued, batting her long eyelashes at him and caressing his fleshy nipple. Remmi's complexion looked dark upon his flesh, which reminded her of uncooked bacon. Usually her men were dark and cocoa-hued. But she did not discriminate. She enjoyed redbones as well, the classic Shamar Moore and Boris Kodjoe pretty boys. But even they tended to be browner than she was. Her skin with Evret's looked like a poster for Spike Lee's *Jungle Fever* in reverse.

Evret laughed, "Do you even want go, babe?"

Remmi sat up in the bed and questioned with wonder, "Of course I want to go. I *have* to go. I have a major role. Why wouldn't I go?"

"Oh, I don't know. You're in preproduction for a film with a major Hollywood film studio. You're acting alongside the renowned Oscar-nominated thespian, Brendon O'Hare. At this point, you don't really need to be associated with a film like *Butta* . . . *Butta*," he snickered. "Who on earth came up with a name like that? Those rappers absolutely amaze me. They do have their own language indeed."

"Well, don't forget that it was these so-called rappers that gave your ass a break when white Hollywood wouldn't, Evret," Remmi snapped.

Sensing her agitation, Evret tried to clean his statement up and began to gently stroke her hair. "Oh, I'm not trying insult you, babe. You know I absolutely adore the black youth and their culture. I just feel that you are special. That you need not do any more films of that caliber. That you are a Hollywood starlet—like

Lena Horne or Dorothy Dandridge. You need not be associated with a little low-budget film that goes by the name of *Butta* . . . *Butta* is not the name of a film. It is the name of something you put on a piece of toast." Evret shook his head with a chuckle.

"Look, Evret. Whether you like it or not, that little low-budget film gave me a name in Hollywood. That little low-budget film made *you* wanna put me in *Moon Circles the Sun*. In fact, that little *low-budget film*—as you call it—has you fucking me here right now!" Remmi irately retorted.

"Rementa, calm down, babe. I mean not to upset you. I apologize. You are correct. *Butta* served its purpose. Your portrayal of Dorene was remarkable. And if you want me to attend the premiere with you, I certainly will, babe. I want you to be happy. That's all I want," he cooed as he gently kissed her stomach, slowly inching his way down to her thighs, licking her triangle and finally spreading the plump lips of her vagina apart with his thick slimy tongue before plunging it deep inside her moistened tunnel.

"Remember that . . . ," Remmi genuinely moaned, feeling electricity for the first time between them and hoping that what Evret was clearly unable to do with his dick, he was able to do with his tongue.

17

the lighting is poor!" Evret yelled through the megaphone from his black-and-white canvas director's chair. "For the tenth time, fix the goddamn lighting!"

Remmi, in full Samantha garb, looked up from the café table at which she sat. It was the beginning of Scene 2, and she wondered why Evret was yelling yet again at the crew—the tenth time in the past hour. They'd change the lighting to accommodate his request, then five minutes later he would have them change it back to the way it was originally. This must have gone on almost a dozen times, and Remmi was clearly annoyed. Each time they had to change the lighting, she had to do the scene over, and not only was she getting tired, but she also felt she had lost some pretty good footage. So what the lighting wasn't perfect? Couldn't they fix that later? She was tired of lighting up a new cigarette every time Evret roared the word "Cut!" While she was a nonsmoker, Samantha was not, and Remmi feared that if Evret kept making her repeat the scenes, she'd either have lung cancer or a nicotine addiction by the time the film wrapped.

While the crew adjusted the lighting once again, Luci took the opportunity to hustle onto the set and powder Remmi's face with a thick puff brush, catching her in the eye by accident.

"Damn, Luci!" Remmi snapped, blinking profusely, her eye watering from irritation.

"Ooh, sweetie, I'm so sorry!" Luci gasped, dabbing Remmi's eye with a soft white tissue.

"Ya know whut?" Remmi snarled in her best New York voice, not caring about all the hours she had spent with Evret's linguist. "I'm outta here for the day. This muthafucka and his lighting issues are driving me crazy!"

Remmi picked herself up from her chair, tossed the lit cigarette as well as the tissue upon the tabletop before disappearing from the set. Moments later, a small puff of smoke began to rise from the table, the cigarette burning a hole through the cloth. From her dressing room, Remmi heard someone yell, "Fire!" in the distance, but felt no need to turn around. At that moment, she couldn't have cared less if the entire set burned to the ground. She was sick of Scene 2, she was sick of smoking cigarettes, and most of all she was sick of Evret VonShayne.

Ever since they began filming, it was like Evret had turned into someone she didn't even know. He yelled at everyone constantly—especially Remmi—and lacked any sort of patience when it came to any technical difficulties. She could never do a scene he liked in the first or second take, and he frequently criticized Remmi's performances—even telling her that she needed to lose five pounds.

"You're looking kinda chunky on camera, babe," he told her in front of everyone.

"I have my period this week, Evret, as you already know," Remmi replied with an attitude, tired of his badgering and deliberately trying to anger him. Although the rumors had already begun to fly before the camera had filmed its first take, the two of them had agreed to keep their personal relationship private when on set. But even that was starting to get on Remmi's nerves. She simply could not understand how this man who did all he could to please her every night seemingly went out of his way to publicly humiliate her every day. It was like she was dealing with another bona fide Dr. Jeckyll and Mr. Hyde, and Remmi was definitely getting tired of it. So, that day after the tenth take of a two-minute scene that wasn't even a significant part of the film, Remmi had had enough. She wanted to meet Shannelle at the spa and get a massage. She *needed* to. Her neck was in knots, and she could feel the pressure of stress building in the small of her lower back. She rationalized that she had to keep herself in top physical condition—which meant being stress free—if she was going to perform at her highest level. *I'm doing them all a favor by getting rubbed on a little*, she told herself. And after all of Evret's badgering, she felt she deserved it.

"Yeah, meet me at LePetite, girl. I'm outta here," Remmi said to Shannelle through the receiver of her silver cell phone. There was no way Remmi was going back out on the set that day. They would just have to shoot without her.

As she zipped up the jacket of her Applebottoms oversized hoodie—a little gift that came in a huge box sent by Nelly himself—there was a gentle knock on the door of her dressing room.

Simon, a young red-haired intern, stuck his freckled face in and, with a look of apprehension, said softly, "Mr. VonShayne wants you back out on the set immediately, Miss Broughton."

"You tell *Mr. VonShayne* to kiss my black ass. I've listened to his last rant for the day. His last insult. Tell him I'll be back tomorrow." Remmi nonchalantly shrugged, without looking up at the snotty-nosed intern. Giving him a prime view of her heart-shaped behind, she administered a dismissive wave while swiftly tying up the laces on her Prada boots.

"Miss Broughton, I can't tell Mr. VonShayne that! He'll fire me!" Simon replied.

"Why is everyone so afraid of that man? That muthafucka puts his pants on one leg at a time like everybody else!" Remmi said. "Fuck it." She grabbed her bag and pushed past the intern. "I'll tell him myself."

Remmi stormed onto the set, where she found Evret intensely viewing the scene they had just done on the director's monitor. Before she could open her mouth and let him have it, Evret interrupted her, his European accent tickling her eardrums, "This last take is actually a good one. We will keep it."

Ready to attack, Remmi instantly backed down instead, changing her tone and stuttering a bit. "Good," she managed to utter.

"It's been a difficult day for all of us. Call your girlfriend and take the rest of the day off. Just be certain to arrive here at five A.M. tomorrow morning. It's going to be a long day," Evret continued, without making eye contact.

A huge smile came over Remmi's face as she gently pecked Evret on the cheek and whispered in his ear, "I love you, Evvy."

Evret looked straight ahead, failing to respond to Remmi's words of endearment. He was serious about not confirming any of the rumors. And Remmi was okay with that. She knew Evret VonShayne loved her. The suite he had booked for her at the Four Seasons proved that. Her own credit card with the name R. VON-SHAYNE printed on it, proved that. The way he'd perfected his tongue game to give her multiple orgasms each night proved it as well. As far as she was concerned, he never had to say it. All he had to do was keep it coming.

much to Remmi's delight, the next few weeks of filming went quite well. As each day rolled into the next, Evret became more and more pleased with her acting, adding to the spice of their already intense off-camera relationship. Many days Remmi felt as though she truly was Mrs. VonShayne—a fantasy come true, as she had often dreamed of marrying a man of wealth and stature. Of course, on the other side of the door of her luxury Four Seasons suite, reality reared its ugly head, and they had to behave as though their relationship was strictly business. But people knew. They could tell from the way she sassed him like an annoyed lover does when her man gets on her nerves. And the tabloids had a field day with it as he showered her dressing room daily with expensive gifts—each one more elaborate than the previous—all accompanied by little notes signed by a so-called biggest fan. He was a romantic, and Remmi wasn't used to a man who took courting so seriously. The way he treated her when their clothes were on helped her become accustomed to and even almost enjoy intercourse with him, although she was used to more endowed men. But Evret was eager to please and always went out of his way to do the extra things an ordinary man who felt he was laying the pipe right might have neglected and ignored. He enjoyed her body more than he had ever enjoyed a woman's. She knew he still loved his slightly overweight, boring wife, but she simply could not compete with Remmi's exotic, primal sex drive and beauty. Even with her surgically altered breasts, Evret had told her that his wife was no match for Remmi's spontaneity and uninhibited spirit, which kept Evret's miniature uncircumcised dick standing at attention as soon as he neared her. It was these attributes that kept Evret coming to Remmi's suite every night without fail, lying to his overcompensating, overly trusting, overly supportive spouse about late-night editing and review sessions that never actually took place. But he was captivated by Rementa Broughton and could not bring himself to go twenty-four hours without softly placing his thin pink lips around her copper-colored areolae. There was something addicting about the taste of her nipples. So addicting that he was convinced they actually contained some sort of sweet syrup that sent shivers down his spine the moment it hit his tongue. Her breasts were so delicious that they could never be duplicated on any operating table. No, Remmi's splendor was God-given, never touched by a knife or scarred by painful incisions. To Evret VonShayne, Rementa Broughton was a goddess, and he could not get enough of her. On the other hand, he was Remmi's sugadaddy, giving her the finest things life had to offer—treating her like the queen she knew she was. And it worked well for both of them. After all, they were both getting exactly what their hearts desired.

the long day of filming in an urban section of San Fernando Valley had wrapped, and Remmi had retired to her trailer with a yawn. She'd been up since daybreak, and her bones were weary. She was glad it was Friday—a day off was clearly called for. A weekend where she could lay up in bed with her man was what she needed. She needed to be pampered. She needed to be peeled a grape. She needed to lie around the house in nothing but a La Perla thong. She needed to feel free. As she gathered her belongings, placing them into her Louis Vuitton duffle, she envisioned herself nude, up to her neck in Victoria's Secret pear-scented bubble bath, relaxing in the whirlpool in her luxury suite. The thought made her quicken her pace, as she hurried to make that vision a reality—when all of a sudden there was a soft knock on her trailer door. Without turning around to see who it was, she summoned her visitor to enter, continuing to gather the things from her dressing room that she could not live without for the weekend.

"Rementa Broughton?" a gently accented whispery voice questioned from behind. Remmi turned around to see a slightly overweight red-haired middle-aged woman with enormous breasts dressed in a matronly floral-printed muumuu. A self-appointed fashion police officer, Remmi's first inclination was to write the woman a summons for her blatant violation, but she managed to control herself and simply let out a gasp.

"Who's asking?" Remmi inquired with a raised brow, as she could not imagine what this swollen Lucille Ball wannabe could possibly want with her.

The woman stepped inside the trailer and swiftly shut the door behind herself without taking her eyes off Remmi or blinking.

"Do I know you?" Remmi asked with an attitude. She was really in a rush and had no time to give autographs to lonely housewives who'd somehow found their way past security.

"They are right. You are very beautiful," the woman stated, her lips trembling with a nervous quiver.

"Again—do I know you?" Remmi impatiently questioned.

"You know my husband too well for my liking," the woman found the nerve to mutter.

"And who is your husband?"

"My name is Isabella VonShayne. And I am here to ask you to stop fucking my husband." Isabella revealed a shiny silver

.22-caliber pistol in the palm of her chubby right hand. Looking into the green eyes of her lover's wife, Remmi realized that this woman was a perfect match for Evret. She figured that Isabella's bright red mane and strategically placed freckles probably complemented his thinning dark hair and pale complexion. Remmi assumed that Isabella must have been attractive once in her own Lucky Charms–type way, and her implants revealed that at one time this woman must have cared about her appearance enough to surgically alter her body.

Choking on her own saliva, Remmi took a step back from the woman and nervously grabbed her designer satchel, using it as a shield—as if a bullet from a .22 couldn't penetrate right through the bag. She began to feel flushed, her temperature rising with anxiety beneath the collar of her buttoned-down blouse. It wasn't that Isabella appeared dangerous or threatening; in fact, being from the hood, Remmi was sure that if she lunged at Isabella's portly body at full speed, she could crack her skull just as Humpty Dumpty had cracked his when he'd taken that infamous fall. But the echo of the conversation Remmi had had with Shannelle about deranged spouses resonated throughout her psyche, and she suddenly wondered if her life might be in danger. Remmi's trailer was secluded to ensure the utmost privacy—just in case she and her beloved Evret needed some time alone. Thus, being situated away from the rest of the cast and crew would give Evret's wife the opportunity to kill Remmi without anyone finding her lifeless corpse until after all her blood had completely emptied itself upon the trailer floor.

"What makes you think your husband and I are having any kind of inappropriate relationship?" Remmi nervously uttered.

"Lying will only make me angry," Isabella glared, her aqua

green eyes turning the color of an emerald shamrock. "Everyone knows, Miss Broughton, that you and my husband are having an affair. The media, our friends, our colleagues . . . everyone. So, please. Do not attempt to deny it."

It was amazing to Remmi that this woman whose husband she'd been fucking the brains out of still had enough respect for her to refer to her as Miss Broughton, even as she held a gun aimed at her torso. White women were amazing. Like Shannelle had said, they were definitely on some other shit when it came to their men. A sista would have just jumped on her. A sista wouldn't generally pull a gun on you. A sista wouldn't politely request that you stop fucking her husband. And a sista definitely wouldn't refer to her husband's ho as *Miss* anybody. No—black women and white women were indeed different. Shannelle was right.

"Mrs. VonShayne, please don't listen to the ugly rumors of ignorant people who need to get lives of their own. Evret loves you. He tells me all the time. He would never cheat on you. He has no need. Look at you. You're beautiful," Remmi lied without a blink, her eyes watering from being held open so long. Remmi feared that if she made one move, even a blink, Isabella's nervous index finger that rested gently on the shiny trigger would pull inward. Knowing the possibility that she was about to take a bullet for her indiscretion, Remmi's mind raced with thoughts of how she could get herself out of the situation she had gotten herself into. Remmi knew that she had to make Isabella comfortable enough to let down her guard so that she could attack her, Latin King style, and give her a full-fledged El Barrio beatdown. After all, how dare this deranged, insanely jealous homely looking woman come into her dressing room and threaten her? Now more annoyed than scared, Remmi knew that if she could get herself out of this life-threatening situation, it would be great for publicity, sending her that much closer to the Hollywood stardom she so urgently craved. For a moment, Remmi almost wanted to thank Isabella. That was until a dose of reality juice spilled on her.

What if this shit doesn't go my way? What if this crazy bitch actually pulls the goddamn trigger? Remmi thought. She was not about to go out like this. After all she had survived, Remmi was determined not to lose her life in some lonely, sterile, nonpersonalized dressing room trailer on the grounds of a movie set. She wanted immortality, but not like that. She wasn't about to follow in the footsteps of Aaliyah or Left Eye, cut down in her prime, just as she was about to soar to the next level of stardom. No, she'd take Isabella's gun and shove it up her fat ass first. As a million and one thoughts scurried rapidly through her head, the wife of her lover remained erect, nonflinching and self-assured as she pointed the silver nickel-plated pistol at her nemesis.

I bet that steel in her hand makes this bitch feel strong, Remmi thought. She managed to crack an innocent smile as she made another attempt to convince Isabella that the relationship she was having with Evret was nothing close to what anyone had speculated.

"Why would he wanna cheat on you? You're way more than any man could want," Remmi earnestly reasoned.

"He wants babies. I can't have any," Isabella replied, her eyes swelling with water.

"What about adoption? It's the latest celebrity thing! Angelina and Brad. Madonna. There are beautiful babies available for adoption! And they come in all shapes, sizes, and colors these days, too!" Remmi explained, concealing the fact that she really didn't give a shit about this woman's desire to be a mother. A trickle of salty perspiration slowly formed upon Isabella's Botox-injected forehead, and as she used her left hand to wipe it before it slid into her brow, she lost focus of her victim for a millisecond, giving Remmi the opportunity to pounce with all fours, administering all the blows and self-defense tactics she had learned in the six-week kickboxing class she had taken at the New York Sports Club right before she moved to L.A. Hoping to prepare herself for the streets of L.A., Remmi had signed up for the class after watching *Boyz n the Hood* one too many times on cable. Truth be told, she'd never entered South Central one time since she'd been in Cali. And she had no idea that she'd have to use what she'd learned on the 250-pound deranged silicone-breasted spouse of her lover.

As Isabella's chunky frame forcefully plummeted to the trailer floor, the shiny .22 slid like water across the blond pseudo-wood linoleum with the ease of a glass marble. She let out a heinous yelp, agonizing in pain and paralyzed in Remmi's unyielding headlock grip. Remmi was mad now. Men like Evret cheated all the time. Remmi was sure she had not been Evret's first mistress, so why on earth was Isabella trippin'? They both knew that this was what men in Hollywood did and that while Evret laid with Remmi each night, there was no question about the fact that it would be cheaper to keep Isabella. They all knew he would never divorce her and frankly, Remmi did not want him to. Isabella's marriage and money were safe. Remmi didn't want to marry Evret, so him staying with his wife was not a problem. As far as Remmi was concerned, if Isabella didn't mind sharing, the three of them could go on like this forever—or at least until Remmi was the biggest star she could possibly be.

Remmi's hands tightly clutched a huge clump of Isabella's thick red hair as she forcefully hammered her attacker's cranium into the floor. Isabella's cries for help echoed throughout the trailer, mimicking a scene from a bad B movie.

Just as Remmi was about to smash Isabella's head once more,

the door of the trailer flew open, and in ran security, who peeled Remmi from Isabella's flattened, battered body.

"She tried to kill me!" Remmi cried, physically showing signs that she had engaged in some sort of struggle.

"That's her gun!" she continued as she pointed to the floor where the shiny handgun glistened beneath the small window as the sun beamed off its barrel.

"Miss Broughton, are you all right?" one of the guards asked. Remmi was obviously shaken. Her usually perfect tresses were in disarray, and a small scratch gleamed from her left cheek. The crisp white Brooks Brothers shirt she had changed into now looked as though it had been callously tossed from the window of a moving truck. Just for that alone, Remmi was definitely planning to make sure this woman would be prosecuted to the fullest extent of the law. She couldn't have cared less that Isabella was Evret's wife. She cared not about the scandal it would cost him, his family, and perhaps his career. She didn't even care that Isabella was right. All Remmi could see was the fact that this woman had threatened her life with a gun just like the one her mother had used to kill herself—and somebody was going to pay for it.

The uniformed guards apprehended a dazed and bloated Isabella as she screamed out in terror, "I'm Mrs. Evret VonShayne! You cannot do this to me!"

As security gripped her tightly on both sides, Isabella wriggled around, making it difficult for them to keep her in place.

"If you don't remain still, miss, we'll have no choice but to cuff you," the tall dark-skinned guard sternly informed her. It was quite obvious that he didn't care one bit who her husband was, and Remmi couldn't help but notice how attractive the guard, whose name tag read HARRIS, looked in his uniform.

He could moonlight as a stripper if he wanted to, Remmi thought, noticing his firm pecs. *Arrest me. . . .*

"Did you hear what I said? Do you know who I *am*! I am Mrs. Evret VonShayne—the wife of the producer and director of this God-forsaken film! If you bumbling idiots don't unhand me right now, my husband will terminate each of your measly jobs!" Isabella barked at high volume.

"Don't you *dare* let this bitch go," Remmi ordered as she fumbled to flip open her cell phone. "This maniac tried to kill me! I'm getting Evret on the phone right now!"

"You do that, you homewrecking Jezebel!" Isabella yelled. The guards looked stunned and uneasy, suddenly realizing they had stumbled into a conflict between a mistress and a wife.

"Yes," Remmi spoke into the tiny receiver. "She's crazier than you said, Evret. She held a gun to my chest and threatened to murder me. If these officers had not busted in when they did, she would have killed me! . . . Oh, yes she would have! She had the most terrifying look in her eyes! A deranged look! She's totally nuts!"

Remmi closed the phone and beamed at Isabella, whom the guards had now forced to sit on the sofa in the living area of the trailer. Isabella sobbed frantically into the palms of her chubby hands. The officers, not knowing what to do, stood silently above her, shrugging at each other and trying not to burst into laughter. This incident had indeed been the most exciting thing they had experienced since production began—other than witnessing an occasional cursing out between Remmi and Evret. It was no secret that Remmi and Evret had a sexual relationship. Still, no one expected Isabella VonShayne to show up to the set wielding a .22-caliber pistol.

"Your *husband* is on his way . . . and so is the LAPD." Remmi smirked as she smoothed down her hair, suddenly realizing that the press might be on their way as well. It was only moments before the trailer door burst open once again, this time blowing in Evret VonShayne himself, the object of both women's desire.

"Isabella, my sweet. Are you all right?" Evret panted, walking right past Remmi, windblown and out of breath from running from the other side of the set. Remmi stood still as a statue, her arms tightly interlocked. She was pissed that Evret ignored her presence when it was *she* who was the victim.

"Is *she* all right? Excuse me, but she pulled a gun on *me*. . . . Helloo?" Remmi spat, interrupting Isabella's ridiculous sobs. Remmi could not imagine why this woman was crying. After all, she was not the one whose life had been threatened.

"I'm sorry, Rementa," Evret began, finally turning to Remmi, his accent suddenly more pronounced than Remmi was used to hearing it. She quickly wondered if this was the way he spoke only around his wife—for her fragile benefit, of course. "But my wife has been having a difficult time as of late. She meant nothing by her actions," he continued.

"Excuse me? There's a .22-caliber handgun laying five feet away from me that says she did. It was just pointed at my heart ten minutes ago. I'd say she *meant* something, all right! She meant to make me a muthafuckin' memory—had I not jumped on the bitch and whupped dat ass!" Remmi fumed. As she spoke, Isabella began to bawl harder.

"Oh, shut the fuck up!" Remmi yelled. By this time, the two uniformed guards were doing all they could to keep from cracking up.

"Rementa, please refrain from using that kind of language in the prescence of my wife," Evret instructed, as if he were behind the camera directing a scene. Totally bewildered and insulted by Evret's concern for his wife, Remmi's rage continued to escalate.

"You gotta be fuckin' kiddin' me," Remmi ranted. Looking at the Cellissima Rolex Evret had given her for their two-week anniversary, Remmi continued, "Ya know whut? Since I *obviously* can't get an *ounce* of concern for my well-being from your ass, maybe I'll be able to get some from the cops who should have been here by now!"

"Rementa, there will be no police involvement," Evret snapped, looking up from where he sat embracing his pathetic spouse, who continued to slobber all over his arm with her snotty, demented tears.

The fury in Remmi's hazel eyes turned them the color of dark chocolate Godiva raspberry drops. And as she raised her right brow, like a defiant child challenging an absentee parent, she announced, "There has been a crime committed here, and I intend to press full charges!"

"There will be no police involvement, Rementa," Evret repeated, this time with more authority.

"Excuse you? You may be in control of this movie, but you are *not* in control of *me*, and in case you haven't heard, attempted murder is a crime—even in L.A.!" Remmi barked, grabbing her bag and preparing to take herself to the nearest police precinct if she had to. Like flies on the wall, the two security guards remained motionless and mute, hoping that the parties involved would forget they were there. They wanted to excuse themselves, as this was clearly a personal domestic issue, but they were intrigued by the events that continued to unfold before them. It was like watching an episode of a popular *novela*, and they wanted to see the conclusion.

In one swift motion, Evret jumped up and forcefully grabbed Remmi's wrist, causing one of the security guards to intervene. Bravely wedging his six-foot-three-inch frame between the two soon-to-be ex-lovers, the same guard who hadn't cared that Isabella was the wife said, "With all due respect, Mr. VonShayne. We can't allow you to put your hands on Miss Broughton with us standing right here."

Remmi snatched her arm from Evret's grip and could not believe how this man, who had lain in bed just the night before, admiring every molecule of her body, could turn on her for his crazy and deranged unattractive wife. Powerful men like Evret Von-Shayne could never be satisfied by one woman—let alone one that looked like Mrs. Garrett, from *The Facts of Life*, on steroids. Isabella should have known her place and accepted it, letting her man do his thing in his world and reaping the benefits and status of being the wife of a successful director. In fact, she should have been glad that he hadn't turned her in for a younger model years ago, as so many others like him in Hollywood had. He'd stayed with her for twenty-two years—a feat Remmi considered quite amazing in itself. Obviously Isabella didn't know how to play the game, and Remmi was determined to punish her for her ignorance.

"How dare you put your hands on me!" Remmi snarled. She could feel the heat rise in her armpits and silently hoped that the Secret she had used that morning truly was strong enough for a man.

"I'm just trying to talk some sense into you, Rementa. If you go to the police, the press will be all over us. *Moon Circles the Sun* will be doomed before it hits the theaters! Don't do this to me! Don't do this to *yourself*! Both of us have worked very hard for this. Don't ruin it for us!" Evret pleaded, sounding like a toddler begging his mother for one more piece of candy. *Now that's what I'm talking about*, Remmi said to herself, enjoying the fact that Evret was now groveling at her feet. Still Remmi continued to appear unfazed.

After neglecting her feelings and well-being the way he had, Evret was going to have to do better than that if he was going to prevent Remmi from talking to the police. As Remmi took in the scene laid out before her, a lightbulb went on in her head brighter than Macy's Fourth of July fireworks.

Turning to the guards—particularly the cute one—Remmi smiled. "You gentlemen have saved my life, and for that I am so grateful. I'm sure Mr. VonShayne will make sure that you are both appropriately rewarded for your courage *and* your silence, won't you, Evret?"

"Oh, yes," Evret agreed. "See me at the top of the week, and I will have handsome bonuses for both of you."

"Especially this one," Remmi added, squeezing the brawny biceps of Officer Harris. "Fellas—if you could give me a moment with the VonShaynes, I'd appreciate it." Remmi smiled. "But stay outside the door—just in case ol' girl here blacks out again," she continued.

The officers did as they were asked but not before picking up the loaded pistol and placing it into a plastic bag.

"Evidence," stated the other officer, who had been silent earlier.

After the door shut tightly behind them, Remmi turned to the couple and began, "Evret, it's quite clear that your wife has mental issues. Look at her—she's still making a fool of herself with those ridiculous crocodile tears."

"Calm down, dear. It's gonna be okay," Evret assured Isabella. Remmi could not help but shake her head and chuckle at the sight of this all-too-pathetic couple.

"She needs to be institutionalized, Evvy. Because quite frankly, she's definitely a threat to society," Remmi added. Isabella continued to sob and slobber upon her husband's shoulder as Remmi stood up with her arms folded, rolling her eyes upward.

"Rementa. My wife had a miscarriage recently, and this has caused a severe mental breakdown. Please try to be a bit more sensitive," Evret pleaded.

"Seems to me like *you're* the one who needs to be more sensitive, Evvy. 'Cause if she really had a miscarriage, how sensitive were *you*, laying up with me every night?" Remmi spat, her temples throbbing at the thought that he'd actually still been having sex with this blob of a woman. At that, Isabella turned up the intensity on her bawling and wailing, causing Remmi to shake her head more vigorously in disgust.

"Look, let's cut the bullshit, folks," Remmi turned, facing Evret eye to eye. "Your prima donna princess here is an attempted murderer. A fact that I'm sure the LAPD will eat up and the press will love, causing you, your business, and your life so much scandal you'll wish you never came to this ruthless town. And as much as I'd love to save your ass, Evret, I would feel like I am doing an injustice to society if I say nothing and allow this woman to go free. She may do this to someone else. Then how am I gonna feel? How would I be able to live with myself?" Remmi sarcastically rationalized.

"We do not have to go to the police, Rementa. Doing that won't only cause problems for me and my business, but you won't be doing your career any good either," Evret firmly told her.

"Well, I actually disagree. I can always tell the press that I thought you were in the middle of a divorce—that that's what you told me. I'll tell them that I would have never been with you had I known that you and your wife were still together—and trying to conceive a child, no less! You'll look like such a dirt bag, no reputable studio in Hollywood will wanna fuck with you. I, on the other hand, will look like a victim *twice*. And you know how much Hollywood *loves* a victim. In fact, I might be able to sell my story to Lifetime behind this shit—after all, if they gave Fantasia a movie, mine would be a shoe-in. But you? You'll look like a skanky Hollywood creep who takes advantage of young girls looking for their big break. Not to mention the fact that I *will* play the race card—and have every black activist—from Sharpton to Jesse Jackson—blackballing your ass for taking advantage of a young black girl trying to make it in Hollywood. I'll even call the NAACP and get a couple of other girls to come out saying you did it to them, too. And when all is said and done, your beloved princess here will be thrown in a dark, cold cell for her crime . . . No. Evvy—what could be the biggest scandal of *your* career, could be the biggest boost for *mine!*" Remmi laughed.

Then the room fell so silent, you could hear a pin drop. As Remmi calculated her next move, abruptly, Isabella broke the tranquillity, wailing, "Evret, do something! Do whatever you have to do! I cannot go to prison! You cannot let me go to prison! This is all your fault! If only you could keep your dick in your pants, this would never have happened! I don't care what you do! Pay the bitch! I don't care! I cannot go to prison!"

Evret took a deep breath and, in his most defeated tone, softly, asked "Rementa, what can I do for you to stop you from going to the police?"

"Oh, I don't know . . ." Remmi smirked, stretching her body a bit and gently swaying in a circular motion. "Star billing in *Moon Circles the Sun* . . . and an additional two hundred fifty thousand cash, maybe?"

Evret's eyes widened at Remmi's request. "Star billing! Rementa that would mean rewriting the script, and at this late date, that would put us way behind schedule. And how would I explain it to Brendon? He's an Oscar nominee!" Evret reasoned.

"Nominee, shma-minee. I couldn't care less. The muthafucka

ain't win, so the hell wit' 'em. Look, on the real, Evvy, you don't have to give me shit. We can all just leave this room and head on over to the nearest precinct and tell them what happened. I'm sure they'd love to hear about it." Remmi shrugged, tightening the clutch on her Louis and heading toward the trailer door.

"Evret!" Isabella shrieked. Nervously, Remmi's soon-to-be ex-lover ran toward the door to prevent her exit.

"Okay," he soothed. "I'll call for an emergency rewrite as soon as this evening. They'll bump up your character. Give you more visibility. More lines."

"Star billing," Remmi firmly requested, refusing to accept anything less.

"I'll have to meet with the powers that be, but with my endorsement, they should consent. Of course, I don't think Brendon will be too happy sharing the bill with you."

"Fuck Brendon. He's on his way down anyway. I'm probably doing you a favor," Remmi huffed. "What about the two hundred fifty grand?"

"Rementa, there's no money left in the budget to give you an additional two hundred fifty thousand dollars. You're already making more than any other new actress in Hollywood right now anyway!" Evret snarled, disgusted, but also surprised by the Gestapo tactics used by what he thought was a young, dumb, ex–video ho from New York City.

"Excuse you? Let's get something clear. What you're paying me is my acting fee for performing in your film in the first place. The additional two hundred fifty is to keep my black ass from going to the cops. That's not coming out of the movie budget. That's coming outta *your* personal bank account!" Remmi retorted, now losing patience with the entire situation. In sixty minutes, her life had been threatened at gunpoint, she had tackled a would-be murderer, found interest in a security guard, and now she was negotiating a deal with her ex-lover, who also happened to be the husband of her attacker. She'd already taken far too long to get to the bubble bath that awaited her back at her suite, but it would all be worth it if she walked out of that trailer with a starring role and a quarter of a million dollars.

"Where do you think I'm gonna get that kind of money? Do you think I just have two hundred fifty thousand dollars *lying around*?" Evret screeched.

"I don't know. Where will you get the money to pay for your wife's defense? You might wanna tap that account," Remmi calmly suggested. After a momentary stare-down, Remmi shrugged her shoulders and smiled. "Look, it's on you. Why don't you and wifey poo here discuss it. But if I don't have that money wired into my bank account in twenty-four hours, I'm going to the cops." Turning to Evret and staring so intensely, she could practically see the wall behind him, she continued, "You know the account number, babe. You've done it so many times in the past."

Proud of the way she had once again made lemonade out of some very sour lemons, Remmi left the trailer. On her way out, she convinced the guards to hold on to the evidence and exchanged cell phone numbers with Officer Harris, as she could really use some black dick. She'd missed it so much messing around with Evret. Driving toward Century Boulevard, Remmi figured she would call the guard, whose first name was Orlando, just to keep him in pocket, in case Evret was stupid enough not to comply with her requests.

Sometimes Remmi amazed herself, and this was one of those times. Once a struggling temp turned hip-hop video dancer, Remmi was truly making a name for herself in Hollywood. The bumps and bruises along the way really didn't matter to her. All that was important was where she was right then and where she was headed. And with star billing on a major Hollywood film and more money than she'd ever had in her life in the bank, Rementa Broughton was headed in a pretty good direction.

18

*O*rlando's *manhood* pushed in and out of Remmi's saturated loins with incredible intensity. The once-crisp Yves Dolerme hand-embroidered sheets were dampened with perspiration—a result of over ninety minutes of intense lovemaking. The windows of Remmi's suite were fogged beyond visibility, and she'd had to open the balcony door so that they would not suffocate from passion. Orlando's skills were so exquisite that Remmi had to be very careful not to confuse his sexual expertise with love. His mocha-colored penis was so perfect that it resembled something in a display case at the Pink PussyCat Boutique. About nine and a half inches, it was perfect in length, width, and shade—its skin smooth, unblemished, and screaming to be received. Unable to resist him, she had done it in her trailer on the set, in his makeshift office behind the set, at her suite at the Four Seasons, and even in his Toyota Avalon. Remmi was addicted to the thrill of doing it with him in public places, where the threat of being photographed by the paparazzi made the encounter all the more forbidden.

"You're phenomenal," Orlando moaned, catching his breath after climaxing for the third time. The slight gap in his two front teeth only added to his sexy. She glanced at his euphoric grin, and couldn't help but place a soft and tiny peck on his succulent lips. The moonlight bounced brightly off his dimpled cheeks as he lay there naked beside her upon the sweaty sheets. He gazed at her, and Remmi admired his masculine form. She'd recognized his fineness in her trailer the day Isabella VonShayne had tried to kill her, but she had no idea what an incredible specimen he was beneath his navy blue uniform.

Orlando Harris was a twelve-year veteran with the Los Angeles Police Department. A respected officer, Orlando was moonlighting on the set of *Moon Circles the Sun* when he and Remmi met. At thirty-five years old, Orlando didn't look a day over twenty-four, taking pride in his body enough to hit the gym three hours a day, five days a week. His frame was perfect for Remmi, as he wasn't too short or too tall. His washboard abs turned Remmi on to the point where she would sometimes douse them with honey and lick them for twenty minutes at a time. Needless to say, he was a very good catch. He'd never been married and he had no kids. And while he'd never had any trouble getting the ladies, never in his wildest dreams would he have thought that he'd be laying up with Rementa Broughton. He figured she went for the sugadaddy types—which of course she did—but deep down inside, what she really wanted was a kind, sensitive brotha who knew how to handle his business in the bedroom.

As she lay there basking in the afterglow of passion, Remmi was on cloud nine. Life was good, and she was in a great place both professionally and personally. Evret had wired the money into her account, so her finances were not an issue, which allowed Remmi to be selective about the many projects she was now being offered. The industry was already buzzing about the anticipated success of *Moon Circles the Sun*, and there was even talk of a best actress Oscar nomination. Thus, she'd already been signed to two more major films with huge paychecks attached. With that in mind, Remmi's search for a sugadaddy was put on the back burner. No more screwing to get ahead. She finally *was* ahead, and fine-ass Officer Orlando Harris was her current dick of choice. Not bad for an ex–video ho from a New York City housing project, huh?

"No, *you're* the one who's phenomenal. Four orgasms in one night? I'd say that's pretty phenomenal," Remmi moaned, pressing her exposed, moistened flesh against his. A gentle breeze cast over the room, cooling them. They were both exhausted from pleasing each other but still willing to go one more round.

With ease and grace, Orlando rolled over and, in one gentle motion, softly placed his tongue upon Remmi's erect nipple. He then led his muscular fingertips across her tight abdomen and, with a slow circular motion, traced her navel before tenderly walking his fingers down to her neatly shaven triangle. As he lightly stroked the sweetened zone, he found his way to her opening and caressed the outer skin of her slippery vulva before plunging his forefinger deeply inside its crevices. He thrust his fingers in and out of her with ease, interchanging from pointer to middle to ring finger and back as Remmi moaned with sheer delight. When she could no longer stand the fact that he was not inside her, Remmi tossed her tanned, lean legs over his iron rock-hard dick and propelled his pulsating penis into her swollen vagina.

"Yeah, that's it, baby. Work that shit." Orlando smiled as Remmi slid up and down on his magnificent dick. Remmi giggled, tightening the walls of her saturated pussy, giving him even more pleasure and pulling him deeper into her. By the time they reached orgasm simultaneously, they both knew they'd need the rest of the day to recuperate.

"This is unbelievable," Orlando finally sighed as Remmi placed her head on his chiseled mocha-colored chest.

"Yeah. Our chemistry is pretty amazing," Remmi giggled.

"Yeah, but not only that. I mean, me even being here with you. It's crazy."

"Oh, it's not so crazy."

"And I still can't believe you got dude to give you that money. Beauty, brains, and slick as BP gasoline. What a deadly combination," he continued, running his finger through her wild mane.

"Well, I didn't do it completely alone. You did hold the gun for me as collateral. If Evret ever decides to get stupid, we still have that as evidence, and it has her prints all over it." Remmi yawned, rolling over just a bit and hoping to change the subject. She really wasn't interested in discussing the issue, since she wasn't too big on talking or bragging about the dirt she sometimes did, which was one of the reasons she had been able to get away with so much. *Loose lips sink ships*, she remembered her mother saying. So she made it a point never to tell on herself, only momentarily breaking that rule when she immaturely tried to impress Lamard Fisher—who probably didn't believe her anyway.

"I like how you said the word *we*." He laughed nervously.

Oh, here it comes, Remmi said to herself. She had wondered how long it was gonna take Orlando to ask for a cut of her money. Remmi knew men rarely did anything for free even if she was fucking them. It had taken him a minute, but here he was nearly three months later trying to get a piece of her pie—as if laying up cost-free in the penthouse suite of one of the best hotels in L.A.

and getting the best sex of his life wasn't more than enough payment.

"So how much did the old geezer give you?" Orlando casually questioned.

"Not much. Ya know, contrary to what you may think, I really had feelings for Evret, so I cut him a break." Remmi shrugged, rolling over on her side and giving him her back so she didn't have to lie in his face.

"Not much? For an attempted murder cover-up? You could have gotten him for at least a half a mil. That cracka got dough. You saved him from serious legal fees and scandal that would probably have ruined his career!"

"Yeah, I know. But Evret was so good to me, and I really didn't feel right extorting him. I do have a conscience and *some* morals, ya know," Remmi lied.

"So what's 'not much'? 'Cause not for nuthin', but I kinda think I deserve a little cut—for holding the weapon and all, if ya know what I mean," Orlando reasoned.

"Oh, of course you do. I totally agree, and I was planning on giving you something, too. Truth be told, with everything that needed to be done to finish the film and preparing for its release and all that, I actually just got the money last week. And since this is the first time I'm seeing you since I got it, I was gonna talk to you about it today—after we made each other feel good," Remmi cooed, rubbing her hand gently across his chest. "Things have just been so hectic for me since the movie wrapped. But you know that," she continued to lie.

Remmi suddenly realized that no matter how good a lay Orlando was, he'd never be the king in her castle. In her opinion, men who asked women for money—under any circumstances—were lower than the scum of the earth. Had he just kept his mouth closed, she would have probably let him ride the wave of success with her. He definitely looked good on her arm, and that's all she really needed him for. By expecting some sort of *payment* for his involvement with her dirt, he had given her a permanent bad taste in her mouth.

"So what did you make out with?" Orlando continued, forcing the issue.

"Twenty grand," Remmi huffed, now totally put off. "Plus he's still paying for this suite. And of course, I got star billing in the film."

Remmi's words were phonier than a three-dollar bill. Not sure if he really believed her, Orlando lay very still. Remmi was beautiful and a great piece of ass, but seeing her in action that day in her trailer showed him that as lovely as she was, she was also as slick and cold as ice. Still, her skills were so good and she was so convincing that she made him question his own instincts.

"Does five thousand dollars sound fair to you?" Remmi asked with bated breath. She could tell that he was skeptical about what she was telling him, but she wasn't about to give him one penny more. After all, he'd just *happened* to be at the right place at the right time. Why should he get more for a scheme that was totally her creation? He should be glad she was offering his ass anything.

"Yeah, I guess. I think you coulda got more outta him, though. You sold yourself short," he replied with an attitude.

"Probably. But blackmail ain't really my thing," Remmi lied once more.

Realizing that he wasn't going to get anything other than great sex from her, Orlando remained silent. Remmi, on the other hand, quickly put out of her mind all thoughts of him being a permanent fixture in her life. His request had put a screeching halt on any real relationship they might have had and she was glad he had given her the key to the safety deposit box where the gun was stashed. She'd still keep him around, though—or at least his dick.

Remmi let out a good stretch, exposing her bare skin from beneath the sheets. She was ready to go one more round. As her nipples hit the chilled air, they hardened, and her breasts resembled a pair of ripened, succulent plums, immediately drawing Orlando to them. Placing his masculine fingers around the breast nearest to him, he began sucking and licking the crevices of the areola, his saliva marinating each and every miniature valley. Unable to contain herself, Remmi climbed upon his face and silently craved for him to place his tongue gently inside her throbbing pink walls. Without hesitation he obliged her, bringing her once again to an incredible level of ecstasy. *Yeah, I have to keep him around*, Remmi thought. Even if he did cost her five thousand dollars. Little did he know that, for what he was giving, if he had been a better negotiator, she'd have probably paid ten.

he fluorescent bulbs beamed down from the ceiling like spotlights above Remmi's and Shannelle's heads. Remmi tried to concentrate on the *Ebony* magazine in her hands, but the glare from above made it difficult to read. *Funny how you could have a light so bright and still be unable to see anything*, Remmi thought. But bigger than the lighting Remmi's thoughts were preoccupied with the reason she and Shannelle sat in the sterile blue waiting room of Dr. Foster's office to begin with. He had called Shannelle earlier that morning to say that he had gotten her blood work back. He obviously saw something he didn't like, because he refused to discuss the results over the phone, telling her that it was—as he put it—"imperative that you come to my office at your earliest convenience."

This, of course, had Shannelle shitting big red New York City housing project bricks. Shannelle was so shook up, Remmi canceled her entire day so that she could go to the doctor's office with her. The whole ride over, Remmi tried to reassure her best friend that Dr. Foster's request was standard procedure—even though that was bullshit. But it was her job to make her friend feel better, not worse, and if she had to tell a little white lie to do it, so be it. The black-and-white print from a story on celebrity weddings stared back at Remmi from the glossy page. Remmi could see them, but she was unfocused. What if Shannelle really was sick? How would she manage in L.A. without her road dog? Remmi shook the thought out of her mind and was snapped back into reality when the "too old to be wearing that outfit" receptionist called Shannelle's name. When they both rose to walk down the corridor toward the examination rooms, the woman stopped the two in their tracks with a nasal, gum-smacking, "Patient only."

"This is my sister, and anything Dr. Foster has to say can be said in front of her," Shannelle spat with a quiver. She was really scared now. Something had to be wrong.

"Suit yourself," the receptionist replied, walking back around the cream-colored Formica desk. Remmi noticed that she was far too old to have breasts so perky.

Remmi and Shannelle waited in silence in Dr. Foster's office. Both of them wanted to say something, but couldn't. Remmi had a frog the size of Kermit in her throat, and Shannelle had suddenly caught a temporary case of laryngitis.

"If you need a transplant or anything like that, you know I got you, girl," Remmi finally managed to mutter. Shannelle blinked hard, folded her lips inward, and shook her head up and down as if to say, *I know.*

"And they got cures for all kinds of cancers these days, so a little chemo and you'll be back to your old self in no time ... bald as an eight-ball, but they got them lace front wigs now too. Beyoncé and 'em live in 'em, girl. You can't even tell." Remmi nervously chuckled, causing Shannelle to do the same. The ice was broken a bit, and they both seemed a little more relaxed after letting out their giggles.

Dr. Foster, a very handsome middle-aged man with smooth cinnamon-colored skin, entered the room wearing a crisp white coat on top of a navy blue Armani suit. He was stylish, built, and fine. A distinguished-looking older gentleman, he stood about six feet even with a thick low-cut salt-and-pepper fro and silky black eyebrows. His broad shoulders, muscular arms, and trim waist indicated that he still regularly hit the gym, and Remmi envisioned him naked for a moment. She'd never had sex with a doctor before, and looking at Dr. Foster, she'd definitely be willing to let him give her a checkup.

"Good afternoon, Ms. Anderson, and ... ," Dr. Foster began, noticing Remmi's presence.

"This is my sister, Rementa," Shannelle informed him.

"Um, Ms. Anderson, what I have to say is confidential," Dr. Foster stated, barely acknowledging Remmi. "You may want to have this conversation in private," he continued.

"No, Doctor. This is my sister—the only family I really have. Whatever you have to say, she can hear. After all, she's gonna be the one to help me deal with it," Shannelle said firmly.

"So be it," Dr. Foster replied. He walked behind his mahogany desk and situated himself upon his plush black leather swivel chair. He then began to thumb through Shannelle's chart. When he looked up from the folder with intensity in his dark eyes, he began, "The results from your blood work, Ms. Anderson, indicate that you have been infected with HIV, the virus that causes AIDS."

You could have heard a pin drop in the room. Both Remmi and Shannelle were speechless. The atmosphere suddenly became very hot and the room very dark. Remmi could feel a tiny bead of perspiration trickling down the fold of her back. Though the words that fell from Dr. Foster's lips were spoken in soft and even tones, they pierced the inside of Remmi's chest like a kitchen knife, cold and blunt, like a rip, rather than a stab—making them much more violent and painful.

He paused, and then seemed like he wanted to continue, but the looks on their faces forced him to take a deep breath instead. The only thing Remmi could hear was the unusually loud ticking of the circular brass wooden clock that sat on the left-hand side of the doctor's desk.

"Of course, you know," Dr. Foster began once more, finally breaking the silence. "HIV is not a death sentence these days. Medical breakthroughs have made it possible for patients to live for many years with the right lifestyle adjustments and medication."

"I don't know what to say," Shannelle replied.

"Well, the sooner you get started with the drug cocktails, the sooner we can get you on the road to stabilizing the illness. Now I noticed that you paid out of pocket for your visit. Do you have medical coverage?" Dr. Foster questioned.

"I'll be taking care of all expenses," Remmi interjected.

"HIV drug therapy is very expensive. If you have no coverage, I suggest that you apply for public assistance. After all, the enormous cost of medication could bankrupt even the healthiest bank account after a while," he continued.

"I said I'll be taking care of everything. Just let us know what the first step is," Remmi snapped, annoyed that Dr. Foster obviously didn't recognize her celebrity.

"Okay, well, first I think it would be helpful for you to join a support group or a local AIDS service organization so that you can talk to individuals who understand what you are going through firsthand. I can recommend one here in the area if you like," Dr. Foster explained.

"I don't need no damn support group," Shannelle barked, her eyes glossed over with tears ready to fall.

"Okay, suit yourself. I just think many people who are dealing with the disease find it helpful to surround themselves with others who are dealing with it also," he suggested.

Shannelle glared at the doctor—angry with the messenger for delivering such a life-altering message, angry with the world, angry with the nasty brotha who gave it to her, and most of all, angry with herself. She tried to do a mental checklist of all the men she'd had unprotected sex with but soon lost count. Shannelle could not believe this was happening to her. On TV, AIDS victims were junkies, homos, and those people in Africa who let flies swarm around their faces without swatting them. Every once in a while there was a case like West Coast rapper Eazy-E, but Shannelle and Remmi had rationalized that he had probably been one of those down-low brothas. AIDS happened to people like that. Not sexy, voluptuous dancers with perfect bodies and faces. No— AIDS was something that happened only to somebody else. Unfortunately, Shannelle had failed to realize that to somebody else, she was somebody else.

The next forty-eight hours were agonizing for both Remmi and Shannelle as they tried to come to grips with Shannelle's prognosis. They stayed locked up inside Remmi's suite, reminiscing about the things they had done in their past, ordering plenty of food and alcohol from room service. Evret was still footing the bill for the room, but Remmi knew it would probably be coming to an end soon. Good thing she still had her flat over on the other side of town until she could find a more cushy place, given her newfound financial security. She wanted Shannelle to be as comfortable as possible and decided that she would hire a housekeeper to make sure things were taken care of for her best friend if she had to go out of town. The saddest part was the two of them having to admit that Shannelle might not be able to be Remmi's assistant anymore. They had made so many plans, and Remmi wanted Shannelle to be right by her side every step of the way. Of course, Shannelle promised to do the job as long as she could. She wasn't showing any physical signs of being sick and still looked and felt great the majority of the time. But Remmi didn't want traveling and long hours to accelerate the disease. Still, Shannelle made Remmi swear that she would give her the opportunity until it became impossible for her to fulfill it.

Although she had been against joining a support group, Shannelle eventually decided that it might actually be a good idea to take Dr. Foster's advice and sign up with AIDS Project Los Angeles. She was hesitant, but promised Remmi that she would go to the facility first thing Monday morning. Ignorant, uninformed, and uneducated about the disease, Shannelle didn't want to be in an AA- or NA-like group, sharing her most intimate feelings with a bunch of ex-druggies and prostitutes.

"I have nothing in common with those people," Shannelle snapped, waving off the idea of connecting with anyone else who was living with the virus.

"Shannelle, you *are* one of *those* people," Remmi reminded her in her most honest "let's break it down to the curb" way.

Over pastel-colored frosted tumblers filled to the brim with Dom Pérignon Rosé Vintage 1995, the two best friends tried to take the gloom out of the atmosphere by making light of all the lovers they had had over the years. The champagne helped to lift their spirits and made it easier for them to discuss the upside of sex rather than the down. They never actually realized how much sex had played a role in their lives and how often they'd used it as a bargaining tool to get what they wanted from men without a thought to any repercussions. They had been reckless, careless, and immature, and Remmi knew how easily it could have been her dealing with such a diagnosis when she had been just as promiscuous as Shannelle, if not more. Shannelle's condition definitely forced Remmi to question her own habits. She didn't always force her partner to wear condoms, and even then, condoms sometimes failed. Had she not remembered the fact that her mother had died with the same disease? Had she become such a master at blocking things that she failed to remember things of great importance?

As Beyoncé whined in the background about wanting a son she hadn't even conceived yet to be just like her daddy, the two sister friends cuddled up on the opposite ends of the plush sofa in the living room of Remmi's suite. They sat, nursing their drinks ghetto-style like they used to do back in Spanish Harlem, both puffy-eyed from crying, from laughing, and from crying some more. It was like their lives were flashing right before their eyes.

"See, that's why that bitch is so damn successful," Remmi moaned, swishing the Dom between her cheeks as if it were Listerine before swallowing hard.

"Who?" Shannelle asked, her head feeling light from the champagne.

"Beyoncé. That bitch daddy ain't no joke. You don't realize it, but not having a daddy makes a chick start out automatically behind the game," Remmi explained. She was feeling the bubbly hard by now, but the words she spoke came from a place of deep pondering and logic.

"You might be right. Plus she went right from her daddy's arms to that nigga, Jay-Z. What a transition. . . ."

"Yeah, but it's more than that. True—Jay's cool and all, I guess, even though I heard rumors about him fuckin' around on her, but they look happy as shit when you see 'em . . . but not for nuthin'— if she stops feelin' that nigga, she can bounce. She don't have to take his shit unless she wants to, 'cause she got her own bank and a daddy who loves the shit outta her. When you have a daddy that loves you like that, ain't no other man that really matters. Even if the rumors about him fucking on her mama are true."

"Well, I don't know shit about that. I ain't neva even met my daddy. That nigga could walk past me on the street and I wouldn't know it," Shannelle spewed with a drunken shrug.

"I know who mine is—the evil son of bitch. Never met him. Never seen him. But my mama told me who he was the day she died. He ain't even come to my mama's funeral—the useless bastard. Ain't never seen the muthafucka and don't wanna neva see the muthafucka," Remmi snapped.

"He ain't come to your mama's funeral!" Shannelle slurred.

"Nope . . . the rat bastard . . . ," Remmi spat.

"Well," Shannelle slurred, "ain't that some shit? Neither of us ever seen our sperm donors. Girl, we might really be sisters!" Shannelle cackled before continuing, "Man, for all I know, my daddy probably was watching me drop it like it's hot up in Shirley's Temple . . . and that's some ol' disgusting-assed incest shit."

"That ain't even nothing to joke about," Remmi calmly whispered, remembering her mother's words the day she committed suicide. "Ever thought about trying to find the jerk?" Remmi questioned.

"Naaah. I mean, what the fuck do we really have to talk about? What would I say to him? . . . Why you left me? . . . Get real."

"That's exactly what you should ask the nigga." Remmi rose from the sofa and unsteadily climbed upon the glass-topped coffee table as if she were climbing a stage to make a very important announcement. She then placed the nearly empty champagne bottle beneath her lip like a microphone and broadcast at the top of her lungs: "How you just make a baby and bounce? Don't you ever think about the kid you brought into this world? Don't you ever wonder if I'm hungry? If I'm cold? How the hell I'm doing in school? If I'm even *in* school? . . . Don't you give a fuck about me? Or do you hate my mama so much that you hate my black ass, too? The black ass you made? . . . That's what the fuck *I* would say to *that* nigga."

There was an uncomfortable silence in the room as Shannelle gazed up at Remmi in awe, confused but humored at the same time, before both of them burst into a heap of drunken laughter and Remmi fell off the tabletop, spilling what was left of the champagne onto the carpet as she plunged down upon the sofa.

"Seriously though . . . ," Shannelle softly said. "What good would it do me to curse him out now? He wasn't there when I was born, he wasn't there throughout my life, and now I want you to make sure that he ain't at my funeral."

"You serious?"

"As serious as the HIV-infected blood that's running through my veins. Promise me you'll make sure he ain't at my funeral."

After thinking about it for a moment, Remmi figured that her best friend had every right to choose whom she wanted to exclude from her funeral, and it was her duty to make sure that those wishes were honored. Remmi sternly replied, "If it's the last thing I do, I'll make sure that the muthafucka ain't there."

"Thanks, girl," Shannelle said with a smile and hugged Remmi tightly. "I always knew I could count on you."

19

remmi *waited* patiently in the reception area of her agent's office, thumbing through the most current issue of *Black Enterprise* magazine. Allen had requested that she come in to discuss some matters and a few new projects that were on the table. He seemed slightly agitated when they spoke on the phone and didn't want to talk about anything specific until they met. He just kept saying there were issues that needed to be addressed and told Remmi to rearrange her schedule so she could be in his office at three o'clock. She could not imagine what was so pressing that Allen could not talk to her about it over the telephone, but Remmi did as she was asked and rescheduled her day.

"He's ready to see you now, Rementa." Diane, Allen's secretary said, smiling.

Remmi entered Allen's sunny office to see him sitting behind his auburn-colored desk intensely reading from a copy of *Variety*.

His pale bony fingers tightly gripped the pages, causing the tips to turn purplish red. He wasn't an ugly man but definitely not someone you would call handsome. And while he did well for himself, he didn't exude the confidence, the bank account, or the poise of Evret VonShayne, nor did he have the arrogance of Arthur Haddox. He was seemingly very much in love with his Pamela Anderson–look-alike wife, and Remmi was glad about that. He was one of the few men Remmi had encountered that she didn't have to have sex with in order to get favors. He was her agent, and her success was his, so working his ass off to better her career was in the best interest of both of them.

It was at a charity event for Sean Combs's Daddy's House organization that he was introduced to Remmi by a colleague. She had just been signed on to play Dorene in Bad Boy's first film, and he'd remembered seeing her JCPenney commercial. After chatting with her for a while, he realized the tremendous potential of this young actress and asked if he could represent her. Remmi eagerly jumped at the chance to be represented by a former star of the William Morris Agency—a seasoned agent who had helped shape the careers of several celebrities whom she admired. Much to Remmi's delight, their relationship had proved to be quite fruitful for both of them and looked like it had no intention of slowing down.

Remmi strutted into the art deco European-furnished office donned in a casually classic shrimp-colored Betsey Johnson jumpsuit and gave Allen the standard Hollywood kiss—one touch of her right cheek to his left, one touch of her left cheek to his right. A pair of Gucci Palladium Pinks shielded her from the intense California sun, while making her appear all the more the Hollywood starlet that she was on her way to becoming. Allen smiled at her, but his face appeared troubled as he instructed Remmi to have a seat before him.

"Remmi, on the set of *Butta*, did something happen between you and Arthur Haddox?" Allen quizzed with a tilt of his head. Remmi gave him a slightly confused look before he continued, "I mean, I know you two were rumored to be having an affair, but there's always so much gossip in the air that it's really senseless to pay attention to anything. So I figured I'd cut the chase and go right to the source."

"Why do you ask?" Remmi questioned.

"Well, it seems that Mr. Haddox has been making a very huge effort to blacklist you," Allen explained.

Shocked that Art would be bold enough to start talking about their tryst, Remmi was totally taken aback. She knew he had been salty about the fact that she'd screwed Lamard, but after he had kicked her ass, Remmi figured they were even. Plus, since Art had been married the whole time they were dealing, her stepping out was a fair part of the game they were playing. She could not believe he would have the audacity to speak badly about her in public—not after the rave reviews she had gotten for herself *and* his movie at the Sundance Film Festival. Remmi had made *Butta*. She had been the critics' favorite and the only reason the movie was getting released nationwide. Until her reviews, the plan was to release it only in limited urban markets. Remmi's portrayal of Dorene had without a doubt taken the film mainstream. And this was how he repaid her?

"Are you serious?" Remmi managed to utter, her words peppered with agitation.

"Very. For some reason, he seems to have a vendetta out on you, despite all you've done to help *Butta* become a success. I don't quite understand it. I mean the numbers on the film were tremendous, especially for an independent. But he's been spreading the word that you're an unprofessional temperamental diva who thinks she's more talented than she actually is, amongst other things."

"Gethefuckouttahere! Well, nobody's actually *listening* to him are they? I mean, how much weight could his opinion really hold?" Remmi asked.

"More than it should, evidently. I mean, on the independent film circuit, particularly films of the urban genre—it's really no big deal. In fact, in that environment, a bad attitude could almost be viewed as more 'ghetto' or 'black' or even 'New York,'" Allen rambled.

Remmi didn't know if she should be relieved or insulted. Was a bad attitude really synonymous with *blackness* or *New Yorkness*?

"But we're taking your career mainstream, Remmi. You'll probably never do another film like *Butta*, especially if *Moon Circles the Sun* is the hit we expect it to be," Allen continued.

"So what are you saying, Allen?"

"I'm saying that this asshole has some personal beef with you for some reason—and while I don't wanna get into your private affairs, when I'm hearing negative shit about your personality from the suits up at Dreamtracks, I'd say we need to nip this thing in the bud before it really gets started," Allen remarked, fingering a small silver octagon-shaped paperweight that rested to the left-hand side of his paper-covered desk. There was some sort of engraved plate on its face, but Remmi couldn't make out the writing at a glance, nor did she care enough to focus on its words.

"Dreamtracks?" Remmi repeated, removing the expensive frames from her face.

"Yes—the big boys. They contacted my office to say they've been considering casting you for the lead in the film adaptation of that novel *Nyagra's Falls*. It'll be a made-for-TV movie—a major television movie event, actually. Catapulting you into millions of homes. You'll be a household name on the big and small screen and the envy of every black actress in Hollywood. Damn, you'll be the envy of every actress, period."

"Get outta here! I read that book. It was crazy! And if they do the movie right, it'll be incredible! Are you serious?" Remmi said with excitement.

"And incredible for your career. But evidently this asshole and one of the senior VPs go to the same gym. So you see how important it is for us to get this bastard to stop spreading these vicious rumors about you? It really could affect your career, Rementa. Hollywood is a big town, but it's a small town. There's a lot of 'six degrees of separation' in this industry."

"So what do you suggest I do?"

"I suggest you reach out to the asswipe personally. One on one. I don't know what went on between the two of you, but if he has a human side, talk to it. Your career depends on it."

"All right, Allen. I'll reach out to him. But to tell you the truth, I haven't seen the prick since *Butta*'s screening. I don't even know if his numbers are the same."

"I'm sure they're the same. Assholes like that always want to be reached."

"Well, I'll get on it ASAP. In the meanwhile, please reach out to the powers that be over at Dreamtracks and tell them how much I *loved* that book."

"Will do."

to Remmi's delight, it didn't take much for her to get Arthur Haddox to agree to meet with her. Remmi had been ready to stroke his ego when she called him as she cruised along the highway after leaving Allen's office. But it wasn't necessary. Art was in

New York, but would be returning to the West Coast later that week. Fortunately she didn't have to throw on the fake charm, as he was seemingly happy to hear from her. In fact, he had actually been the one to suggest that they get together for Sunday brunch. She was a little confused by his positive response, figuring that if he had been trying to ruin her career, she obviously was not one of his favorite people. However, once Art recognized Remmi's voice on the other end of the phone, his demeanor went from surprised to excited. Maybe what he was doing was some sort of call for attention from Remmi.

Still, she reminded herself that Arthur Haddox was an undercover borderline psychopath whom she should meet only in a public place. She suggested they meet at noon at Cobalt Cantina on Sunset Boulevard. He eagerly agreed and promised to be there on time. As Remmi touched the END button on her micro flip phone, she shook her head in amazement. How could a man who had assaulted her and who was currently trying to blacklist her seem so excited about meeting her for lunch? Remmi had no idea what Arthur Haddox had up his sleeve, but she was determined to cut it off even if he lost a limb in the process.

anxious to get it over with, Remmi arrived at the restaurant a little early. She wanted to get there before Art so she could watch him walk in and assess his attitude before he sat down. She'd called ahead to ensure that they were given a table in the patio area, not only because she knew Art liked to smoke, but also because there was only one way in and one way out. She didn't want him to sneak up behind her. She wanted to make sure she saw him from the moment he entered the establishment. And if things got hairy, he would not be able to easily escape.

Elegantly dressed in a sunflower-colored formfitting spaghetti-strapped baby doll sundress, Remmi looked absolutely lovely. The Californian sun agreed with her, and she now sported a permanently bronzed complexion, which contrasted with her hazel eyes, making them appear even more beautiful. Her cinnamon-highlighted bone-straight hair hung just above the middle of her back, with soft wispy bangs gently framing her face. She wore little makeup other than heavily mascaraed eyes and magnolia-tinted lips but looked as though she had stepped out of a fashion magazine, her natural beauty radiating so.

The dial on her Movado Harmony had barely struck twelve when Arthur Haddox strolled toward her sporting a blue-and-white pin-striped Ralph Lauren seersucker suit. His perfectly sized muscles bulged beneath the deliberately crinkled cotton. Remmi could not deny the fact that he was gorgeous and graceful in his form. His smile suggested that he had been wearing Crest Whitestrips longer than the manufacturer recommendation of one hour per day. His haircut appeared to be barely fifteen minutes old, its lines straighter than an arrow shaft. His ebony-colored almond-shaped eyes were concealed behind a pair of Giorgio Armani mirrored sunglasses, giving him an air of mystique and making him all the more intriguing. Remmi could not help but notice that every female eye on the patio was directed at him, just as every man's had been drawn to her when she'd entered.

How could a man so physically beautiful be so mentally deranged? Remmi asked herself with a soft chuckle.

"Remmi—oh, or is it *Rementa* now?" he sarcastically asked.

"Remmi is fine. We have history."

"Yes, we sure do," he laughed, and licked his lips as if he were ready to devour her at any moment. "You look so good, I just wanna eat you up."

Had that statement come from any other man, it might have been flattering, but since it came from Arthur Haddox, Remmi wondered if he secretly possessed cannibalistic tendencies to go with all his other demonic and violent behaviors.

"Long time no see, Art." Remmi smiled. They gently hugged and took their seats, ordering a bottle of Piper-Heidsieck Rosé Sauvage champagne to begin their brunch.

"Well, L.A. has obviously been good to you. You look great. You've gotten rid of your hood tendencies. Charm school?"

"I've been diligent about improving myself," Remmi softly responded, ignoring his subtle attempts to get under her skin.

"Well, whatever it is, it's working. If it weren't for those eyes, I'd hardly recognize the girl I met backstage at the Sean John fashion show inhaling a chicken wing. . . . Not bad for a crazy little girl from Spanish Harlem," he continued, grinning from ear to ear as though he'd just bumped into his high school girlfriend.

"Yeah, well, things have been going pretty good for me lately."

"I hear you just completed Evret VonShayne's *Moon Circles the Sun*."

"Yes. We wrapped a few weeks ago. I think it's gonna be a huge box office smash."

"Well, look who's in it. How can it lose?" he humored her.

Remmi let out a choreographed chuckle.

"By the way, I'm having my birthday party at White Lotus tomorrow night, and if you're not busy, I'd love for you to stop by." He smiled as he slipped his arm across the table and placed his fingers upon her hand.

"Put me and a guest on the list, and I'll be there," Remmi assured him.

"Now, you're not bringing your boyfriend, are you?" He winked.

"No . . . no boyfriends for me. My career is my man." She smirked. After an awkward moment of silence, Remmi removed a sesame-seeded braided roll from the breadbasket before her and smeared a pat of butter upon its porous surface.

"Same ol' Remmi . . ."

"Art," she began with a breath. "Ya know. I'm really glad you asked me to join you for brunch today because I don't think I ever really got the chance to officially thank you for everything you've done for me."

"I knew you were a star from the moment I laid eyes on you. If I hadn't discovered you, somebody eventually would have." He shrugged, taking a sip of champagne.

"Well, *Butta* was a tremendous learning experience, and I was really grateful to be a part of that project. Still am."

"Well, the production was lucky to have you. You brought a lot to the project."

What is up with dude? Remmi thought to herself. *Is Allen sure that he's the one spreading lies?*

"I know we ended on kind of a bad note, you and me, but I want you to know that I don't have any hard feelings about what you did to me. I know how people can lose it when they feel they've been disrespected," Remmi justified, looking down at the white tablecloth and fiddling with her butter knife. She was suddenly feeling a bit nervous about approaching the real reason she had called him in the first place.

"About what I *did* to *you*?" Art calmly asked. "Tell me, what did I do to you, Remmi?"

Remmi softly laughed. She found it hard to believe that he was going to act as though the assault that took place in his condo never happened, and she was amazed that he actually thought they were not going to discuss it.

"Oh, you forgot? Does it happen so often that you can't remember when it happened between us?" Remmi sarcastically asked. "Well, to put it bluntly," she continued. "The way I remember it is that you pretty much beat the shit outta me then had sex with my battered body. Remember that?" Remmi announced without a flinch, her piercing hazels now turning a dark copper.

"Sounds pretty brutal. Are you sure it was me? I mean, you *do* have quite a reputation in Hollywood. Maybe it was one of the johns you brought home late one night," he snickered.

"Are you serious?" Remmi wheezed.

"Or maybe you just took something the wrong way. I know how much you like it rough and tough. Did I get outta hand with you one time and not realize it?" he asked with a hint of sarcasm.

"I see you're still not living in the real world," Remmi huffed, more agitated.

"No, kiddo, I think *you're* the one not living in the real world. 'Cause if you thought you were gonna get away with fucking the next nigga in *my* place without repercussions, *you're* the one who's being unreal." Art sharply sneered as Remmi glared at her own slightly distorted reflection in his shades. Not wanting to draw attention to their table or discussion, Remmi backed down but figured it would be best to address the issue and cut the brunch short.

"Well, it's in the past, and I just wanted to let you know that I don't have any hard feelings about it," Remmi nodded, taking a small sip of the freshly poured champagne.

"Good for you," Art nonchalantly said.

"And, um, I was hoping that since I have decided to let it go, I was kinda hoping that you would, too," she suggested.

"Come again?"

"Look, Art. We both did things that we shouldn't have done

during the course of our, um, *relationship*. But it's not like either of us ever felt like we had something that was gonna last forever. After all, you *are* a married man."

"So what's your point?"

"My point is, I want us to put everything that happened behind us so that we'll both be able to move on with our lives. We both have tremendous careers ahead of us, and I wouldn't want our anger for each other to hurt either of our futures in any way."

"I don't know what you're talking about," Art snickered.

"Oh, I think you do."

"Look, you always were a little crazy, but okay. I forgive you, if that's what you want. But you know that's all part of the game. I might have a wife, but you were my woman. It really didn't matter how many other bitches I fucked. I brought you to L.A. just like I brought my Gucci luggage. You belonged to me."

"While I'm flattered that you considered me your property, didn't you know that slavery was abolished a long time ago?"

"Not in L.A."

"And *I'm* crazy? Okay, nigga. Let's cut the fuckin' bullshit," Remmi began, now annoyed by his nerve and audacity and unable to implement her charm school teachings any further. "If you don't stop bad-mouthing and talking shit about me all over Hollywood, I'll be having a little meeting with Mrs. Haddox real soon. By the way, she still teaches at the Excelsior School, right? I've been asked to be a guest speaker at their next assembly . . . and you know how much I love the kids." She glared.

"Are you threatening me?" Art questioned, slightly raising his voice and removing his shades from his face.

Remmi remained silent but replied with an incline in her eyebrow; not only was she threatening him, she was making him a promise.

"Look at me real good as I speak. . . . You can meet with my wife, my mother, my mother-*in-law* and even the mother of Jesus Christ himself! I don't give a shit who you meet with! You think my wife don't know I fuck around? We been married twelve muthafuckin' years. You think you were my first trick? Or my last? Remmi, you're a gutter rat—a skank and a high-class prostitute— and I happen to think that anyone in this town who is *remotely* thinking about working with you deserves to be schooled! That's my contribution to this Hollywood game—hippin' niggas to yo shit before they get caught the fuck out there like I did. You fucked me to get the part in *Butta*, you fucked that old cracka to get your role in *Moon Circles the Sun*, and you'll fuck whoever else you need to fuck to secure your next gig! Now don't get me wrong, I ain't complaining." He let out a hearty laugh. "I mean, you're a great fuck, and that bitch they call Superhead ain't got *nuthin'* on you—so we both got what we wanted out the deal, but don't play yourself by coming in here trying to threaten a nigga 'cause you already got burned by this fire once before and don't think I won't hesitate to burn that ass again!" Art's monologue was cold as ice. While his voice never got louder, his now dark and sinister eyes danced like little black coals on the floor of Satan's mansion. Remmi knew Art's deranged ass meant business. She also wasn't very surprised that his wife was aware of the kind of dog she was married to. The wife always knew. Essentially, Remmi didn't have a leg to stand on. At the end of the day, what could she really do to stop this fool from trying to hurt her career? Angry and flustered, Remmi felt her blood pump rapidly through her veins. As her mind raced a mile a minute, she knew she had to get away from Art and devise another plan. He had to be stopped. As Allen had said, her career depended on it.

Without saying another word, Remmi rose from her seat, tossed the contents of her champagne glass into Art's face with a splash, and headed for the front door of the eatery. Remmi knew she was presenting the paparazzi with a huge photo op and even making herself vulnerable to another beatdown, but she was so ticked off that she simply didn't care. Still she moved swiftly enough to get out of Art's way in case he started whaling on her. But when the liquid from her flute had splattered upon Art's chiseled mug, he'd calmly lifted the white linen napkin from his lap and dried himself off, shaking his head from left to right with a chuckle.

As Remmi strutted toward the exit of the establishment, in the distance she could hear Arthur Haddox calling, "Don't forget to stop by tomorrow night and wish me happy birthday! You'll be on the list plus one!"

20

hannelle sat quietly at the kitchen table thumbing through pamphlets on the AIDS crisis in America when Remmi stormed through the front door of the suite. She'd spent the whole day with her counselor and had ultimately been glad that she decided to join the center. It made her feel better to speak with people who were living with the disease, but it also saddened her to hear stories of many victims who had passed on. Still, it empowered her to know that there were things she could do to decelerate her disease. She wasn't as helpless as she'd originally thought. Even though her blood work had indicated that she had been infected for a while, it made her feel better to know that her illness was not an automatic death sentence. Dr. Foster told her that she could still live for many years without the disease turning into full-blown AIDS, if she was lucky and smart. And physically, other than being about ten pounds lighter, Shannelle looked really good. No one would ever be able to tell from looking at her that she was HIV positive, a fact that made the disease all the more frightening.

It had been Remmi's intention to rant and rave about her day's events, but she quickly stopped dead in her tracks once she remembered what her best friend was dealing with. In the scheme of things, Remmi's issue suddenly didn't seem so important. Still, her blood flowed like acid through her veins when she finally began to describe what had happened. Together they knew they had to come up with a way to stop Arthur Haddox, and they pledged not to stop at anything until his lips were silenced.

"Look, we both know that I been wanting to plot revenge on the muthafucka since he did that shit to you, so you know I'm with any- and everything to screw him over," Shannelle huffed.

"I know. But we gotta be smart. He's vicious, and one false move could mess up everything," Remmi said.

"Look, if we got away with all that money from Shirley's Temple, I think we can get away with damn near anything." Shannelle shrugged. "Not to mention the fact I really have nothing to lose, so I volunteer to do all the dirty work."

"You have nothing to lose? What's *that* supposed to mean?"

"Let's just get real, Remmi. I'm sick. Truth be told, I'm probably not gonna grow old and have grandkids. So whatever happens, happens."

"Don't talk like that. You might outlive me! Every day they're getting closer to a cure. Isn't that what they tell you at the center?" Remmi asked, pointing toward the pamphlets.

"Yeah. They also have a corkboard with new obituaries posted every day."

Silence ensued, and as hard as Remmi tried to find a response for Shannelle's comment, she couldn't.

"Look," Shannelle continued. "I don't even know how long I've been infected with the damn virus. For all I know, at my next checkup they could tell me that I have full-blown AIDS."

"That's not gonna happen," Remmi huffed angrily.

"It could. And you gotta prepare yourself for that. We been there for each other since the second grade. When I die, you basically gonna be alone. After everything we been through, it's my job to make sure you gonna be all right in this world without me. I can't have no nigga trying to fuck up your career. I ain't having that shit."

"I don't wanna talk about you dying," Remmi mumbled, agitated and unsettled.

"Then let's not talk about it. But what we do need to talk about is how we gon' stop that nigga. I have an idea. I have this friend named Rocky that I met at the center. Real cool. Used to be in the industry but now hates anything that has to do with the business. I'm one hundred percent sure Rocky would be willing to help us get that nigga."

"Since when are you making friends at the center?" Remmi huffed, slightly jealous that Shannelle had a friend she didn't know about.

"I don't tell you *everything*, bitch!"

"Since when?"

"Look, do wanna get this nigga or not?"

"Of course I do."

"Then shut up and listen."

Shannelle and Remmi walked into White Lotus looking like movie stars. It didn't matter that Remmi was the celebrity. When they were together, heads could not help but turn. Under ordinary circumstances, Remmi would never have shown up to

Art's birthday party, especially after what had happened at Cobalt Cantina. But she needed to be there to set their plan in motion. If Shannelle could have gone alone, it would have been better, but Remmi's name was the one on the list. It was her intention to just get Shannelle into the party so that she could leave, which was exactly what she did.

After being given VIP passes and standing in for a few photo ops in the foyer of the club, Remmi made a hasty exit, promising everyone that she would return shortly. Of course that was a lie, but a lot of lying was about to go down that night.

As Shannelle strolled toward the red velvet rope, which separated the so-called VIPs from the "ordinary" folk, all eyes were on her. Her eucalyptus green silk strapless dress fit every curve of her figure, hugging all the right places. Despite her diagnosis and weight loss, her body was still cut, showing remnants of all the years she'd spent dancing. Draped in Remmi's genuine emerald jewelry—compliments of Evret VonShayne, Shannelle glided through the foggy club. She headed in Art's direction with a one-track mind, ordered a cranberry juice, and scoped out the place. She wanted to see him first and hoped he didn't show up with his wife, but figured the Mrs. would be only a minor roadblock for a pussy hound like him. If Art went for her bait, which Shannelle had no doubt he would, she was sure that he'd find a way to get rid of the ol' ball and chain.

The VIP room was filled with important people, proving just how much of a big shot Arthur Haddox truly was. She had no idea he was such a major player in L.A. and became even more determined to stop him, figuring that he could do some real damage to Remmi's career. With her eye on the prize, Shannelle remained focused despite the fact that every five minutes some jerk was tugging at her arm offering alcohol, sex, or stardom. She thought about how just a year ago she would have accepted almost any offer from any celebrity to do anything they wanted her to do. But so much had changed for her since leaving New York. It was almost as if she had become another person. She started to want more out of life, although her future seemed so uncertain—so grim—and almost nonexistent. When she finally found an empty barstool, Shannelle scanned the room but didn't see Art anywhere. Momentarily forgetting why she was there, she stared into space as she sipped the deep red liquid and envisioned herself in a cap and gown marching down a narrow aisle to receive her degree. She imagined her mother in the audience cheering and realized that she hadn't even told her mother about her illness. While she had picked up the phone several times to dial it, each time it was about to ring, she'd place the receiver back upon its cradle.

Carol Anderson was one of those old project women who was a landmark in the neighborhood. Born and raised in the East River housing projects, she'd reared Shannelle in the same apartment she'd grown up in herself. She was a tough cookie who didn't take shit from anyone but whose heart was made of gold—if she liked you.

Shannelle thought about how much it was gonna break her mother's heart when she found out about her illness. She was Carol's only living child. When she was seven, her older brother, Shawn, had gotten killed by a gypsy cab while crossing the street on his way home from school. Since then, Shannelle had become Carol's life. Although they didn't see each other too much since she started working at the Temple, Shannelle worried about what would happen to her mother if she passed away, hoping that Carol would be able to go on after losing both of her children.

"Excuse me, but you look really familiar. Have we met?" a deep, sexy voice asked Shannelle, snapping her out of her train of thought. When she looked up, she found herself staring right into the sparkling ebony eyes of Arthur Haddox. He was far more handsome than the photos Remmi had given her and she could see why her best friend had been so open. He had a confidence about him that made you look, take notice, and want to know him better. He was impeccably dressed and groomed, with the whitest teeth Shannelle had ever seen. In a word, the nigga was *fi-yon*. Too bad he was about to go down.

"I've seen you around town before," Shannelle replied, extending her hand. Art gently gripped her fingers and kissed the tips, his soft perfectly shaped lips sending a small electrical charge up Shannelle's spine.

This is gonna be easier than I thought, she told herself.

"Really? What do you do?" Art asked.

"I'm a personal assistant slash manager slash celebrity babysitter," she giggled.

"Probably more babysitter than assistant and manager," he laughed.

"You got that right," she agreed.

"So do you have any clients I might have heard of?" he asked.

"Well, actually I'm just getting started, but I've got a few very talented prospects." Shannelle replied, trying to sound as poised as her suitor.

"Well, no matter what you do, always be sure to have an airtight contract."

"No doubt. My mama ain't raise no fool." Shannelle smiled.

"Or no ugly duckling." He paused for a moment as something behind her seemed to grab his attention.

"So what kinds of clients are you looking for?" Art inquired, directing his concentration back to Shannelle, still holding her hand in his.

"Well, since I just started, I figure I can't be too picky. I figure in this town, it can't be too hard to get clients. Everybody's a wannabe somebody."

"That's true."

"I worked briefly with Rementa Broughton. She was the best. Said I could use her as a reference if I needed to."

"I know Rementa well. Yeah. Me and Remmi are old friends. In fact, she's probably in here somewhere, I gave her her start, ya know." He chuckled, looking around as if he thought he would see her. "But, maybe I can help you. I know a lot of people here in this town."

"Well, you can help me by telling folks that I played a big role in Rementa's success. And then reminding those same people of how talented she is and how much influence I had on her as her personal manager," Shannelle requested.

"You sound more like a publicist than a manager. You sure Remmi didn't send you here?" he joked.

Before she could respond, a broadly built middle-aged white guy with piercing blue eyes came up to them and gave Art a manly hug. He was dressed far too young for his age, seeming not to know that middle-aged white guys aren't supposed to wear sagging Rocawear jeans.

"Happy birthday, man!" the man barked.

"Thanks, Lyor. Glad you could make it. Order something from the bar. It's open." Art grinned. Shannelle stood quietly as she observed the scene and waited for Art to get back to their conversation.

"Well, I'd like to get your expertise on anything I can do to officially establish my company." Shannelle smiled.

"Well, that can be arranged. But don't you go forgetting a brotha when you blow up." He breathed heavily in her ear, his

tongue gently licking the fine hairs on her lobe. "So," he continued, now backing up to face her. "How'd you get into my party? I
had a pretty exclusive guest list. Is my security slippin'?" Art questioned with a raised brow.

"No, actually, your security is right on point. I just have my
ways, that's all." Shannelle smiled.

"I'm sure you do," Art slyly replied, looking Shannelle up and
down as if he wanted to do her right there in the club. "Well,
however you got in, I'm glad you did. You're someone I definitely
wanna get to know better," he continued.

"Well, maybe we can make that happen."

"Oh, it's *gonna* happen."

As the night moved on, Shannelle remained at the bar as Art
came and went, strolling throughout the nightclub, mingling
amongst his guests. He had assured her that they would leave the
club together at the end of the night, and Shannelle had called
both Remmi and Rocky to let them know that the evening was
moving forward just as they had planned.

Shannelle took in the atmosphere around her as she patiently
waited on Art to be ready to leave the party, ignoring the advances
of every man who'd attempted to make her acquaintance. By
the time Art returned to where Shannelle sat perched stat-
uesquely upon a gold-and-scarlet-colored leather barstool nursing her fourth Cosmopolitan, it was 2 A.M. and she was more than
anxious to vacate.

"I see you're one of the good ones, Shannelle. Waiting for me
all this time. I been watching you. I thought you mighta gotten
tired and bounced with the next cat." Art grinned, stroking the
fold of Shannelle's back with his fingers.

"I told you I'd be here waiting, didn't I?" Shannelle purred
with a bat of her extra-long lashes.

"Yes, you did. . . . I like that. A woman of her word." Art snickered.

As he helped Shannelle from her seat, his hand made its way to her ample backside, where it found a comfortable home. She then followed him outside to a sparkling iridium silver metallic Mercedes-Benz SLK. The top was down on the luxury vehicle, revealing its black-and-red leather interior. The two-seater itself was orgasmic, making Shannelle moist between her legs just from the thought of riding it. It also kicked Art's fineness up another two notches, making Shannelle feel almost sorry for what she was about to do to him. Almost.

This is the muthafucka who's trying to ruin Remmi's career, she reminded herself as her body sank into the butter-soft crimson-colored seat.

Steadying his dream machine with his left hand as he pushed eighty up Cahuenga Boulevard, Art slowly licked his lips as he grew increasingly excited by Shannelle's presence.

"Damn you wearing that green, girl," he moaned, shaking his head from side to side.

"Green is so common. I'd like to call it *emerald,*" Shannelle corrected.

"Call it what you want. Anybody else would look like they should be carrying a box of Lucky Charms, wearing some green shit like that. But not you. You look like a precious gem." Art grinned.

Wanting to blush at his charm, Shannelle knew she had to remain focused on the job she had come to do. After a moment of silence, as he continued to steer the car with his left hand, Art's right hand eagerly inched up Shannelle's dress, pulling aside her Victoria's Secret thong, where he found her saturated vagina ready to receive his pulsating index finger. Feeling someone touch her middle for the first time in so long, Shannelle couldn't lie to herself. She was definitely enjoying the sensations as she continued to tell herself that Art deserved what was about to go down.

Nearly thirty minutes later, the car came to a screeching halt in front of the Mondrian Hotel in West Hollywood. Art jumped out of the driver's seat and ran into the five-star establishment, assuring his next conquest that it would take only a few minutes to secure a room. As he disappeared beyond the glass doors, Shannelle quickly dialed Remmi's phone to inform her accomplice of her exact whereabouts so that Remmi could call Rocky and let her know where she needed to go. The mission was to get it, hit it, and quit it.

Shannelle could barely contain herself in the elevator as she and Art rode up twenty-three floors to a beautiful one-bedroom suite. Art made everything so easy, being so fine, charming, and rich.

The deluxe king suite at the Mondrian was gorgeous. The sophisticated but sparsely furnished room glimmered by the golden light of a perfectly circular brightly illuminated moon. It was an amazingly clear night, and the enormous floor-to-ceiling windows offered a magnificently unobstructed view of the Los Angeles skyline. If the night's agenda had not been one of such wickedness, the elegant surroundings would have made the perfect backdrop for an incredibly romantic encounter.

As they crossed the threshold, Art's feet slid across the pale maple floors, wasting no time or words as he laid Shannelle down on the cream-colored king-sized duvet. Revenge or not, Shannelle hadn't felt such an intense burning between her legs in a long time. Her diagnosis had killed all her sexual desire and made her actually promise herself that she would never let another man touch her for as long as she lived. But promises were sometimes made to be broken.

As Art plunged his tongue deeply into Shannelle's mouth, she felt a tingly sensation in her veins. She understood why Remmi had been sprung. Arthur Haddox definitely had it going on. Strategically placing her in the center of the bed, Art began to remove her dress with his teeth before tracing the outline of her silhouette with his vibrating tongue. As if he had recently been listening to the 1990s R & B hit song "Freak Me," Art licked Shannelle up and down, letting his fingers find their way inside her slippery sugar walls, where he set up shop for more than fifteen minutes. Feeling good and unable to move, Shannelle allowed him to finger-fuck her as long as he was willing. However, when he was ready to go to the next level, she knew the time had come to get the plan rolling.

"I want this pussy now," he moaned. "You on the pill?"

"Yeah," she lied, not knowing what else to say.

"Good. I know I'm safe, and your pussy's too sweet to be rotten. If a woman like you is on the pill, we don't need a condom 'cause I ain't no faggot or junkie," he proudly announced.

Once upon a time that would have been all she needed to hear to let a dude run up inside her without using protection, but after getting educated at the center, Shannelle couldn't believe how stupid she had been. This was exactly how she'd contracted HIV, and if she could go back in time, she would have done so many things differently. Twenty minutes of passion certainly wasn't worth getting cut down in her prime. Her newfound education caused her to be amazed at what an ignorant and easy target Art was. Had she, too, once been that stupid?

Reveling in her third orgasm, ready to move forward, Shannelle closed her eyes tightly and whispered in Art's ear, "Slow down. I want to savor every moment. Let's make this last all night. Lemme make you a drink, baby."

"Definitely," Art moaned as he released her from his grasp and allowed her to get up from the bed.

As she headed over to the minibar, Shannelle glanced at Art's throbbing penis and sighed. *What a waste*, she thought as she opened a tiny bottle of Seagram's Gin and poured it into a nearby glass. "We need juice, baby," Shannelle cooed.

"Juice? Just gimme that shit straight," he sighed, massaging his crotch in an attempt to tame his eager and overzealous dick.

"I can't drink this straight! I'll get sick. And if I get sick, I won't be able to fuck. You do want me to be able to fuck, don't you?"

"Yeah, yeah . . . I definitely do . . . ," Art replied, jumping up and fastening his pants. Barefoot and sloppy, Art headed for the door of the suite. "I'll be right back. I'll get something from the machine down the hall. Be naked when I get back," he ordered.

No sooner had the door closed behind him, Shannelle rushed over to her purse and pulled out a tiny bottle of what she and Remmi liked to refer to as Love Potion Number 9—a man-made liquid concoction of the drugs GHB and Rohypnol, powerful enough to put an elephant to sleep. She emptied the contents into the glass of gin with only enough time to toss the empty container beneath the minibar before he thrust back into the room with a hard-on leading the way.

"You still got that dress on?" he asked.

"I'm sorry, baby. I was just about to take it off," Shannelle stuttered as she reached for her zipper.

"Okay, I got a can of Coke and a can of Minute Maid OJ. Take your pick," he offered, out of breath. He must have run like a bat out of hell to get back to what he felt was waiting for him.

"Don't worry about me. I wanna be nice and sober when I fuck your brains out!" Shannelle groaned like a wild beast. "But gimme the juice and I'll add it to your glass." She smiled with a wink.

Unsuspectingly, Art opened the can of juice and handed it over. "Such a gentleman," Shannelle teased.

As he stripped himself down on the way to the bed, Shannelle rushed over with his drink in hand.

"Have some. You're so anxious. Like a teenage boy. I want you to relax so you can enjoy me to the fullest," she sexily soothed.

Art grabbed the tumbler and emptied its contents into his mouth with one gulp. As she waited for the potion to work, Shannelle continued to undress him before gently pushing him down onto the wrinkled bed. Without resistance, he watched her slide his pants and boxers down to the floor and gently kiss his thighs before giving him a hand job he would never forget. As Art whimpered in ecstasy and began to throb from preejaculation, Shannelle slipped his pulsating dick inside her mouth and sucked it like it was an incredibly rich and chocolaty Tootsie Roll Pop with a prize in the center. It didn't take long for him to reach his climax, and when he did, his left leg began to shake uncontrollably while he cracked his neck and let out a yelp that almost frightened her, until she realized that that was his way of indicating his satisfaction. Already filled with plenty of Hennessy and chronic, now combined with a large dose of Love Potion Number 9, Art's body slumped over, leaving Shannelle with a suddenly limp dick in the side of her jaw.

Shannelle looked around the now silent room and took a deep breath. She then forcefully punched him in the chest to make sure he was completely spent before running over to her cell phone and dialing as quickly as she could.

"Rocky? You here?" she whispered into the receiver.

"You know it," Rocky replied.

"Room 2306," Shannelle said.

Within moments, there was a soft knock at the door of the

suite. As if her life depended on it, Shannelle opened it, and in strolled Rocky Banks, a six-foot-eight-inch drag queen, dressed in a hot pink satin corset and a silk chiffon full-length skirt. In eight-inch platform stiletto slides, Rocky stood nearly seven feet tall, towering over Shannelle like the Empire State Building, as her size 38 triple D silicone bosom seductively protruded from her bodice. Her honey-colored lace front wig flowed effortlessly down her back, and her makeup was tight. She was a beautiful sight to see—in a freak show kind of way. A pre-op transsexual, Rocky had been ready to take the final step into womanhood when her blood work indicated that she had been infected with HIV, putting a screeching halt on her plans. The surgery no longer an option, Rocky decided to dedicate her life to helping others with the virus and outing the down-low brothas who had once been her main suitors. With a vendetta against men in common, she and Shannelle had become fast friends at the center, and when Rocky heard about what Art was trying to do to Remmi, she was willing to do anything she could to help.

"Humm. He *is* a cute one." Rocky laughed, standing over Art's body.

"Yeah. I know. Too bad he's such a dick," Shannelle laughed.

"Well," Rocky said as she proceeded to position Art's naked body the way she wanted it. "Cute or not, he needs to be taught a lesson."

"I agree. Where's the camera?" Shannelle asked.

Rocky lifted up her skirt, exposing a tiny black holster that was attached to her right thigh, unsnapped it at the top, removed a Sony Cyber Shot DSC-T10, and handed it to Shannelle. She then proceeded to jerk Art off, bringing his dick to rock-hard status once again. Shannelle snapped away as Rocky changed positions multiple times—catching shots of what appeared to be Rocky giving Art a blow job, them embracing and kissing passionately, and Rocky nibbling at Art's ass. Rocky even removed her skirt so they could get a shot of what looked like Art fucking Rocky in her ass. If he even uttered a negative word about Remmi again, those pictures would be sent to his wife, his job, and every industry head in the country. Oh, yes. They had that nigga now! Revenge was *never* so sweet. . . .

After the extensive photo shoot, Shannelle checked her cell for Remmi's text message indicating that she was in the parking lot waiting. Shannelle and Rocky quietly slipped their clothes back on and did their best to remove all signs of their presence before tiptoeing out of the suite, stilettos in hand, careful not to disturb their still comatosed victim. Just like the heist at Shirley's Temple, it had all gone according to plan.

As the clock struck 5 A.M. and the sun began to show up for yet another day, Thelma, Louise, and their new sidekick in the middle cruised up North LaCienega Boulevard into the sunrise with smiles of accomplishment splashed across all of their seemingly angelic faces.

i don't know what you said to that Arthur Haddox prick, but whatever you told him, it worked. Seems he's been singing a very different tune when it comes to you these days. Telling folks how much he enjoyed working with you and how professional you are. And I guess the suits at Dreamtracks have forgotten about whatever it was that he did say because they definitely want you to come in for a reading," Allen informed Remmi over her speakerphone as she did twenty-five miles per hour uphill on her Precor treadmill. Dr. Phil held her interest on the living room TV before her, but Allen's news forced her to turn her attention to their conversation.

"Really?" Remmi asked with little surprise. After she'd printed out the pictures of Art and Rocky, a nice little care package was overnighted to his office with a large stamp that read CONFIDEN-TIAL on the front. Shannelle followed up with a call letting Art know what he would and would not be saying about Remmi from that point forward. Of course he went ballistic at first, threatening to do everything and anything to bring death upon Remmi and Shannelle, who he now knew were in cahoots. But he was power-less. He didn't know any real details about either of them at that point, and all he could do was live with his fury and comply with their demands. And when Rocky called him and threatened to go public with their "relationship," he really knew they meant business.

"Yeah. They want you in their offices tomorrow at eleven."

"Tomorrow at eleven! Allen, that's too soon! I'll never be ready to read that soon. I need to get the book and brush up on the char-acter. I need to do my research!" Remmi squealed, pressing the COOL DOWN button on the treadmill control panel.

"Remmi. When Dreamtracks calls, you answer. I thought you said you read the book."

"I did. But that was a few years ago!"

"Well, pick it up, dust it off, and refresh your memory. You have exactly twenty hours to prepare. That should be more than enough time."

"More than enough time!"

"Look, Remmi. You've done two movies in less than a year. You'll be fine. You're a natural, remember?"

"All right. I'll be there," she sighed.

"Good. And by the way, some man came here looking for you. Said he's some relative of yours. I don't know how he found my office, but since he had your last name and those same piercing hazel eyes you got—I told him I'd pass on the message. He said his name was Charles. Charles Broughton. Didn't leave any information but said he'd stop by again. I told him I didn't know when the next time you'd be up here, but he said he'd keep trying till he caught you. Truth be told, he was a little weird," Allen told her. There was a moment of silence before he asked if she was still on the line.

"Yeah, um, yeah, I'm still here," Remmi replied in a daze.

"Know anybody by that name?"

"No, but my family's kinda spread out and we're not very close. There's a lotta Broughtons in this world," Remmi lied.

"Yeah, he's probably some distant cousin wanting to borrow money or something like that. You know how family can be. Everybody's got a hand out these days. He looked like he was in his fifties. Good-looking man but no spring chicken. And like I said, he had those same eyes you have. Must run in your family. Looked old enough to be your father, but you've probably got all kinds of people looking for you since *Butta* came out. Wait until *Moon Circles the Sun* hits. *People* magazine is already begging to do a story on you, and *Essence* wants you for the September cover," Allen said.

"Wow," Remmi nervously answered.

"You might really wanna consider hiring a real business manager. I don't think your friend is gonna be equipped to handle the momentum your career is about to pick up," Allen continued.

"Yeah, maybe you're right," Remmi robotically replied, blankly staring into space. In the distant land of fiber optics, Remmi could hear Allen talking about how her schedule was about to go into overtime and how much promise her career had, et cetera, until she said good-bye on autopilot and clicked the OFF button on her cordless phone.

After she hung up, Remmi drove to the nearest bookstore to pick up another copy of *Nyagra's Falls* to replace the one she'd mislaid. She had to prepare herself for her meeting and begin her research on the next character she would become. Distracted by the memory of Allen's final comments, Remmi wiped perspiration from her forehead and turned up the air-conditioner in her car. Allen's voice kept echoing in her mind.

Charles. Charles Broughton, a voice repeated in Remmi's head, amplified with vibrato and bass. She sat at a stop sign longer than necessary as her eyes slowly blinked and she heard it again.

Charles. Charles Broughton.

A faceless person Remmi could remember her mother mentioning by name on only one occasion—an occasion so heated that it would stay etched in Remmi's mind forever. A man her mother always referred to as "the devil himself"—a man whom Remmi had heard Rita describe as "my mother's son"—but never "my brother." Remmi could never understand why her mother hated her own brother so. She could not comprehend what a person's own flesh and blood could do to deserve the hatred her mother felt for that man. Until the day of her mother's death, Remmi was confused by the depth of Rita's loathing for her only sibling.

Remmi could remember her mother hitting her only two times in her life. Once when she'd gotten caught in the staircase of Shannelle's building smoking weed and once when she'd found a wooden chest in the back of her mother's closet while looking for clothes to play dress-up in. The trunk, a medium-sized wooden chest, contained all kinds of paraphernalia, from Remmi's birth certificate to her mother's first bra. As Remmi sorted through the trunk's contents, she rummaged through everything from sex toys to old photographs. It was in this chest that Remmi found a picture of her mother dressed in a beautiful pink frilly dress and shiny black patent leather shoes. Beside her in the picture stood a handsome young man, approximately the same age, at what appeared to be some sort of dance or party. Both children were dressed up and looked as though they were having the time of their lives. On the back of the picture, in pretty cursive writing was *The Twins, Rita & Charles—13 years old.* Up until that point, Remmi had never even known that her mother was a twin. In fact, she did not even know that she had an uncle. She had never met any of her mother's family except for a great-aunt who passed away when Remmi was only six years old. And whenever Remmi would ask her mother about her grandparents, Rita would always reply, "Some people are better off being strangers." She refused to say any more than that, and it was made clear that the topic was not open for discussion. So when Remmi inquired about the photograph labeled "the twins," her mother, slapped her into eternal silence regarding the topic. A fire in Rita's eyes sent a warning to Remmi never to mention the issue again. And she didn't. On the day Rita committed suicide, she mentioned her twin again, referring to him as the person who had impregnated her with Remmi. All her life, Rita had carried around the pain of the abuse she had endured at the hands of her very own brother. And for the last seven years, Remmi had been burying the fact that her father had indeed been her uncle.

"Uncle Daddy," she muttered aloud as the soft echo of her voice gently bounced off the car windows.

She hadn't talked about the way she was conceived with anyone on the planet—not even Shannelle. She'd never repeated what Rita had said to her on the day that she died. Remmi merely kept her mother's revelation beneath a thick shell of scar tissue, never to be stated aloud for anyone else to hear. Remmi figured that as long as she was the only one who knew the facts, then no one else ever had to know. But now, here this man was—the monster who had raped her mother, the man who was her father *and* her uncle—a man Remmi considered so evil and vile, she wished him dead. Here he was trying to reach out to her, showing up at her agent's office and trying to connect for some unknown reason. This was truly not someone Remmi wanted to face. He was her dirty secret, and he represented the shame she had successfully hidden from the world for so long, reminding her that she was a product not only of rape, but of incest as well. Remmi decided right then and there that if their eyes ever did meet, Charles Broughton had best be ready to meet his maker, who she was quite sure was the devil himself.

21

*t*he *rapid* pace at which Remmi's life was going had her in a whirlwind. Everything was surreal, and she felt as if she were having an out-of-body experience—like she was watching an image of herself from a distance. Her life was beginning to unfold right before her eyes, and she was living her dream—a dream she once could only have imagined. At twenty-five years old, she was on her way to becoming an official Hollywood starlet. She'd been in Cali only eighteen months, had already completed two films, and was attacking a role that would land her amongst Hollywood's black elite—and the elite in general. Most actresses struggled for years to acquire such a pivotal role. Here she was, less than two years in, being given a job coveted by every black actress in Hollywood. She had no doubt that Rita was seated at the right side of the Most High asking God for every blessing. Remmi felt her mother's presence and each night talked to Rita before going to bed, hoping that eventually Rita might visit in a dream. Like a little girl on the first day of school, Remmi often yearned for her mother, no matter how turbulent their relationship had been. She wished that she could share all her blessings with Rita and make up for some of the pain her mother must have had in her own life. But she knew Rita was present, and she was never without the feeling of her mother's constant watchful eye.

Despite being distracted by the mention of Charles Broughton, Remmi managed to focus long enough to nail the role of Nyagra Ensley from the moment she walked into the audition at Dreamtrack's headquarters. She looked the part, she spoke the part, she *was* the part. As soon as they laid eyes on her, the powers that be had decided that Rementa Broughton was the only actress who could truly bring the role to life. It seemed that in a matter of moments, she was thrust from urban video vixen to major Hollywood player. And she was about to embark on the next level of her career—a level that would toss her into the homes of millions.

Shannelle, you have to eat! And why do you have this air-conditioner on full blast? It's freezing in here!" Remmi shouted at her best friend as she waltzed over to the window and shut down the cooling apparatus. The shrimp Parmesan Remmi had brought home sat untouched beside Shannelle's bed. For the past two weeks, Remmi had been trying to get Shannelle to eat, and for the past two weeks Shannelle had been tossing the food into the trash, which caused her weight to drop and her illness to accelerate. Shannelle had also stopped taking her medication. It was as if she had fully given up and wanted actually to die.

"I eat," Shannelle dryly replied, not taking her eyes off the television.

Annoyed at the fact that she was being dismissed, Remmi walked over to Shannelle's bed and yanked the comforter from her friend's body, tossing it violently upon the floor. Shannelle was dressed in a Victoria's Secret cotton tank and boxers, and Remmi could see the protruding bones of her best friend, a woman whose meaty and voluptuous assets had once made her a top earner at Shirley's Temple. As if she had just seen the ghost of Christmas past, Remmi let out a gasp. Her partner in crime looked like a refugee from a third-world country. It was as if she'd dropped 20 pounds overnight—or had Remmi been so busy rehearsing for her new film that she had not noticed that her only sister was withering away right before her very eyes?

Like a drug addict who'd dropped her syringe, Shannelle scrambled to the floor, grabbing at the blanket that had covered her emaciated bones, attempting to hide behind its fluffiness.

"Shannelle, you are wasting away to nothing! Have you looked in the mirror lately?" Remmi screamed, grabbing her best friend and forcing her to face the oval mirror, which rested above the dresser. Shannelle refused to look at her own reflection, tightly closing her eyes.

"Where's your medication?" Remmi barked, heading over to Shannelle's Gucci knapsack, which sat beneath the bedroom window. Shannelle did not answer, but watched in terror as her friend went through the bag and pulled out a brown medicine bottle filled to the rim with pills.

"You haven't even been taking these, have you?" she yelled once again.

"No! No, I haven't! And I'm not!" Shannelle finally replied, tears streaming down her sallow face. "Why should I? In case you haven't heard, there's no cure for AIDS, Remmi! Do I wanna live like this? Do I wanna live another five years not being able to have a relationship or get my groove on with any nigga I choose? *No!* If I have to live like this, I'd rather be dead!"

"Bitch, you gonna take these fuckin' pills! And you gonna get better! And they *gonna* find a cure. Every single day they're getting closer. And I'm gonna make sure you get the best care money can buy. But you have to take this medicine. And you have to eat! And you have to get up outta this bed! 'Cause, bitch, you can't leave me all alone in this fuckin' world by myself. I won't let you!" Remmi screeched, her own cheeks now soaked with tears as her hands trembled with fury and fear. The two best friends sobbed uncontrollably on each other's shoulder. They cried for themselves and for each other. They cried for the past and for the present. But most of all, they cried for the future—a future that was unknown and uncertain.

ehearsals for the film adaptation of *Nyagra's Falls* were going surprisingly well. The crew and cast were wonderful, and Remmi was having the time of her life. Despite worrying about Shannelle, she managed to show up to the studio each day with a smile on her face, ready to embark on another day of transformation into a character she could truly identify with.

The ensemble cast consisted of quite a few Hollywood veterans who were happy and eager to embrace her and take her beneath their wings. It was a family-like environment unlike any Remmi had ever experienced, complete with a maternal figure, who was cast as the mother of the lead character. Remmi looked forward to sitting with Mima during breaks and listening to her stories. She was one of those old Hollywood actresses who came up with the likes of Ruby Dee and Ossie Davis, and boy did she always have a story to tell about the early days of black Hollywood. Needless to say, Remmi was enamored of her and eager to hear all that Mima had to say, secretly wishing that she could have grown up with a grandmother like this woman—or at least an aunt. The only person who was a bit less inviting was Remmi's old nemesis, Gayle Ford, who had somehow gotten lucky enough to be given the role of Nyagra's best friend, Trish.

Remmi had heard through the rap-video grapevine that Gayle had pretty much taken her slot amongst all the urban video directors once Remmi had made her move to Hollywood. After her success in *Butta*, under the advice of her agent, Remmi refused to do any more music videos—a move that was actually very good for her career in Hollywood. But Remmi's absence made way for Gayle's star to shine, allowing her to secure herself amongst video-ho royalty and even appearing in a few uncensored clips baring her ample breasts. For the life of her, Remmi could not figure out how Gayle had gotten the role of Trish but assumed that she had merely sucked or fucked the right Dreamtracks executive.

Remmi was not threatened or impressed. No matter how much beauty Gayle possessed, she could never be the starlet Remmi was. She didn't have the charisma, the skills, the drive, or the brains. And most important, she did not have a mama up in heaven watching out for her. Remmi almost fell off her seat the day Gayle walked onto the rehearsal set dressed in a silk yellow painter's shirt and jeans. The director, Richard Ratzenberg, made the swift introduction, and both actresses offered unenthusiastic salutations. Although Remmi knew that playing the part of best friends with her archnemesis would be a huge challenge, she reminded herself of her talents, her paycheck, and professionalism—as well as of the fact that she was indeed the star and would not be upstaged by the supporting role of a "friend." After all, the film was titled *Nyagra's Falls*, and she was Nyagra.

Like the professional that she clearly was, Remmi arrived on the set at her normal 5 A.M. call time. Although rehearsals didn't begin until six, Remmi liked to relax as she ate breakfast and reviewed her lines. This particular day she would be rehearsing a "sister girl" sequence with Gayle—a scene that she wasn't particularly looking forward to. Due to their history, Remmi and Gayle had chosen to remain on the opposite ends of the set unless they had to interact. Remmi had no desire to befriend her, and Gayle was even less eager. While no one on the set knew the reason why the two despised each other, the tension was evident. Every time Remmi looked at Gayle, she would remember the gorilla of a security guard with his dirty hands between Gayle's legs, and she'd chuckle. But there was a part of her that respected Gayle's gangsta. She had no doubt that Gayle was a certified hustler who would do anything and anyone to further her career, and Remmi knew a bitch like that could never be trusted. After all, *she* was a bitch like that.

The morning had gone smoothly, and each day the movie was closer to its first day of shooting. The cast had incredible chemistry, and even Remmi and Gayle's scripted friendship appeared genuine.

As everyone headed for lunch, Remmi decided to spend a few moments alone in her dressing room to mentally regroup. She was tired from staying up the previous night with Shannelle but refused to let it affect her performance. As she strolled off set, Remmi could hear a voice having a conversation behind a stairwell door. Leaning in closer, she realized that the voice belonged to Gayle. The fact that she was chatting behind the closed staircase door made Remmi raise an eyebrow, curious about the words she heard falling from the lips of her competition.

"Well, if something *were* to happen, I *know* I'd be the only one they'd consider for the lead. I've been practicing with her, and I know all her lines," Remmi heard Gayle say. She did not hear another voice and assumed Gayle was speaking into a cell phone. Gayle's statement made Remmi lean in even closer.

"Nothing that would get us into too much trouble. Just something to throw her performance off. Something that would break Little Miss Perfect's concentration. Something to make her late or not show up to the set at all. But it has to happen soon. We start filming next week, ya know," Gayle continued. There was a pause, as if she were listening to the person on the other end of the line, until her voice finally softly echoed once again, "Well, I think I have just the thing. I've been doing my research on Little Miss Black Hollywood for a minute now. Everyone seems to think that she's some sort of golden child. Up until now she's never had a scandal in the tabloids. Not even an ounce of bad press. Now's the time," Gayle laughed.

Remmi heard Gayle flip her cell phone shut, so she quickly shuffled away from the hollow door. She was angry that Gayle was scheming on her role, but not surprised. Controlling the urge to jump on Gayle with all fours, Remmi rushed down the hallway toward her dressing room. She would never be able to prove what she had heard, so she had to devise a plan to ruin Gayle first, and she had to be very smart about it.

Emotions are the stupid woman's downfall, Remmi could hear Rita say. And stupid Remmi was not.

"thanks for coming over on such short notice, Officer Harris." Remmi smiled that million-dollar smile that was carrying her to the top. She wore a canary yellow halter-top-and-shorts set without any undergarments. Her muscular but feminine legs sparkled from the Johnson's Baby Oil gel she had smoothed on ten minutes before his arrival, while her succulent breasts jiggled like a bowl of strawberry Jell-O. She'd set the air-conditioner on HIGH ensuring that her nipples stood fully erect to entice her former lover even more.

"Damn, baby. Every time I see you, you look better and better. You know I can't resist you." Orlando grinned.

"I would have called sooner, I've just been so busy with the new film and all. But you know I can never resist you either. Can I get you a glass of wine?" With a smile, Remmi headed toward the kitchen.

"Oh, no thanks. I'm still on duty. But I'd love to take a rain check," Orlando answered.

"Yeah, we have to get together when you have some time to get loose," Remmi suggested returning to the living room with a glass of merlot for herself. Orlando had made himself quite comfortable on her sofa, and Remmi placed herself beside him. She wanted him fully aroused before she moved in for the kill. Plus, he still looked damn good in his uniform, and she hadn't had any in a while. Yeah, Orlando Harris was an opportunist, but his bedroom skills were impeccable. And although she was definitely planning to give him a little middle-of-the-day booty, that day she needed more from him than a good stiff one between her legs.

"Oh, I have a little time. I just don't wanna smell like liquor when I get back to the precinct," he laughed.

Remmi tossed her right leg over his left, and he began to vigorously rub her thigh. She in turn gently kissed his neck and loosened the collar of his uniform. His fingers moved to her heated middle, and he rubbed her like a dog in heat before sliding his dark blue crisply creased trousers beneath his buttocks. His nine and a half inches stood at attention as if saluting the president before Officer Harris pulled a Trojan from his crumpled pocket and placed it into the palm of Remmi's hand. In one motion, she ripped it open with her front teeth, straddled him with both her legs, and slid the lubricated condom upon his throbbing penis. A pool of fluid awaited him between her legs, allowing him to slide inside her with the greatest of ease. She then proceeded to lay it on him as only she could, in and out, up and down, Remmi style—a style that always kept them coming back for more.

When they were finished twenty minutes later, Officer Harris lay limp on Remmi's sofa with a smile of satisfaction splashed upon his face. She figured he was more than ready to hear her request and definitely in no position to refuse her.

"So," Remmi began, removing the condom and wiping off his slippery penis with a warm damp towel. "I know it's been a minute since we laid up. But I'm always thinking of you," she lied.

"Yeah, me, too," he sighed with closed eyes.

"Baby, I just been so stressed out with this new movie," Remmi explained, gently stroking his coarse black pubic hairs and walking her fingertips up and down his inner thigh.

"Relax, baby. You're a star. You know that. Whenever you feel stressed, just call big poppa, and I'll help you release it." He grinned, kissing her breast.

"I know. You always make me feel better."

"And I always will. You name it. I'll fix it."

"Really?"

"Really."

"Well, there is this one itty-bitty issue I've been dealing with. But I bet *you* could make it go away for me."

"Name it."

"Well, there's this actress in the movie I'm doing. She's so jealous of me. It's just making her do crazy things! And I have no idea why she hates me so!" Remmi innocently squeaked.

"Bitches are like that, ma. You should be used to it. I'm sure chicks been hatin' on you your whole life."

"I am. But this one is psycho! She wants to ruin my career! I overheard her saying it. And to tell you the truth, I'm kinda scared," Remmi lied again.

"You? Scared?" Orlando chuckled. "Girl, you don't seem like you scared of nothing."

"Well, I am. I'm scared of losing my career. A career I've worked so hard to build," she replied matter-of-factly, actually telling the truth.

"So whaddaya want me to do?" Orlando asked.

"Well, if I could have it my way, I'd ruin her first—you know—beat her to the punch." Remmi laughed, as if she was joking, although she wasn't.

"Are you serious?"

"No, I'm joking. Unless you gon' do it," Remmi teased as she began to softly jerk the tip of his dick, causing it to rise again.

Orlando grinned like a Cheshire cat, not only at the conversation they were engaged in, but also at the incredible sensation spreading throughout his groin.

"So what do you think would ruin this bitch?" he asked, his eyes closed in pleasure.

"Oh, I don't know," Remmi cooed. "I mean, it's not like I've ever actually done anything like this before. I'm really not even built like that. I really try to let things go. My mama taught me to turn the other cheek. But this bitch has been asking for it for a minute."

Now taking Orlando's manhood deeply into her mouth with a

sopping gulp, she tenderly licked the fold where his testicles began, sending a sensation through the officer's nerves and simultaneously forcing all the sperm in his body to rise to the very tip of his penis just one pulse short of ejaculation. In a word, Remmi had caused Officer Harris to have an orgasm without coming, causing him to become so physically and mentally debilitated that all he could do was comply with any request she was about to make.

"But I was thinking," she began, now stroking him once again with her hands and bringing him back into consciousness. "Maybe we could set her up or something . . . I don't know. Maybe a fine. Or I'm sure an upstanding highly decorated officer of the law like yourself could find something illegal in her car or hotel room or something like that," Remmi softly suggested, caressing the tip of his penis that was now harder than a piece of frozen chocolate.

"Yeah, that would do it," Orlando moaned, relishing in the pleasure Remmi was giving him once again.

"So whaddaya say, baby? Can you make that happen for me? Maybe a ziplock bag filled with crack or something like that might *magically* appear in her car? Enough to get her kicked off the project, out of Hollywood, and sent to rehab for six months?" Remmi inquired with a raised brow as she now engaged in a full-fledged jerk-off session.

"You really think she's trying to ruin you, baby?" Orlando managed to mutter through his ecstasy.

"I'm sure of it."

"Well, we can't let that happen."

"No, we certainly can't," she retorted. With his penis now fully erect and ready, Remmi prepped him with another prophylactic and climbed upon him once again, bringing L.A.'s finest to the height of passion and sealing the deal between them. She was glad she hadn't fully cut him off two months ago. She knew his badge would come in handy one day.

the anchor on the morning news looked emotionlessly into the camera as if he were speaking directly to Remmi. The newspaper left on her front door step confirmed his story, its headline announcing to the world that her problem had indeed been taken care of.

ASPIRING HOLLYWOOD ACTRESS ARRESTED ON DRUG CHARGES flashed like a neon light above a full-body photo of Gayle Ford wearing a pair of shiny handcuffs compliments of the Los Angeles Police Department. Beside her, the arresting officer, Officer Orlando Harris, stood dutifully. All Remmi could do was smile. Of course, filming would be pushed back, as they would have to find another actress to play the role of Trish. But it would be well worth the delay. Remmi did not know what Gayle had planned to do to her, but she was sure that she was the last thing on Gayle's mind now.

Orlando had assured her that he would handle the situation, and he did. Less than seventy-two hours after Remmi had given him Gayle's address—which she managed to obtain by suggesting that she and Gayle get together outside of rehearsal to go over the script—Orlando made sure that her costar was no longer a threat to Remmi or her career. Almost amazed at herself, Remmi savored the taste of her freshly squeezed orange juice as she watched the story unfold on the early morning news. It was at that moment that it occurred to her that anything and anyone could be sabotaged at any time should they make the wrong enemy. As the cold pulp hit the back of her throat, Remmi giggled and shook her head. She had not realized how much of a force she was to be reckoned with, and as she patted herself on the back for a job well done, she told herself that this was only the beginning.

With Gayle's drug possession charge pending, as Remmi had planned, the powers that be had no choice but to eject her from the project. She clearly had more important things to worry about—like her freedom—and the studio did not want negative publicity sabotaging the film. Of course, this made Remmi very happy and quite eager for the studio to find a replacement, as she was anxious to get on with the process.

After a tireless fifteen-day search for someone to take on the role, it was finally narrowed down to three actresses, Remmi's favorite being a young thespian by the name of Kara Sweeting. Kara, a pretty girl about five years younger than Remmi, hailed from Baltimore and could actually have passed for Remmi's sister. They had a similar look and an uncanny chemistry. Eager to make Gayle a distant memory in the minds of the producers, Remmi was so determined to get Kara the role that she made it a point to meet with her secretly to rehearse. Thus, when the time came for what was supposed to be an impromptu screen test, the two actresses played off each other flawlessly, effortlessly, and naturally—making the director's decision very easy. With extra preparation under her belt, Kara's performance soared miles above those of the other candidates, proving that their clandestine rehearsals had paid off. And what had started out as Remmi sealing the coffin on the acting career of Gayle Ford ultimately resulted in the acquisition of a protégée. Remmi herself could not deny the fact that she had not clicked with another female in the way that she and Kara had clicked since she and Shannelle had pricked their fingers and smashed them together in the second grade. With Remmi's support and endorsement, Kara was handed the role of Trish with a big red bow on top, and the silhouette of Remmi's biggest rival was quickly forgotten.

As if the production had not been touched by scandal, filming began without further hesitation once Kara was a secured member of the cast. Having to make up the time lost, the movie was scheduled to be shot in a mere eight weeks; which suited Remmi just fine. And although Allen had three potential blockbuster scripts sitting on his desk with Remmi's name on them, she knew she had to take some time off to spend with Shannelle, who seemed to be getting weaker by the day.

As the sixth week of filming came to a close, Remmi grabbed her bag from her dressing room and headed to her car. She was pooped and needed a way to truly unwind. Her days had been filled with long hours on the set and her nights were occupied with long nights taking care of Shannelle. Strolling toward her little BMW 3 series coupe, a monthly rental she had recently obtained, Remmi heard her name called from behind. Turning around to see Kara's brightly lit face beneath the California sun, Remmi smiled.

"Rementa," Kara began.

"Remmi," she warmly instructed.

"Okay—Remmi." Kara blushed. "I wanted to ask you if you wouldn't mind us getting together sometime. I'm pretty new here in L.A., and I could use some camaraderie with someone who's been here for a while. I also haven't really had a chance to thank you for everything you did for me."

"Okay, sure . . . when?"

"Um, well, I don't know about you, but I'm pretty hungry . . . ," Kara replied patting her stomach. Remmi looked at her watch and thought for a minute. It had been a while since she'd been anywhere other than the set, home, and the gym. She could actually use a little social activity. After all, Shannelle was at the crisis center and would not be home until later.

"Okay, why not? I could eat." Remmi shrugged. They jumped in Remmi's car and, at Kara's suggestion, headed toward West Pico Boulevard to Roscoe's House of Chicken n Waffles. After eating rabbit food all week, they were both in the mood for something hearty. Roscoe's would hit the spot.

Greeted by a buff and friendly security guard, the two women found an empty table and buried their faces in the grease-stained menus. Roscoe's was a place that served breakfast all day long, and Remmi's stomach rumbled as she craved the big mama special. She knew she'd have to spend an extra forty-five minutes on the treadmill the next morning, but satisfying her palate, which often craved high-calorie treats, was worth having to do extra every once in a while. As she thanked herself for being focused enough to give herself that periodic additional push and Rita for giving her pretty good genes, Remmi placed the order for the mega meal with the buxom light-skinned waitress, while Kara requested the candy yam special.

While they waited for the food to arrive, they chatted about the film. They were both excited about Kara being added to the cast and how good their chemistry was. Kara was so grateful that she had Remmi's stamp of approval, not only because this was her first real role, but also because she looked up to Remmi and aspired to be like her.

"I still can't believe I'm here," Kara said in awe. "I mean other than a few local commercials in Baltimore, this is the first thing I've auditioned for since I've been in L.A. It's crazy. . . . I came out here with my dad a few months ago and, by the grace of God, got an agent really fast . . . but I feel like I owe this all to you for taking me under your wing."

"No, not really. I only embraced you 'cause I recognized your skills. So you really owe it all to your talent. I just helped speed up the process."

"You're being really modest, but I do feel like I owe you so much. I mean one day I was in the PGC mall shopping for luggage to come here, and two months later I'm in a network television movie playing the best friend of a well-known Hollywood actress! I'm just amazed that it's all happening so fast."

"Well, that's how this business is. I mean, one day I was modeling in a fashion show, and five days later I was heading out here to be in *Butta*," Remmi remembered.

"Yeah—but you were a video vixen for a while. I've watched your career for a long time. From your videos with Ludacris to Jay-Z all the way to your JCPenney commercial. It's because of you that I even started acting at all."

"Thanks for the compliment, girl. But honestly, you do have skills. You remind me a lot of myself when I first got out here. The fact of the matter is that when you got it, you got it." Remmi laughed.

"Man, do I got it?" Kara questioned with a snicker.

"Well, you definitely got somethin'."

The waitress placed their heart attack–inducing food before them, and without another word, they both began digging in as if they were death row inmates savoring their final meal the night before execution.

"A lotta luck," Kara finally responded, her chin dripping with the sugary sweet syrup that drowned an otherwise nutritionally sound sweet potato.

"I don't believe in luck. I think things are celestially planned for you, and it's up to you to seek them out," Remmi matter-of-factly said.

"Celestially planned?" Kara laughed. "What's that?"

"Celestial—as in the stars? Astrology? YaknowhatImean."

"Oh—so like I'm a Virgo, right? And does that mean that as a Virgo, Virgo-like things happen to me?"

Remmi chuckled and sipped on her cranberry orange juice before responding. "No—not really. I guess I just believe in fate. What's for you is for you. What's meant to be, will be. Ya know? . . . I think you were meant to be here in Hollywood with me doing this movie. I think this role is for you. Part of your destiny. Part of your fate."

"Okay. I can get with that. I mean I definitely feel a connection between me and you. Kinda like we've known each other already."

"Yeah, I feel it, too. It's kinda weird though 'cause I don't really have too many female friends. Only one, actually. And I consider her more of a sister than a friend. But you're right. You and I pretty much clicked right away."

Kara smiled. Although she wanted so much to delve deeper into the connection that she and Remmi shared, she remained silent. Common sense told her that it was definitely too soon to talk to Remmi about anything serious. Sure—the two of them had hit it off quickly and were seemingly on their way to becoming fast friends, but the real reason Kara had come to L.A. needed to be concealed for a while longer. It had been her mission when she purchased her plane ticket and headed out West not only to jump-start her acting career, but also to seek Remmi out. Landing the role as Trish only made the excursion that much sweeter. She had been prepared to be in California for months—or maybe even years—before coming face-to-face with Rementa Broughton. Kara had never dreamed that it wouldn't even take two months for them to share a set. Perhaps Remmi was right—maybe it was part of a celestial plan. But Kara knew she had to play her cards right, for the wrong move could ruin everything for everyone. What she really wanted to discuss with Remmi needed to wait until their friendship was firmly established. She wanted Remmi to really get to know and like her as a person. Kara felt it was imperative for Remmi to trust her as a confidante before she discussed anything significant with her. Only then, Kara believed, would she be able to receive the response from her hero that she was truly looking for.

22

Shannelle's fragile body lay motionless beneath the sterile white sheets. The glare from the halogen light, coupled with the sun beaming brightly from the sky through the east-side window nearly blinded Remmi as she observed her best friend resting so still in the aluminum-framed hospital bed. Shannelle's doe-shaped eyes were now reduced to mere slits upon her face, leaving only a small hint of the brilliance they once possessed. Watching the person closest to her deteriorate right before her eyes was the most difficult thing Remmi had ever experienced. She wanted so desperately to jump on Shannelle, tightly wrap her fingers around her neck, and choke her to her senses, begging her not to give up. But Remmi stood like a statue, almost paralyzed, tears streaming down her face and her heart breaking in two at the sight of her only family member giving up on life.

Determined not to live her life combating the disease, and

refusing to be a burden on Remmi, Shannelle had done everything in her power to accelerate the virus spreading throughout her body. Unbeknownst to Remmi, who had been consumed with the movie, for nearly two months, Shannelle had been pouring her cocktails down the bathroom drain within moments of their delivery from the pharmacy, while her other meds were flushed down the toilet with the same urgency seconds later. She rarely ate, and when she did, it was processed fast food that greased the inside of her already weakened stomach, forcing her to violently regurgitate soon after ingestion. From the moment Remmi left the condo in the morning until she returned in the evening, Shannelle made frequent trips to the patio, where she smoked unfiltered Black & Mild cigars and even weed—which she justified was acting as a natural painkiller. For additional numbing, Shannelle also made it a point to stay drunk, keeping a flask filled with Hennessey close to her side at all times—she no longer cared about living. Because Remmi was gone most of the day, Shannelle was at liberty to behave as she chose without having to deal with the constant nagging and reprimands of her best sister friend. Still, Remmi knew something was up because each and every day Shannelle looked worse than she had the day before. Shannelle's complexion became sallow, her hair limp; Remmi could smell the stench of liquor on her breath, and ugly lesions had begun to form on her arms and legs. Her behavior had caused the virus to turn into full-blown AIDS, and almost overnight Shannelle had begun to look not only like a woman battling the disease, but also a woman who was clearly losing the fight.

"Ms. Broughton, can we please speak privately?" Dr. Foster requested. His baritone voice startled Remmi, snapping her out of deep thoughts about a happier past and back into a much gloomier present.

"Sure," Remmi replied, following the doctor out into the busy hallway. Her honey-colored eyes burned from sobbing and sleep deprivation, making it difficult for her to focus on the face of the man who was about to inform her of the fate of the one person on the planet who had always been there for her.

Believing that Shannelle and Remmi were truly blood relatives, the physician began, "Your sister's condition is deteriorating quickly."

"I can see that," Remmi managed to mutter, though the lump in her throat had reduced her voice to a simple murmur.

"While there's not too much we can do about the acceleration of her decline—especially now that she has developed pneumonia, I definitely believe her mental state has a great deal to do with how quickly she is going to go."

Remmi stood silently as the doctor's monotone voice hit her ears like a ton of bricks. Up until that moment, Shannelle's fate had never been verbalized, allowing Remmi to tightly hold on to a hope that her best friend would get better. After all, there were many cases of people who had been able to live relatively normal lives with the virus for many years. With new medical technology developing each and every day, Remmi believed Shannelle would live long enough to benefit from a cure. If only she could just get her best friend to *want* to live—to *want* to get better—and to *want* to conquer her illness.

"Guaranteed, if Shannelle does not want to live, she will not," Dr. Foster continued. Remmi shook her head in agreement. She knew the doctor's words were true, and Remmi was a huge believer of mind over matter.

"I have to be honest with you, though. It does not look good. I believe Shannelle had been living with the disease for quite some time before she was diagnosed. Her condition has progressed too rapidly for someone who was only recently infected. And to make matters worse, her blood work has indicated that before she was admitted to the hospital, she had not been taking any of her medication. She's also been doing things that are detrimental to a healthy person's immune system—never mind someone battling the AIDS virus. The results of her tests show that she's been consuming plenty of toxins. Were you aware that she's been drinking alcohol and smoking marijuana?"

"I knew about the alcohol. But I didn't know about the weed. I'm gone most of the day. I hired someone to stay with her during the hours that I was gone, but she fired them."

"Yes. I see your sister's very headstrong and stubborn. If only she could use those attributes to conquer this disease, she could probably live a very full life," Dr. Foster said. "But to be honest, if she keeps this defeatist attitude, she won't see the first of next month." Dr. Foster was straightforward and honest, and Remmi didn't know what to say. Her first inclination was to run back into Shannelle's room, grab her limp body from the bed, and kick the shit out of her ass for putting her through this. Remmi could deal with Shannelle's illness, but she couldn't deal with Shannelle deliberately trying to kill herself. *Booze? Weed? Where did she even get this stuff?* Remmi wondered.

"Shannelle instructed me not to share the details of her illness with anyone other than you, and since you're the only one who's been here supporting her, I'm assuming that you are the only person who knows about her condition. I know you must have other family members—parents? Aunts? Uncles? I know it's none of my business, but I think you should call any other important family members, as well as anyone that she's been intimate with. We can pray for a miracle, but if things continue as they are, your sister really doesn't have much longer," Dr. Foster suggested.

"I'll make some calls today," Remmi sighed.

"If you really want to help your sister, get her to think posi-tively. I've seen miraculous turnarounds in patients who possess an upbeat and optimistic outlook. The mind is an incredible thing. Don't underestimate it." Dr. Foster half smiled as he gently patted Remmi on her shoulder.

that evening, Remmi did what she dreaded most and called Shannelle's mother. Even before she'd told Dr. Foster that she would, Remmi had already been planning to call the woman she had referred to as Auntie C for the majority of her life. As Remmi expected, Carol was devastated by the news, cursing the world to damnation and asking the Lord why He felt the need to take both her babies before He took her.

"It should be me. Not my baby girl. That chile ain't never did nuthin' to nobody. She don't deserve this. I'm the one who's been out there doin' what I gotta do. It should be me, Rementa. . . . It should be me," Carol bawled.

"It shouldn't be anybody, Auntie C. Nobody deserves this. No-body," Remmi replied.

Remmi and Carrol made arrangements for her to fly in from New York on the next available flight. It was Remmi's hope that her mother's prescence would give Shannelle a much-needed boost in attitude. After all, she would have given anything to have her own mother there right now. Auntie C was the next best thing to Rita, and Remmi asked herself why she hadn't called her sooner. Had Carol been there, she could have forced Shannelle to take her medicine. She could also have prevented her from drinking alco-hol and smoking by monitoring her every move. Since you can't exactly fire your mother, Carol would have been able to keep a close watch on her daughter while Remmi was on the set. After giving it a moment's thought, she couldn't wait for Shannelle's mom to arrive in L.A.

Despite the toll that Shannelle's condition had taken on her, Remmi had managed to finish filming the movie and gave a stellar performance in her portrayal of Nyagra Ensley. But as much as she was enjoying her job, she was only too glad to be finished. The daily running from the set to the hospital was starting to wear her out. Carol's arrival made it easier, but she still felt it was her duty to show up every day without fail. Unfortunately the paparazzi had caught up with Remmi coming out of Cedars-Sinai Medical Center one sunny afternoon, and it was only a matter of hours before a story was plastered on the cover of a local rag that masqueraded as a respectable newspaper. HOLLYWOOD'S NEWEST DARLING FIGHTS FOR THE LIFE OF HER SISTER was the headline of a story that chronologically detailed all the events of her best friend's illness. At first, Remmi was taken aback, not knowing how they had gotten the surprisingly accurate information. The story had dates and details that only someone close to Remmi or Shannelle could have known, including the day of diagnosis. Remmi was baffled about where they had gotten their information, as she thought she had been pretty successful in keeping her personal life private. She knew Shannelle would be furious if she got wind that her condition was now public knowledge because of Remmi's celebrity.

The story listed legal names, both first and last, and even mentioned Shannelle's prior profession back in New York. It brought to mind the dirt she and her partner in crime had engaged in the not-so-distant past. Remmi became worried about the public attention the two were now getting. She didn't want Lopez or Shirley showing up in L.A. to retrieve what had been taken from them, and she didn't want Art to start talking about how he had been set up by a modern-day Thelma and Louise. Angered and concerned, Remmi racked her brain trying to figure out who would have leaked such a story to the media, until she remembered the day she and her onscreen best friend had gotten tipsy over Long Island iced teas one Sunday afternoon at Remmi's flat.

Needing someone to talk to and feeling as though she had been growing closer to Kara, Remmi had confided in her new friend about Shannelle's deterioration. Kara, who had dropped by Remmi's condo unexpectedly to return a jacket she'd borrowed, was greeted by a very depressed actress who was engaged in a rare moment of breaking down. Coming at the right time, Kara was able to comfort the woman who had helped give her a start in Tinsel Town. Remmi wept uncontrollably on her shoulder. With Carol at the hospital and an empty house, the CD player spewed Maxwell's "Lifetime" at such an incredibly high volume that Remmi failed to hear Kara's knocking or subsequent entrance through the unlocked door. Usually tight as a virgin about her business, on this day with a pitcher of homemade Long Island iced teas in her left hand and an old photo of her mother in her right, Remmi poured her guts out to Kara. She spoke of Rita and her love for Shannelle, the only other person she could ever rely on.

"I ain't no dyke, now. But that girl is my bitch. If God made a man like that girl, I would marry him in a New York minute. I'd even propose! . . . That girl is my dawg. My homie pastromie from Wyoming. My confidante. Thelma to my Louise. My best friend. Ain't nobody ever been there for me just because. She ain't never asked me for nuthin'—ain't never done no backstabbing, jealous-ass, trifling shit that bitches usually do. All she did was be my sister, and for that I love her so much," Remmi rambled.

Kara didn't really know what to say. She wanted to be there for

Remmi, but her mentor's drunkenness made her uncomfortable. She had never seen Remmi in such a state and was surprised. It was contradictory to the strong superwoman image that Kara had of her, and she wanted that impression to remain intact. Still, as Remmi continued to rattle on, Kara became aware of how much pain her idol had experienced. She felt sorry for her. But with a dry mouth, Kara remained silent, riddled with guilt about the fact that she, too, had an ulterior motive for becoming up close and personal with Remmi.

"I'm sure she'll get better," Kara finally managed to utter.

"That's the thing!" Remmi spat. "It's like she don't wanna get better! She ain't even been taking her medicine! How she expect to get better if she ain't even taking her medicine?"

There was a moment of silence between them as Remmi gulped the brown juice directly from its glass pitcher. She gently swayed to the melodious tempo of Maxwell's music as if every word that flowed from his supple lips was meant solely for her. The lyrics felt deeply personal to Remmi that Sunday afternoon. Remmi could have penned "This Woman's Work" herself; the words took on special meaning to her as she reflected on all the years of her life—more than half of them spent as Shannelle's ace boom coom. Cut number ten was one of Shannelle's favorites, and Remmi remembered the rainy Tuesday night when her best friend had dipped out of Shirley's Temple to go with her to the Ziegfeld for the premiere of *Love & Basketball*, the movie from which the song came. She remembered them joking about how Omar Epps looked like he could have been the love child of Wesley Snipes and Johnny Gill and how she'd complained to Shannelle about ordering the popcorn swimming in butter. She even recalled what she was wearing that night and how her best friend had begged her to introduce her to the actor Darrin Henson from the Showtime series *Soul Food*. Yes, the memories made her smile, and she wondered if she would ever have any others to make her laugh. With the image of Shannelle's frail body fresh on her brain, she was beginning to accept the fact that the past might be all she was going to have to hold on to.

Thinking back to that day and the intricate details she had shared with Kara, Remmi realized that this new "friend" of hers was the most probable culprit. The article in the paper also had details of Remmi's breakdown—an occurrence that only one other person was there to witness, and that was her *Nyagra's Falls* costar, Kara Sweeting. Remmi could not believe that Kara had taken her anguish and shared it with the media. She really believed they were developing a friendship and had no idea that confiding in Kara was going to cost her her privacy. She'd thought the woman was her friend.

Remmi was so angry that she grabbed the flimsy rag from the countertop, jumped in her coupe, and headed toward the Eagle Rock apartment complex. After doing eighty on the freeway and finally hitting Yosemite Drive, Remmi made a right onto Eagle Rock Boulevard. As she approached the white-bricked buildings, her blood pumped forcefully through her veins and she could feel her temperature rise beneath her cotton T-shirt. Since she'd been in Hollywood, Remmi had grown to hate confrontation, but felt that Kara's betrayal could not be ignored. She had taken this girl under her wing, and this was the thanks she got? The way Remmi saw it, Kara owed her an ounce of loyalty. In fact, had Remmi not devised the plan to rid *Nyagra's Falls* of Gayle Ford and pushed so hard for Kara to be a replacement, that girl would still be waiting tables at some corny eatery on the Sunset Strip.

Determined to pick a bone with her newly exposed faux friend, Remmi ran up the stairs to the second floor. Her swift gait led her to apartment 211, where she forcefully knocked on Kara's door. The noise of the television resonated from beyond, and the sound of heavy footsteps grew louder as they neared her. Just as she was about to knock again, the white door flew open, and a dark-haired middle-aged man with a medium build stood eye to eye with her. Remmi looked the man in his face, thinking she had knocked on the wrong door. Confused, she asked for Kara, but before he could answer, Remmi took a better look at the man who stood before her.

His intense almond-shaped hazel eyes flickered with yellow specks beneath the thickest and shapeliest brows she had ever seen on a man. In silence, she momentarily observed him. He stood speechless, observing her as well, unable to answer her question about whether or not she indeed had the correct apartment. In a moment's time that seemed to last forever, they studied each other without uttering a word. Remmi's heartbeat suddenly began to accelerate. She knew she'd seen those eyes before. Racking her brain and trying to place the man's face, she finally realized where she had seen them. Those light brown eyes with honey-colored splashes and golden dancing specks were all too familiar to her. She'd seen them just a little while ago before she'd left her condo. In fact, she'd seen them every morning in her own mirror. They were eyes that she thought she had gotten from her mother.

"You are as beautiful before me as you are in pictures," he softly stated, slowly inching forward as if he wanted to embrace her. Breaking the thickness in the air, Kara suddenly appeared behind Charles, surprised to see Remmi standing at the door.

"Oh my God—Remmi!" Kara gasped. Like a flash of lightning, before she knew it and without any premeditation whatsoever, Remmi punched Kara in the face with the tightest fist she could build, dropping Kara to the floor with a thump. The man tried to help her as blood spewed violently from her mouth. Incomprehensible screams filled the air before Remmi raced down the concrete steps two at a time. Like an addict on speed, Remmi tossed open her car door, shoved the key in the ignition, and smashed the gas pedal into the floor, hauling ass out of the Eagle Rock parking lot like it was nobody's business.

i t was crazy, girl," Remmi chuckled. Her chair was pulled as close to Shannelle's bed as it could get. Remmi had no one else to talk to and hoped Shannelle could still hear her. Now attached to a ventilator, her best friend's body lay still as a corpse with the exception of the slight rise in her chest each time she took a breath. Shannelle's condition had gone from bad to worse almost overnight, and it was clear that the end was quickly approaching. The pneumonia had caused her lungs to collapse, and she now needed a machine to keep her alive. Remmi knew Shannelle had told her she didn't want to live like that, but she sure wasn't going to be the one to tell Carol to let her go. Even though she hadn't talked to God in a while, Remmi still believed in miracles. And because her closed eyes still seemed to move beneath their lids from time to time, Remmi figured she could tell Shannelle what happened, hoping that somehow her girl could hear her words.

"This man," Remmi continued, almost as if she and Shannelle were really chatting. "Or should I say—this monster—my mother's rapist—and murderer, 'cause I truly believe if he hadn't raped her, her life woulda been different and she still woulda been alive—my father—my uncle—wants to have a relationship with me. Like why the fuck would I wanna know him? He raped my mother, for Christsake! . . . I mean, he said he was sick. That he loved my mother but he had a mental disease. And after six years of jail and counseling for doing it to somebody else, he's cured. But I don't believe that shit. Just like nobody ever believed my mother when she told them what he did to her—that's why I don't have no family. My mama's own mama ain't believe her baby boy could do that shit. So my mama left 'em all. Every last one of 'em. And we moved away. A fifteen-year-old girl with a baby out in the world on her own. By herself. And she never looked back either . . . Girl, I ain't know it then, but Rita was a strong bitch." Remmi adjusted the pillow behind Shannelle's head just enough to make her look a little more comfortable. Not that Shannelle didn't look content. Remmi just knew how she liked it.

"Oh, and did I tell you that that bitch, Kara—Kara Sweeting— and that ain't even the skank's real name . . . she's his daughter. That bitch is my so-called half sister-cousin—whatever the fuck you wanna call her. They come telling me that shit like I was supposed to be excited about it or something. Woo woo—I have a sister!" Remmi sarcastically raised her hands to do a phony cheer. "That bitch ain't my sister," she continued, sucking her teeth. "You my only sister. That bitch'll never be my sister, 'cause that bastard ain't my father. I ain't *never* gonna claim either of 'em. . . . Yeah, girl. And it's in all the gossip magazines and shit: *Hollywood Newcomer Finds Sister She Never Knew She Had*, *Newest Hollywood Black Brat Pack Member Comes from Despaired Beginnings*, *Rementa Broughton Rises from a Dark Past*. Good thing they haven't mentioned that my uncle is my father. They only keep talking about my mother's suicide. But those are just some of the headlines I've seen. I told Allen to stop sending them to me. I'm embarrassed— but he says it's great for my career. I guess it is. . . . Oprah wants me to tell my story on her show. Ain't that some shit? Me on *Oprah*?" Remmi let out a hearty laugh. "Man, my family's dysfunction is making the Jacksons look like the Cosbys right about now. You always said that I wasn't the shit till I was on Oprah. . . . Well, I guess I'm about to be the shit." Remmi rose from the chair, kissed Shannelle on her forehead, and walked over to the huge glass window.

It was an amazingly clear day, especially for L.A. Remmi had gotten used to the smog and appreciated the sunshine when it dared to peek through the haze. The beep of the ventilator echoed behind her as she continued to talk. "I can't believe these muthafuckas actually expect me to embrace them with open arms. Like some long-lost relatives. Has this nigga forgotten that he raped my mother?" Remmi acknowledged, her voice higher now. She wanted so badly to get a response from Shannelle, the only person on the planet she could ever confide in. A joke, an insult, a "Bitch, you crazy." Anything. But she got nothing except for the annoying beep of that damn metal machine that looked like something off the set of *Star Wars*. Suddenly the beep from the ventilator, the noise from the hallway, and the sound of Shannelle's breathing all became magnified, and Remmi's emotions took over. She became so angry with herself, with Shannelle, with God— with the *world*—that she wanted to rip the tubes out of Shannelle herself and kick her out of the bed onto the cold tile floor.

On more than one occasion, they'd promised they would never abandon each other. When Carol's on-again, off-again boyfriend, John would come to the house drunk, and Carol would pull a butcher knife on him as a reminder to sober up, they would cower in Shannelle's bedroom and promise they'd always be there for each other. And now Shannelle was reneging. How could she? What was Remmi going to do without Shannelle? How would she make it?

Without warning, Remmi began to sob uncontrollably, beating her clenched fists against the thick glass of the window. Her anguish rumbled ferociously through the tranquil air, causing such a ruckus that the nurse raced into the room and grabbed Remmi's shoulders to calm and settle her down.

"Ms. Broughton, you cannot do this in here! Think of the patient!" the hefty brunette admonished in a loud, raspy whisper.

"I'm sorry . . . so sorry," Remmi howled, gathering her belongings and rushing past the nurse's chubby arm, nearly knocking down Shannelle's mother, who had suddenly appeared in the doorway.

Again she found herself in her car—a place that seemed to be more like home to her of late than her condo—speeding off to nowhere and running from the reality of what her life was about to become as Shannelle lay unmoving in room 1215 at Cedars-Sinai Medical Center.

"I'm really alone," Remmi said out loud.

The speedometer climbed passed ninety miles an hour while tears obstructed Remmi's vision. As she recklessly zoomed up the coast highway, she was tempted to drive her car over the edge of the thinly railed cliff. Instead she swerved around the edge of its sharpness as if tempting death was a game she had played many times. The only thing standing between her and the endless drop was a cracked and weathered balustrade—a barrier so frail and fragile that Remmi could probably have kicked it from its anchor with her tiny foot. And at that moment, ending it all seemed like a reasonable and likely conclusion to her story. *Them muthafuckas would really get some good headlines if I did that*, Remmi thought. *Hollywood's Newest Star Plunges to Her Suicidal Death. Yeah, that would probably make the* Times.

Remmi pushed the gas pedal deeper into the rug, causing the slender red dial to creep toward its maximum position on the speedometer. An evil and deranged voice echoed in her head, telling her to turn the wheel just enough to the right to send her over the edge. It wasn't her voice, nor was it a voice she had ever heard. Yet it completely entranced her. Just as she was about to do as instructed, while spellbound, Remmi slammed on the brakes, causing the silver car to slide, scrape the rocks of the freeway wall, and flip on its side before crashing to a screeching halt against a tree. Then there was silence.

23

W e've been in a bit of an accident, Miss Broughton," the balding Caucasian man informed Remmi as he stood above the bed where she lay motionless. He was wearing a white cotton coat and holding some sort of chart, so through her groggy daze, Remmi concluded that he was a doctor. She had been in the presence of far too many physicians of late and really didn't want to chat it up with another. As she lifted her head to reply, a sharp pain shot through her right temple, and she was forced to fall back upon her pillow. Slowly raising her hands to her aching head, Remmi realized that her throbbing head was wrapped in gauze. A quick assessment of her surroundings told her that she was once again in somebody's hospital room. Since she was still bewildered and slightly disoriented, it failed to dawn on her that the room was her own.

"Ms. Broughton. I know we're probably a little sore, but we're gonna be fine. Looking at your vehicle, it's a miracle that we came out with only a bump on our little head," the doctor continued.

"I, I . . . ," Remmi stuttered.

"Don't say anything. We need to rest."

What is all of this "we" shit? Remmi asked herself, but managed to say aloud, "How long have I been here?"

"Since yesterday. From what I understand, you ran from your sister's room distraught and somehow lost control of your car, causing it to smash through the railings on the side of the highway. We really should never drive under distress, you know . . . ," he continued, scribbling something onto the medical chart he gripped tightly in his hand. The silver clip that held it in place caught a gleam of the California sun and reflected the rays across the room, nearly blinding Remmi's weakened vision.

"I didn't try to kill myself. It was an accident," Remmi tried to explain. Even though she couldn't quite grasp her bearings, Remmi was determined to set the record straight, knowing that if the tabloids had gotten wind of her accident—her "attempted suicide"—it would be a media fiasco. The truth was that she had actually thought about killing herself but changed her mind at the last second.

"We know you've been under an incredible amount of stress lately, Miss Broughton. That's why we're going to get you some help. Even the strongest people on earth need help every once in a while, and we have an excellent mental health physician you can talk to."

"A psychatrist? I don't need to talk to no shrink! I'm not crazy! I just told you that the accident was just that—*an accident!*" Remmi indignantly snapped. She wanted to get up from the bed and walk straight out of the cold and sterile room, but her body felt as though she had been dragged by an eighteen-wheeler.

"It's just procedure. Nobody's saying you're crazy," the doctor assured her. They were then joined by a slender black woman with well-kept sandy blond dreadlocks flowing down her back. Through squinted eyes, Remmi glared at them but said nothing. The woman stood still as a statue above Remmi's bed. She wore a very conservative navy blue outfit that appeared to be separate articles purchased individually off a clearance rack at Wal-Mart. Still, even though the woman wore a cheap suit, Remmi could not deny the fact that her presence commanded attention. Yet Remmi wanted to ignore her. She felt like she was trapped on the planet of the white coats and desperately wanted to return to civilization. It seemed as though every person who wasn't laying up in a bed was wearing a white coat. Remmi wanted out.

"This is Elena Toussaint," the doctor stated with a smile, as though he was smitten with her.

Elena extended a slender mocha-colored hand, but Remmi turned away. She had no desire to speak to anyone, let alone some dreadlocked Dr. Phil wannabe that she didn't need.

"And who the hell are you?" Remmi questioned the doctor.

"Oh—I apologize. I'm Dr. Webber. I was the physician on duty when they brought you in," he responded, ignoring her tone.

"Ms. Broughton," Elena began. Her raspy voice was peppered with a heavy West Indian accent, making her words all the more emphatic. "I know you hev been chrough a lat. But I em 'ear to 'elp you."

"I told you people I don't need no help. I had a headache and lost control of my car! That is it!" Remmi snapped. The doctor made eye contact with Elena, who remained silent with a soft smirk upon her face. She was used to being treated with less respect than she knew she deserved in her line of work. After all, trauma victims didn't usually like to discuss their pain, and folks with suicidal tendencies often lived in denial.

"You assholes are just waiting for me to admit that I tried to kill myself so that you can run to the nearest newspaper and tell them all my damn business! Well, that ain't gonna happen! My mama ain't raise no fool, so y'all can just take your white-coat-wearing asses up on outta here. I was in an accident—ya hear me? An acci-muthafuckin-dent! It happens every day! Don't nobody need no psychiatrist up in this bitch! Now if you'll just gimme some of that one-million-milligram Motrin, I'll be able to walk up outta here in a little while!"

"Ms. Broughton, you've been unconscious for nearly twelve hours and have suffered a mild concussion. I really suggest that you stay here for at least another twenty-four hours for observation," the doctor calmly advised, ignoring Remmi's incensed demeanor.

"No can do. My sister is dying and I need to be by her side," Remmi huffed, adjusting her blanket and looking around the room for her belongings. Nothing was in view, and she wondered where her clothes were. Clad in an uncomplimentary blue-and-white medical gown, she could think only of finding the brand-new Citizen of the Humanities low-rise jeans she had been wearing when she'd left Shannelle's room on the day of the accident.

"Where's my stuff?" Remmi asked the medical professionals standing before her.

"Ya cloting was destroyed in de accident. Ya should not worry 'bout anyting material. Ya should just be 'appy ya were not kilt," the psychiatrist firmly said, her accent more pronounced as she grew impatient with Remmi.

"Don't tell me what the hell I should or shouldn't worry about!

I wanna know where my shit is!" Remmi barked, more viciously than before. She was pissed now. She had paid over two hundred dollars for those jeans, and here was this woman who, from the way she was dressed, obviously knew very little about fashion, telling her that she should be unconcerned about them. The nerve!

The woman bit her lower lip as if she were using all the patience she possessed within and resisted the urge to address Remmi's rudeness.

Dr. Webber didn't hold his tongue. "Look, Ms. Broughton. I am the doctor attending to your matter. My orders are for you to stay here another twenty-four hours, but I cannot stay by your side to ensure that you follow them. If you choose to do something different, it will be on you. And if you don't want to talk to Ms. Toussaint, that is also your prerogative," the doctor, now annoyed, stated.

Remmi glared at him. It wasn't that she was angry with Dr. Webber. She was really angry with herself for having twisted up her car. She could only imagine what her beloved Betsy looked like after crashing through a wooden fence and slamming into a hundred-year-old tree. With very little strength to continue challenging the doctors, Remmi just placed her head back upon the pillow.

While most of the facts were blurred she remembered that she had changed her mind about going over the edge of the cliff moments after she had decided to end it all. She'd heard her own voice reasoning with her that if she could join her mother and wait for Shannelle to arrive, they could all be together again. And then another unrecognizable, almost demonic voice told her to "Just do it!"

As she forcefully pressed the leather sole of her Manolo Blahnik floral thong sandal into the silver gas pedal, she heard a voice she hadn't heard since she and Shannelle had been caught smoking weed in the staircase of the projects.

Don't you dare! the voice had roared. *Don't you dare be a coward and take the easy way out!*

Startled by her mother's voice, in a fraction of an instant, Remmi twisted the steering wheel to the left, swaying the car off the direct path to a mammoth birch tree whose trunk spanned well over three feet wide. Sideswiping the tree on the passenger's side, she managed to escape with a minor concussion and a few bumps and bruises—evidence that God and Rita were truly watching over her. The car, on the other hand, had not been quite so lucky.

With a cotton gauze bandage still tightly swaddling the right side of her head, Remmi quietly walked into Shannelle's sterile whitewashed room. Luckily they were being treated at the same facility and when Remmi was released from her own bed she had not hesitated to go to the other side of the hospital, where her best friend remained unconscious, her life being prolonged by a cold silver ventilator. Auntie C sat beside the bed with her face in her hands, lifting her head as Remmi neared. Her eyes were bloodshot, and tears stained her cheeks. She looked tired and weary, as if she had not slept in weeks. Remmi tightly wrapped her arms around Carol's torso and hugged her, whispering in her ear that she was there.

"You girls are gonna drive me to an early grave," Auntie C sighed. Remmi let out a soft, nervous laugh as she released the embrace. "Since when can't you drive a car?" her aunt continued, gazing at Remmi.

"It was just a little accident. I'm fine. Really . . . ," Remmi replied.

Auntie C slowly blinked her eyes and sucked her teeth. She then turned her attention back to her daughter who lay beneath a spotless white sheet. Small tears fell from her swollen red eyes and cascaded down her already blemished face as she wearily shook her head from side to side. "What am I gonna do with you girls?" Auntie C managed to mutter. Remmi remained silent, her eyes glued on the fragile shell that now housed the woman who used to be her closest friend and confidante. She could not believe how much Shannelle's voluptuous body had deteriorated in less than thirty days, and it pained her to see her sister lying there motionless, at death's door. As Remmi focused on Shannelle, scenes from everything they had experienced together replayed vividly in her mind. From their Theo Huxtable lunch boxes to the heist they pulled at Shirley's Temple and everything in between—it all played through Remmi's mind like a major motion picture. Remmi didn't know if she should laugh, cry, or scream as the memories flooded her psyche. Her head still throbbed from the bump that sat noticeably upon her noggin, but she refused to pay attention to its pain. Her thoughts were too preoccupied with the condition of her best friend and the fact that she knew it was time to resolve herself to going on without Shannelle.

"I was trying to wait for you to come," Auntie C began, breaking the silence and interrupting Remmi's train of thought. "We're taking her off the machine today. It's time to lay her to rest."

"*We* who?" Remmi asked. Remmi knew the decision to disconnect the ventilator was hundred percent Carol's, but she could not help feeling like she should have a say. After all, over the past five years, she and Shannelle had been the only family each of them had really had. Carol had not approved of Shannelle's choice to dance at the Temple, and her decision created quite a rift in their relationship. It was Remmi whom Shannelle had grown to depend on, confide in, and communicate with on a daily basis. In fact, Shannelle had not even told her mother that she was relocating to L.A., and Carol hadn't even known her daughter was no longer living in New York. Remmi could not help feeling like she should have some say about such a major decision. After all, she had been the one paying all the hospital bills.

"The doctors and me," Auntie C replied as she straightened out Shannelle's bedsheet. She could see the disapproval in Remmi's eyes but chose not to make eye contact with her daughter's childhood friend. As far as she was concerned, Remmi had no place in the decision to keep Shannelle's body alive when her mind had already gone on to Heaven. She didn't care that Remmi was footing the bills. She didn't care that they had been best friends since the first day of the second grade. Remmi was not a blood relative, and as Shannelle's mother, Carol was the only one who could make the decision to end her physical life, regardless of the history the two young women shared.

"Auntie C . . . Don't you think we should wait just a little while longer? I mean, her eyes move beneath her lids, and she's still breathing. She could wake up at any time. God could give us a miracle," Remmi pleaded.

"Girl, I know you love my daughter. But you don't love her more than me. You think I wanna put another one of my babies in the ground? I don't. But we can't stay here every day looking at a dead body that's only breathin' because of a machine. I'd rather give her on to the Lord so that she'll be able to rest. The doctors did all they could. There ain't no more to do. I don't think my daughter would wanna live like this. Keeping her body here is for us. She's already gone. And I'm sure she'd wanna rest in peace," Carol replied.

As tears poured from Remmi's face, she tried to bring herself to understand why this was happening. She knew Auntie C must have been going through a hard time, too, and that the decision to disconnect the ventilator was probably the most difficult one she'd have to make in her entire life. Remmi tried to remind herself that her Auntie C had already lost one child, and now here she was about to lose another. Remmi couldn't imagine giving birth to two children and then having to bury both of them.

Things like this aren't supposed to happen, Remmi thought. *Children are supposed to bury their parents. Not the other way around.* With these thoughts in her mind, she decided not to fight Auntie C on the issue. She didn't want to make it any harder on her aunt—or on herself—than it already was. After all, if the woman who had given birth to Shannelle decided that it was truly time to lay her daughter to rest, then it probably was.

a t 8:39 P.M., the sky began its transformation from soft azure to cobalt. Shades of pink and purple streaked across the heavens as the sun lowered its position to brighten someone else's day on the other side of the earth. As the sky became a beautiful sapphire blanket with brightly glistening stars throughout, Shannelle Marie Anderson took her last breath and secured her position in Heaven beside Rita. Yet another angel would be dutifully watching over Rementa Renee Broughton.

24

the echo of the loudly ringing telephone jolted Remmi out of a deep sleep. She reached from beneath the covers only to grasp an empty base. Quickly rising from the bed, she scanned the room for the receiver, which she spotted resting faceup on the dresser.

"Hello?" she groggily spoke before realizing that she had not pushed the TALK button. "Hello?" she asked again, now connected to her caller.

"Rementa, where have you been?" Allen spewed, an annoyed tone peppering his voice.

"Allen . . ." Remmi sighed as she headed back toward the bed.

"Yes, Rementa. It's me—Allen Young—your agent, remember me?"

"Don't start," she huffed, crawling back beneath the covers. "You know I was in New York for my sister's funeral."

"I know, but that was nearly three weeks ago. You know how

much happens in Hollywood in three weeks! You've been off the scene for nearly two months. In a lot of ways, you're still up and coming, Rementa. You need to stay visible. And furthermore, it's one thing to be MIA, but you haven't been returning any of my calls!" Allen rambled.

"Allen, did you hear what I said? My sister died, for Chrissake! I think three fuckin' weeks of mourning is more than reasonable! Give me a fuckin' break!"

"I'm sorry for your loss, Rementa," Allen replied, softening his tone. "It's just that there's been so much speculation in the media about the accident, and now you disappearing—I've really had to do quite a bit of damage control."

"I couldn't give a shit about the media, Allen. I just lost my sister," Remmi barked.

"Okay, well, maybe this is something that will cheer you up. ABC is interested in creating a sitcom around you. You and an up-and-coming New York comedian named Capone. They call him 'the gangster of comedy.'"

"I've heard of him. Seen him at the Laugh Factory in New York. He does *Showtime at the Apollo*, too, doesn't he?"

"That'd be the one."

"Yeah. He's funny as hell."

"I think it'll be a great opportunity for you. They want to do a meeting with you tomorrow at ten A.M."

"All right. Send the info to my BlackBerry, and I'll be there."

"And let's not forget that Oprah is waiting for a confirmation for your interview, which is supposed to take place at the top of next month."

"I wouldn't stand up Oprah, Allen," Remmi huffed, feeling like he should already know that. Damn, even Oprah would understand that she had to lay her sister to rest.

"Oh, and Remmi," Allen began, as an afterthought. "There have been some rumors circulating about a physical altercation that you allegedly had with your *Nyagra's Falls* co-star, Kara Sweeting."

Remmi remained silent as she wondered what Allen really knew. She had no intention of announcing to the world what her connection to Kara Sweeting was, but with Shannelle's death, the craziness of her funeral, and having to stay in New York for close to two weeks, Remmi had almost forgotten about the incident.

Shannelle's funeral, which had taken place in Harlem, had been a fiasco to top all fiascos. The ultimate stereotypical black service, there was plenty of hooting, hollering, and fighting. It was standing room only, as ex-lovers, friends, colleagues, and family members from near and far came to pay their respects to a young woman who really was hard not to like. Even Shannelle's old boss, Shirley, had shown up. But the bold and brazen bitch that she was, Shirley felt the need to inform Shannelle's mother that had Shannelle not died from AIDS, she surely would have killed her for setting up her club. Of course, this announcement caused quite an uproar in the Unity Funeral Home, resulting in the entire Anderson clan jumping on Shirley and beating her to a pulp. Remmi couldn't help but wonder why Shirley would have ventured into enemy territory to defame the beloved deceased whose life was being honored at the front of the room.

It proved what Shannelle had told her for so many years about Shirley, who truly thought she was invincible. The woman got the crap knocked out of her for underestimating the craziness of Shannelle's ghetto-ass clan. As she approached Auntie C, who sat weeping in the first seat of the first row, Shannelle's mother initially assumed that Shirley was one of her daughter's friends who wanted to extend heartfelt condolences. However, as soon as Shirley's malice-filled words hit her ears, Auntie C hauled off and pummeled her daughter's ex-boss with the Nextel cell phone she had been speaking on just moments before. Without explanation, the entire room proceeded to jump on Shirley, stomping her to the ground and causing the undertaker to call the police. They figured if Carol was whipping someone's ass at her own daughter's funeral, she must have had a good reason.

Remmi couldn't believe the nerve of this fool and continued to look over her shoulder for the duration of the service, just in case anyone else decided to bring it. She was particularly looking to see if Lopez was going to show up, but was told by one of Shannelle's ex-coworkers that Lopez was doing fifteen years at an upstate correctional facility, much to Remmi's relief.

With all the drama surrounding Shannelle's funeral, including a lack of funds and Auntie C begging her to stay with her, Remmi had all but forgotten about her scandalous half sister and trifling uncle daddy. But forgetting did not make it go away, and here it was back to haunt her.

"Evidently, Kara did an interview with the L.A. *Times*, claiming that you guys are half sisters. Is that true?" Allen asked, breaking Remmi's train of thought.

"I'm my mother's only child. As far as where else my biological father might have put his dick, I have no clue," Remmi firmly answered.

"Well, Dreamtracks quickly deaded the story and informed her that she better not bring any bad press to the project or else. But you know once it's out there, the public starts to speculate. And since you've not been around to comment—"

"Well, I'm back now."

"You might wanna talk to her about it. I thought you two were friends."

"*Were* is the key word. Look, I'll be there tomorrow at ten."

"See you there."

Once again Remmi found herself standing before apartment number 211 at the Eagle Rock apartment complex. She had decided that it was in the interest of her career to confront her fake friend/half sister/cousin one last time. Despite her risqué start in music videos and her reputation for hooking up with whoever was going to help her further her career, Remmi had been embraced by Hollywood as the new black "it" girl. She had a squeaky-clean image in town. If word got out that she was the result of an incestuous rape, it could take her career in a direction she might not want it to go. Of course, the masses could either embrace her plight, sympathize with her, and make her the poster child for incest survivors, but on the other end of the spectrum, they could label her as some sort of freak. And no telling how Hollywood would feel if they found out the why Rita had killed herself. People might have been willing to embrace AIDs awareness, but not in their own backyards. Remmi didn't want to take any chances. She didn't want to end up as some *Surreal Life* has-been before her career even really got started. She had worked far too hard to get where she was and wasn't about to let these people ruin her life or her career. Now that Shannelle was gone, her career was all she had, and she was determined to do whatever she had to do to preserve it.

When Remmi reached the dingy white and slightly dented door, she stood firmly upon the AstroTurf welcome mat and leaned in close for a listen before knocking. There was no sound or movement coming from inside the apartment, but Remmi used her knuckles to gently thump anyway. Leaning in once again and wishing she had a glass to place against it, Remmi waited a moment and knocked once more. With a sigh, Remmi turned to leave until she heard an opening sound from behind.

"Remmi?" a voice softly said. Remmi turned around to stare into Kara's eyes, and a moment of silence ensued. Kara stood perfectly still, clad in a short black silk robe.

Looking her enemy up and down, Remmi began, "We need to talk."

"Um, yes, we do. But it's not really a good time. I, um, have company," Kara stuttered.

"I don't give a—"

"Look, I never meant to hurt you. I just wanted you to know that we have a connection," Kara began as Remmi stepped across the threshold. "I wanted to tell you from the start, but Daddy said you'd reject me. That you'd reject *us*. He said it'd be better if you and I developed some sort of friendship. That it'd be easier for you to accept if you already liked me as a person," she continued.

"You wanted me to know that you and I have a *connection*? Bitch, you and I have no connection! You are the daughter of the muthafucka who raped my mother, impregnated her, and ultimately caused her death! Am I supposed to embrace you monsters? Am I supposed to consider you people *family*?" Remmi spat.

"Remmi, I know Daddy did some awful things. I know it. But he's paid his debt to society, and he's really, really sorry. He's different now. He's changed. He really has. You need to give him a chance. You need to give *us* a chance," Kara tried to explain.

"I don't give a damn if he died and came back as Martin Luther King! He ruined my mother's life! She was never the same after he did what he did to her. Why on earth would I want to know him! And why on earth would I want to know *you*, for that matter?"

Kara walked toward the left of the living room, to the kitchen area. Removing a can of Diet Coke from the refrigerator, she answered, " 'Cause we all the family you got."

"Then I have no family. The only sister I had passed away three weeks ago, and I am here to warn you and that rapist father of yours that if you both do not stay away from me and if you do not crawl back under whatever rock y'all niggas came from, you *will* be sorry."

"Don't threaten me, Rementa," Kara huffed before taking a swig from the soda can. "Look, all I wanted was a connection with my big sister. And if you don't want that, then fine. I won't bother you anymore. In fact, Daddy's already gone back home. He figured you've been through a lot lately, and he didn't wanna hurt your life any more than he already had. But I, on the other hand, haven't done shit to you, so I'm staying right here in Cali. So get used to it. I have a career to build. And if I have to do it by telling the world that I'm your sister, then so be it. For some reason, Hollywood is interested in everything that has anything to do with you. And that includes the baby sister that you've rejected," Kara indignantly spewed.

"I promise you. If you use my name to try to come up, you *will* be sorry," Remmi threatened with fire in her eyes.

"I'll take my chances." Kara smugly shrugged. "And if I were you, I'd cool it with the threats. Whether you like it or not, we *are* sisters—which means we're cut from the same cloth. I'm made from the same shit you are. So stop trying to scare somebody."

Remmi wanted so badly to lunge at her adversary with both hands and choke the last breath from her. However, she knew she had far too much to lose and didn't want to ultimately wreck the very career she had gone there to save by catching a murder charge. No, again, she had to be smart, not emotional. She and Shannelle would never have reacted emotionally when logic and planning could get the job done without risk or repercussion.

"You're an amateur fucking with a pro, little girl." Remmi slyly smiled.

"Ya know, when I got here, I was hoping that as sisters we could take Hollywood by storm and do something creatively that no two siblings have ever done in the history of this town—especially as two black women. But since you wanna reject me, I guess that idea is down the drain." Kara shrugged with exaggerated disappointment. "But I'm not gonna let that stop me. Just like you, I'm a survivor. In fact, I look up to you. You're my big sis, and I always wanted to be like you. Used to watch you in those videos on BET and wished I could be just like you."

"You could neva be like me, bitch. There's only one me," Remmi snapped, her arms folded tightly upon her chest.

"Yeah, well, we're more alike than different, girlfriend. The difference is that I'm not as oblivious as you."

"Oblivious?"

"Yes. I watched you closely over the years, Ms. Rementa Renee Broughton, and you never even saw or *felt* my eyeballs." Kara laughed heartily.

Remmi could see that the kind, sweet, and innocent girl she had believed Kara to be, was all just part of an act to get her to let down her guard. She had used that tactic herself in the past and was annoyed that she had fallen for it. Now seeing her for what she really was, Remmi crinkled her eyebrows up above her long black lashes as her hazels focused on the devil in the black robe standing before her.

"But I guess that's how it is when you're so fuckin' into yourself. You just don't have time to notice anyone else. You think you're so smart and cunning and beautiful," Kara sarcastically declared.

"I'm not the only one who thinks I'm smart and cunning and beautiful," Remmi smugly said.

"Yeah, well I wonder what those same people will think about you once they know about your family history, your promiscuous past, or your involvement with the heist at that strip club in the Bronx with your equally bitchy dead friend."

Kara's words splattered Remmi like hot grease from a frying pan. It took all the control Remmi had to keep from throwing Kara to the hardwood floor and using her size 7s to stomp her to an early grave. How on earth did this girl know about what had happened at Shirley's Temple? Had Kara truly been watching Remmi all these years without her knowledge? Had Remmi really been that self-consumed?

Remmi clenched her jaw and racked her brain for a solution to this problem. Not only was Kara threatening to divulge her entire dysfunctional family and personal history, but now she was also blackmailing her about revealing her involvement in a federal crime. Should people like Shirley or Lopez learn of her connection to the heist, it could truly cost her her life. On the other side of that coin, if Kara went to the police, Remmi's freedom would surely be stripped from her. It would be the biggest Hollywood scandal of the new millennium. And these were two prices Remmi was not willing to pay.

"Baby girl, you all right?" a familiar voice summoned from the back of the apartment, snapping Remmi out of her train of thought. Remmi turned around to see the infamous Arthur Haddox standing in the doorway of Kara's hall. He stood bare-chested, a green-and-white-striped towel wrapped around his waist, his ample half-erect penis slightly bulging from beneath the terry cloth. No wonder Kara had taken so long to open the door. Remmi laughed at the sight of him and then smiled, armed with the knowledge that she still had pictures of him and Rocky locked away in a Citibank safe deposit box.

"Oh, what's up, Remmi? Looking good, as usual." Arthur grinned, his arms now raised above his head and gripping the frame of the doorway. His rippled torso momentarily took her back to their days as an item, before a vivid image of him beating her with a leather strap came crashing down on her previous memory. A mental slide show then took her to an image of the description Shannelle had given her of Rocky sucking him off. Oh, how Remmi wished she could send those pictures to *The Enquirer.* But they had a deal, and she had to honor it.

"Remmi, I think you know Artie," Kara smirked as if she had acquired one of Remmi's prized possessions.

"I do." Remmi smiled.

"Well, Artie's helping me build my career. I watched how he helped you and felt that he could be an asset in my life, too," Kara smugly informed her.

Remmi gleamed. "And what a perfect pair you two are."

With stars in her eyes, Kara walked over to Art, wrapped her arms around his chest, and kissed him on the cheek.

"I had no idea you two were sisters, although now that I know, I do see a resemblance." Art sarcastically grinned, suggesting that he knew Kara's version of the grueling details.

"We're not—," Remmi interrupted.

"Small world." Art beamed, ignoring Remmi's reply.

"Small people make small worlds," Remmi spat with a glare in her eye as she slammed the door behind her with a bang.

K nowing that she had not seen the last of Kara, Remmi was determined to come up with a plan to run old girl out of Hollywood. Kara Sweeting needed to be stopped, and she needed to be stopped now, before she did some real damage to Remmi's career.

Day in and day out, Remmi racked her brain but still could not seem to come up with something that would rid her of her problem. Hiring someone to kill Kara was far too risky now that Remmi had attracted some notoriety. And getting her own hands dirty was not an option. But as long as Kara walked the streets of Hollywood with a mission to build her career on Remmi's back, getting rid of her permanently was Remmi's only solution. How she wished she could brainstorm with Shannelle to come up with something. She knew Shannelle would have had an answer, just like she'd devised the heist at Shirley's Temple and sent Lopez off to jail. All of that had been so brilliant.

Maybe she could incorporate the assistance of Officer Harris as she'd done with that wench, Gayle Ford. But he hadn't been returning her calls of late. *His girlfriend probably finally busted his cheating ass*, Remmi figured. She thought about calling the precinct, but part of her really didn't want to be bothered with him either. No, whatever she was going to do, if Shannelle wasn't there to help execute it, then Remmi needed to do it all by herself—without witnesses or potential blackmailers. After all, Harris had already shown his true colors, and Remmi knew it was only a matter of time before he'd want to really cash in on the favors he had done.

No. The only person she could truly trust was now just a handful of ashes in a silver urn sitting on top of an entertainment center in Auntie C's apartment. It once again became apparent to Remmi that she was definitely on her own and that all she had was herself.

Like Treach from Naughty by Nature once said, Remmi thought as she sped up the highway in a charcoal gray BMW X5—a little loaner from Allen—"*I do my dirt all by my lonely.*"

25

a s a new day was born, Remmi watched the shade of the sky lighten through the heavy slits of her eyes. She had wanted to rise early for a run, but her body felt heavier than two tons of bricks. It was as if the weight of the entire universe had manifested itself in Remmi's impeccably pedicured toes, making her feel like one of Tony Soprano's turncoat enemies, ready to be tossed into the Long Island Sound as fish food.

Although she somehow had been managing to look alive and energetic during the day, the reality was that each night Remmi had tossed and turned, thinking about how she would rid herself—and the world—of Kara Sweeting. The idea began to consume her every thought. She considered everything from setting Kara up with a criminal charge to cutting the brake line in her car—all of which she felt were great ideas, but far too risky.

At the end of the day, she had decided that maybe she should just go public with her entire story herself. That way when Kara told it, no one would really be interested. It would lose its luster and shock value once the details of Remmi's past and upbringing came directly from Remmi. Of course, she'd need to discuss it with Allen and perhaps hire a publicist. After all, they would surely need to strategize a plan of action, ensuring that the gory details resonated from her lips at the right time, with the right words, to the right ears.

Though Remmi would have felt better if she could kick Kara's ass up and down Eagle Rock Boulevard, negative press wasn't the kind of attention Remmi was looking for. And she didn't want to be labeled another Hollywood hothead, à la Naomi Campbell. She was at a very pivotal time in her career, and she knew she had to be smart. If Remmi hurt Kara, but did not kill her, her story would still come out. If she killed her, she would have to risk getting caught, losing her freedom, her career, and everything she had worked so hard for. No, maybe coming clean with the world about her history was the best answer. Maybe it was the *only* answer. She had so much to look forward to and so many opportunities knocking at her door that now was truly not the time to rock the boat with scandal. Perhaps if she told her own story, she could garner some public sympathy and her career would skyrocket even higher.

Remmi's meeting with Allen and the ABC execs had been a complete success. It was evident they had been watching her career and loving every minute of it. They wanted to work with her and were willing to give her carte blanche to secure a commitment. They wanted to develop a television sitcom around her and another one of their newly admired up-and-coming stars—a well-known New York City comedian who went by the name Capone, just as Allen had told her. The "gangsta of comedy" as he was referred to by those on the circuit, Capone was apparently on his way to being the next big Hollywood comedic favorite. With Eddie Murphy struggling with paternity suits, Hollywood seemed to have its arms wide open for a new funny man. And Capone was that man.

As her popularity steadily increased—and now with a proposal for her own sitcom—Remmi knew that getting her story out before Kara did was of paramount importance. But what would she do? Talking to the girl was obviously no use. Like a fallen Jackson worse than La Toya, Kara was determined to use Remmi's success as a platform to boost her own career. Still, Remmi believed there had to be something she could do to stop this blackmailing half sibling and cousin.

Deeply in thought, Remmi propped the down pillow up behind her head and blankly stared at the thirty-six-inch plasma television before her. Although the sound was muted, the picture tube gave an image of the opening credits of Remmi's favorite morning show, while her tension-filled neck grew stiff and Remmi's brain continued to ponder. After nearly twenty minutes of deep contemplation as the voiceless reflections of Barbara Walters and her crew stared back at her, Remmi came to a decision. It was difficult, it was scary, but it was very necessary.

The drive to Allen's office seemed longer than usual. Traffic was thick, and the clouds that had suddenly moved in over the California sky were even thicker. The half-speaking half-singing voice of Jill Scott bounced off the walls of the X5 and seeped through Remmi's ears. The words "whatever, whatever" provided a backdrop for Remmi's thoughts as she played her anticipated speech over and over again in her mind. The night before, she had divulged her entire story to Allen, who was shocked, astonished, and then in awe of Remmi as the words fell from her mouth.

"I had no idea" was all Allen could say, amazed that Remmi could excel as far as she had with such a sordid and dysfunctional history. People with less horrific pasts had ended up homeless, jailed, or institutionalized. For Remmi to have become as successful as she had, she must have been made of the strongest African diamond—unbreakable, unshakable, and brilliant.

"It's amazing that you've made it as far as you have, Rementa," Allen softly stated.

"I know. I been real lucky. Things always seem to turn out okay for me in the end. I think my guardian angel is best friends with Gabriel," Remmi nervously laughed, referring to God's archangel.

After much discussion and rehashing, Remmi and Allen had decided to hire a publicist, alert ABC and Dreamtracks, call a press conference, and confirm with Oprah. It was a unanimous decision: This was the only way to go.

Remmi finally walked into Allen's office nearly forty minutes later than scheduled, tired from sitting in traffic but eager to get the ball rolling. Yvette Hayward, one half of the renowned publicity firm Flowers & Hayward, sat patiently before Allen's desk awaiting Remmi's arrival. Yvette, a nicely built, leggy woman with a shoulder-length bob, appeared younger than Remmi thought she would have been. From Allen's description, Remmi had assumed her redeemer would be a fifty-something-year-old white woman, with a Joan Crawford voice and a Virginia Slim in her hand. She had no idea that Yvette Hayward was a thirty-something-year-old sista—a true sista—with chocolate-brown skin and ample hips, doing her thing in the dog-eat-dog, mostly single-white-female-dominated world of publicity.

Remmi was pleasantly surprised that the industry had even let

Hayward in. But with over ten years of experience in the publicity game, Yvette's witty and feisty reputation preceded her, causing Remmi and Allen to believe that she was the perfect publicist for the job of damage control, even if she did charge an arm and a leg, a foot and a toe.

"She's well worth her price," Allen assured Remmi after explaining that Yvette's prices were a little higher than the average Hollywood publicist—but that her clients got far more from her services than they bargained for. Flowers & Hayward had been the mastermind behind many downplayed celebrity scandals where their clients were always made out to be the victims of some incident that in reality was actually true or their fault. Allen trusted Yvette to be perfect for the job. They were prepared to pay her handsomely to be their press tainter, bad publicity controller, and ultimate career saver.

As Remmi crossed the threshold of her agent's office, Yvette turned around with a bright smile and friendly salutation. She rose from her chair, offered Remmi a firm handshake, and towered over her by at least three inches. She had classic girl-next-door good looks and a "trust me" type of face—perfect for manipulation and sweet-talk and ideal for reshaping reality.

"Sorry I'm late. L.A. traffic," Remmi explained.

"Not a problem. Yvette and I were just talking about the new season *American Idol.* Have you been watching?" Allen asked with a laugh.

"No. I can't say that I have." Remmi replied.

"They're one of our clients," Yvette replied.

"I can see why they would need you, after missing the ball on Jennifer Hudson." Remmi shook her head.

With a chuckle, Remmi took a seat on Allen's burgundy leather sofa before tossing her white Coach signature tie-dyed camera bag upon the glass-topped magazine table.

"So, Yvette," Remmi began. "I hear you're the woman when it comes to turning bad things into good."

Yvette agreed, with a sly grin. "That's what they say."

"And they all can't be wrong," Allen interjected.

"Well, I'm sure Allen has told you what's going on. As you know, I have quite a career that's brewing, but I also have a crazy past. It hasn't affected me so far, but now I have this psycho half sister/cousin that wants to make it big by telling my story," Remmi explained.

"Your problem really isn't as big as it seems, Rementa. I know it doesn't seem like it, but this girl is probably more of a pain in your ass than she is a threat to your career," Yvette replied, tapping her natural-colored square-tipped nails upon the desk.

"Ya think?" Remmi questioned, her head tilted to the side.

"Yeah . . . Well, let's see. . . . Do we have anything on her?" Yvette asked.

"Anything like what?" Remmi inquired, wondering what her new publicist had up her sleeve.

"Anything like anything? Rumors of homosexuality? Chick-on-chick pictures? Abuse of her own? Crimes committed? Connection to the wrong man? Above-average promiscuity and let's not forget—your psycho father is hers too," Yvette rambled.

"I don't really know too much about her, to be honest. I wouldn't know any of her personal business. We were just getting to know each other when all of this happened. But she's been scoping me out for years," Remmi answered.

"Well, I can see from the start that she definitely has stalker tendencies. And with incidents like John Lennon and even Janet

Jackson, folks don't take that too lightly anymore. But we will need more than just that. I have a friend who's a private investigator. The first thing we need to do is an extensive background check on her. Everyone has dirt, and I'm sure Miss Sweeting is no exception. My job is to make her dirt look dirtier than it is and definitely dirtier than yours. In fact, we wanna make her look so dirty that the threat of exposure will make her wanna kept her mouth shut," Yvette explained.

It seemed like a good idea—if Kara had anything to hide. But what if she didn't? Then what?

"Well, that sounds cool if she's got some dirt," Remmi replied.

"Don't we all?" Yvette snickered. "Even dust can be made to look like grime if you put the right spin on it."

"Well, what's the worst-case scenario? If she had no dirt, then what?" Allen questioned, reminded everyone that he was in the room.

"Well, if she's been a model Girl Scout all her life—which, by the way, is very unlikely, considering that she has the balls to do what she's doing to Remmi—the worst-case scenario would be for Remmi to tell her full story on *Oprah*. Which I don't necessarily think would be a bad thing. The public loves adversity and rags-to-riches stories. I don't think Remmi being a product of rape and molestation would in any way hurt her career. I'm sure it's not something you're proud of," she said, turning to Remmi. "But the way we put it out there would result in your story garnering so much public sympathy, you would surely gain some fans by the time we're through."

"What about the strip club robbery?" Allen asked.

"Well, now *that* we'll have to approach a bit more delicately. Unless she's got any proof linking you directly to the crime, it would just be speculation. The police may or may not find it important enough to investigate further. But I don't think we'll ultimately have to worry about that. I'm sure my guy will find out something on her that she doesn't want the world to know. And we'll use that as our leverage to keep her mouth shut," Yvette assured them.

"But then there'll always be the possibility that at some point in time she'll talk. I mean, it'll never really go away," Remmi announced as if the thought had just gone off in her mind like a hundred-watt bulb.

"Well, let's try to think positively. You never know. Girlfriend may get a burst of guilty conscience and decide to back off," Yvette suggested unconvincingly.

Remmi rolled her eyes, quite certain that Kara would not voluntarily stay quiet simply because it was "the right thing to do."

Muffled noise from the traffic outside seeped through the double-glass windows and became background music as the three sat in Allen's office for another thirty minutes. They continued to brainstorm about ways to quiet Kara and protect Remmi's image, keeping some ideas in mind while tossing out those that seemed unreasonable. It was finally decided that Plan A would be to dig up whatever dirt they could find on Kara, while Plan B rested silently in the background. If worst came to worst, Remmi would be telling more than she'd planned to Oprah, hoping that the world would be understanding, sympathetic, and supportive. By the time she'd left the meeting, Remmi had resolved herself to the fact that the world was about to sift through her hamper, examine her dirty clothes, and decide which articles were worthy of being tossed into the wash. Her only concern was what would be left intact when it was all ready to be hung up to dry.

26

Quarter-sized raindrops hammered against Remmi's window sounding like small stones as they connected with the glass. It was only 5 P.M., but the darkened sky howled midnight. The sound of the television buzzed through an otherwise still and silent atmosphere as Remmi soaked her lethargic bones in the whirlpool tub of her master bath. The events of the past several months played in her mind like an old black-and-white Charlie Chaplin film, its muted actors shifting choppily as their mouths moved to communicate. There was no sound, but Remmi could hear each and every word. Looking up from the tub where she lay motionless surrounded by disappearing bubbles, she watched God's tears splash upon and then roll from the skylight above her. Thunder roared through the night, causing the lights to flicker on and off, but she remained still as a statue. The scented candles she'd lit around the edges of the large porcelain basin were more illumination than she needed anyway. As long as the house wasn't pulled from its roots and swept off to the Land of Oz, she was fine. Or maybe a little trip to see the wizard was just what the doctor ordered. Remmi chuckled at the thought and imagined herself standing before Richard Pryor, playing a phony warlock who wouldn't be able to help her anyway. As usual, she was on her own.

Her journey from El Barrio had been a long one with ups and downs, ins and outs, good times and bad, and oh-so-much learning. Never in her wildest dreams would she ever have thought she would be a real Hollywood movie star. After all, most video girls either get caught up or kicked out of the lifestyle way before the world gets to take a good look at them. Remmi was actually one of the few who had gotten a chance to really show Hollywood what she was made of. She often wondered if it was her talent or if it was her mother talking to God on her behalf that had made her go as far she did. Remmi knew her story was a rare one—the queen of all *E! True Hollywood Stories*. A *Behind the Scenes* to end all behind the scenes. *A Diary Of* that would make all other diaries look like they should have been open books. Yes, Rementa Renee Broughton had quite a story. A story that took Maya's words "And still I rise" to a whole 'nother level.

Remmi replayed her last meeting with Kara Sweeting in her mind in Pixar animation. Remmi remembered that Kara's face had been flushed from lovemaking, made more evident by Arthur Haddox's interruption of their discussion. He'd stood before them bare-chested, clad only in a towel, the undercover undiagnosed maniac that he was.

"That's it," Remmi said aloud, sitting up in the tub. She quickly reached the faucet and shut down the whirlpool feature, grabbed her terry cloth robe from the hook on the back of the door, and walked to the kitchen, leaving damp footprints upon the hardwood floor like bread crumbs used to find her way back to where she had just come from. As she pressed the illuminated numbers on her cell phone, Remmi's heart thumped so fiercely against her chest, she felt the vibration at her temples.

"Allen . . . I think I've got the dirt on that bitch that we need. You and Yvette need to get over to my place as soon as possible!" Remmi rambled, her words so rapid, they sounded like one sentence. Allen assured her he'd alert Yvette and they'd be on the way. No sooner had she disconnected the phone, Remmi threw a black Echko Red hooded jumpsuit over her air-dried body, removed the pins from her hair, and waited for her accomplices to arrive. She couldn't believe she hadn't come up with this idea before. It all suddenly seemed too simple. Maybe she wouldn't have to reveal everything after all.

The doorbell chimed in what felt like an hour but what in actuality was only twenty minutes. Dampened from the rain, Allen and Yvette entered the condo with eyes brightened from excitement and anticipation of what Remmi claimed was a solution to their problem.

"So what is it? My investigator found that she's had far too many abortions to ever carry a child full-term, but other than that, we're still gathering information," Yvette began.

"Forget that." Remmi smiled. "I know for a fact that her new boyfriend, the infamous Arthur Haddox of Bad Boy Films, is a down-low brotha of the very worst kind. The kind that knowingly sleeps with HIV-positive drag queens and spreads the disease to all the young up-and-coming wannabes in the industry. It's like he's on a mission to cause an epidemic in Hollywood." Both Allen and Yvette's eyes widened with surprise, as Allen sat down on Remmi's sofa in awe of the information that she just revealed.

"Arthur Haddox is HIV positive?" Yvette questioned. "How do you know this?"

"I can't reveal my sources, but I know for a fact that he's had sex with someone who's living with the AIDS virus," Remmi announced, confident that the digital photos in her camera would confirm her lie. "And since she's sleeping with him," she continued. "Then surely she'll eventually have it, too. Of course, I'm sure she doesn't know about any of this, but I'd just *love* to be the one to tell her. Serves the bitch right, too. God don't like ugly." Remmi laughed hysterically.

Allen and Yvette remained silent as they witnessed another side of Remmi's personality they had never seen before. There was a glimmer of evil in her eye as she appeared totally consumed with revenge. It almost surprised her conspirators that Remmi was actually happy that this girl—no matter how wicked—had probably contracted a disease and didn't even know it.

"But Remmi, Arthur Haddox . . . I mean, were you and he—? I mean, if he has HIV doesn't that mean you—?" Allen inquired with slight hesitation.

"I told you not to listen to silly Hollywood rumors, Allen. I never slept with him," Remmi lied again. Damn, she was good at this.

"Well, are you one hundred percent sure about this?" Allen questioned.

"As sure as the folks who write the Encyclopaedia Britannica. I know this for a fact. I can't believe I didn't think of this before," Remmi snapped, slapping her palm against her forehead.

"Well, if this is true, this information should certainly keep Miss Thang's lips shut tight," Yvette stated.

"That's right. Ol' girl don't want everybody in L.A. to blacklist her ass—quarantine her like she's got leprosy. There's a lot of ignorance out there. Especially in Hollywood. And even if her test comes up negative at first, she'll know that it'll only be a matter of time before it won't. So . . . this is the plan. If she goes to the press on *me*, then I'll air out all my dirty laundry on *Oprah*, including the part about how I lost one sister to AIDS and how my dear old half sister/cousin is now living also with the virus," Remmi spewed, each of her words growing more and more animated by the time she hit the ending punctuation. There was a hush that came over the room, which resonated through the air louder than the thunder that crashed across the sky outside. It was almost as if each of their thoughts were jockeying for position on a crowded expressway during rush hour, silent but screaming at the same time.

"Well," Yvette continued, breaking the stillness of the room. "If this information is in fact true, then we've got her—"

"Oh, we've got her all right. Right by the balls. That'll teach that bitch to bumble with this B." Remmi cackled like a witch who'd just cast a spell that turned her archenemy into an ugly toad. She hadn't felt this hopeful in ages. Armed with a foolproof fabrication that now gave her ammunition of her own, she could actually protect and save her own ass. Once again, she reminded herself that the only people she could truly count on were herself and Shannelle, even from the grave.

"So do you have any idea about how you'd like to proceed? How do you want to let Kara know that you know about this?" Yvette asked.

"But wait a minute, Remmi. How *do you* know about this, and you do realize that this information will not only be detrimental to Kara but also to Art Haddox?" Allen asked.

"Yeah, I know. But so what?" Remmi shrugged. "Art already knows that I know, so once Kara talks to him about it, there's *no way* he'll let her breathe a word of this to anyone. In fact, with him, I'll have *extra* added security!"

"Wow. You're working with some major ammunition, girl-friend," Yvette stated, shaking her head and letting out a sizable huff, as if to say, *Damn, I'm glad my name ain't Kara Sweeting.*

"I'll call her up first thing in the morning. Or maybe even tonight. Tell her I thought about things and decided that she's the only family I got. Tell her that I want her to be my baby sister. Ya know, tell her what she wants to hear—a bunch a bullshit," Remmi explained. "I'll let you both know how it goes," she continued. "But I have no worries. There's no way she'd want the world to know about this. My plan is foolproof."

"Yeah, if all goes the way it should, it's pretty solid." Yvette shook her head.

"Solid enough to earn me a discount on your fee?" Remmi hinted with a half smile.

ain, rain go away, come again another day," Remmi softly chanted. The weatherman had been right. Large drops of water had fallen from gray clouds for the third day straight, and Remmi truly wanted the sun to shine again. Not only in reality, but also metaphorically. She couldn't wait to put Kara's threats behind her so that she could do like Tom Cruise or Will Smith and just enjoy herself on Oprah's couch. She had three weeks before she was scheduled to shoot the pilot for *Esq.* in New York City and wanted desperately to take a brief vacation to some tropical island where she could lie on somebody's beach and eat grapes all day. But she couldn't leave without handling Kara first. She couldn't go back to New York, leaving Hollywood at the disposal of an arch-enemy. No, she would take a vacation, but only *after* all of her business was taken care of. It was the only way she would be able to really enjoy it.

Remmi waited patiently for Kara to arrive at the Fitness Grill, slightly concerned that she wouldn't show. Kara had been apprehensive about meeting her the night before when they briefly chatted on the phone. She made it clear that she didn't trust Remmi's olive branch and would be examining it closely for razor-sharp thorns. But Remmi was good and had years up on her little half sibling when it came to deception, a natural-born actress, which most people don't realize is synonymous with being a tremendously convincing liar. Remmi's skills managed to convince her nemesis that it would be safe to meet for lunch to discuss "family business"; that the tabloids need not be privy to conversations that took place between sisters, even if they were only half and even if they doubled as first cousins. She reminded her of the "connection" they shared. The same connection Remmi had earlier rejected. Finally Kara agreed.

Remmi sat patiently, checking her watch every five minutes. At first Remmi thought maybe Kara had changed her mind. She initially blamed the thunderstorm for Kara's tardiness, but when she failed to answer her cell phone, Remmi began to believe that her half sister had chickened out of their meeting.

When Kara was officially forty minutes late, Remmi decided to leave the eatery and head over to the Eagle Rock apartments yet again. But as she began to gather her belongings, Kara breezed in from the street, her hair, face, and clothing soggy from the torrential wind and rain outside.

"Sorry I'm late. I hate driving in this kind of weather, so I really had to take my time," Kara offered as she slid into the chair across from Remmi.

A sigh of relief came over Remmi as she collected her thoughts and refocused on the reason she'd called the meeting. "No problem." Remmi gave a false smile.

"It's brutal out there. And I think something is wrong with my brakes. I have to press them at the beginning of the block if I wanna stop at the end. Better get them checked out before something bad happens," Kara mumbled, speaking more to herself than to Remmi.

"Yeah, brakes are nothing to mess around with," Remmi replied, not really giving a damn.

The waitress scurried over to take their orders before disappearing off into the kitchen. As if she were trying to figure out where to begin, Kara took a sip of lukewarm water from a glass that had been sitting there since Remmi's arrival.

"I was hesitant at first 'cause I didn't know what to expect, but after thinking about it, I'm actually glad you called this meeting. I really don't wanna be enemies with you, Remmi. Despite what went on between our parents, we are sisters," Kara began.

"And cousins," Remmi reminded her.

Kara didn't reply to Remmi's comment, but stared straight ahead, seemingly trying to think of what else to say.

"Well . . . I've been thinking real hard about the conversation we had that day in your apartment. You know, the one when Arthur Haddox was there—"

"Oh, I hope you're not still salty about that. He told me you guys used to date but it didn't work out," Kara interrupted.

"No, he's right. We were all wrong for each other. In fact, I definitely think you two are a much better match." Remmi smiled.

"Well, it's not serious between us, so—"

"None of my business," Remmi interjected. "But I really don't wanna talk about Art Haddox—right now, anyway. I'd really like to discuss why I brought you here in the first place."

"Okay . . ."

"Well after thinking about what happened that day, I've pretty much come to the conclusion that you kinda insinuated that you're like blackmailing me," Remmi stuttered, not wanting to sound accusatory and put Kara on the defense.

Kara lightly chuckled with a hint of sarcasm. "I am not blackmailing you, Remmi," Kara replied. "But I will tell you this. *The Daily Enquirer* is willing to pay me twenty grand to tell them about our connection. Truth be told, I need the money. I haven't gotten another project since *Nyagra's Falls*, and you know living in L.A. ain't cheap. It's really not personal, Remmi. I know how it seems, but I'm really not trying to hurt you."

"Well, it definitely doesn't *feel* that way, Kara. So, if you're not trying to hurt me, tell me this: How do you know about the incident that happened at Shirley's Temple?" Remmi asked with a raised brow.

The question fell upon deaf ears as Kara fiddled with her butter knife and opted not to respond. A guilty gleam in her eye indicated that Remmi's suggestion of blackmail wasn't entirely off base.

"Ya know, Kara," Remmi continued, as she received her ham-and-cheese croissant from the giddy waitress. "When we first met, I liked you. I guess I saw a little of myself in you. The drive. The determination. Game recognizes game, ya know. But now I see it's because we're cut from a similar cloth."

"I told you that. Believe it or not, I always wanted to be like you, Remmi. For years, I looked up to you from afar ever since I found out that you were my sister. I'd say I'm well on my way, wouldn't you?"

"I said *similar*, Kara. Not *identical*," Remmi snapped, followed by a smile to soften the traces of venom laced throughout the statement. "You have quite a ways to go before you're anything like me, my dear."

As Remmi took a small bite of the flaky stuffed bread, their conversation was momentarily interrupted by the waitress who had served them, apologizing as she pleaded for Remmi's autograph on a folded napkin.

"I'm such a huge fan of yours, Ms. Broughton. And my brother—he has your posters all over his bedroom wall!" the waitress cheesed with a hint of shyness and embarrassment. With her signature smile, Remmi obliged the petite girl before she scurried off to take the orders of other patrons in her station.

"Well, as soon as the world knows of our connection, I'm sure they'll embrace me as much as they've embraced you," Kara continued with a whisper as soon as the waitress was out of earshot. It was evident that the green-eyed monster was rearing its ugly head. It didn't take a rocket scientist to know that Kara craved Remmi's popularity. But she not only wanted to be *like* Remmi, she actually wanted to *be* Remmi.

"Well, I see that you've definitely done your research on me. Guess I was a special project of yours or something. Musta had a lotta time on your hands to keep track of my life over the years the way you have," Remmi replied.

"The world is a hellofa lot smaller than you think . . . and that six degrees of separation shit is real." Kara smirked, twirling the straw around in her glass.

"So, I gather you think you know people who think they know me, huh?"

"Word of advice, sister dear—since you think you know so *damn* much: Pillow talk is a smartest girl's enemy."

"Oh, is it now?" Remmi replied with a raised brow, racking her brain trying to remember whom she'd revealed her secrets to after a night of sweaty lust.

"Remember your *Butta* co-star, Lamard Fisher? Well he's my

play cousin from back in B-more. We went to high school to-gether, and he lived down the block from me since we were eight years old. He told me a little story about you pulling a *Set It Off* at a strip club. Said you told him about it, then tried to laugh it off and take it back like you were joking. But after doing a little inves-tigation of my own—I found out that it was true—you and your girl got away with a ton of cash—and brought the club down like some real life Thelma and Louise bitches. Man, there's a reason I've always looked up to you. Your ass really ain't no joke." Kara smiled, shaking her head in admiration.

Remmi sat quiet, unwilling to confirm or deny the allegations Kara had just set before her. She knew telling Lamard about the heist had been a mistake. That's why she'd retracted the statement as soon as it hit the air. She had no idea he would believe her, run with it, and tell others.

Remmi's pulse quickened from the realization that Kara had far more on her than she initially believed. She could feel the blood pumping through her veins gearing up for an anxiety attack but instantly went into mind-over-matter mode, calming herself down and taking a deep breath before beginning the dialogue once again.

"It's not gonna work," Remmi mumbled.

"Beg your pardon?" Kara questioned.

"This plan of yours. It's not gonna work. Using me to help boost your career. Yeah, it might get you fifteen minutes of fame, but in the end, you'll be going back to B-more with your tail be-tween your legs begging Habib for your job at Dunkin' Donuts back," Remmi snapped.

Kara shrugged. "We'll just see about that."

"I can't believe that after all I've done for you, you're really planning on using me to help boost your career. If I hadn't given your ass *my* stamp of approval, you woulda never even gotten that role in *Nyagra's Falls*. Truth be told, the powers that be wanted this chick from Canada, and I rallied for your ass. And this is the thanks I get? Don't you think there's something dirty about that?" Remmi frowned.

"*Dirty* is such a harsh word."

"Yeah, well, speaking of dirty, how's Art?" Remmi questioned, as she squeezed the juice from her lemon slice into her Sprite.

"He's fine," Kara answered suspiciously.

"Still married?"

"Don't know, don't care. All I know is that he's good for me . . . and my career."

"Yeah, he's special all right . . ."

"Like I said at the beginning of this conversation, I hope you're not salty about that."

"Salty? Puulleezze." Remmi chuckled. "You can have my leftovers. What Art and I had was done long ago. He served his purpose. I got all I could from him. Now I guess it's your turn," Remmi chuckled. There was a moment of silence before she continued. "He's real good in bed, though, isn't he?" Remmi asked, her delivery cynical and sarcastic, making Kara slightly uncomfortable.

"Yeah, he's okay," Kara replied with a hint of *I know I'm not talking to you about my man's skills in bed* in her voice.

"Just hope you're using condoms. He never wanted to use them with me. All he was worried about was whether or not I was on the pill," Remmi added, circling the ice in her Diet Pepsi without making direct eye contact.

The rays from Kara's eyes screamed, *I know you didn't just go there, bitch*, but her lips were paralyzed, unable to respond. It was clear to both of them that although Kara was on her way, she clearly was no match for her older, more experienced mentor.

"Glad I used to force the issue, though 'cause you know he fucks with drag queens on the low, don't you?" Remmi announced as casually as she might ask for a Big Mac and fries.

As Remmi's words hit Kara's ears, Kara started to gag on her iced tea.

"Are you all right?" Remmi dryly and insincerely inquired. As Kara attempted to collect herself, she gasped for air, swallowed hard—needing water or the Heimlich maneuver. However, Remmi failed to make a move but continued to ingest her sandwich without a blink, cleaning her plate more deliberately than hungrily. "Oh, I'm sorry." Remmi grinned, her voice as artificially sweetened as a packet of Equal. "I thought you knew. I thought surely he would have confided in you about his fetishes. I mean he told me and I hit the ceiling—but you seem a little bit more *worldly* than me. I'm a bit of a prude sometimes. He couldn't handle it. That's why we broke up. Thought he woulda told you about that."

"You're lying," Kara accused, clearing her chest and trying to inhale normally.

"If you say so, but I've seen the pictures. You remember my girl, Shannelle, right? The one that you told the tabloids about? Well, when she was diagnosed with HIV she became a part of this support group made up of other people who are either HIV-positive or who have full-blown AIDS, right, and one of the other people in the group, this drag queen named—well his name isn't important, but he and Shannelle became friends," Remmi explained, now lowering her voice to a whisper and moving in closer. "Well, one day we're looking through the guy's photo album, and lo and behold—there's Arthur Haddox getting his groove on with our buddy—man on man, balls on balls, dick on dick!"

Kara's eyes bugged out from her head with surprise, and she

wanted to get up and run from the restaurant but she suddenly couldn't feel her legs. Her throat was dry as a bone, preventing her from formulating a response. A prickly sensation spread throughout her body. Kara's sudden paralysis made her a captive audience for Remmi as she unleashed her verbal assault with a smile, careful not to draw any attention to their table.

"I don't believe you," Kara managed to utter.

"You don't have to. Now I'm not saying *you* got it, and I'm not even saying Art got it, but I know for a fact that our friend—the queen—he's got it and let's see . . . if he and Art were screwing, and you and Art were screwing . . . humm, damn you betta do the math and get tested, *girlfriend*. And you better do it soon. AIDS snuffed my sister out fast, but that's 'cause she ain't wanna live with it. You, on the other hand, might catch it early enough to get it treated. But of course, it's totally up to you," Remmi snarled, the syrupy grin nowhere in sight.

"Why you lying?" Kara irately asked.

"Lying? *Me?* Nope. I speaks the truth, girlfriend. And let's not forget," Remmi snickered. "You started it, bitch. I just figured that while you on your way to tell the tabloids about *my* past, I'll be on my way to tell Oprah about *your* present. But I'm sure every director and producer in Hollywood is looking for an HIV-positive leading lady." Remmi smirked.

"You're just saying this so that I'll back off with my story!" Kara retorted, trying to convince herself of her statement more than she wanted to convince Remmi.

"Fine, don't believe me." Remmi callously shrugged. "Go to the nearest clinic and take a test. It's free and you'll see for yourself. And if I'm lying, you can run to every tabloid in the country—put *all* my business on front street! But if I'm not—you leave me and my career the hell alone! You keep my secrets, I'll keep yours! After all, you might have a couple of years before your test comes back positive."

Taking a deep breath and regaining focus, in an attempt to call Remmi's bluff, Kara retorted, "Well, if what you saying is true, I'll *really* need the twenty-five grand they offered me. And if I'm sick, I'll have nothing to lose. According to you, if Art gave me HIV, I'll eventually die anyway. I may as well go out with a bang."

Remmi had underestimated her enemy's ability to play hard-ball. Maybe her little sister was more like her than she cared to admit. Maybe their similar genes had filtered into their personalities, creating a hustler mentality in Kara that Remmi had slept on. After all, their relation had double-dipped in the gene pool, Kara being her half sister *and* cousin.

"Sweetie, I think you gonna need much more than twenty-five grand, and no one will hire you if they know you're sick. You could live very functionally with the right cocktails. But the meds cost a hell of a lot more than twenty-five grand. Trust me. I paid for my sister's till the end."

There was an awkward silence as the two women engaged in an intense stare-down. Neither of them wanted to take the first step toward some sort of resolution or truce. The activity beyond their table disappeared as the two of them could see only what was before them—each other. A lot was at stake for both of them. Life or death for Kara. Stardom or has-been-ship for Remmi.

When Remmi could no longer take the sight of the woman she had to restrain herself from pulverizing with her bare hands, she rose from her seat, tossing a sealed Manila envelope into Kara's half-empty plate before breaking the silence with a dry and monotone statement. "I figured you'd doubt my words, so I made you a coupla copies of your man with my friend. Of course, I have the negatives in a very safe place," Remmi snapped. "I'm flying to Chicago to do *Oprah* next Thursday. You have until then to contact me. Oh, and lunch is on you. Be sure to tip the waitress nicely. She's a huge fan of mine."

Remmi exited the crowded eatery and disappeared into the soggy streets, umbrellaless and hoping that her mission had been accomplished.

27

remmi's bedroom was illuminated by the light of several scented candles strategically placed in each necessary area. The fragrances of vanilla bean and coconut traveled through the air and tickled her nose as she typed away on the keyboard of her laptop. The storm had zapped the electricity in her condo and boredom had sent her surfing the Net until her battery ran down. Her thoughts still occupied by Kara Sweeting, Remmi needed something to take her mind off the situation.

What if she still doesn't believe me and goes ahead with her plan anyway? Remmi asked herself. *What if she still forges ahead with a vengeance and reveals my secrets?* Although Remmi knew she'd shaken Kara at their lunch, she still wasn't quite sure of which way her nemesis would go. Neither she nor her career were safe as long as Kara Sweeting was on some *Single White Female* shit, with an urban twist, of course. As a diversion, Remmi was drawn to the computer to help take her mind off the nagging thoughts that rested there regarding Kara's threats and promises. Remmi was often curious about the things written about her out in cyber-space, and with nothing else to do in the dark, she was drawn to the information held within the sleekly designed silver case. But as the skylight above shook uncontrollably from the crashing wind, Remmi found it difficult to concentrate on the flat screen before her. Even when she was a little girl, severe storms unnerved her, sending her hiding beneath her blankets, smashed up against her white-flowered headboard.

Now, fifteen years later, not much had changed, as the sound of thunder roaring through the air made the hairs on her neck stand at attention and caused her to wonder if she was in the midst of some sort of West Coast twister. She didn't remember ever ex-periencing such violent storms in New York and eagerly wanted to return to the familiar concrete jungle. Even without the storm, Remmi had had more than enough of California and Hollywood and its relentless paparazzi, and she desperately yearned to get back to the Big Apple, where she could blend in with people who cared very little about her comings and goings. Remmi had come to the realization that New York money was different from L.A. money. The Manhattan skyline was the backdrop for an elite so-cial scene that seemed to encompass all types. Artists, doctors, CEOs, lawyers, and politicians all dined and partied together. Whereas, it seemed that in L.A., everyone from surgeons to park-ing lot attendants was waiting for their big break. It seemed that everyone in L.A. was an aspiring *something*. Thus, she ached to get back to the city that never slept. The fact that her sitcom was scheduled to tape in New York had been a dream come true. In her mind, Remmi and L.A. were now like oil and vinegar, and without Shannelle by her side, she knew she needed to go home.

Since she had given up her small East Harlem apartment, Remmi was unsure about where she would be living when she got back to New York. She had already begun packing and preparing for her exit from Tinsel Town and each square foot of her condo was occupied by a brown cardboard box filled with important contents. While plenty would be left behind, Remmi's personal mementos were scheduled to travel with her. The plan was to head straight to New York after taking *Oprah* and Chicago by storm, as a small but comfortable suite at the Royal Regal Hotel awaited her arrival until she found permanent housing. She was also eager to meet her sitcom co-star, a handsome thickly built comedian and actor with a contagious smile who she'd heard was a natural-born funny man. A little laughter in her life was exactly what Remmi needed. Additionally, it had been a while since she'd been worked out between the sheets, and Remmi's libido certainly had her thinking about what else her co-star might have to offer. Yes, New York had given birth to her and was loudly calling her name. And now that her work in L.A. was done for the time being, Remmi couldn't wait to answer that call.

after seventy-two hours, the sun finally reemerged, brightly and blindingly, brightening Remmi's bedroom like a halogen lamp positioned directly above her face. As she slowly pried her eyelids open, she was able to read the digital numbers on her cable box, which furiously flashed the numbers 1 2 0 0, alerting her that the electricity had returned. She groggily fumbled through the sheets for her remote control before locating it at the bottom of her feather topped mattress.

As she channel surfed to find a program that caught her interest, the chime of the doorbell echoed from beyond her bedroom walls. Not expecting company, Remmi took her time throwing on a robe and heading toward the front door. From the other side, she heard Allen's frantic voice as he simultaneously called for her, rang the bell, and pounded the wood.

"Whut the—!" Remmi barked, flinging the door open.

"Have you seen the morning news?" Allen spewed into her face before she could complete her sentence. It was evident that he had left his home in a rush, as he stood before her in a nylon jacket and navy blue plaid Ralph Lauren pajamas, his pale feet clinging to a pair of Adidas flip-flops. Brushing past her, Allen went straight to the living room set, and frantically searched for a news program to confirm the story he had come tell his favorite client. As his words flooded her ears, Remmi's eyes were filled with the image of her sister cousin's photograph as it was plastered across the plasma screen.

"Aspiring actress is one of many victims of L.A. County's recent mudslides," the stoic anchorman reported.

"Oh, shit," Remmi muttered, her hazel eyes glued to the screen. She listened intently as the reporter's pencil-thin lips mouthed the details of Kara's Volkswagen bug being found alongside the Santa Ana Freeway beneath a mountain of asphyxiating mud and debris, her lifeless body slumped over the steering wheel. The report chronicled her brief career in Hollywood, her life in Baltimore, and her upcoming role "alongside Hollywood's newest darling, Rementa Broughton," as they put it, flashing a picture of Remmi at the premiere of *Butta*.

"You always manage to come out looking beautiful." Allen shook his head in amazement as he glared at Remmi's glowing image on the television screen. Remmi instinctively released a breath from the pit of her abdomen, a breath that screamed a relief she had not known in months. A relief that said she could leave L.A.

without a worry, concern, or regret. A relief that eagerly looked forward to what awaited her in New York City. A relief that said that the details of her past had died with Kara Sweeting. As she continued to listen to the newscaster's words, she felt no guilt or sorrow for the fact that Kara's life had been cut down in its prime. On the contrary, Remmi felt comfort in the fact that she could now sleep that night knowing that the world would only see her as she, her manager, and her publicist desired her to be seen.

"I told you," Remmi beamed at her manager and friend, her eyes brighter than they had been in ages.

"Told me what?"

"My guardian angel is best friends with Gabriel."

"You ain't lyin'."

28

the couch was softer than she imagined it would be. The lights were brighter. But Oprah's voice was warmer, and the entire experience felt surreal. The audience embraced this ex–video chick from El Barrio and felt a connection to her. Remmi's words flowed like liquid, and she revealed more than she had planned just because she found Oprah so easy to talk to. She didn't glorify her days as a video girl. She didn't glorify her sexual escapades. But she was candid as she talked about her career in an industry whose motto is survival of the fittest. She smiled and almost forgot the cameras were running. It just didn't feel like she was telling her story to over twenty million ears. But she was, and they loved her honesty. But bigger than that, they loved *her* and she loved them. The camera loved her and she looked amazing. Not like a movie star, but like a daughter, a sister, or a friend, and the audience felt like they knew her. Her rags-to-riches story gave them hope for their own dreams, no matter what their history.

Remmi talked about losing her mother and even about Shannelle. She became a stiletto-wearing Picasso painting, a picture filled in with the glorious colors she wanted her audience to see. Fate had allowed Remmi to do it her way, and with Oprah's help, surely she'd be the next black woman to take Hollywood by storm.

"You have a truly amazing story. You've risen from nothing and achieved the unachievable. You've accomplished things that individuals with far more resources have been unable to accomplish. What gave you your determination? Your drive?" Oprah questioned her poised guest. With her back arched and her head slightly cocked to the side, Remmi wanted to respond to one of the most influential women of her time with an answer filled with depth and intelligence, poise and sophistication, but from the back of her throat, in classic Remmi form, all she could muster up was, "Well, you know, Oprah, a girl's gotta eat."